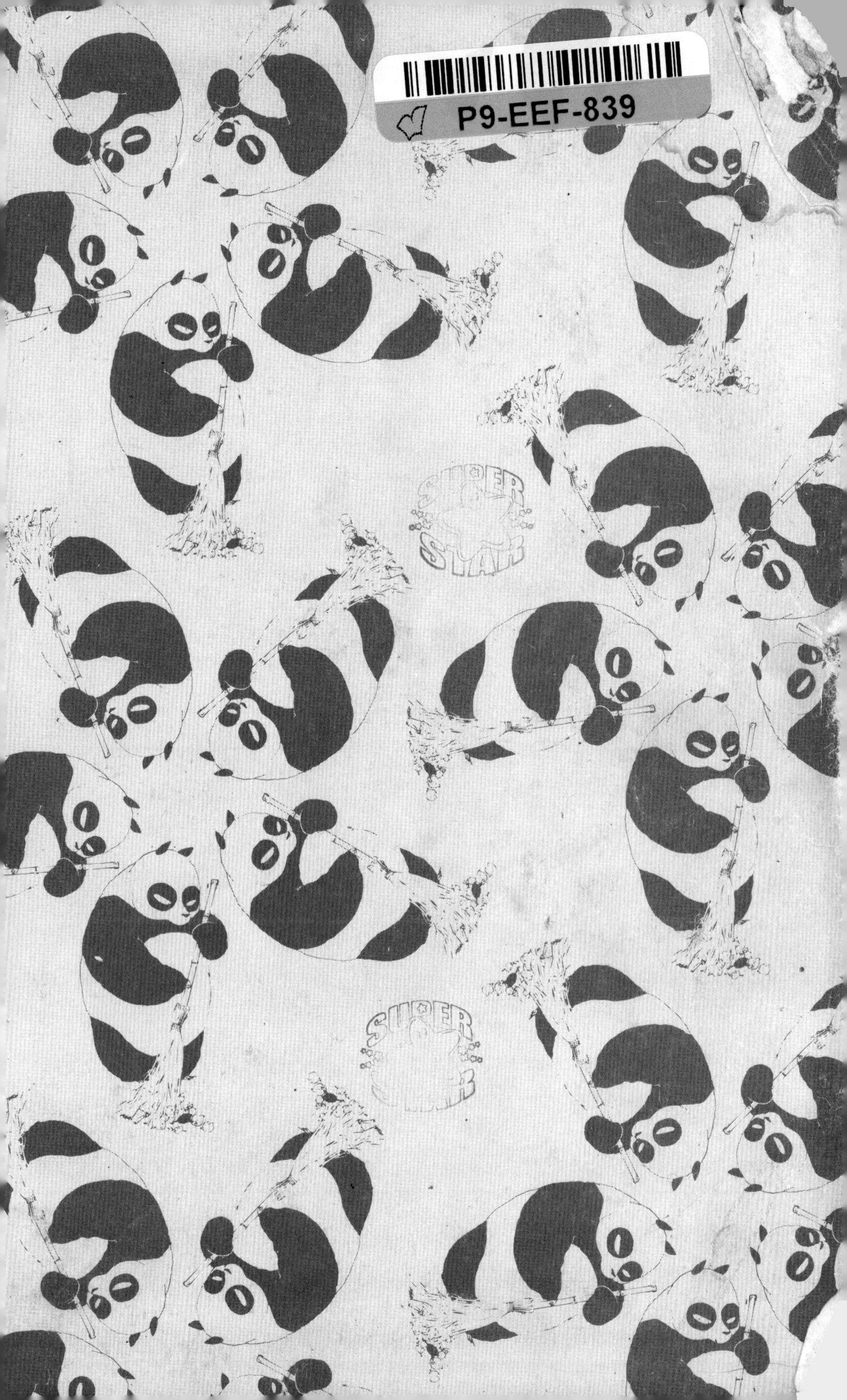
SUPER STAR
SUPER STAR

This volume contains RANMA 1/2 PART FOUR, #1
through the first half of RANMA 1/2 PART FOUR, #6 in their entirety.

Story & Art by Rumiko Takahashi

Translation/Gerard Jones & Toshifumi Yoshida & Matt Thorn
Touch-Up Art & Lettering/Wayne Truman
Cover Design/Viz Graphics
Senior Managing Editor/Annette Roman
*

Editor-in-Chief/Hyoe Narita
V.P. of Sales & Marketing/Rick Bauer
Publisher/Seiji Horibuchi
*

First published by Shogakukan, Inc. in Japan
*

Printed in Canada
*

Published by Viz Communications, Inc.
P.O. Box 77010
San Francisco, CA 94107
*

10 9 8
First printing, July 1996
Seventh printing, July 2001
Eight printing, April 2002

VIZ GRAPHIC NOVEL
RANMA 1/2™

6

"**Rumiko Takahashi** doesn't miss a single farcical opportunity as every volume is crammed with raging hormones, romantic entanglements, gender-swapping, and martial-art silliness. Boy changes to girl, man to panda, girl to cat -- and everybody's kung fu fighting."

Anodyne Magazine

"If you've never watched any of the videos, or read the comic books they are based on, you're missing out on some of the funniest, wackiest, and most character-driven cartoons around."

Tony Isabella, comics critic

"**Ranma 1/2** is a must for anyone who likes a wicked sense of humor."

Gamers' Republic

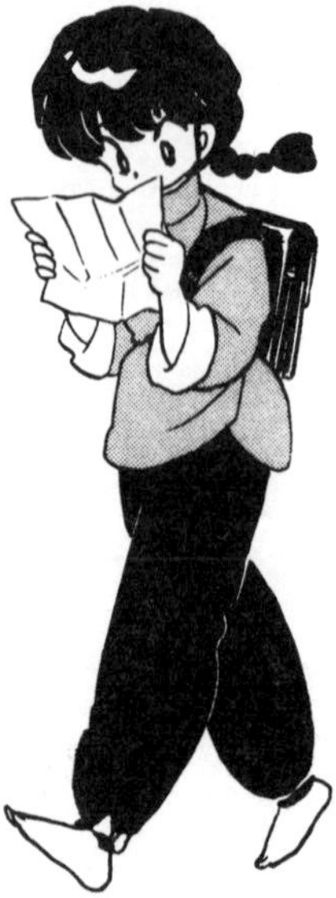

VIZ GRAPHIC NOVEL

RANMA 1/2

STORY & ART BY
RUMIKO TAKAHASHI

CONTENTS

PART 1

THE EVIL WAKES'

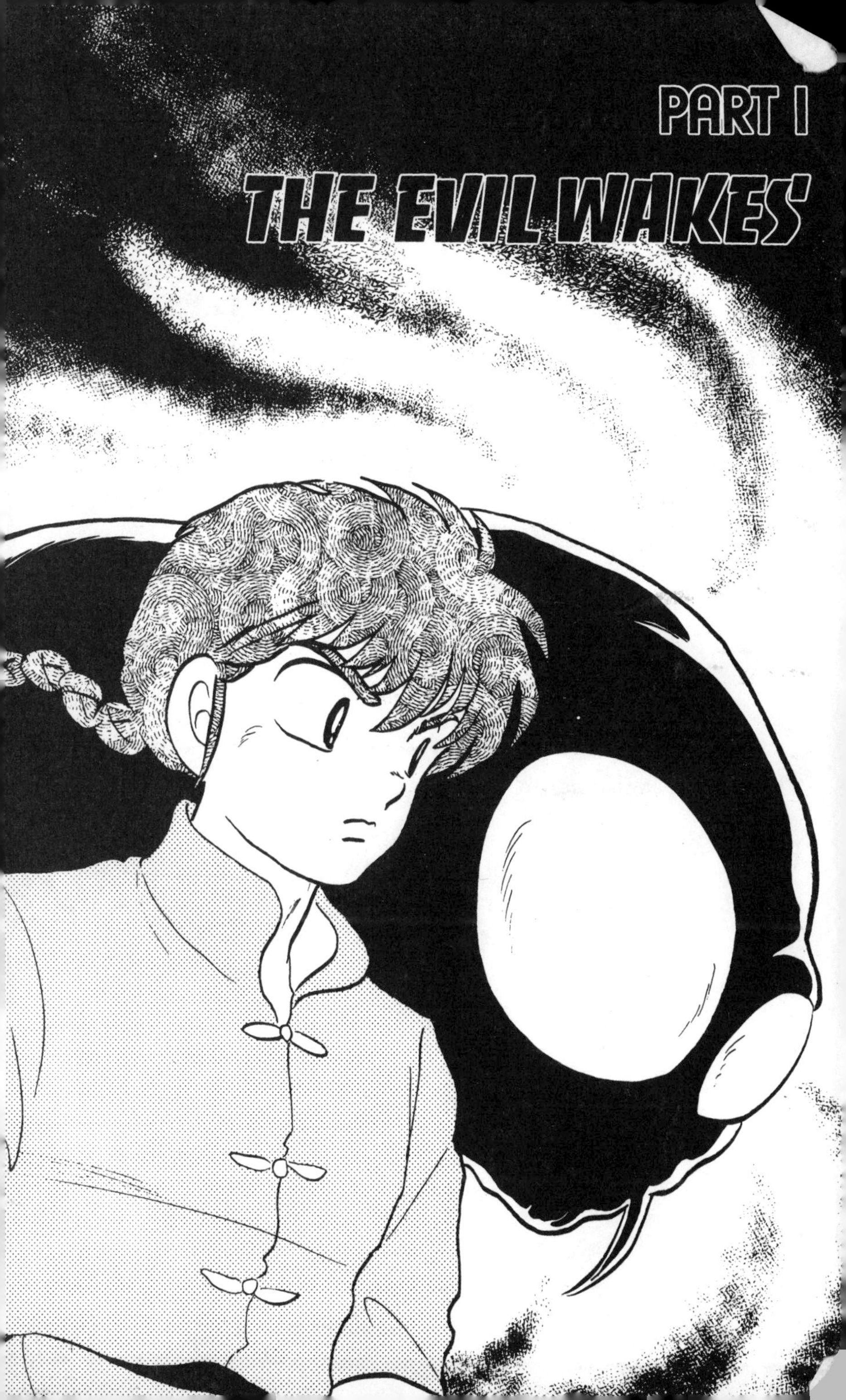

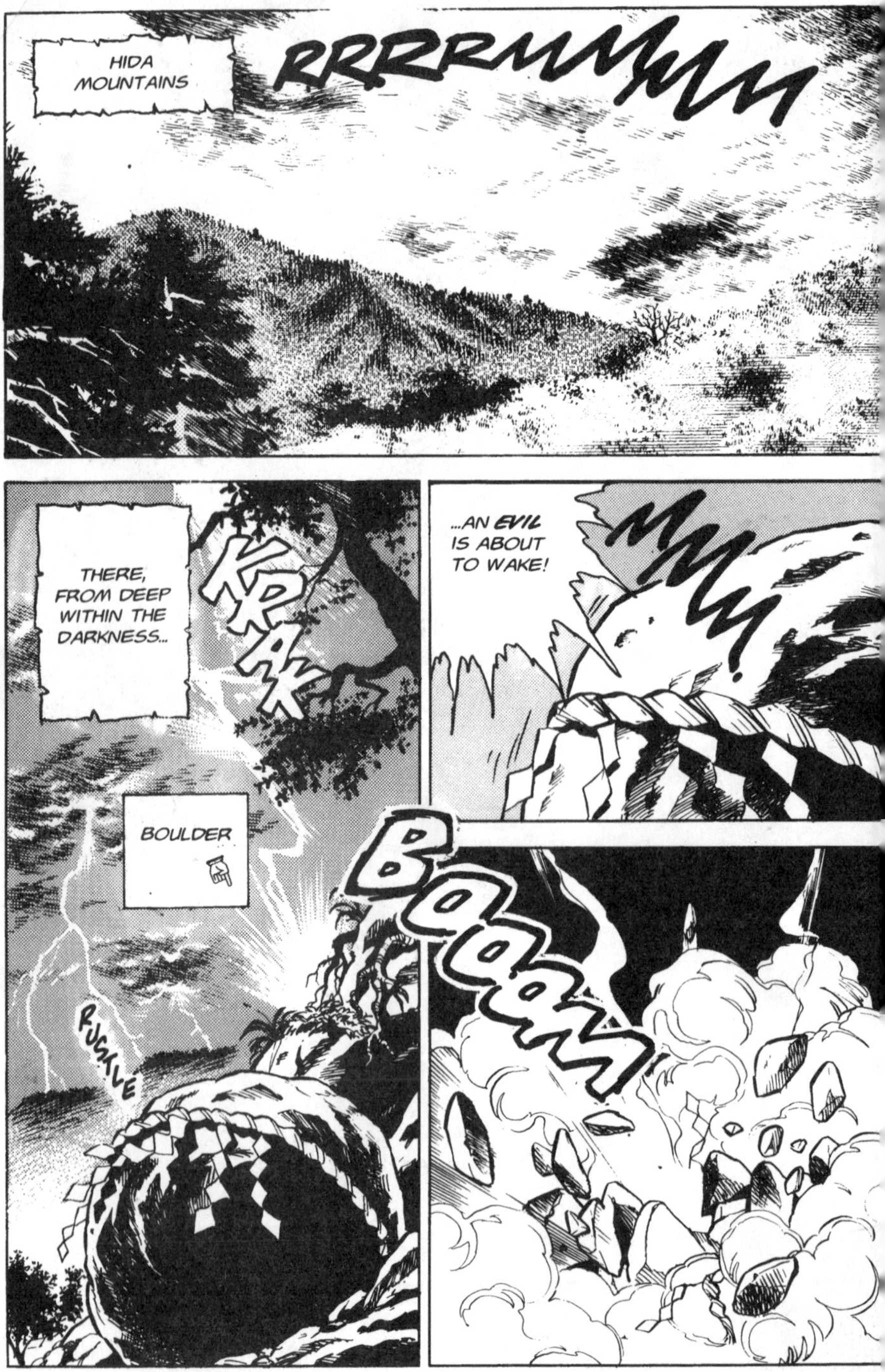

HIDA MOUNTAINS
RRRRMMMMM
THERE, FROM DEEP WITHIN THE DARKNESS...
KRAK
BOULDER
RUSTLE
...AN *EVIL* IS ABOUT TO WAKE!
MMM!
BOOOOM

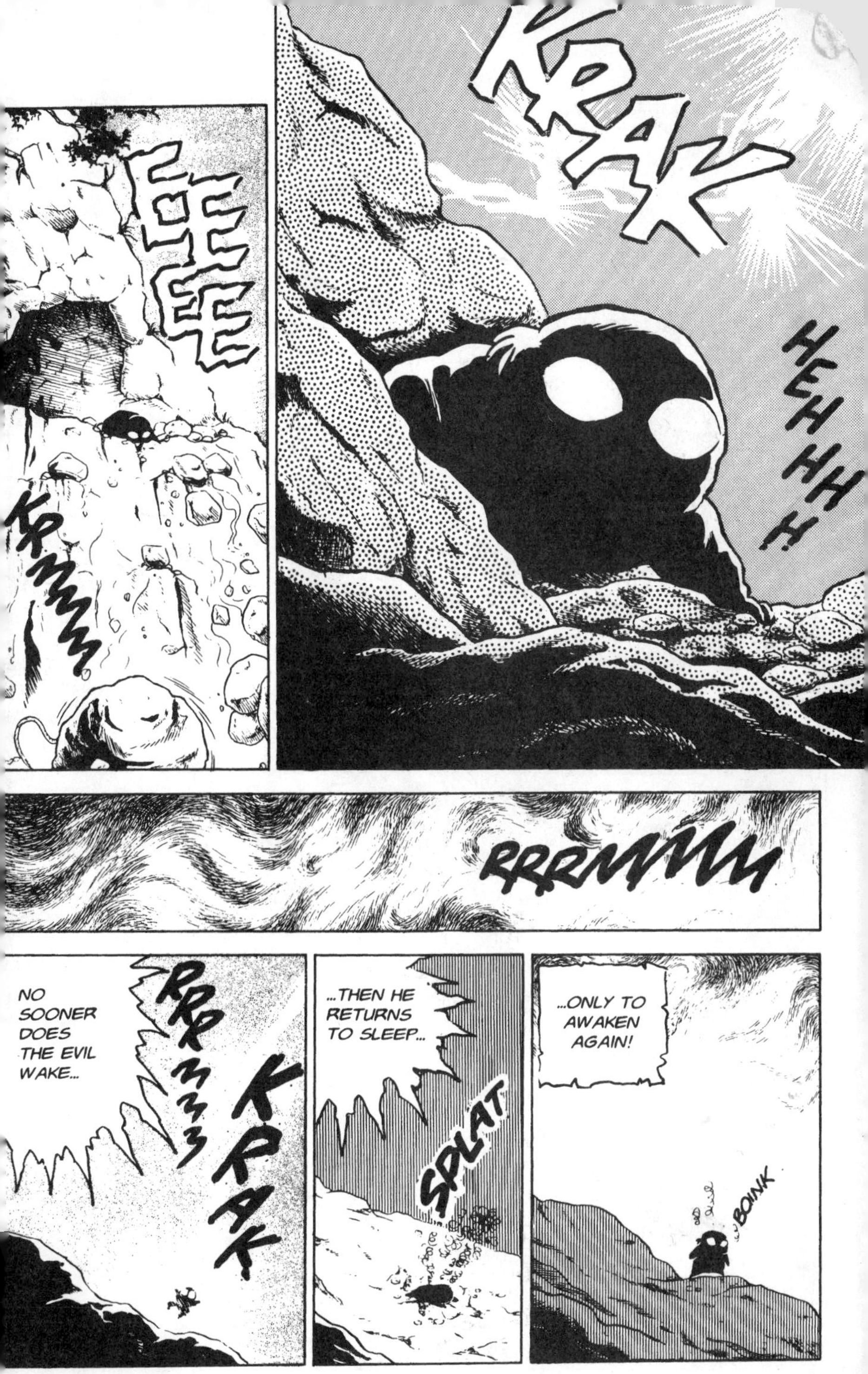
EEE
KRMMMM
KRAK
HEHHHHH
RRRMMMM
NO SOONER DOES THE EVIL WAKE...
RRRMMMM
KRAK
...THEN HE RETURNS TO SLEEP...
SPLAT
...ONLY TO AWAKEN AGAIN!
BOINK

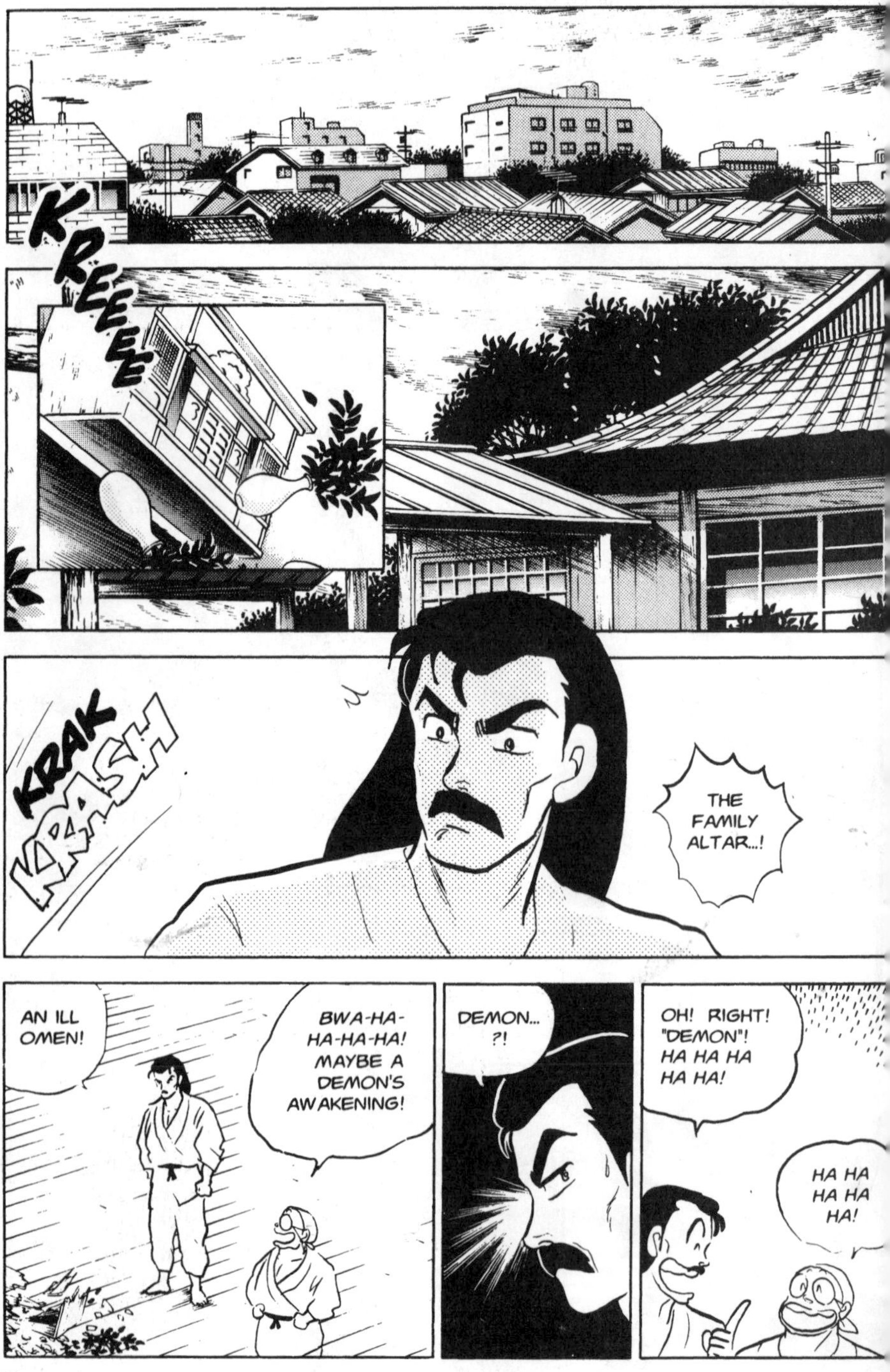
KREEEEE
KRAK
KRASH
THE FAMILY ALTAR...!
AN ILL OMEN!
BWA-HA-HA-HA-HA! MAYBE A DEMON'S AWAKENING!
DEMON... ?!
OH! RIGHT! "DEMON"! HA HA HA HA HA!
HA HA HA HA HA!

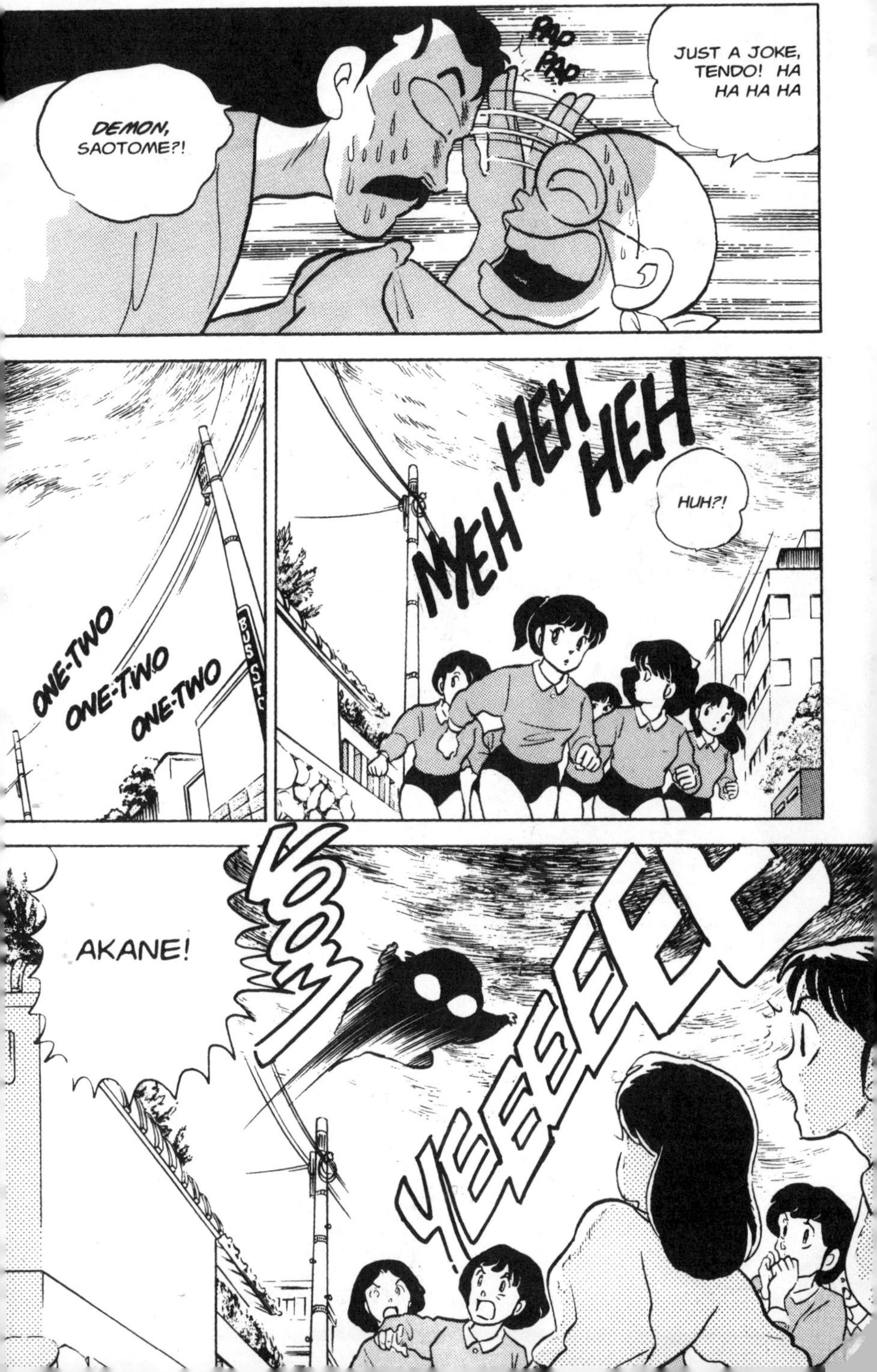
DEMON, SAOTOME?!
PAP PAP
JUST A JOKE, TENDO! HA HA HA HA
ONE-TWO
ONE-TWO
ONE-TWO
BUS STO
NYEH HEH HEH
HUH?!
AKANE!
VOOM
YEEEEEK

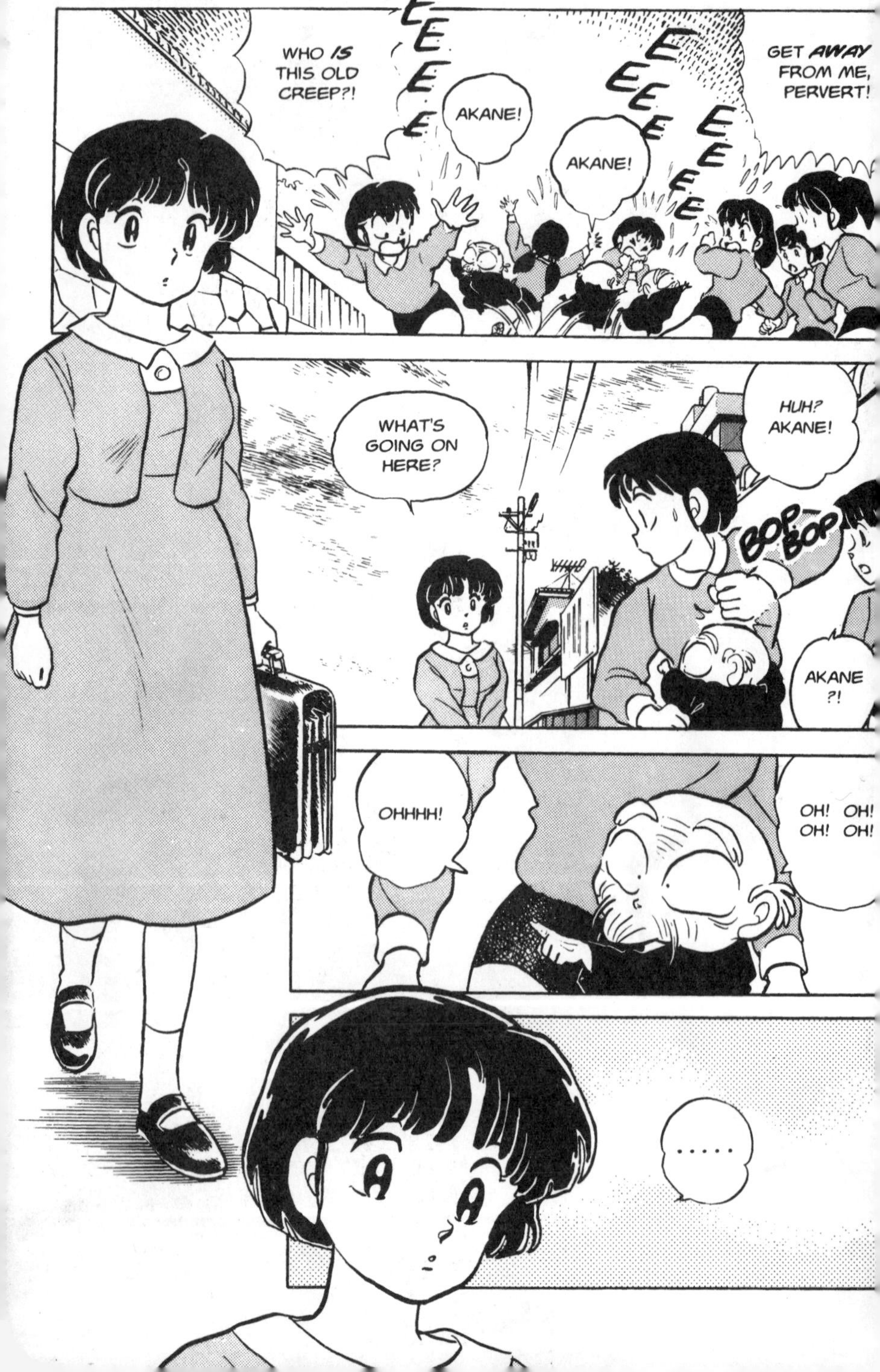
WHO IS THIS OLD CREEP?!
EEEEE
AKANE!
AKANE!
EEEEEEEEE
GET AWAY FROM ME, PERVERT!
WHAT'S GOING ON HERE?
HUH? AKANE!
BOP-BOP
AKANE ?!
OHHHH!
OH! OH! OH! OH!
.....

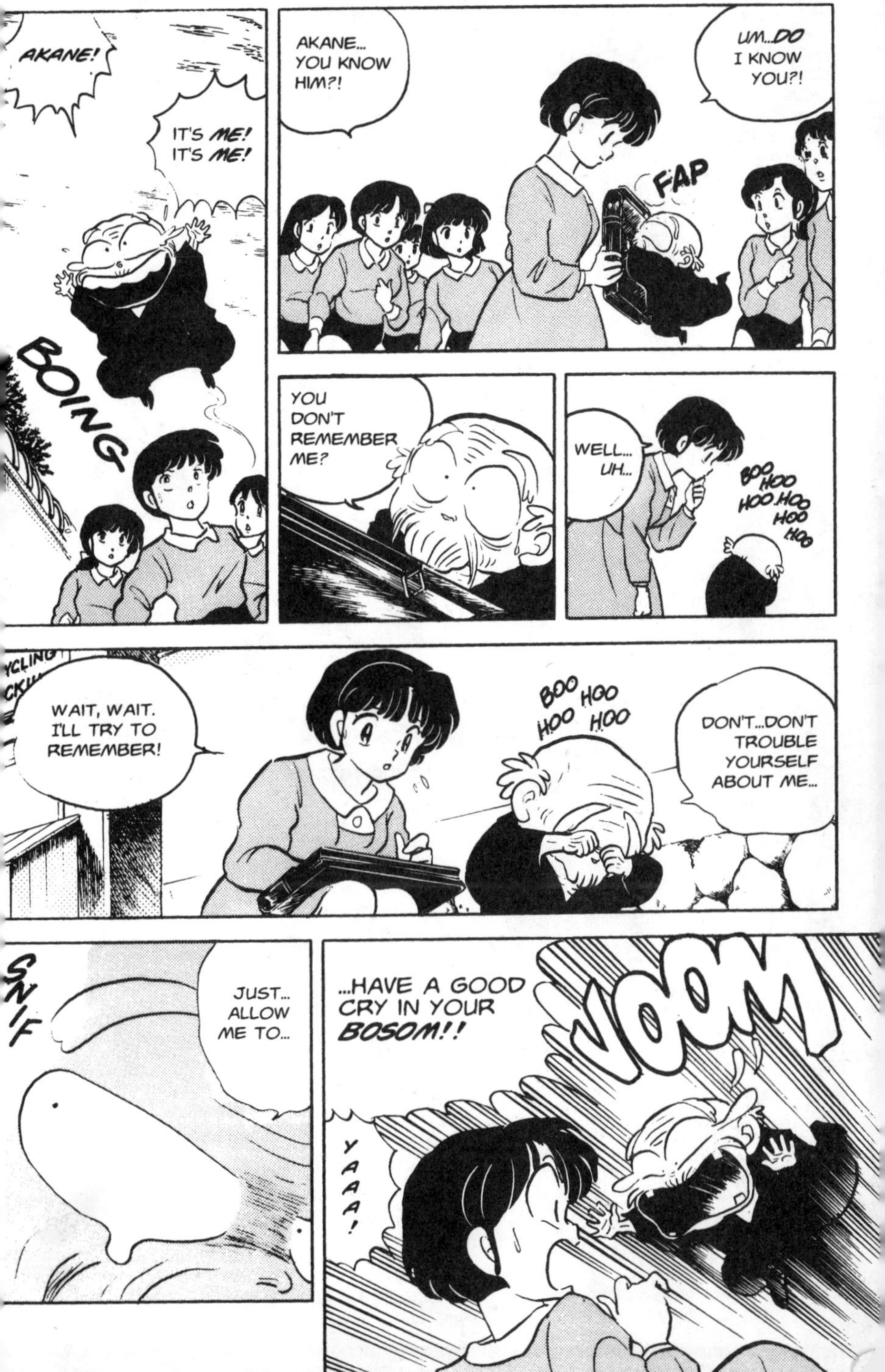
AKANE!
IT'S ME! IT'S ME!
BOING
AKANE... YOU KNOW HIM?!
UM...DO I KNOW YOU?!
FAP
YOU DON'T REMEMBER ME?
WELL... UH...
BOO HOO HOO HOO HOO HOO
WAIT, WAIT. I'LL TRY TO REMEMBER!
BOO HOO HOO HOO
DON'T...DON'T TROUBLE YOURSELF ABOUT ME...
SNIF
JUST... ALLOW ME TO...
...HAVE A GOOD CRY IN YOUR BOSOM!!
VOOM
YAAAA!

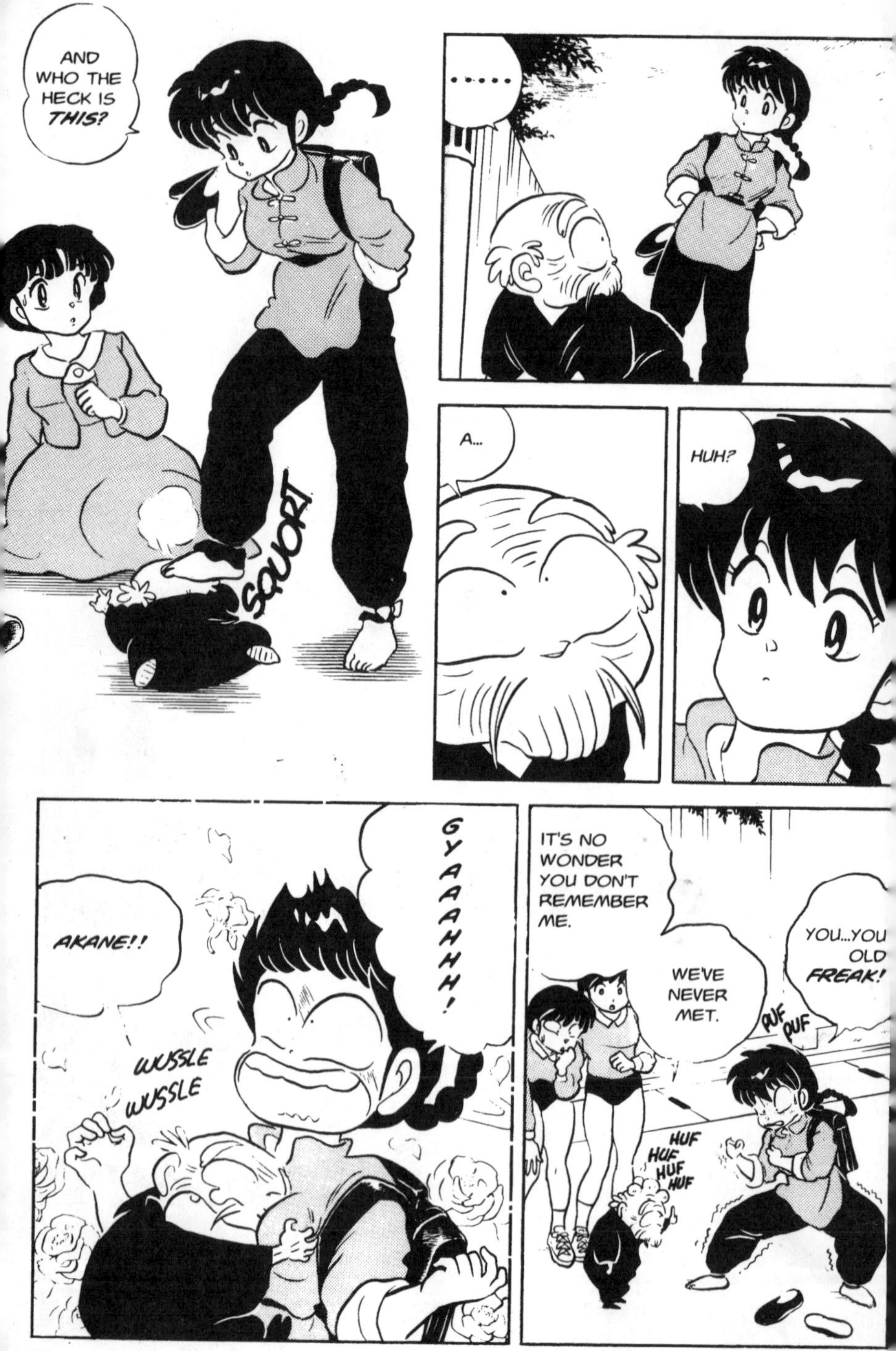
AND WHO THE HECK IS THIS?
SQUORT
. . . . .
A...
HUH?
AKANE!!
WUSSLE WUSSLE
GYAAAAHHH!
IT'S NO WONDER YOU DON'T REMEMBER ME.
WE'VE NEVER MET.
HUF HUF HUF HUF
PUF PUF
YOU...YOU OLD FREAK!

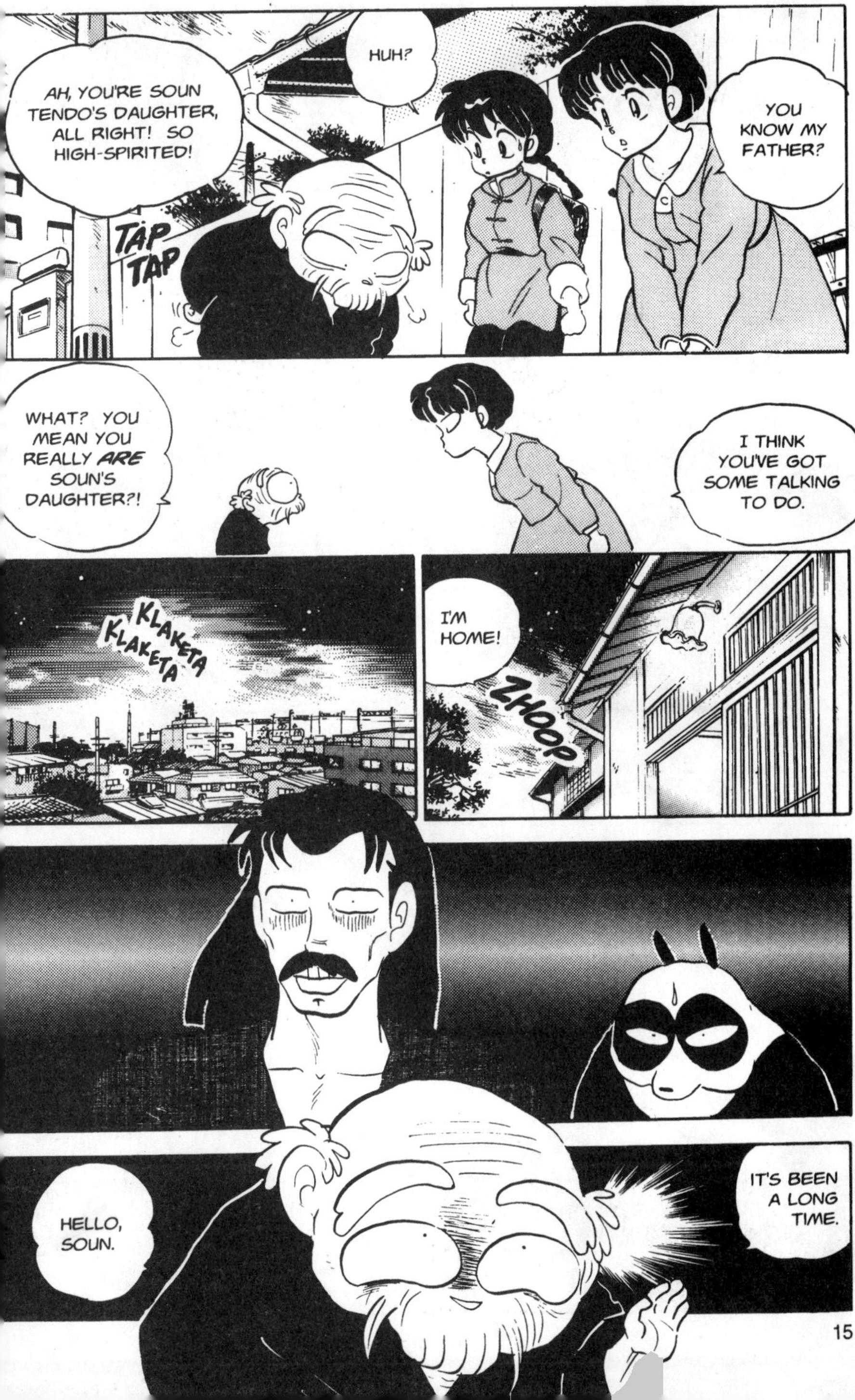
AH, YOU'RE SOUN TENDO'S DAUGHTER, ALL RIGHT! SO HIGH-SPIRITED!
TAP TAP
HUH?
YOU KNOW MY FATHER?
WHAT? YOU MEAN YOU REALLY ARE SOUN'S DAUGHTER?!
I THINK YOU'VE GOT SOME TALKING TO DO.
KLAKETA KLAKETA
I'M HOME!
ZHOOP
HELLO, SOUN.
IT'S BEEN A LONG TIME.

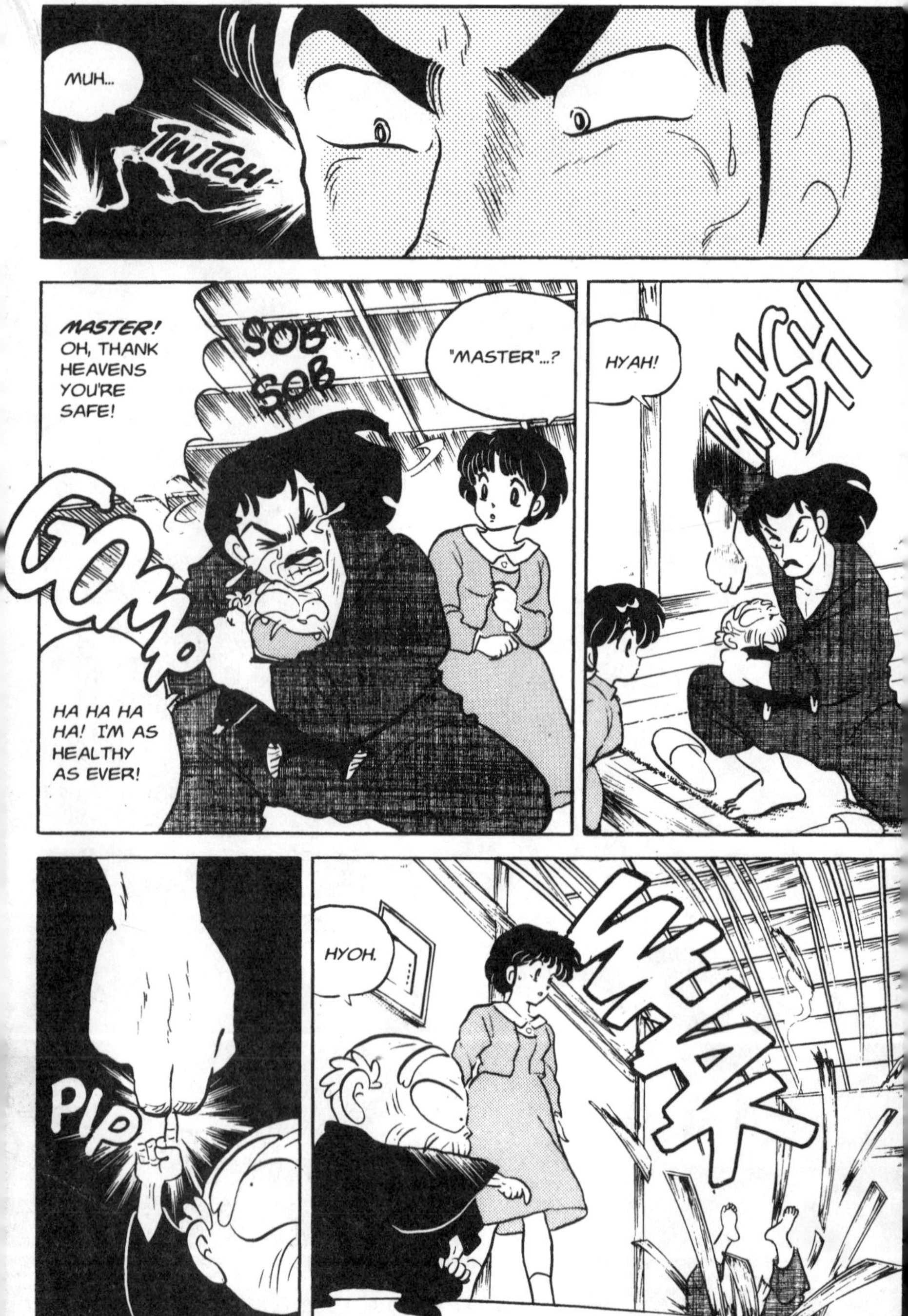
MUH...
TWITCH
MASTER! OH, THANK HEAVENS YOU'RE SAFE!
SOB SOB
"MASTER"...?
GOMP
HA HA HA HA! I'M AS HEALTHY AS EVER!
HYAH!
WHOOSH
PIP
HYOH.
WHAK

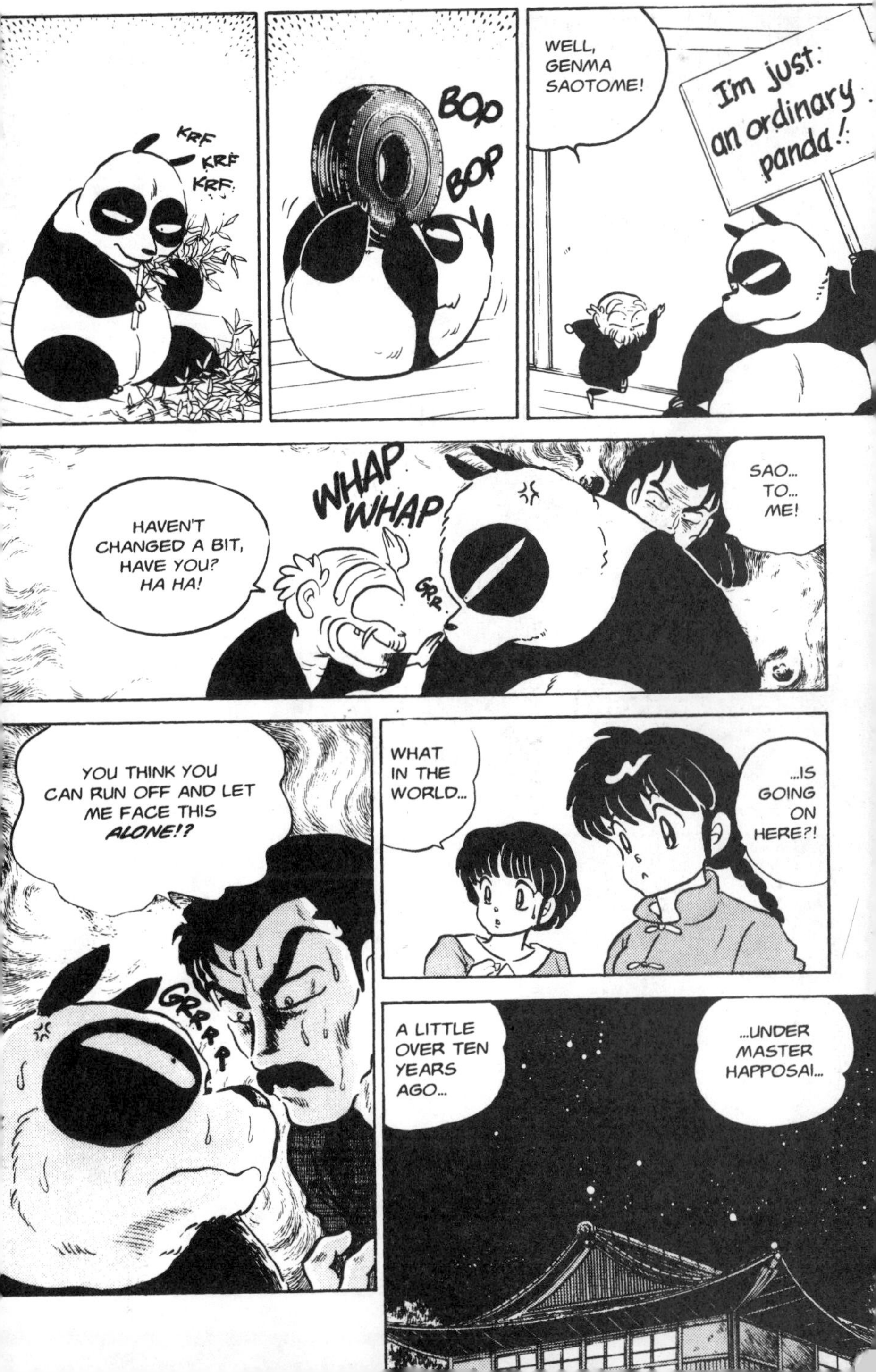
KRF
KRF
KRF
BOP
BOP
WELL, GENMA SAOTOME!
I'm just an ordinary panda!
WHAP WHAP
HAVEN'T CHANGED A BIT, HAVE YOU? HA HA!
GRR
SAO... TO... ME!
YOU THINK YOU CAN RUN OFF AND LET ME FACE THIS ALONE!?
GRRRR
WHAT IN THE WORLD...
...IS GOING ON HERE?!
A LITTLE OVER TEN YEARS AGO...
...UNDER MASTER HAPPOSAI...

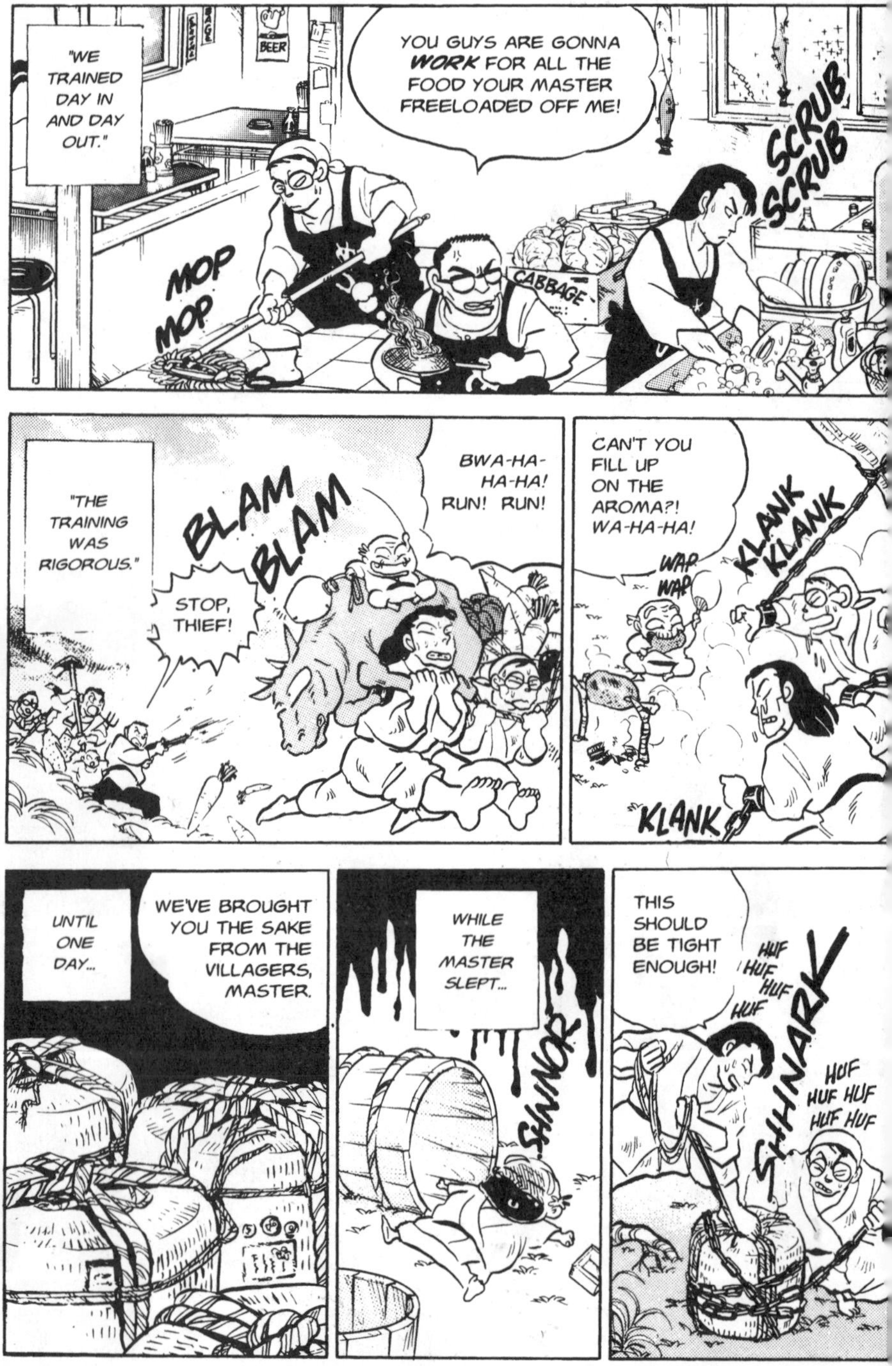
"WE TRAINED DAY IN AND DAY OUT."
YOU GUYS ARE GONNA **WORK** FOR ALL THE FOOD YOUR MASTER FREELOADED OFF ME!
BEER
MOP MOP
CABBAGE
SCRUB SCRUB
"THE TRAINING WAS RIGOROUS."
BLAM BLAM
BWA-HA-HA-HA! RUN! RUN!
STOP, THIEF!
CAN'T YOU FILL UP ON THE AROMA?! WA-HA-HA!
WAP WAP
KLANK KLANK
KLANK
UNTIL ONE DAY...
WE'VE BROUGHT YOU THE SAKE FROM THE VILLAGERS, MASTER.
WHILE THE MASTER SLEPT...
SHNOR
THIS SHOULD BE TIGHT ENOUGH!
HUF HUF HUF HUF
SHHNARK
HUF HUF HUF HUF HUF

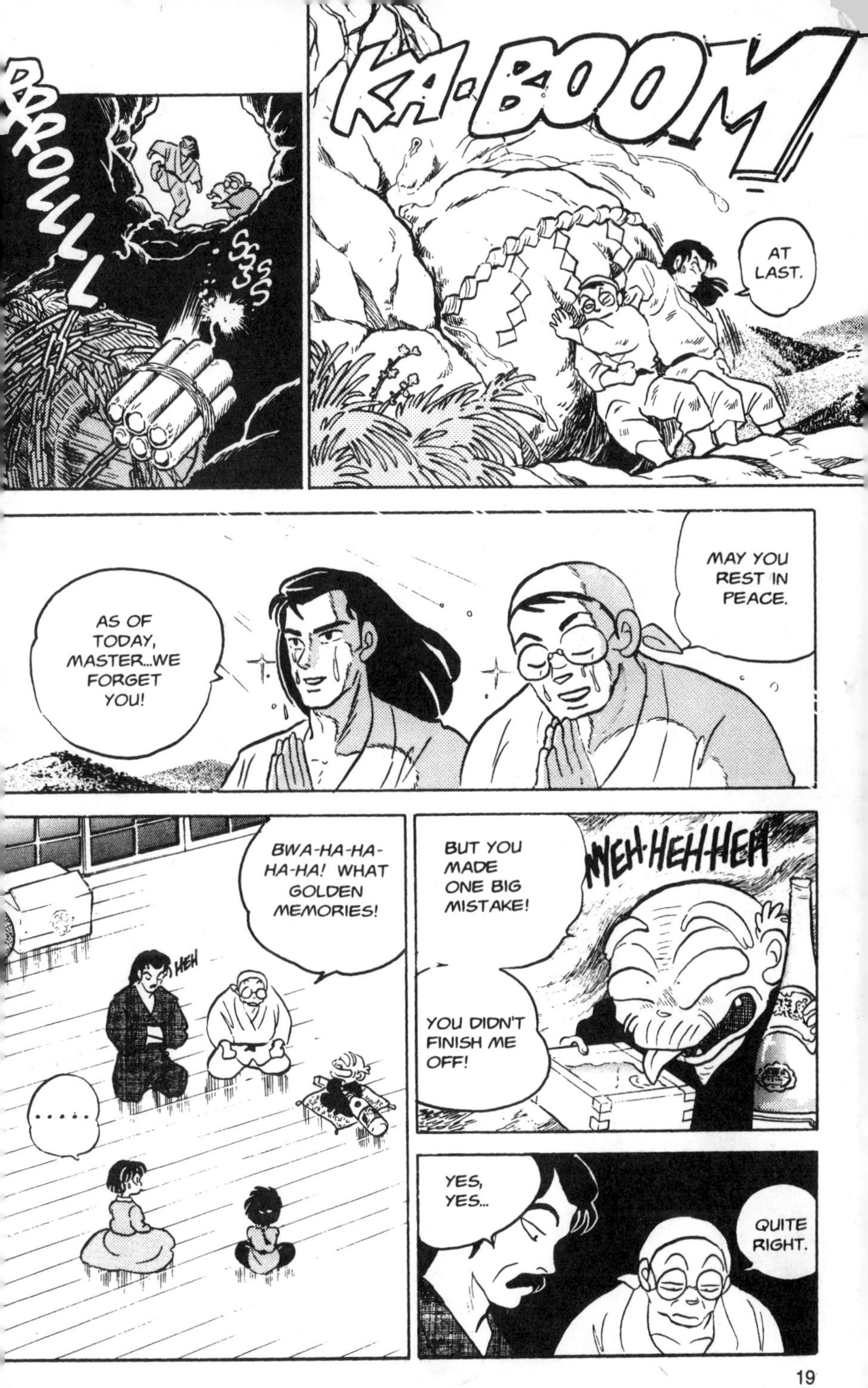
BRROWLLL
SSSSS
KA-BOOM
AT LAST.
AS OF TODAY, MASTER...WE FORGET YOU!
MAY YOU REST IN PEACE.
BWA-HA-HA-HA-HA! WHAT GOLDEN MEMORIES!
HEH
.....
BUT YOU MADE ONE BIG MISTAKE!
NYEH-HEH-HEH
YOU DIDN'T FINISH ME OFF!
YES, YES...
QUITE RIGHT.

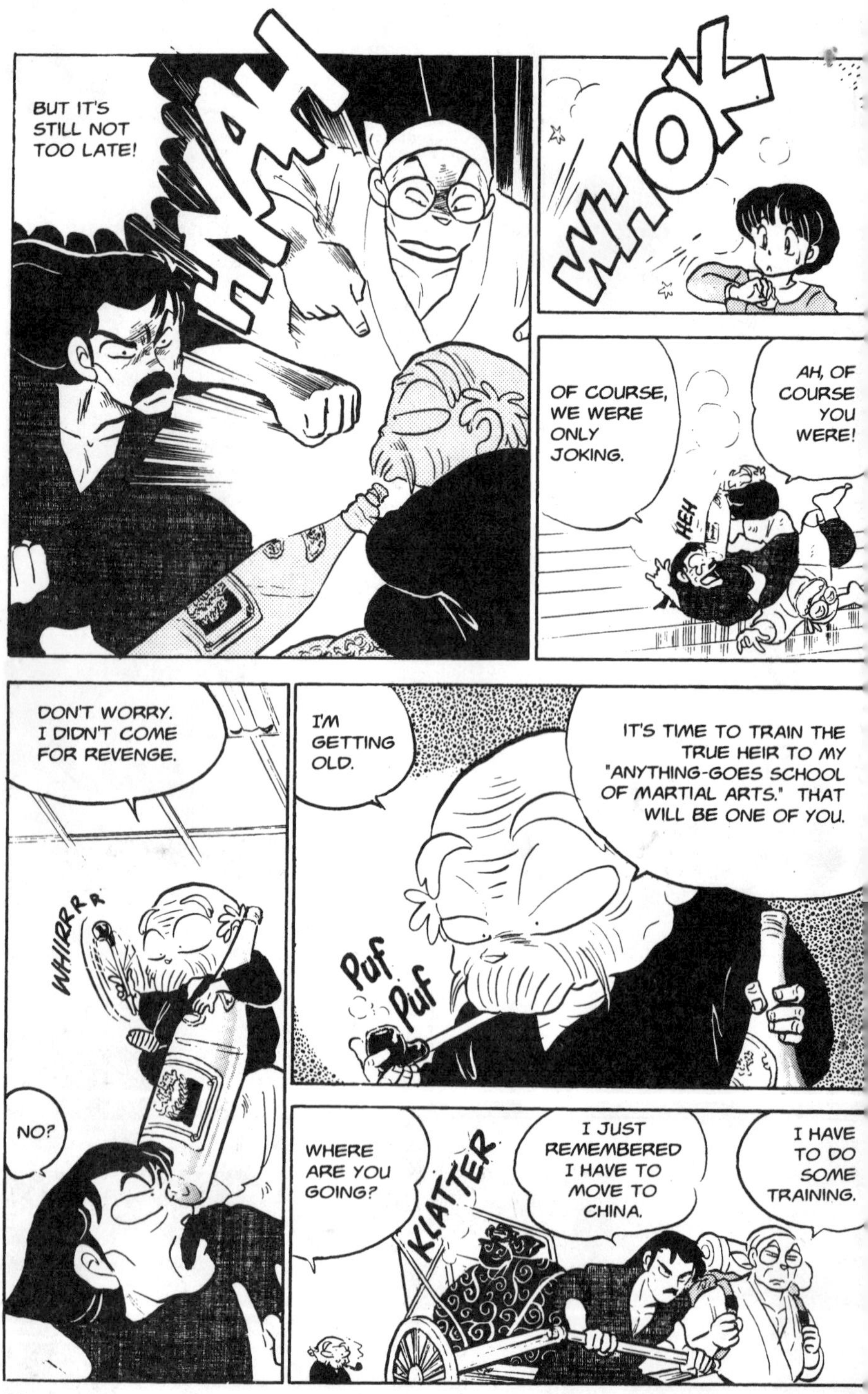

BUT IT'S STILL NOT TOO LATE!
HYAH
WHOK
OF COURSE, WE WERE ONLY JOKING.
AH, OF COURSE YOU WERE!
HEH
DON'T WORRY. I DIDN'T COME FOR REVENGE.
WHIRRRR
NO?
I'M GETTING OLD.
IT'S TIME TO TRAIN THE TRUE HEIR TO MY "ANYTHING-GOES SCHOOL OF MARTIAL ARTS." THAT WILL BE ONE OF YOU.
PUF PUF
WHERE ARE YOU GOING?
KLATTER
I JUST REMEMBERED I HAVE TO MOVE TO CHINA.
I HAVE TO DO SOME TRAINING.

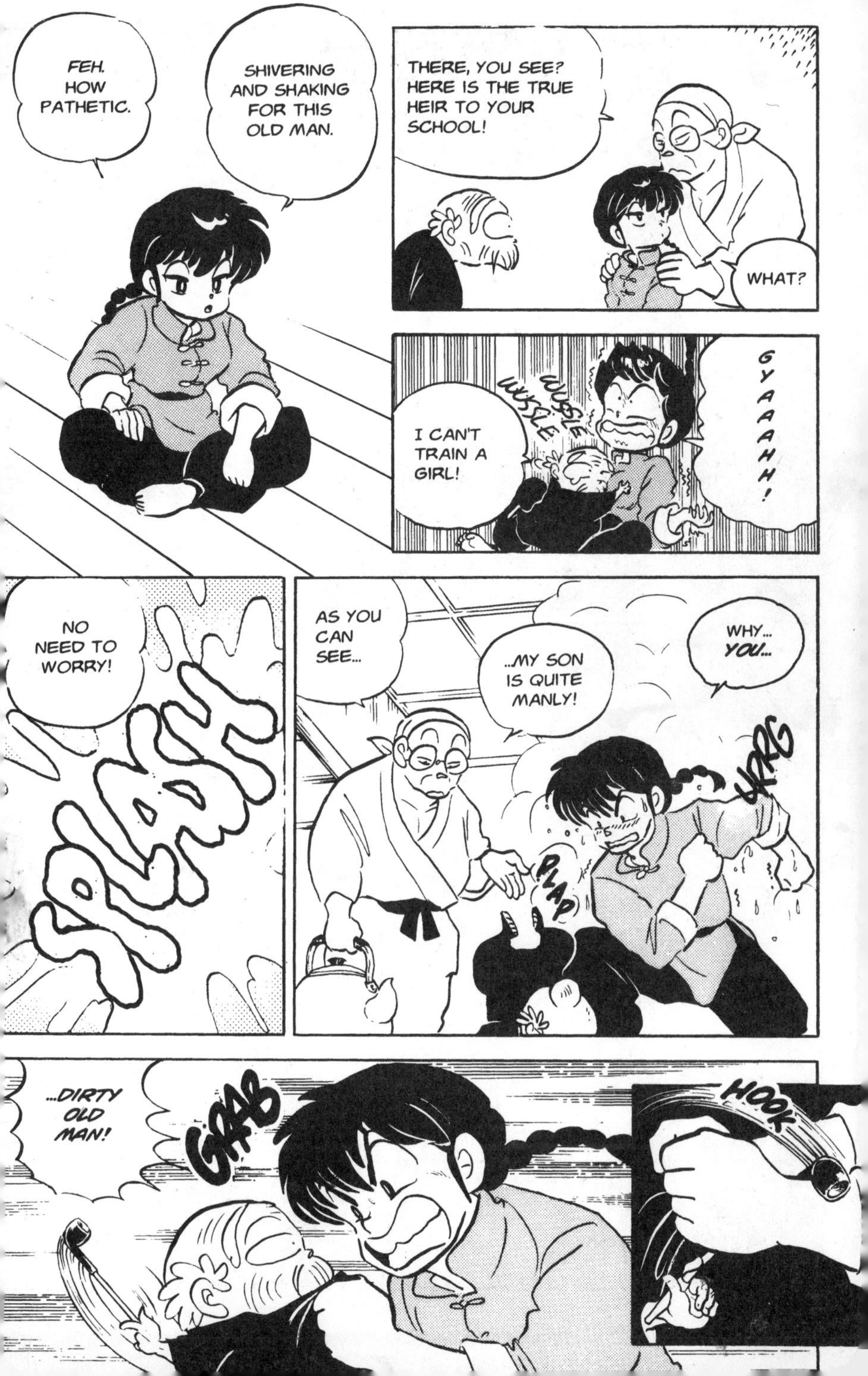
FEH. HOW PATHETIC.
SHIVERING AND SHAKING FOR THIS OLD MAN.
THERE, YOU SEE? HERE IS THE TRUE HEIR TO YOUR SCHOOL!
WHAT?
WUSSLE WUSSLE
I CAN'T TRAIN A GIRL!
GYAAAAHH!
NO NEED TO WORRY!
SPLASH
AS YOU CAN SEE...
...MY SON IS QUITE MANLY!
WHY... YOU...
URRG
PLAP
...DIRTY OLD MAN!
GRAB
HOOK

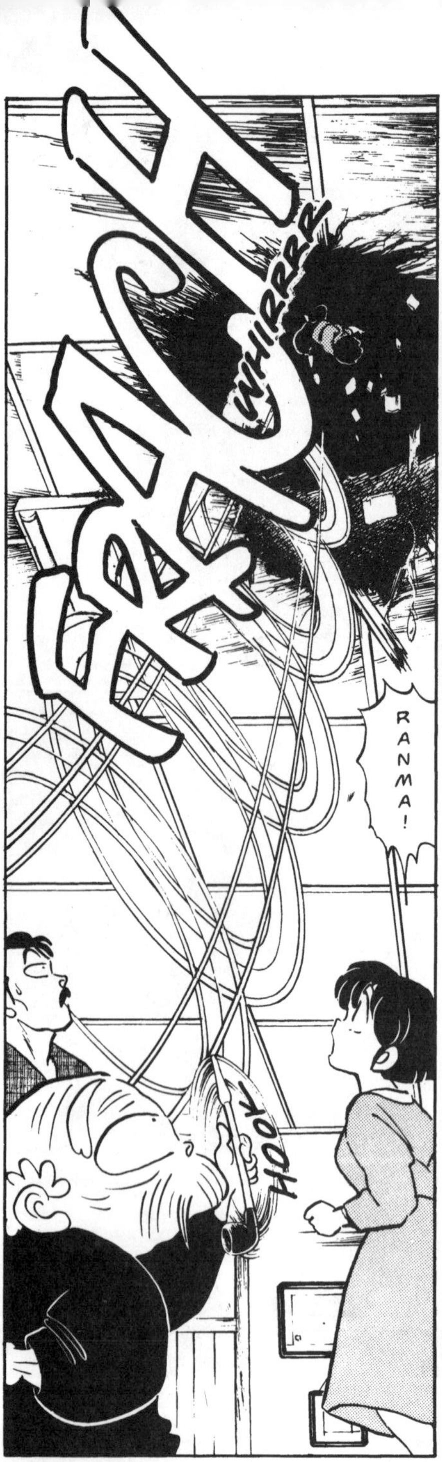
WHIRRRR
RANMA!
HOOK

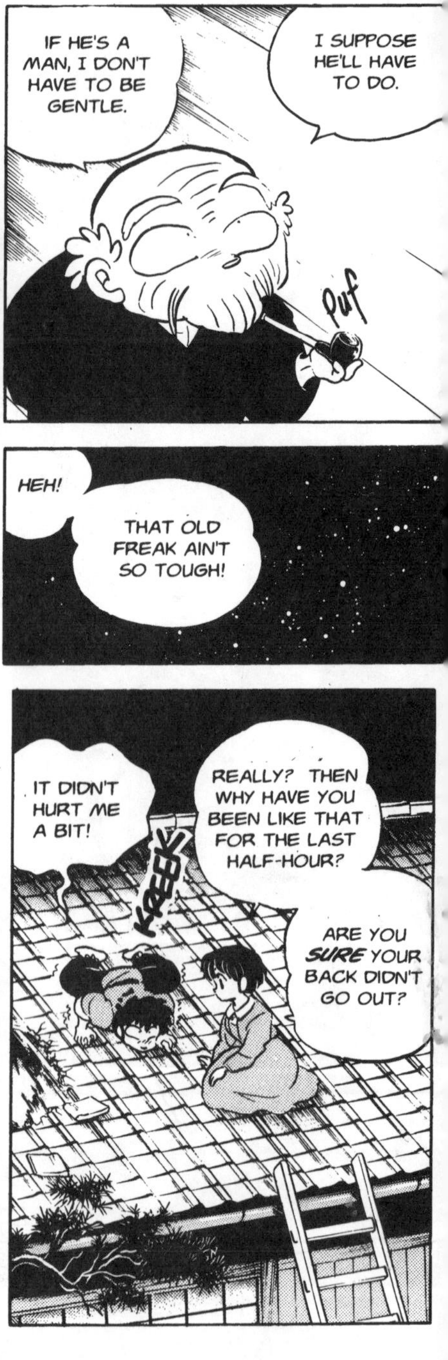
IF HE'S A MAN, I DON'T HAVE TO BE GENTLE.
I SUPPOSE HE'LL HAVE TO DO.
Puf
HEH!
THAT OLD FREAK AIN'T SO TOUGH!
IT DIDN'T HURT ME A BIT!
KREEEK
REALLY? THEN WHY HAVE YOU BEEN LIKE THAT FOR THE LAST HALF-HOUR?
ARE YOU SURE YOUR BACK DIDN'T GO OUT?

PART 2

HE'S SOMETHING ELSE

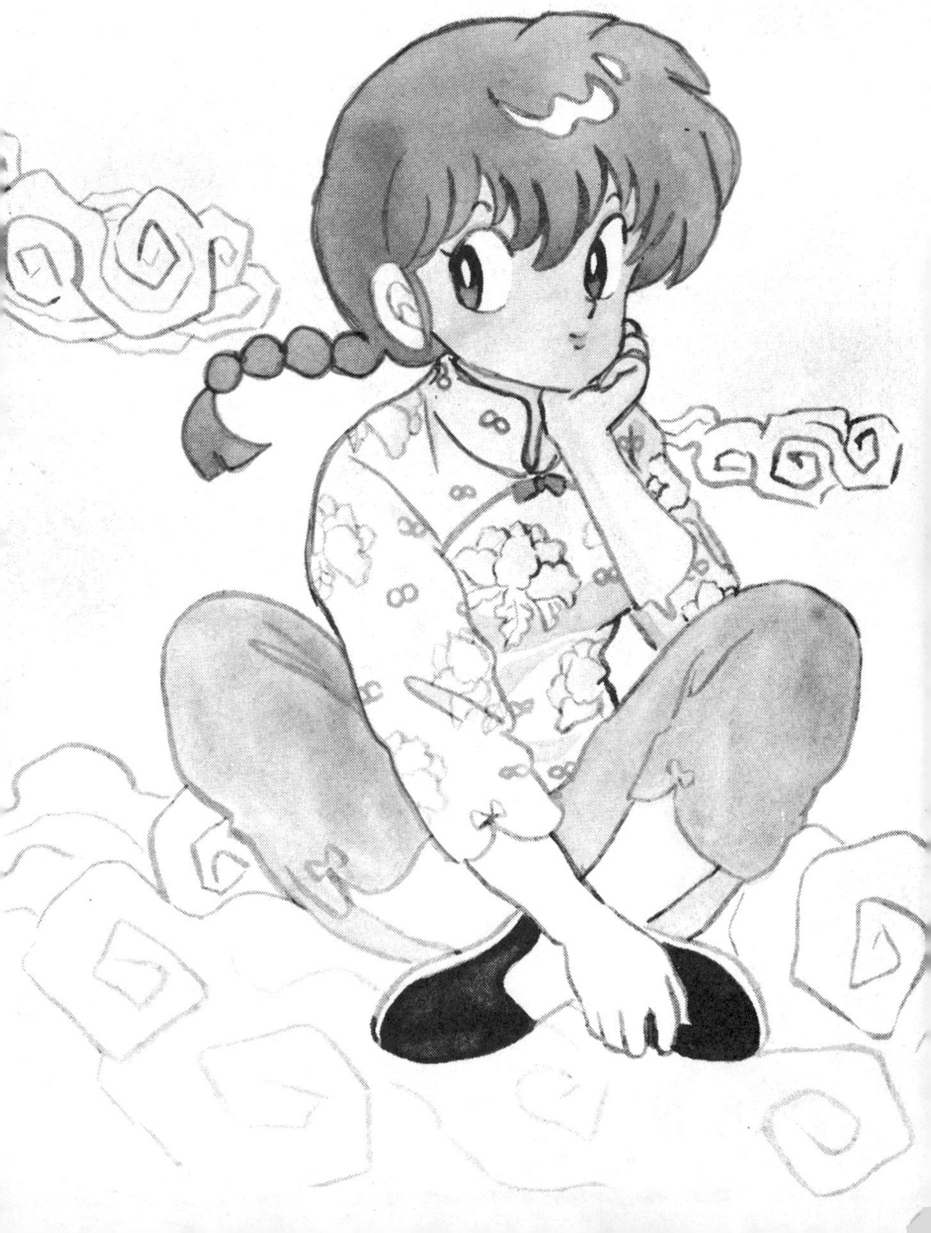

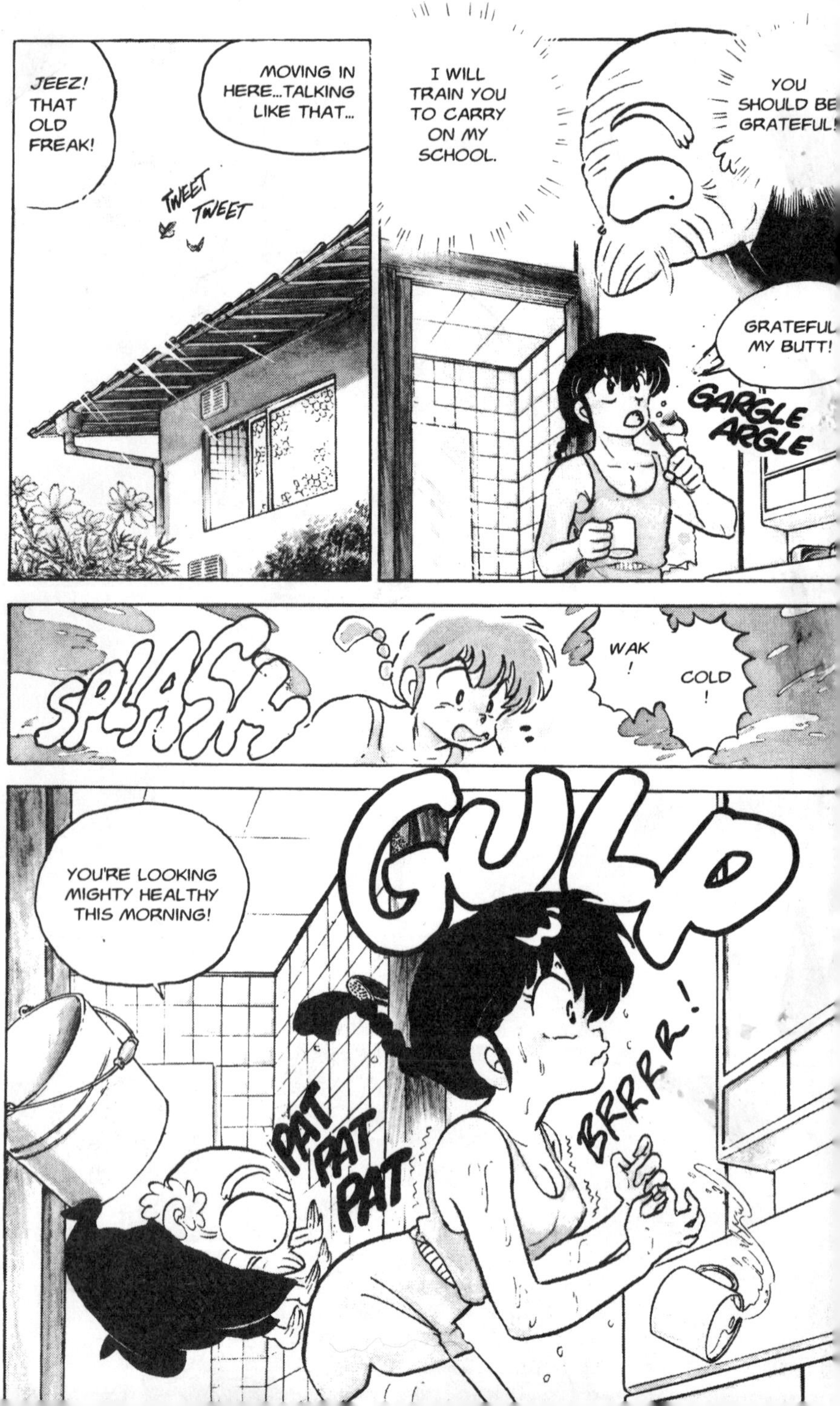
JEEZ! THAT OLD FREAK!
MOVING IN HERE...TALKING LIKE THAT...
TWEET TWEET
I WILL TRAIN YOU TO CARRY ON MY SCHOOL.
YOU SHOULD BE GRATEFUL!
GRATEFUL MY BUTT!
GARGLE ARGLE
SPLASH
WAK!
COLD!
GULP
YOU'RE LOOKING MIGHTY HEALTHY THIS MORNING!
PAT PAT PAT
BRRRR!

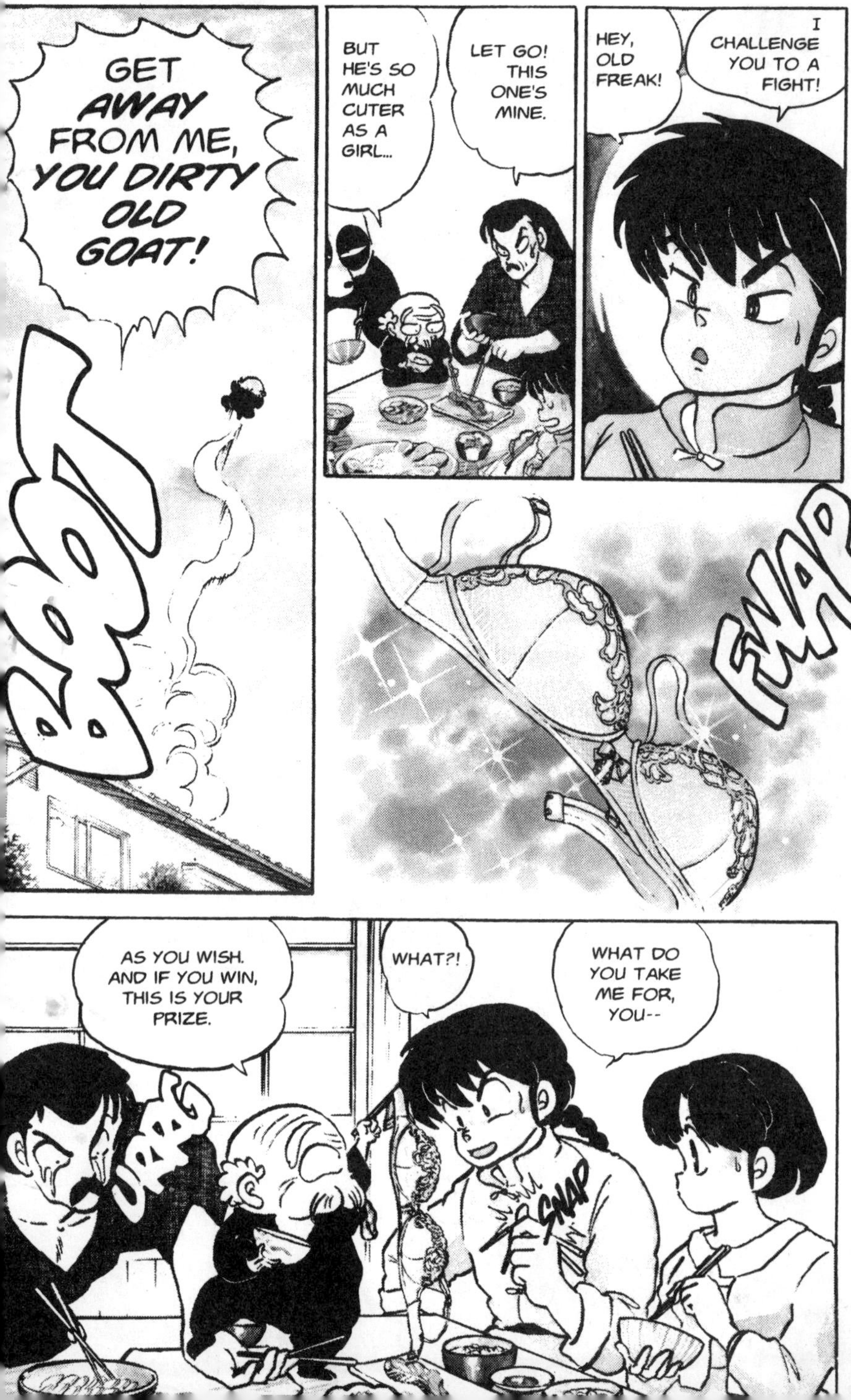
GET *AWAY* FROM ME, *YOU DIRTY OLD GOAT!*
BOOT
BUT HE'S SO MUCH CUTER AS A GIRL...
LET GO! THIS ONE'S MINE.
HEY, OLD FREAK!
I CHALLENGE YOU TO A FIGHT!
FWAP
AS YOU WISH. AND IF YOU WIN, THIS IS YOUR PRIZE.
URRG
WHAT?!
SNAP
WHAT DO YOU TAKE ME FOR, YOU--

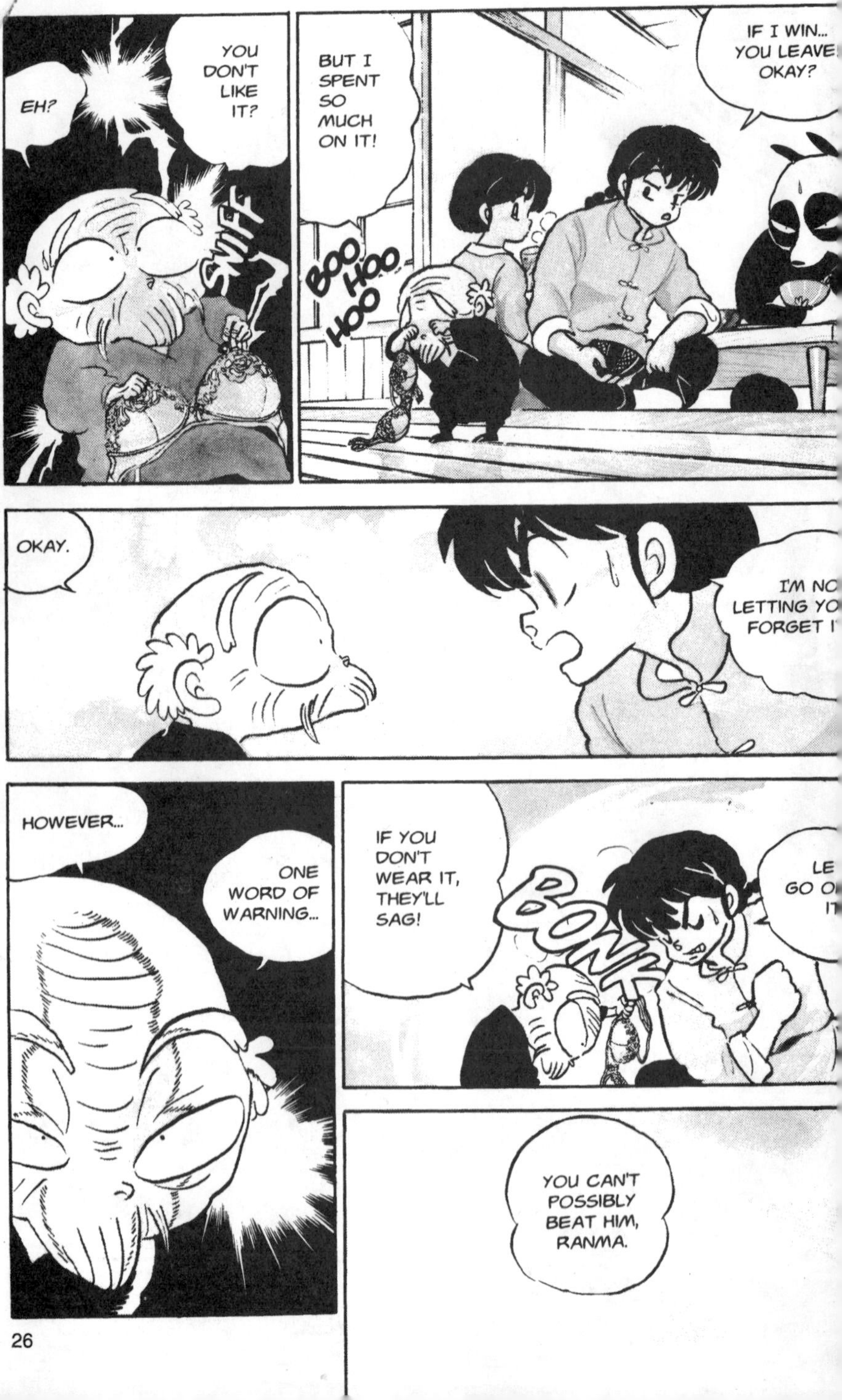
EH?
YOU DON'T LIKE IT?
SNIFF
BUT I SPENT SO MUCH ON IT!
BOO HOO HOO
IF I WIN... YOU LEAVE OKAY?
OKAY.
I'M NO LETTING YO FORGET I
HOWEVER...
ONE WORD OF WARNING...
IF YOU DON'T WEAR IT, THEY'LL SAG!
BONK
YOU CAN'T POSSIBLY BEAT HIM, RANMA.

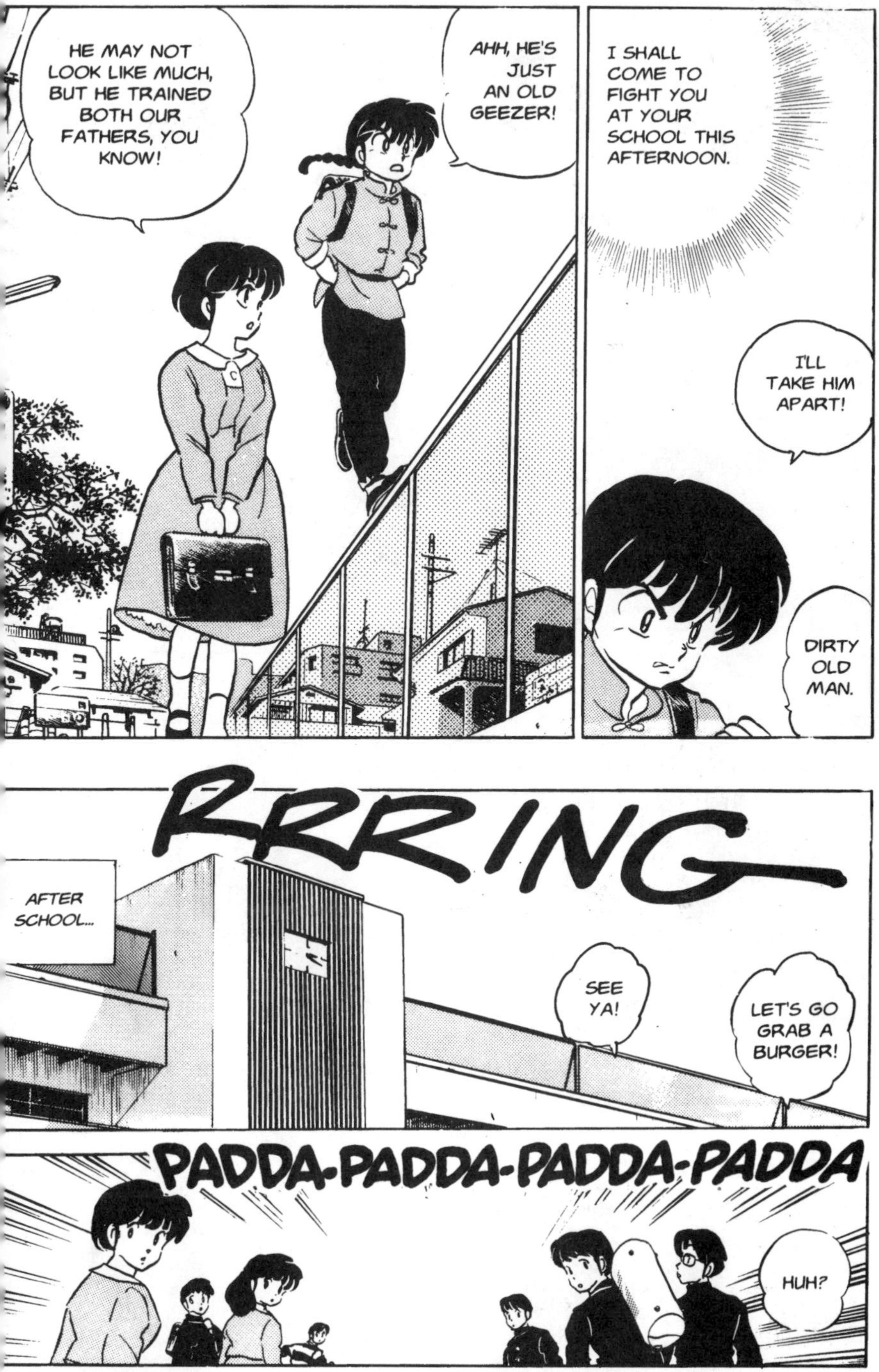
HE MAY NOT LOOK LIKE MUCH, BUT HE TRAINED BOTH OUR FATHERS, YOU KNOW!
AHH, HE'S JUST AN OLD GEEZER!
I SHALL COME TO FIGHT YOU AT YOUR SCHOOL THIS AFTERNOON.
I'LL TAKE HIM APART!
DIRTY OLD MAN.
RRRING
AFTER SCHOOL...
SEE YA!
LET'S GO GRAB A BURGER!
PADDA-PADDA-PADDA-PADDA
HUH?

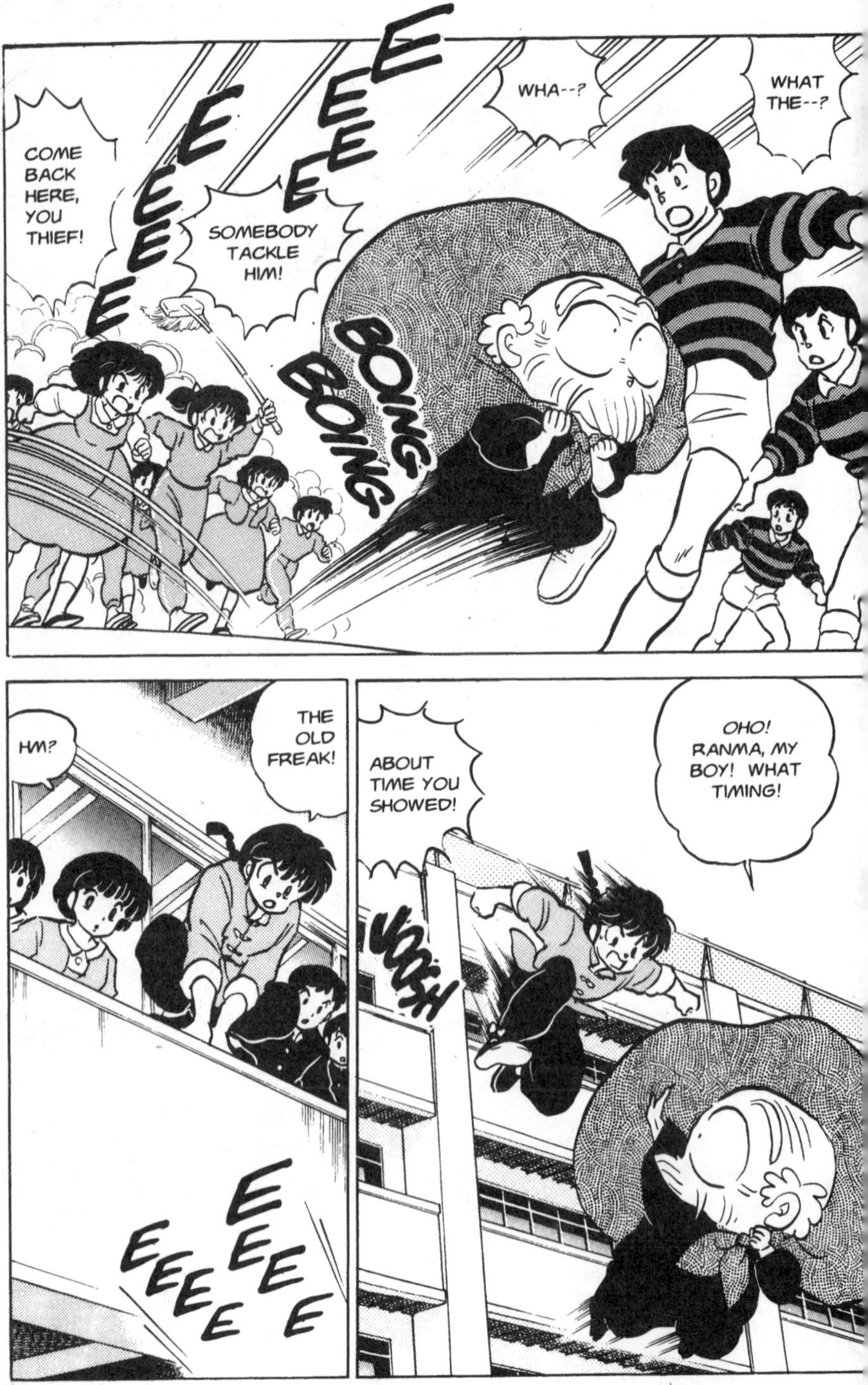
COME BACK HERE, YOU THIEF!
EEEEEEEEEEEE
SOMEBODY TACKLE HIM!
BOING BOING
WHA--?
WHAT THE--?
HM?
THE OLD FREAK!
EEEEEEEEE
ABOUT TIME YOU SHOWED!
OHO! RANMA, MY BOY! WHAT TIMING!
VOOOSH

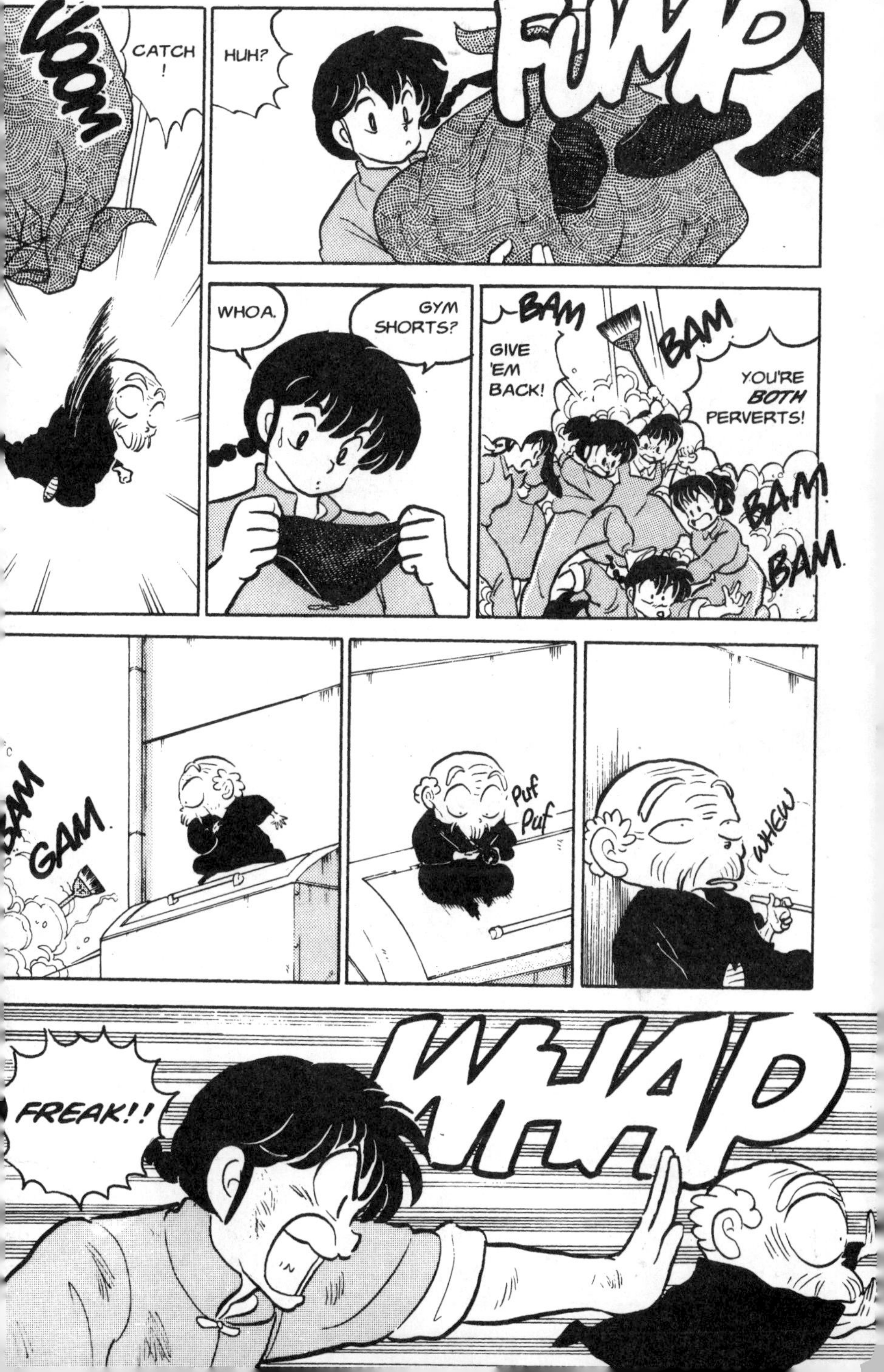
VOOM
CATCH!
HUH?
FUMP
WHOA.
GYM SHORTS?
BAM
GIVE 'EM BACK!
BAM
YOU'RE BOTH PERVERTS!
BAM
BAM
BAM
GAM
Puf Puf
WHEW
FREAK!!
WHAP

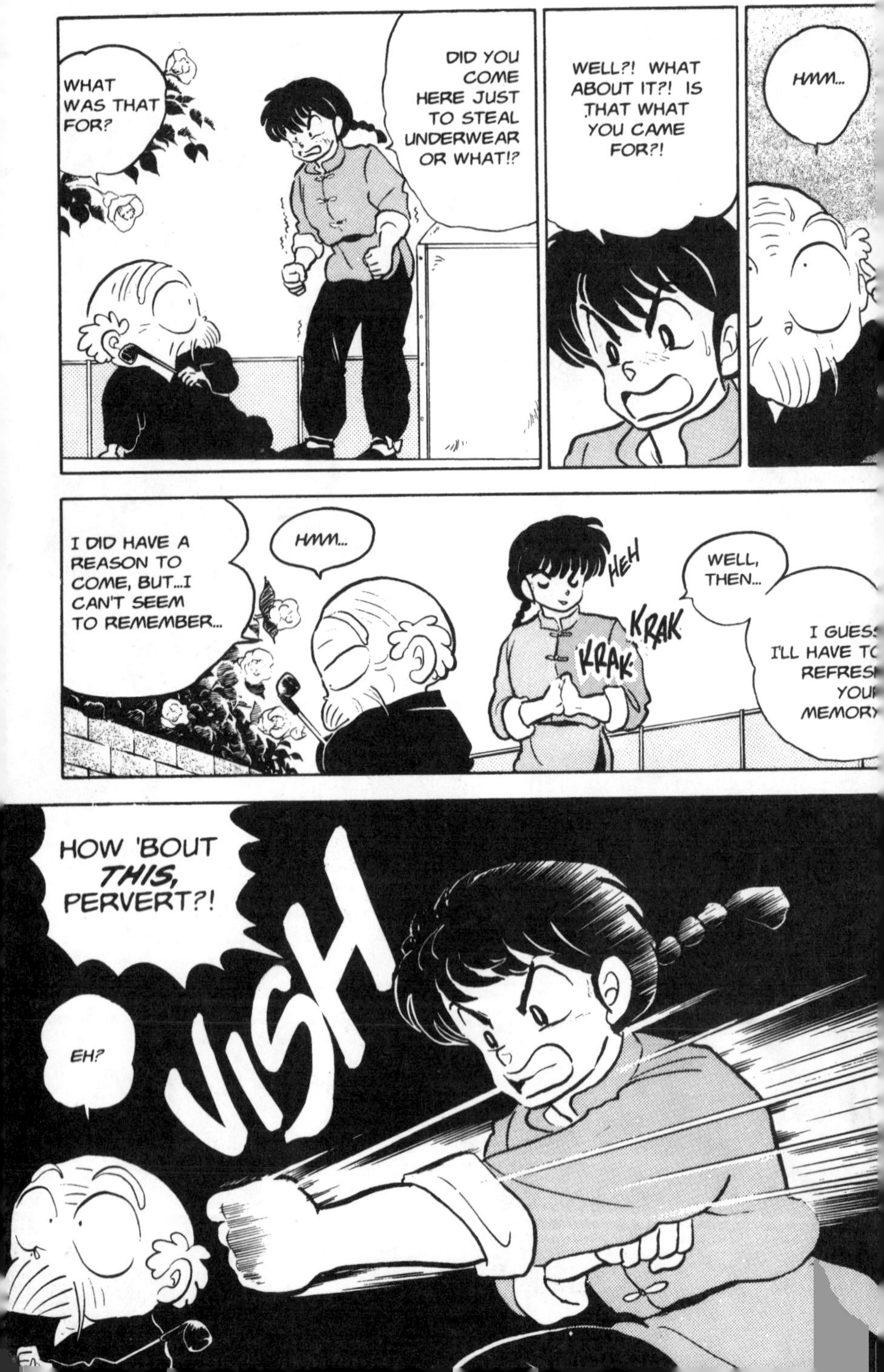

WHAT WAS THAT FOR?
DID YOU COME HERE JUST TO STEAL UNDERWEAR OR WHAT!?
WELL?! WHAT ABOUT IT?! IS THAT WHAT YOU CAME FOR?!
HMM...
I DID HAVE A REASON TO COME, BUT...I CAN'T SEEM TO REMEMBER...
HMM...
HEH
KRAK
KRAK
WELL, THEN...
I GUESS I'LL HAVE TO REFRESH YOUR MEMORY
HOW 'BOUT THIS, PERVERT?!
EH?
VISH

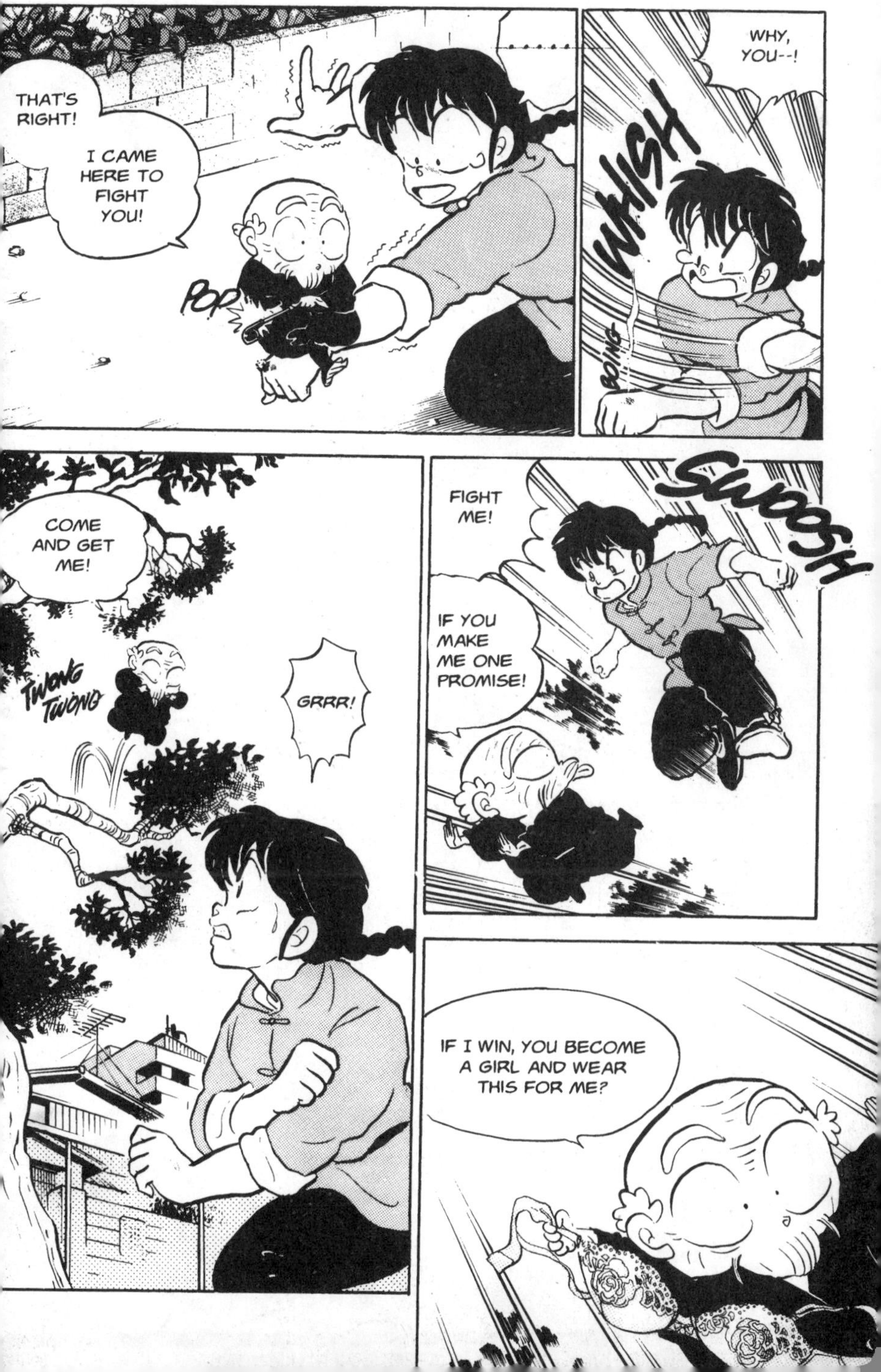
THAT'S RIGHT!
I CAME HERE TO FIGHT YOU!
POP
WHY, YOU--!
WHISH
BOING
COME AND GET ME!
TWONG TWONG
GRRR!
FIGHT ME!
SWOOSH
IF YOU MAKE ME ONE PROMISE!
IF I WIN, YOU BECOME A GIRL AND WEAR THIS FOR ME?

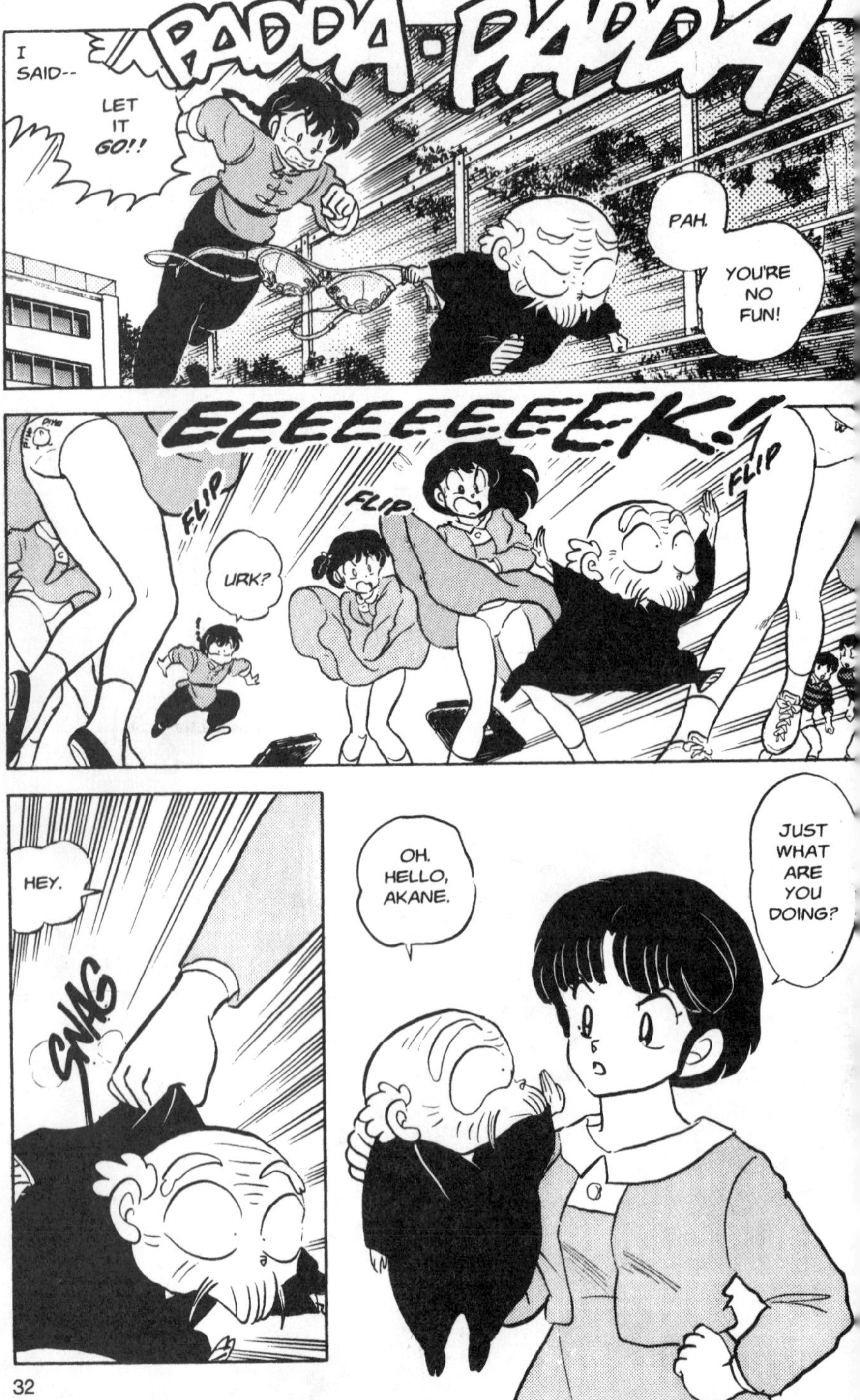
PADDA-PADDA
I SAID--
LET IT GO!!
PAH.
YOU'RE NO FUN!
EEEEEEEEEK!
FLIP
FLIP
URK?
FLIP
HEY.
SNAG
OH. HELLO, AKANE.
JUST WHAT ARE YOU DOING?

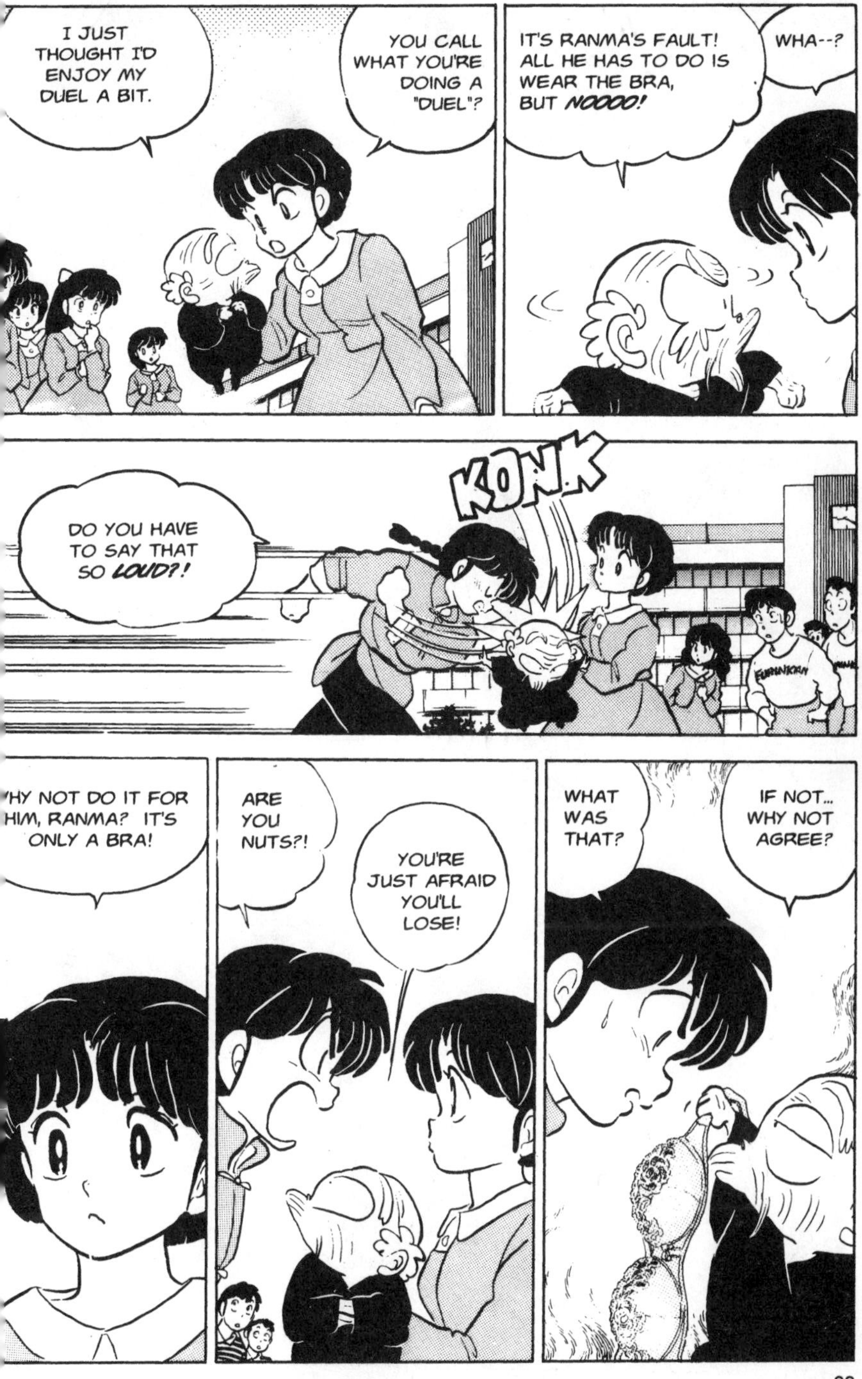
I JUST THOUGHT I'D ENJOY MY DUEL A BIT.
YOU CALL WHAT YOU'RE DOING A "DUEL"?
IT'S RANMA'S FAULT! ALL HE HAS TO DO IS WEAR THE BRA, BUT NOOOO!
WHA--?
KONK
DO YOU HAVE TO SAY THAT SO LOUD?!
'HY NOT DO IT FOR HIM, RANMA? IT'S ONLY A BRA!
ARE YOU NUTS?!
YOU'RE JUST AFRAID YOU'LL LOSE!
WHAT WAS THAT?
IF NOT... WHY NOT AGREE?

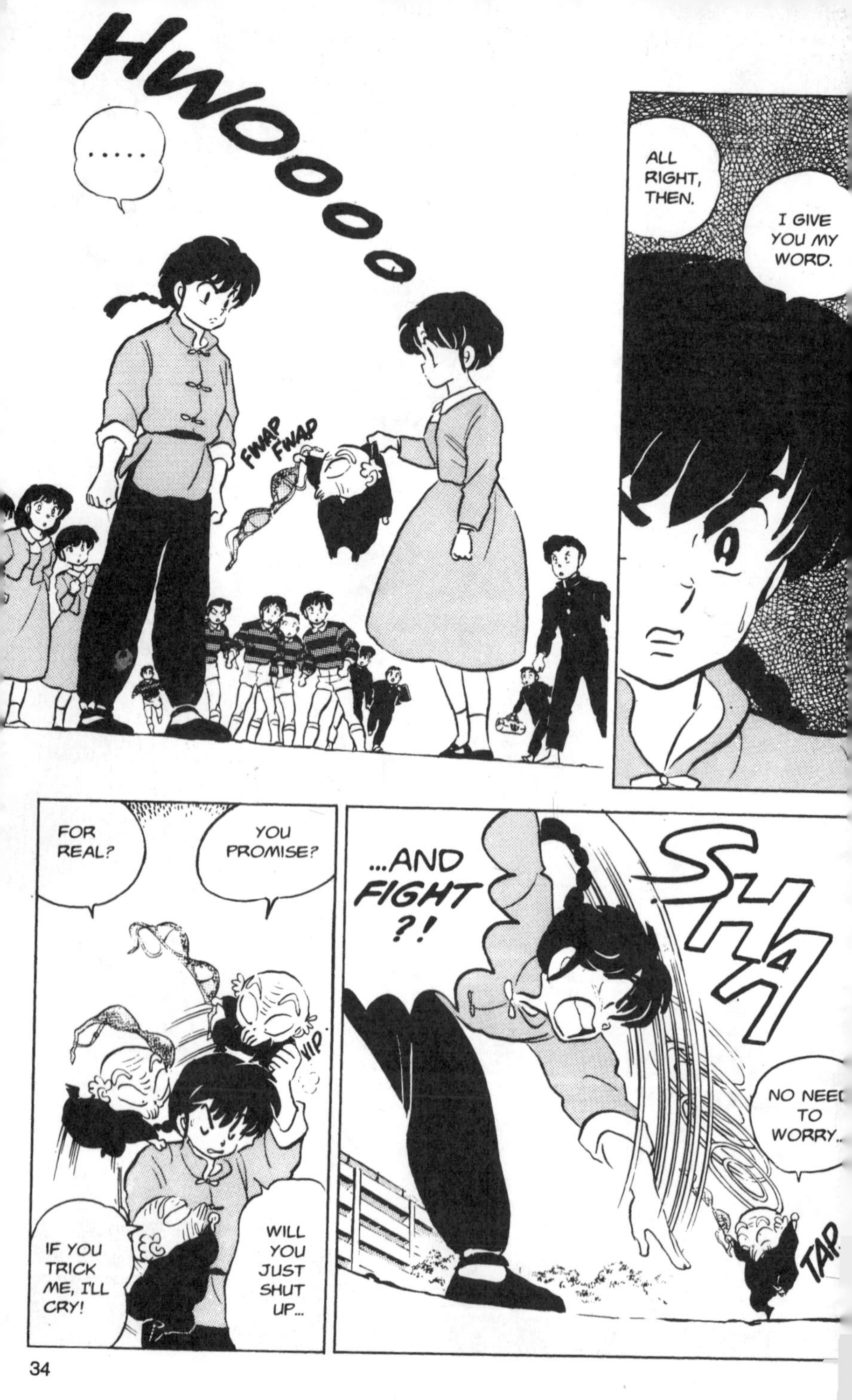
HWOOOOO
......
FWAP FWAP
ALL RIGHT, THEN.
I GIVE YOU MY WORD.
FOR REAL?
YOU PROMISE?
VIP
IF YOU TRICK ME, I'LL CRY!
WILL YOU JUST SHUT UP...
...AND FIGHT?!
SHA
NO NEED TO WORRY..
TAP

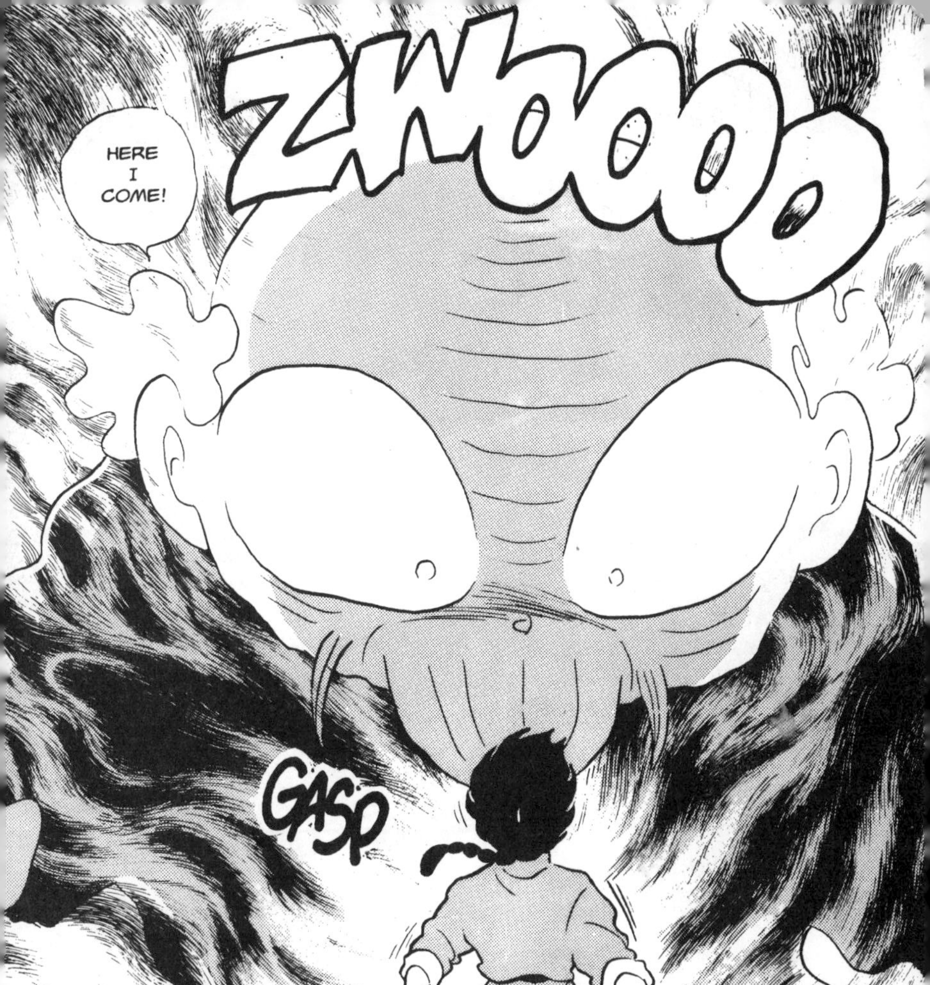
HERE I COME!
ZWOOOO
GASP

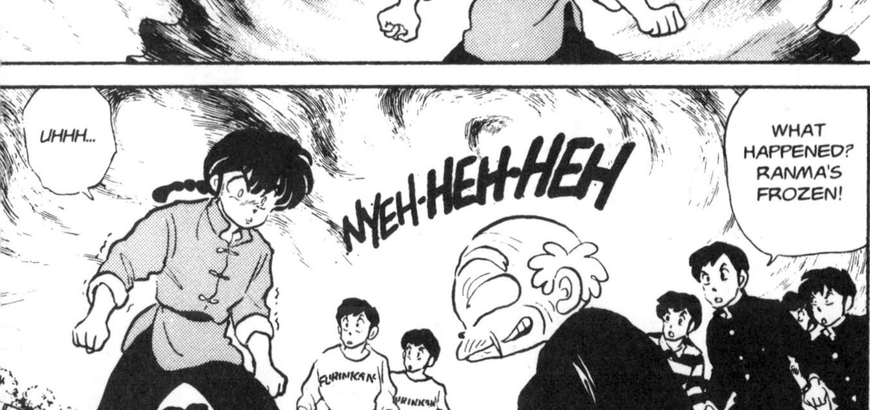
UHHH...
NYEH-HEH-HEH
WHAT HAPPENED? RANMA'S FROZEN!
FURINKAN
FURINKAN

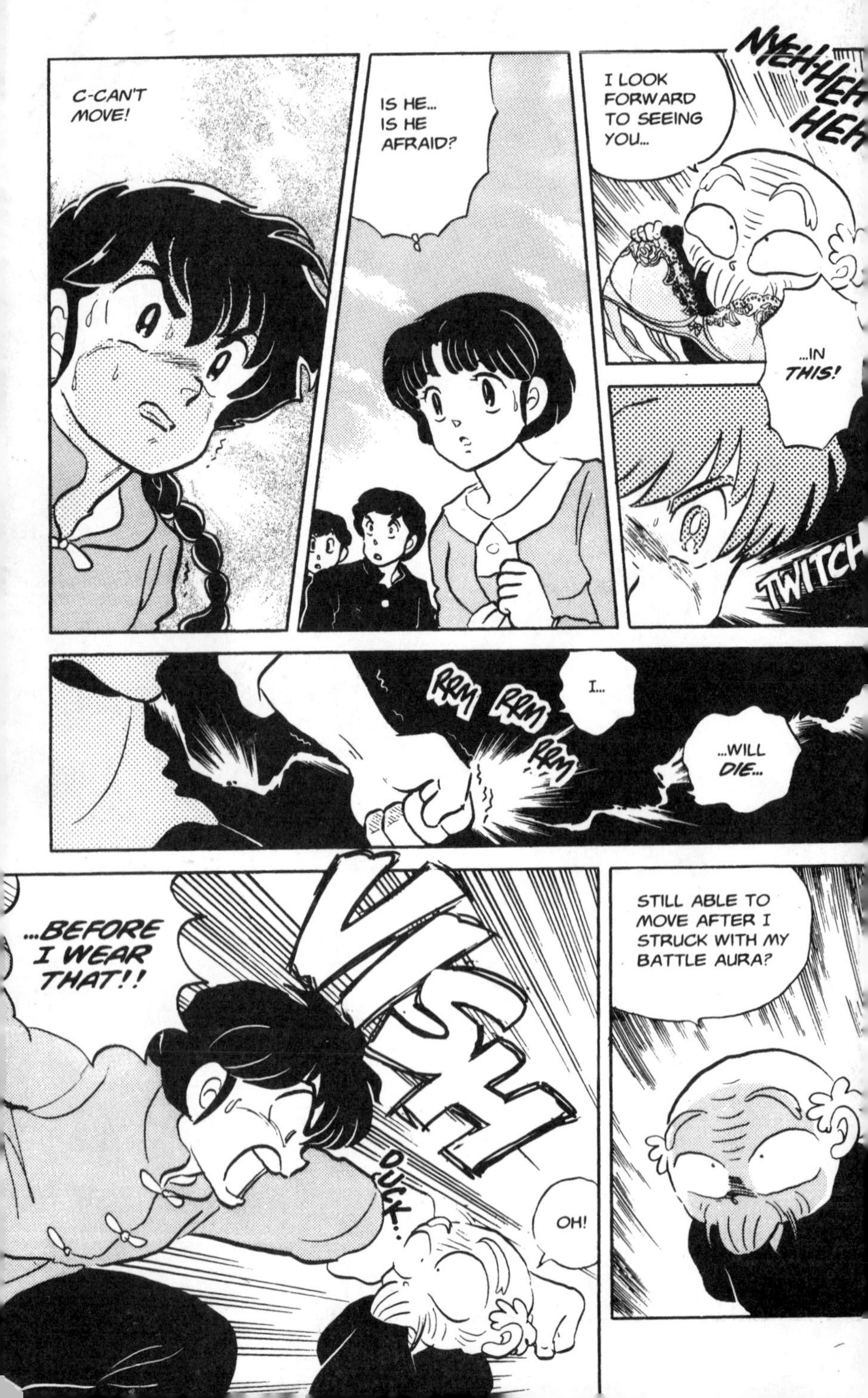
C-CAN'T MOVE!
IS HE... IS HE AFRAID?
I LOOK FORWARD TO SEEING YOU...
NYEH-HEH HEH
...IN THIS!
TWITCH
RRM RRM RRM
I...
...WILL DIE...
...BEFORE I WEAR THAT!!
VISH
DUCK
OH!
STILL ABLE TO MOVE AFTER I STRUCK WITH MY BATTLE AURA?

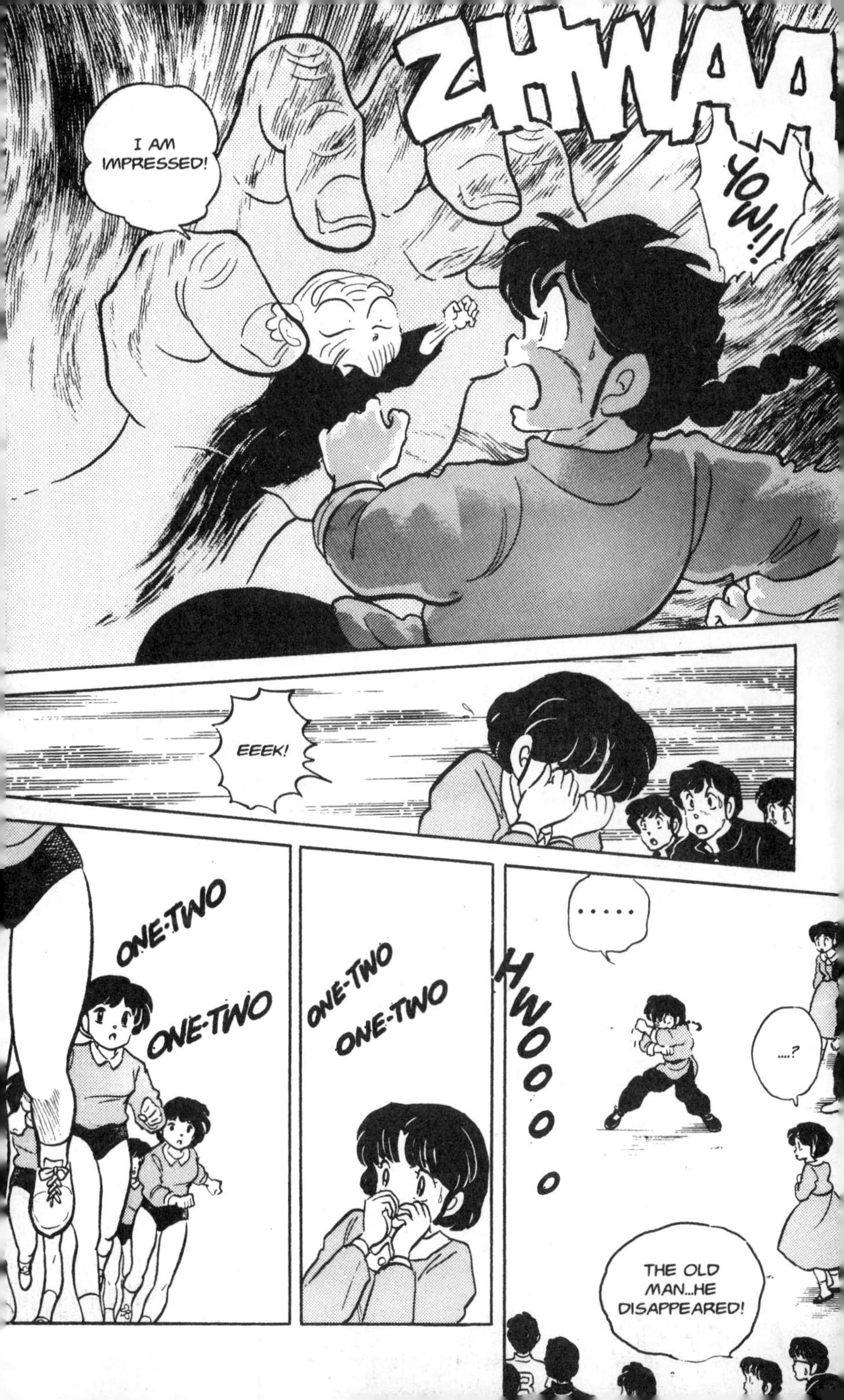
I AM IMPRESSED!
ZHWAA
YOW!!
EEEK!
ONE-TWO
ONE-TWO
ONE-TWO
ONE-TWO
......
HWOOOOO
....?
THE OLD MAN...HE DISAPPEARED!

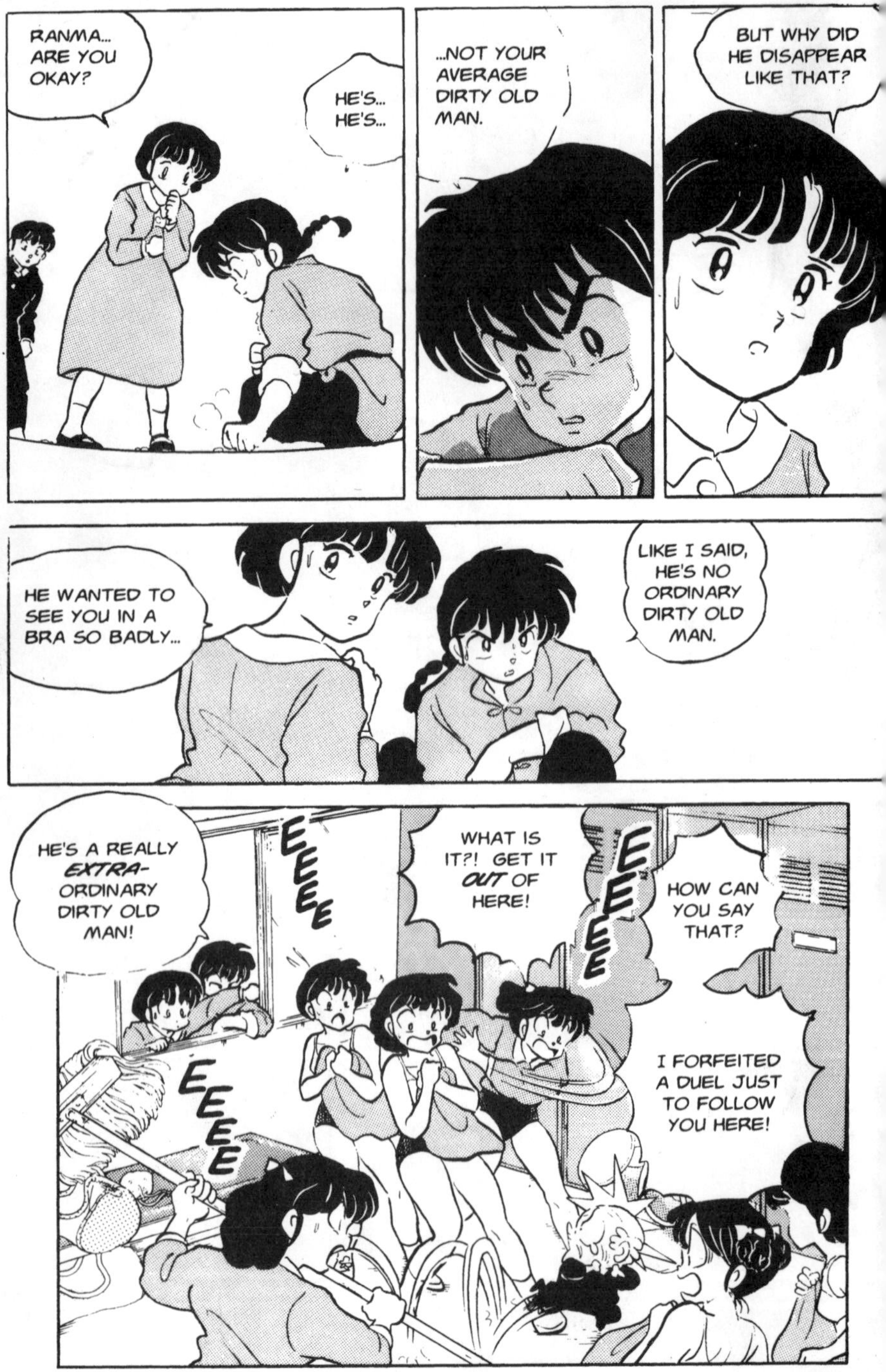
RANMA... ARE YOU OKAY?
HE'S... HE'S...
...NOT YOUR AVERAGE DIRTY OLD MAN.
BUT WHY DID HE DISAPPEAR LIKE THAT?
HE WANTED TO SEE YOU IN A BRA SO BADLY...
LIKE I SAID, HE'S NO ORDINARY DIRTY OLD MAN.
HE'S A REALLY *EXTRA-*ORDINARY DIRTY OLD MAN!
EEEE
WHAT IS IT?! GET IT *OUT* OF HERE!
EEEEE
HOW CAN YOU SAY THAT?
I FORFEITED A DUEL JUST TO FOLLOW YOU HERE!
EEEE

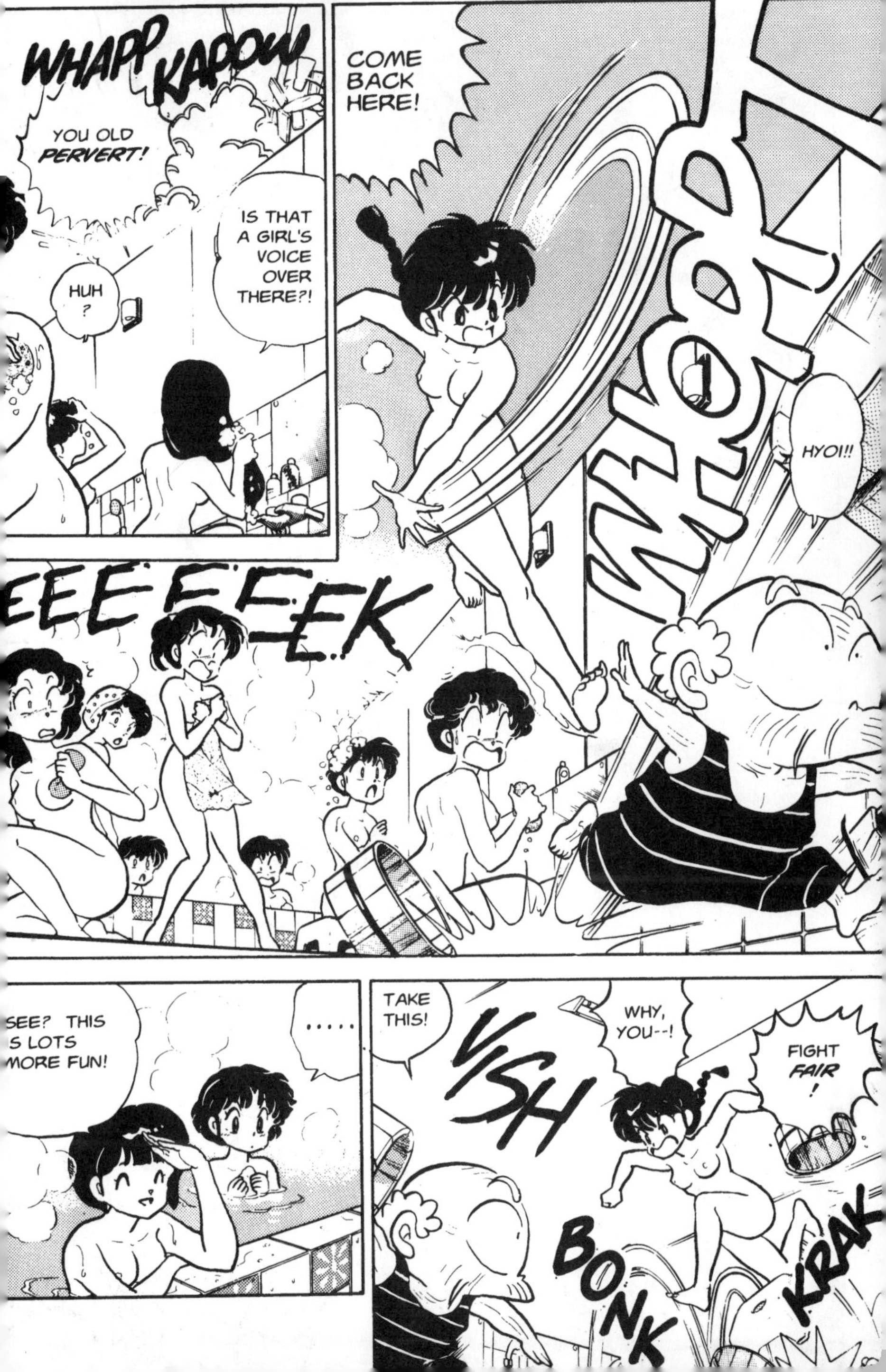
WHAPP
KAPOW
YOU OLD PERVERT!
HUH?
IS THAT A GIRL'S VOICE OVER THERE?!
COME BACK HERE!
WHOP
HYOI!!
EEEEEEEK
SEE? THIS
S LOTS
MORE FUN!
.....
TAKE THIS!
VISH
WHY, YOU--!
FIGHT FAIR!
BONK
KRAK

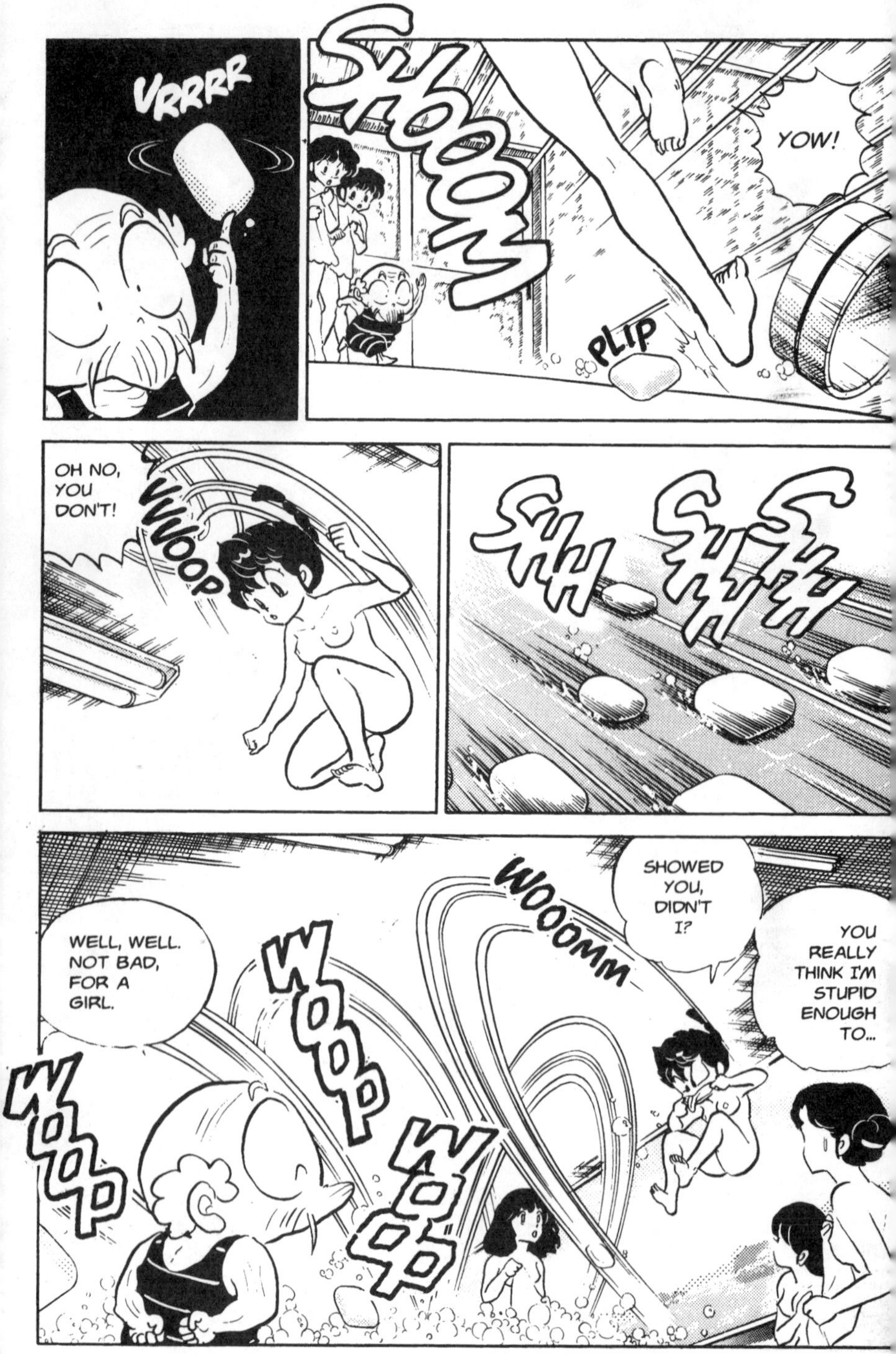
VRRRR
SHOOOM
YOW!
PLIP
OH NO, YOU DON'T!
VWOOP
SHH
SHHH
WELL, WELL. NOT BAD, FOR A GIRL.
WOOP
WOOP
WOOP
WOOOMM
SHOWED YOU, DIDN'T I?
YOU REALLY THINK I'M STUPID ENOUGH TO...

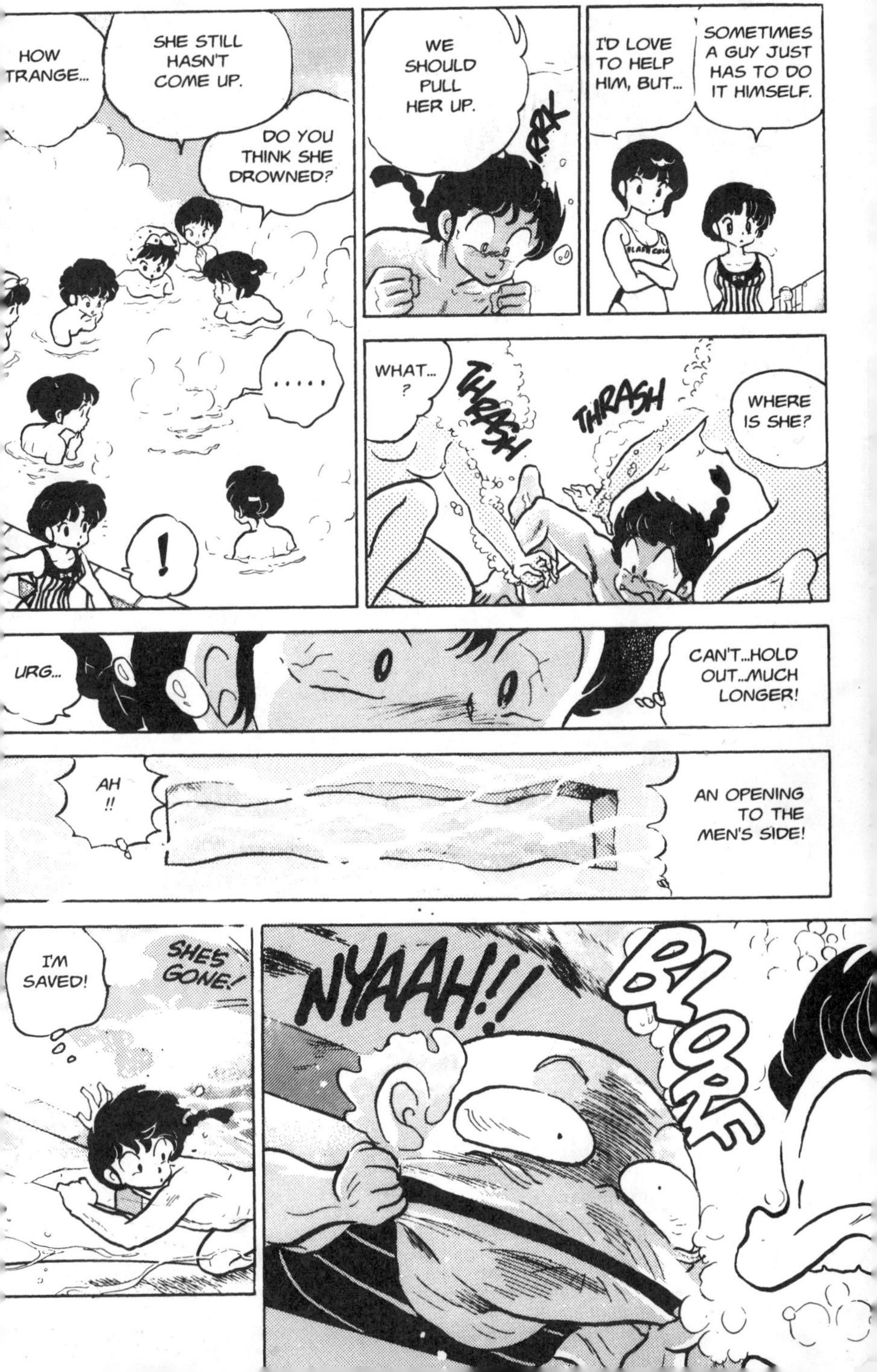
HOW TRANGE...
SHE STILL HASN'T COME UP.
DO YOU THINK SHE DROWNED?
.....
!
WE SHOULD PULL HER UP.
I'D LOVE TO HELP HIM, BUT...
SOMETIMES A GUY JUST HAS TO DO IT HIMSELF.
WHAT... ?
THRASH
THRASH
WHERE IS SHE?
URG...
CAN'T...HOLD OUT...MUCH LONGER!
AH !!
AN OPENING TO THE MEN'S SIDE!
I'M SAVED!
SHE'S GONE!
NYAAH!!
BLORF

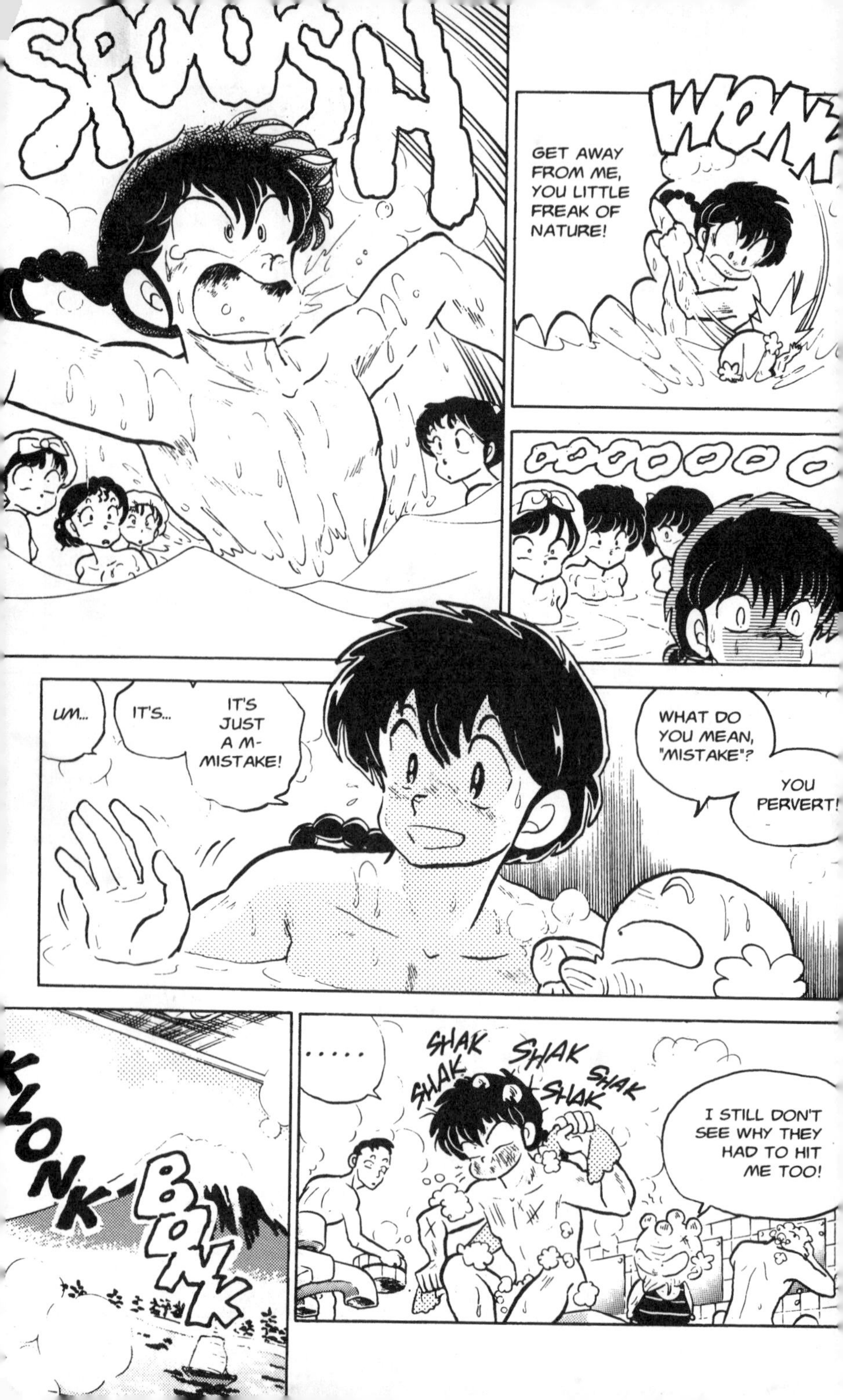
SPOOSH
WONK
GET AWAY FROM ME, YOU LITTLE FREAK OF NATURE!
OOOOOOOOO
UM...
IT'S...
IT'S JUST A M-MISTAKE!
WHAT DO YOU MEAN, "MISTAKE"?
YOU PERVERT!
KLONK
BONK
......
SHAK SHAK SHAK SHAK SHAK
I STILL DON'T SEE WHY THEY HAD TO HIT ME TOO!

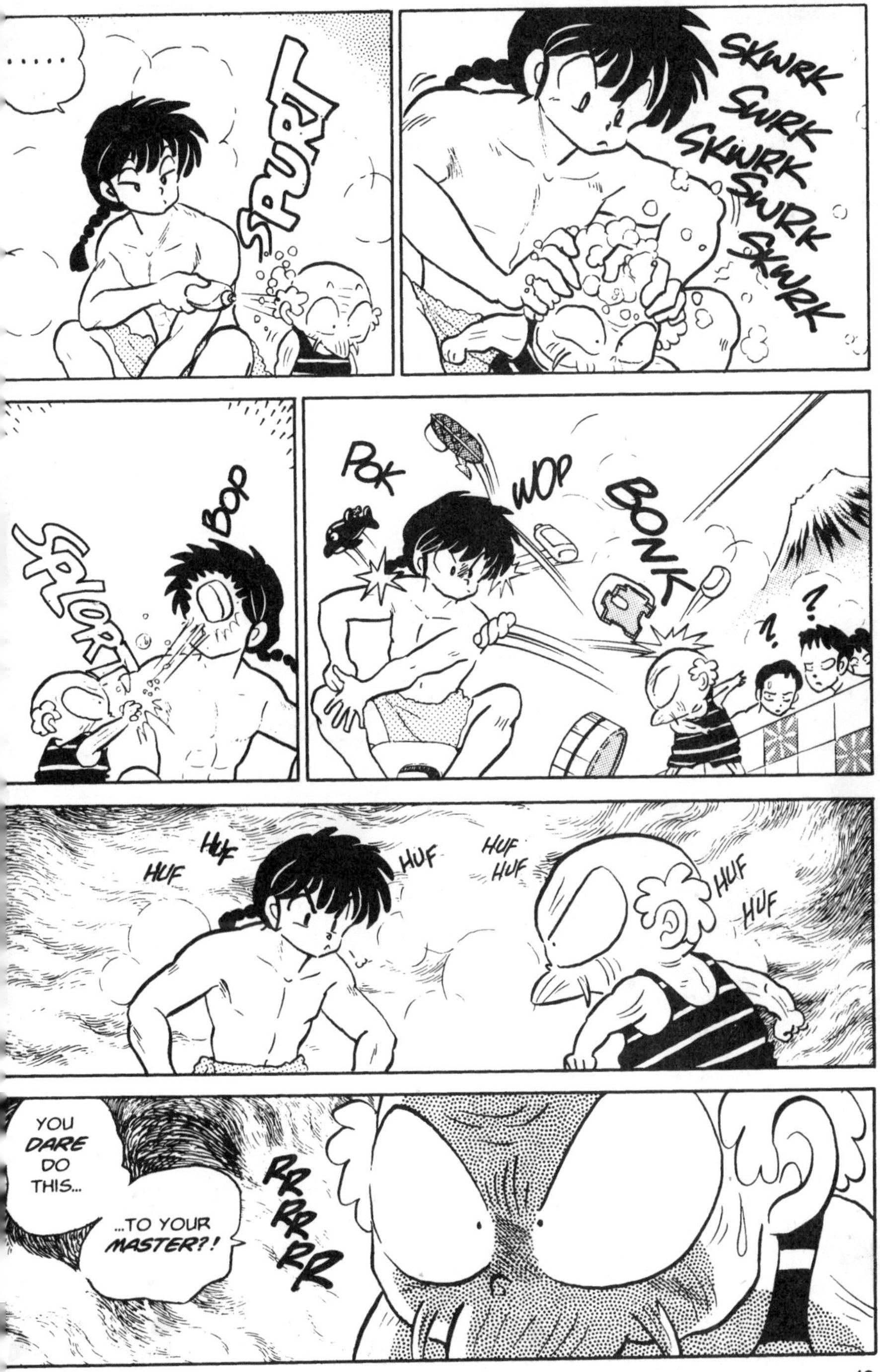

......
SPURT
SKWRK
SWRK
SKWRK
SWRK
SKWRK
BOP
SPLORT
POK
WOP
BONK
?
?
HUF
HUF
HUF
HUF
HUF
HUF
HUF
YOU DARE DO THIS...
...TO YOUR MASTER?!
RRRRRRR

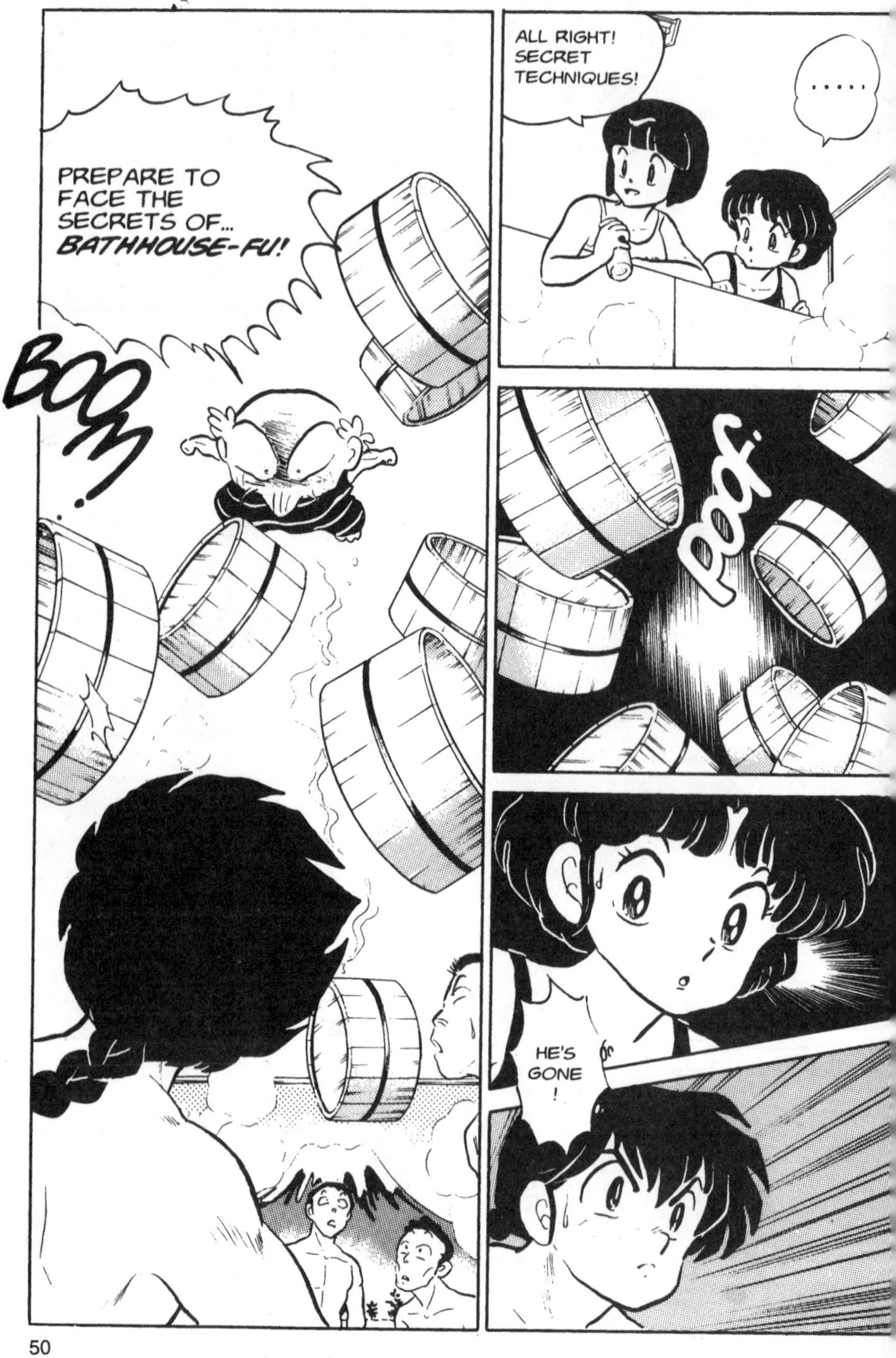
PREPARE TO FACE THE SECRETS OF... *BATHHOUSE-FU!*
BOOM
ALL RIGHT! SECRET TECHNIQUES!
......
POOF!
HE'S GONE !

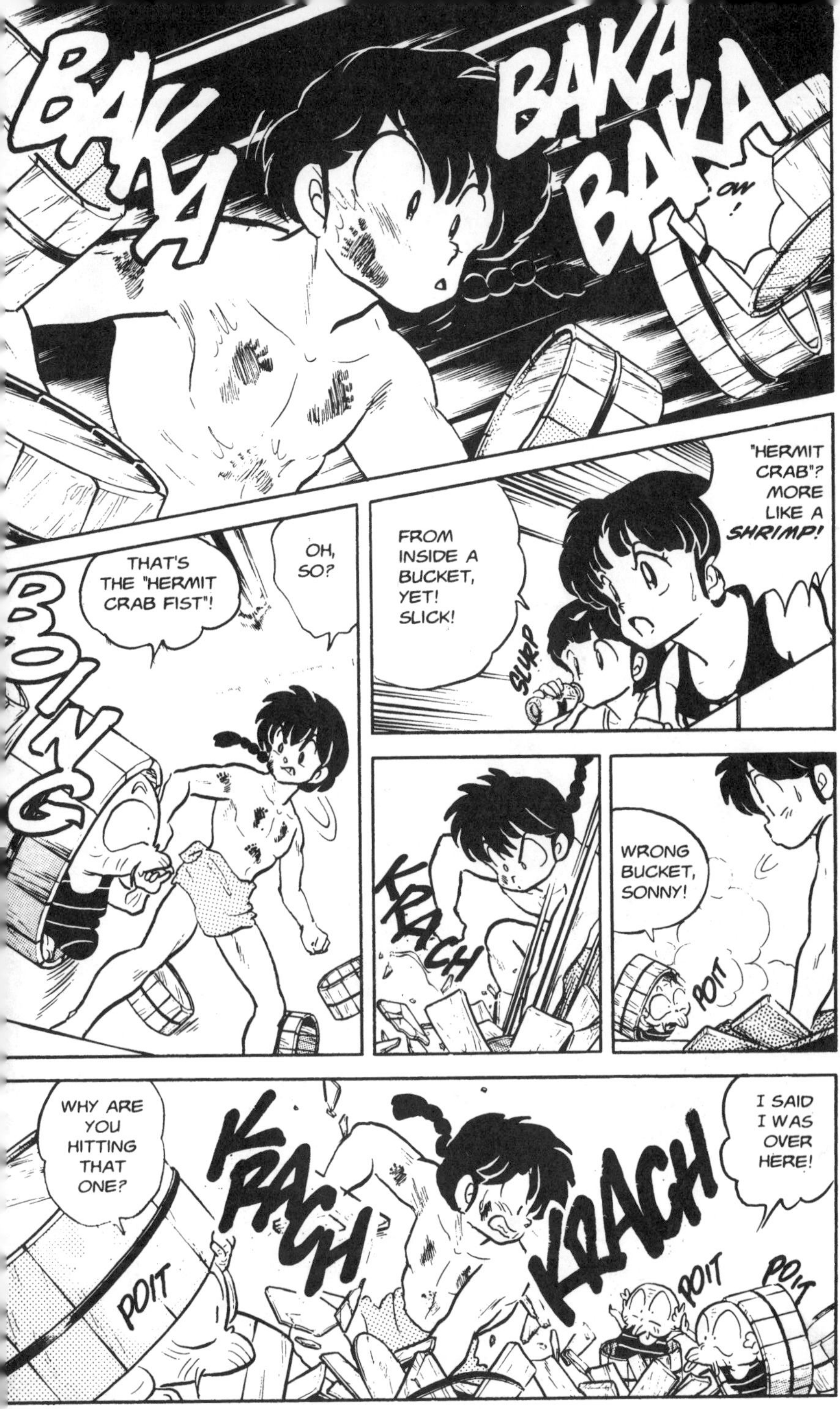
BAKA
BAKA BAKA
OW!
"HERMIT CRAB"? MORE LIKE A SHRIMP!
BOING
THAT'S THE "HERMIT CRAB FIST"!
OH, SO?
FROM INSIDE A BUCKET, YET! SLICK!
SLURP
KRACH
WRONG BUCKET, SONNY!
POIT
WHY ARE YOU HITTING THAT ONE?
KRACH
POIT
KRACH
I SAID I WAS OVER HERE!
POIT
POIT

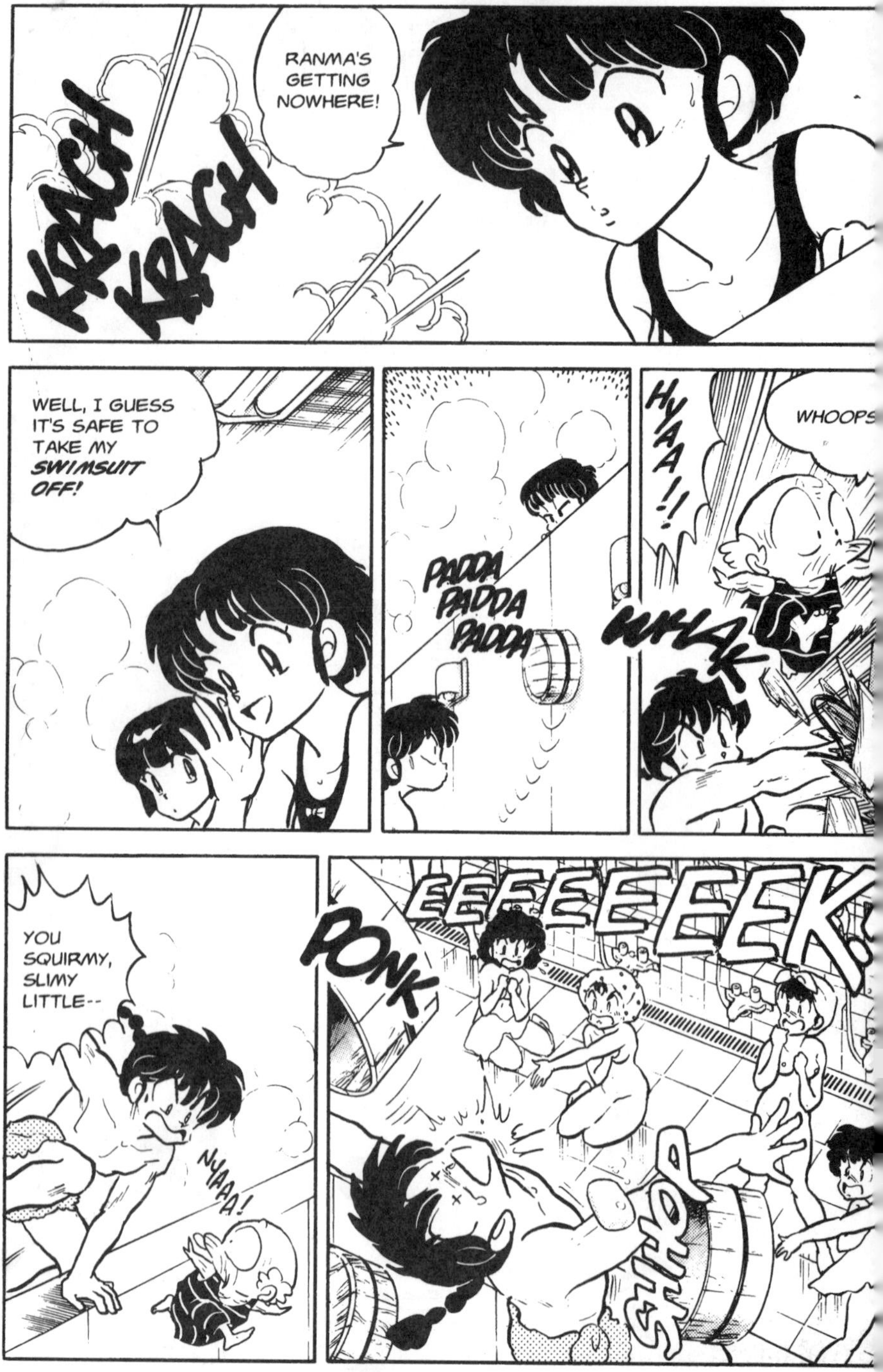
KRACH KRACH
RANMA'S GETTING NOWHERE!
WELL, I GUESS IT'S SAFE TO TAKE MY *SWIMSUIT OFF!*
PADDA PADDA PADDA
HYAAA!!
WHOOPS
WHAK
YOU SQUIRMY, SLIMY LITTLE--
NYAAA!
PONK
EEEEEEEK!
SHPOP

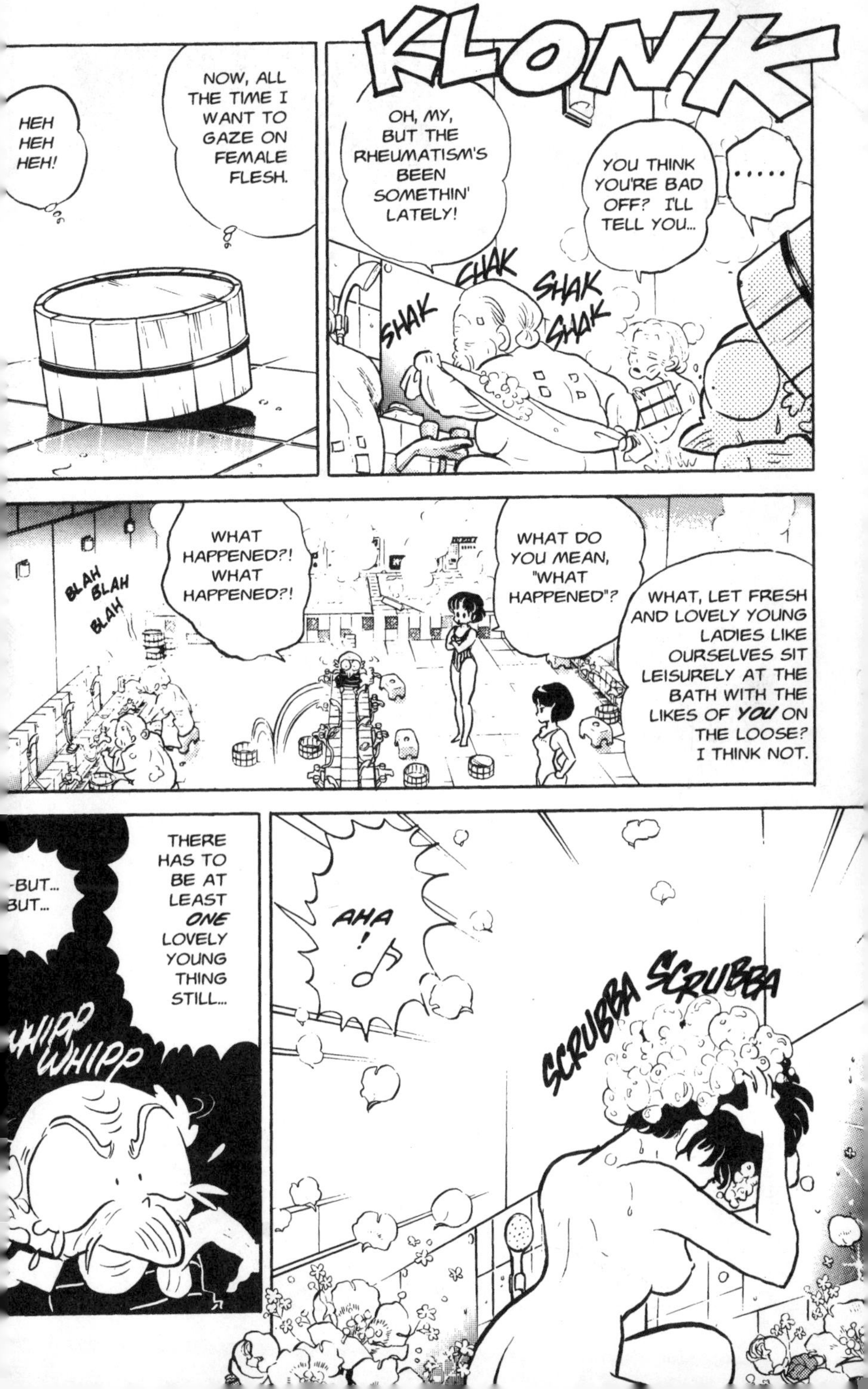
HEH HEH HEH!
NOW, ALL THE TIME I WANT TO GAZE ON FEMALE FLESH.
KLONK
OH, MY, BUT THE RHEUMATISM'S BEEN SOMETHIN' LATELY!
SHAK SHAK
SHAK SHAK
YOU THINK YOU'RE BAD OFF? I'LL TELL YOU...
.....
BLAH BLAH BLAH
WHAT HAPPENED?! WHAT HAPPENED?!
WHAT DO YOU MEAN, "WHAT HAPPENED"?
WHAT, LET FRESH AND LOVELY YOUNG LADIES LIKE OURSELVES SIT LEISURELY AT THE BATH WITH THE LIKES OF YOU ON THE LOOSE? I THINK NOT.
-BUT... BUT...
THERE HAS TO BE AT LEAST ONE LOVELY YOUNG THING STILL...
WHIPP WHIPP
AHA!
SCRUBBA SCRUBBA

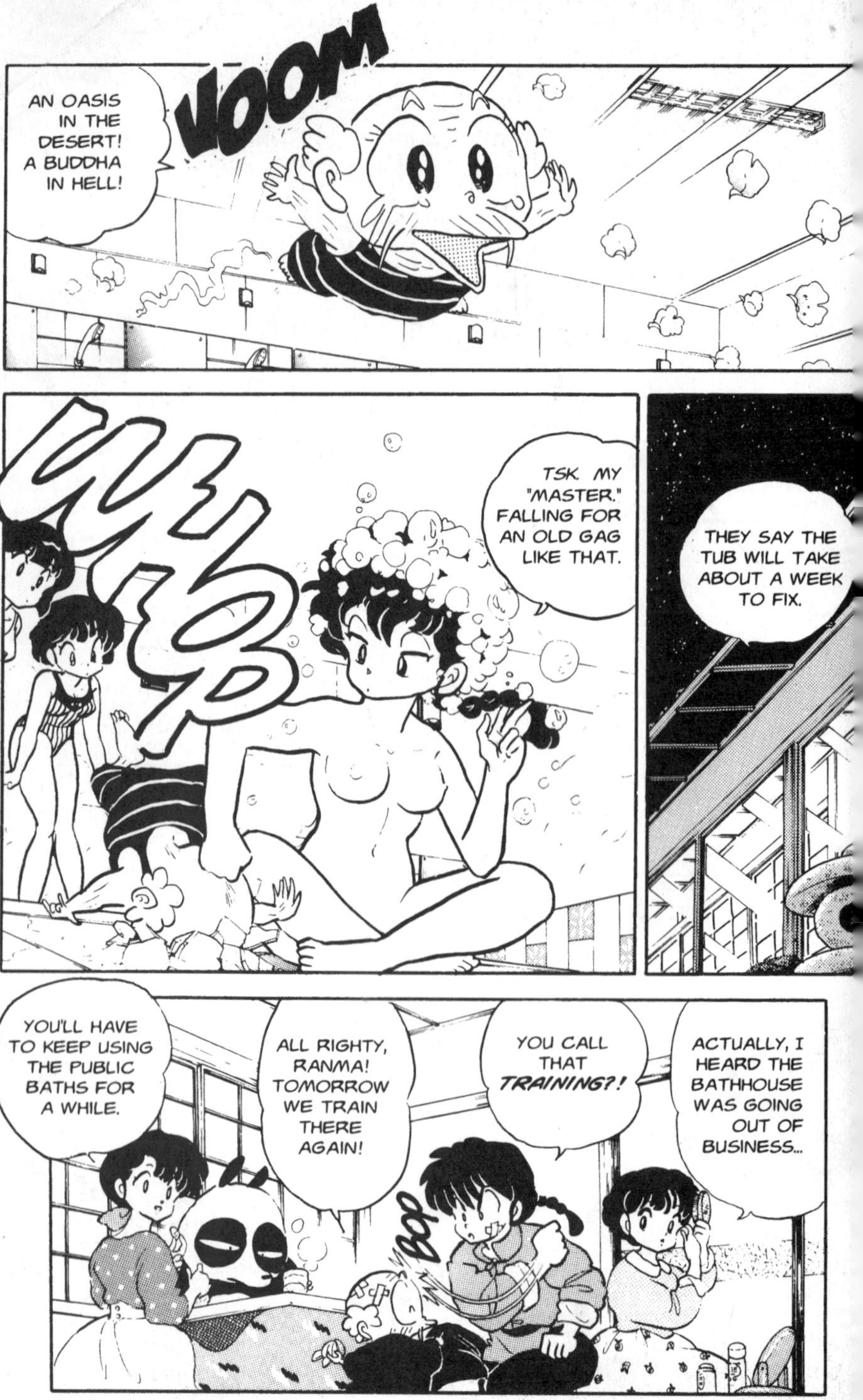

AN OASIS IN THE DESERT! A BUDDHA IN HELL!
VOOM
TSK. MY "MASTER." FALLING FOR AN OLD GAG LIKE THAT.
THEY SAY THE TUB WILL TAKE ABOUT A WEEK TO FIX.
YOU'LL HAVE TO KEEP USING THE PUBLIC BATHS FOR A WHILE.
ALL RIGHTY, RANMA! TOMORROW WE TRAIN THERE AGAIN!
YOU CALL THAT *TRAINING?!*
ACTUALLY, I HEARD THE BATHHOUSE WAS GOING OUT OF BUSINESS...

PART 4

MOONLIGHT SERENADE

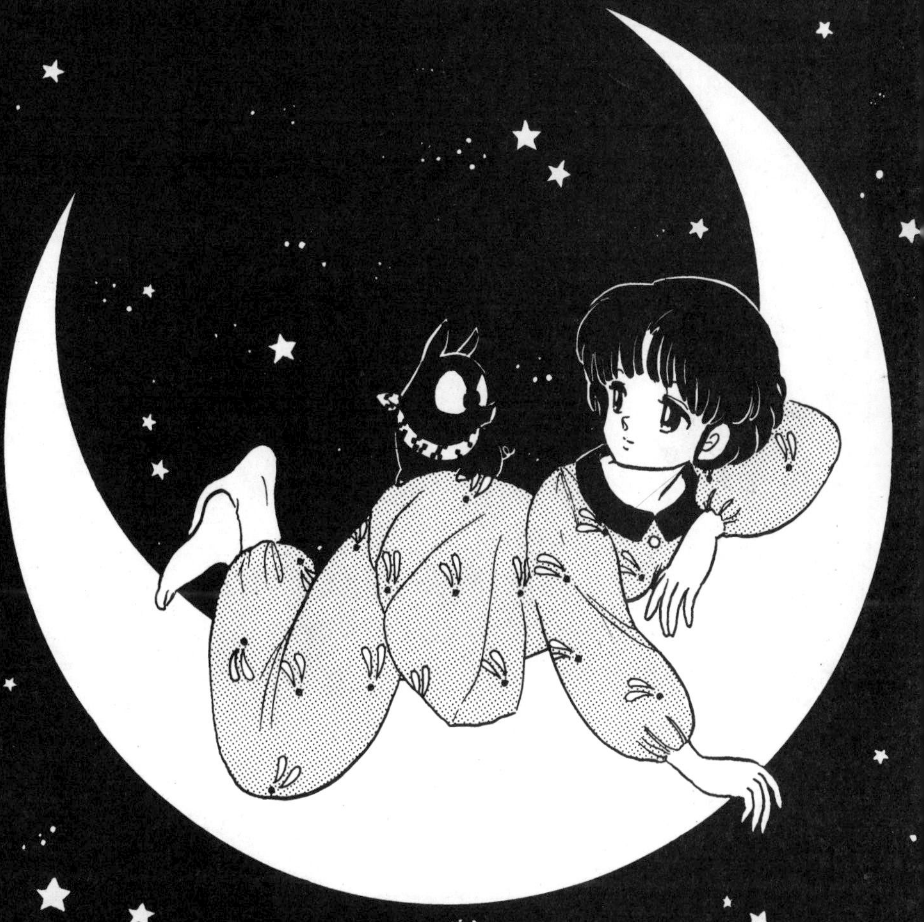

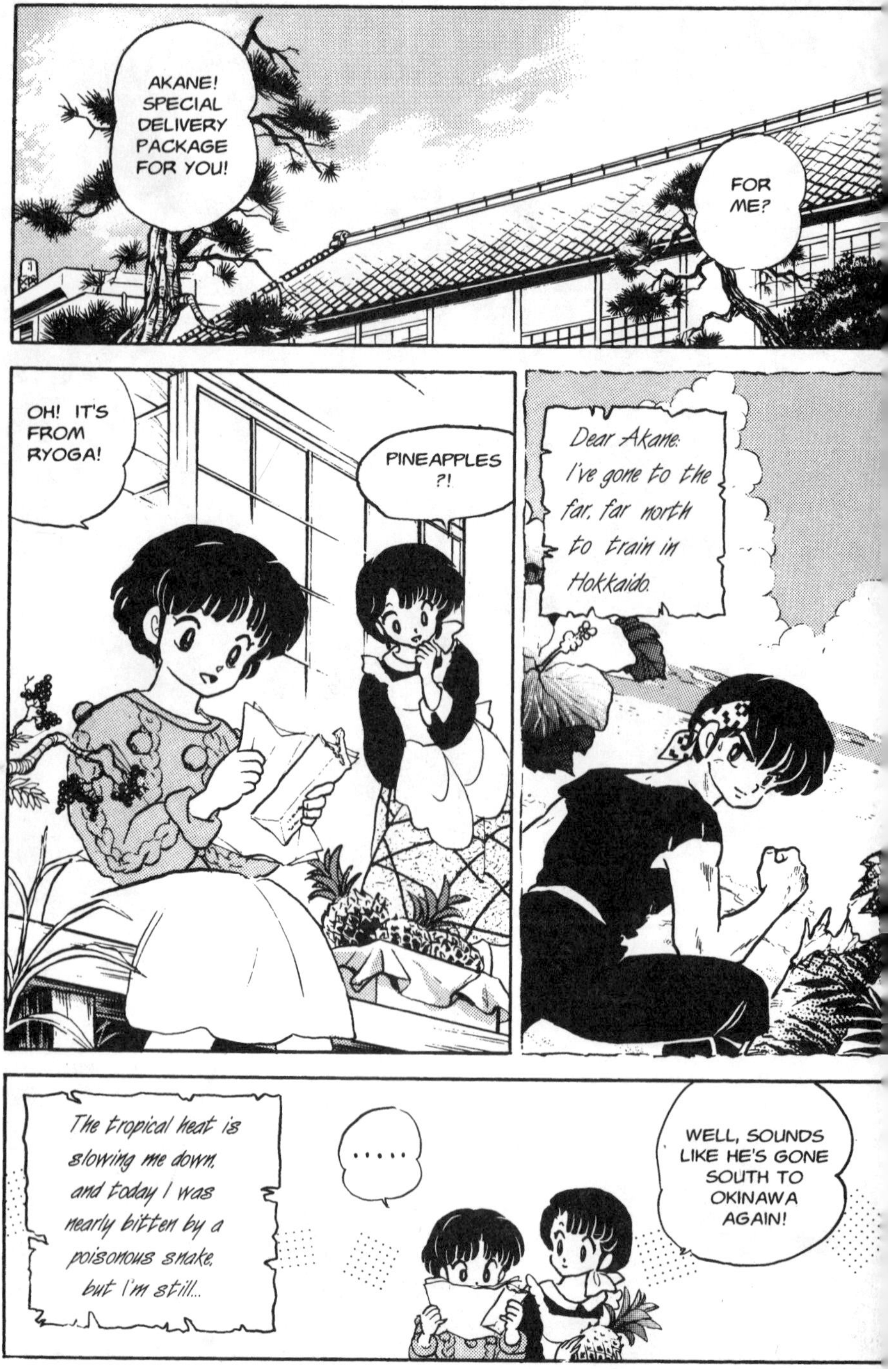
AKANE! SPECIAL DELIVERY PACKAGE FOR YOU!
FOR ME?
OH! IT'S FROM RYOGA!
PINEAPPLES ?!
Dear Akane: I've gone to the far, far north to train in Hokkaido.
The tropical heat is slowing me down, and today I was nearly bitten by a poisonous snake, but I'm still...
.....
WELL, SOUNDS LIKE HE'S GONE SOUTH TO OKINAWA AGAIN!

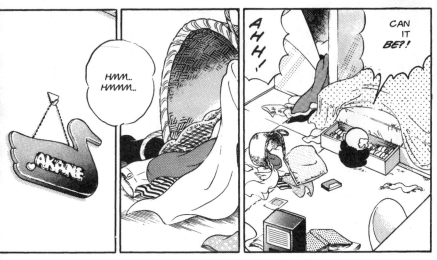

HMM... HMMM...

AHH!

CAN IT *BE?!*

YES, OH, YES!

AKANE'S PANTIES!

AH, FOR SUCH A TREASURE TO BE DELIVERED INTO MY LOWLY HANDS!

IT MUST BE A GIFT FROM GOD!

ZOOM

EH ?!

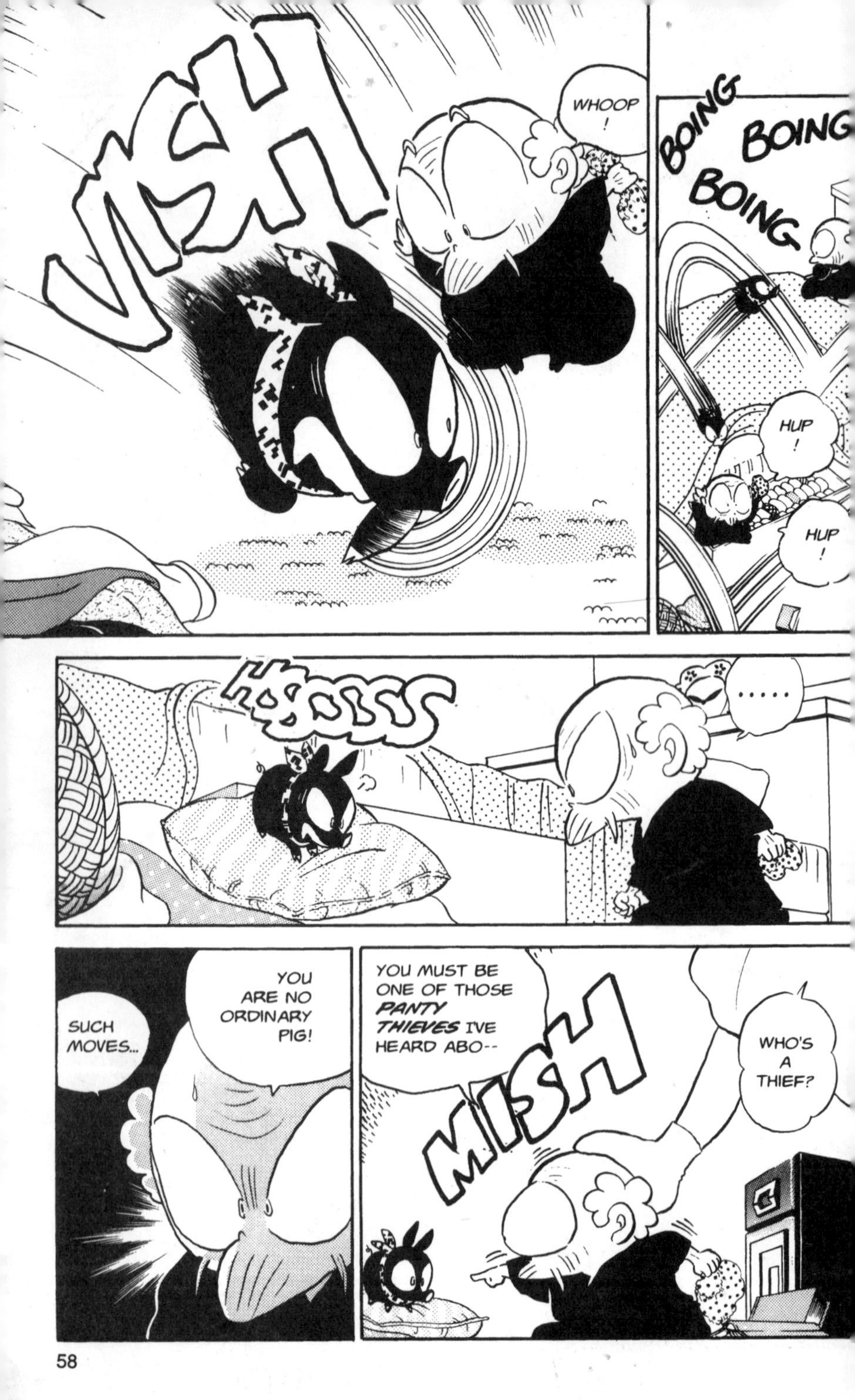
VISH
WHOOP!
BOING
BOING
BOING
HUP!
HUP!
.....
SUCH MOVES...
YOU ARE NO ORDINARY PIG!
YOU MUST BE ONE OF THOSE *PANTY THIEVES* I'VE HEARD ABO--
MISH
WHO'S A THIEF?

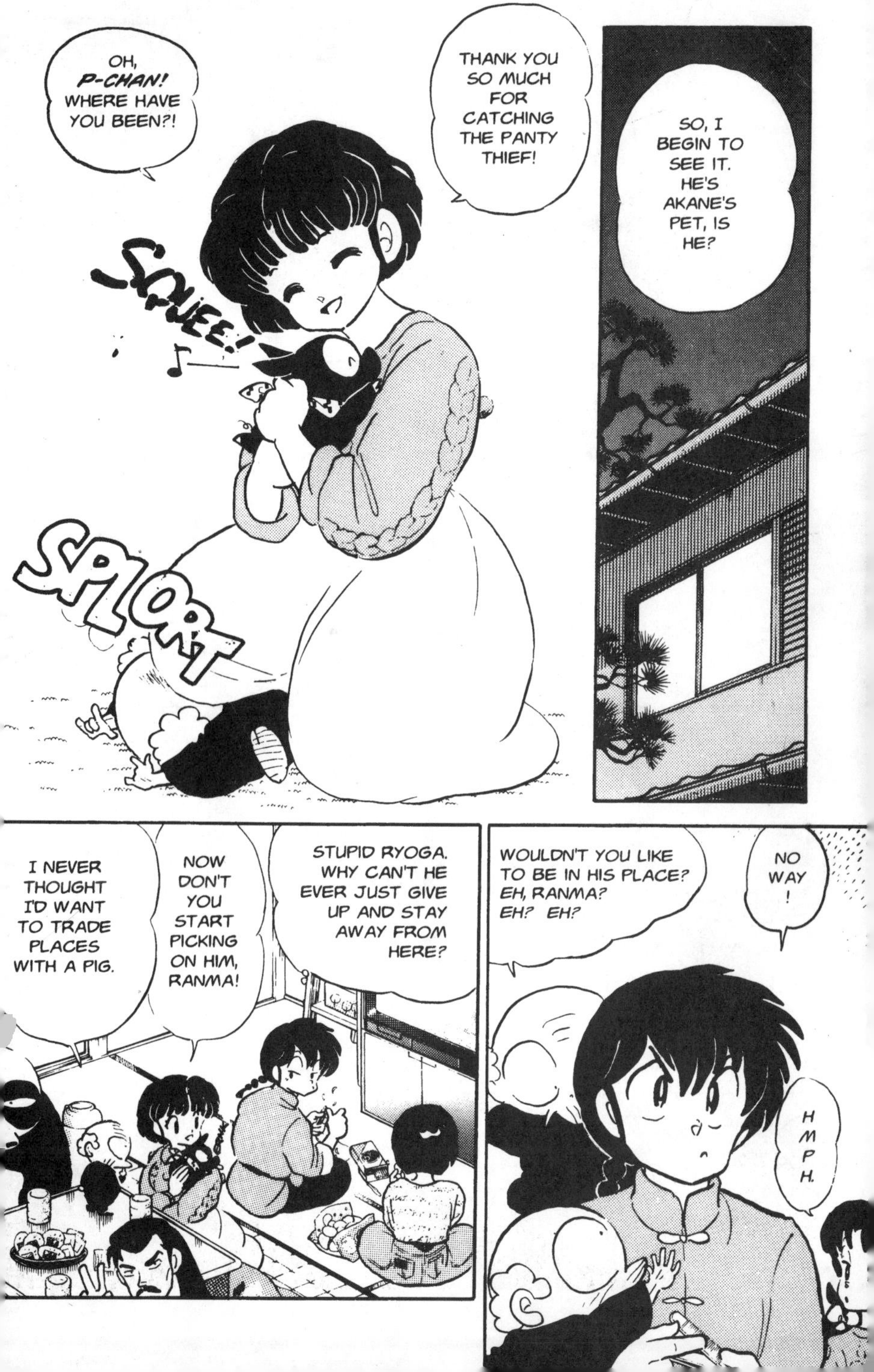
OH, P-CHAN! WHERE HAVE YOU BEEN?!
THANK YOU SO MUCH FOR CATCHING THE PANTY THIEF!
SQUEE!
SPLORT
SO, I BEGIN TO SEE IT. HE'S AKANE'S PET, IS HE?
I NEVER THOUGHT I'D WANT TO TRADE PLACES WITH A PIG.
NOW DON'T YOU START PICKING ON HIM, RANMA!
STUPID RYOGA. WHY CAN'T HE EVER JUST GIVE UP AND STAY AWAY FROM HERE?
WOULDN'T YOU LIKE TO BE IN HIS PLACE? EH, RANMA? EH? EH?
NO WAY!
HMPH.

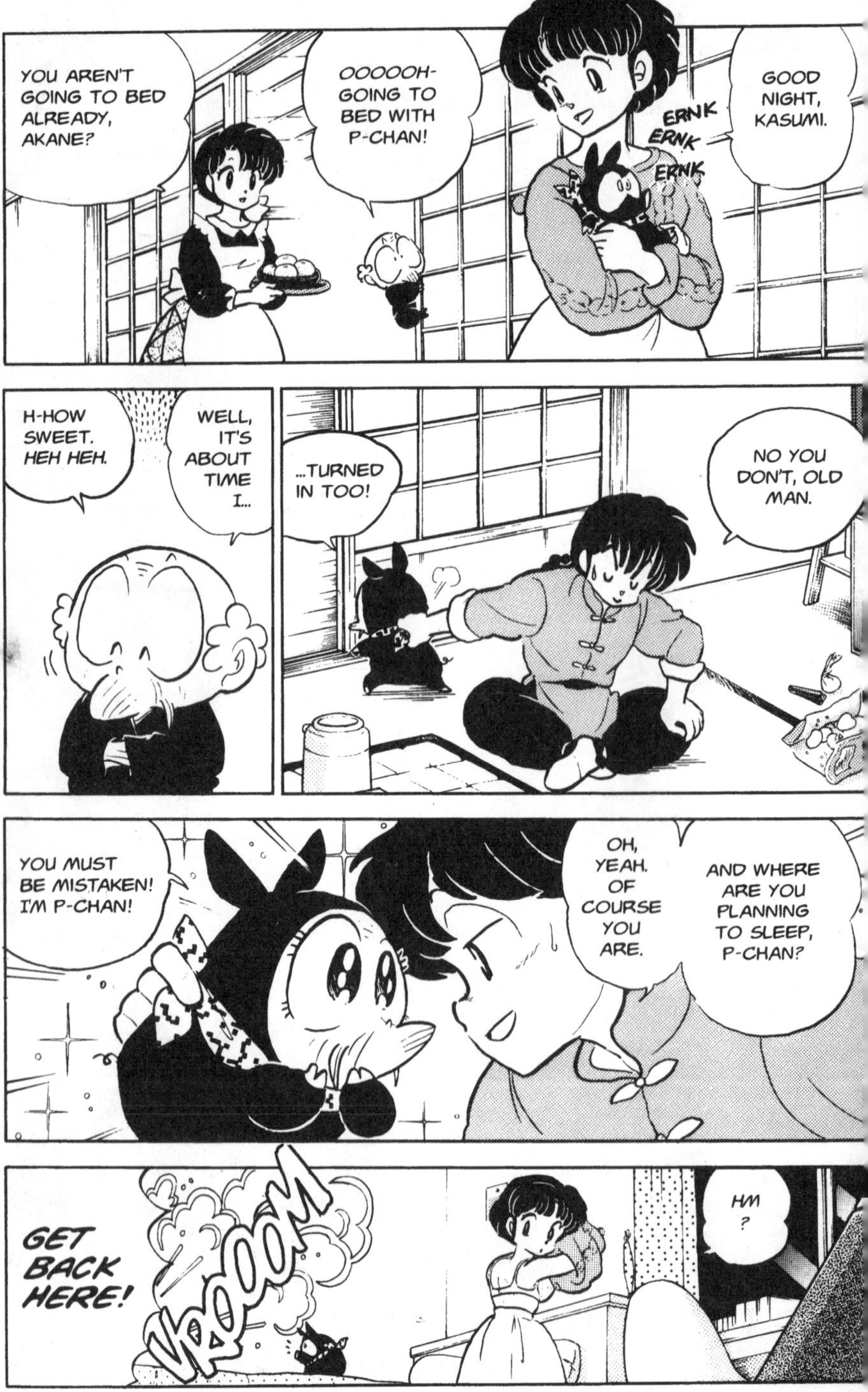

YOU AREN'T GOING TO BED ALREADY, AKANE?
OOOOOH- GOING TO BED WITH P-CHAN!
ERNK
ERNK
ERNK
GOOD NIGHT, KASUMI.
H-HOW SWEET. HEH HEH.
WELL, IT'S ABOUT TIME I...
...TURNED IN TOO!
NO YOU DON'T, OLD MAN.
YOU MUST BE MISTAKEN! I'M P-CHAN!
OH, YEAH. OF COURSE YOU ARE.
AND WHERE ARE YOU PLANNING TO SLEEP, P-CHAN?
GET BACK HERE!
VROOOM
HM ?

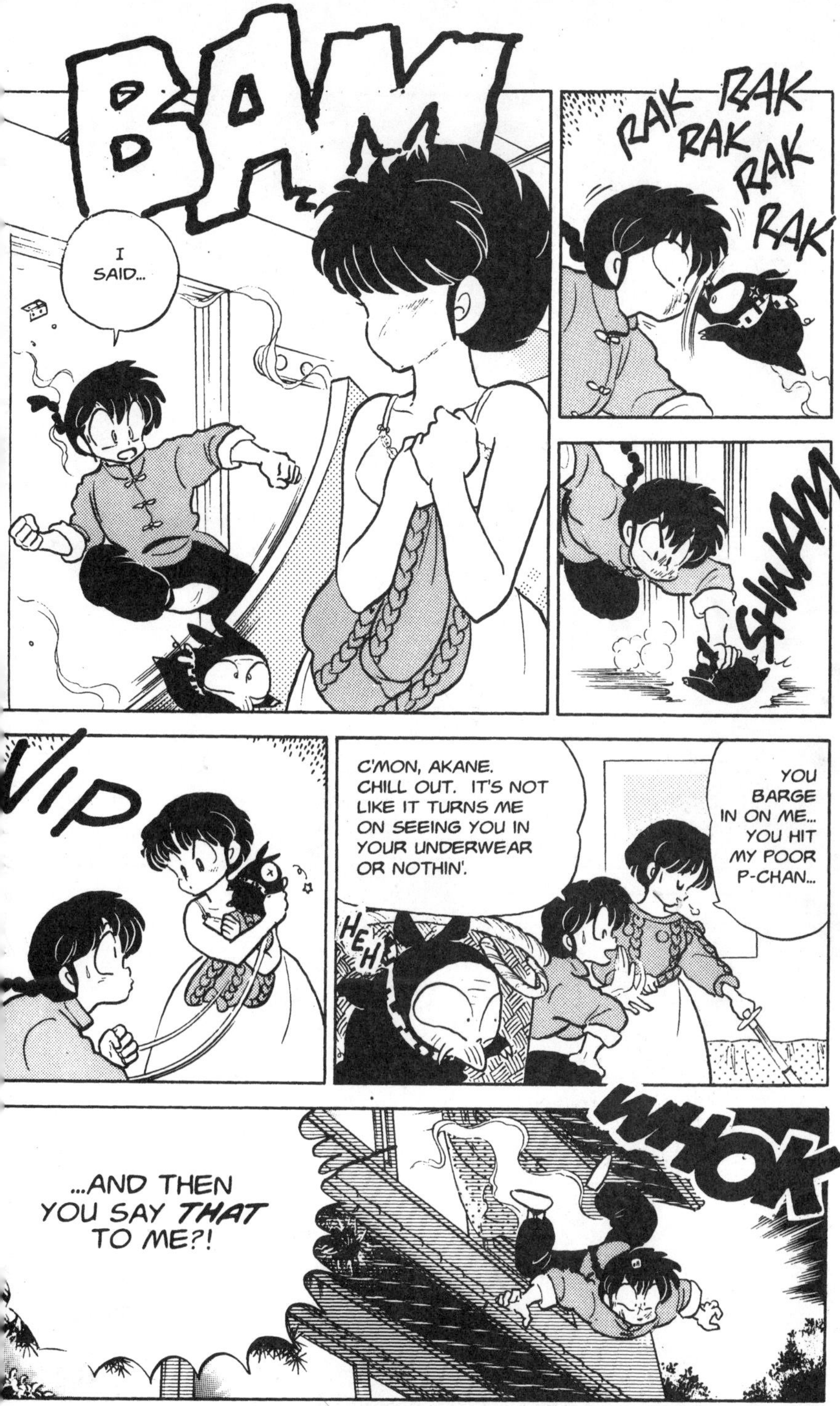
BAM
I SAID...
RAK RAK RAK RAK RAK RAK
SHWAM
VIP
C'MON, AKANE. CHILL OUT. IT'S NOT LIKE IT TURNS ME ON SEEING YOU IN YOUR UNDERWEAR OR NOTHIN'.
HEHE
YOU BARGE IN ON ME... YOU HIT MY POOR P-CHAN...
...AND THEN YOU SAY *THAT* TO ME?!
WHOK

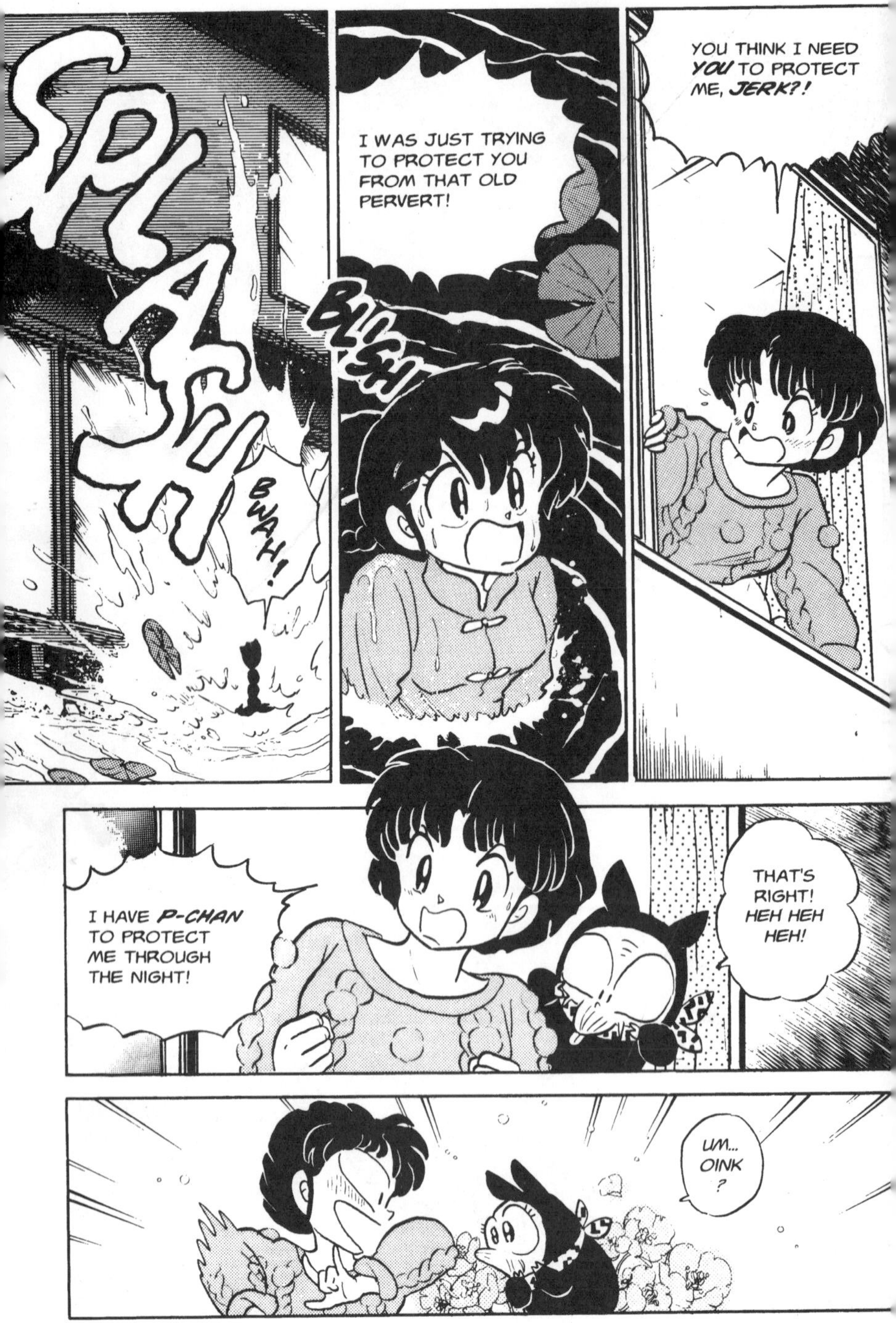
SPLASH
BWAH!
I WAS JUST TRYING TO PROTECT YOU FROM THAT OLD PERVERT!
BLUSH
YOU THINK I NEED *YOU* TO PROTECT ME, *JERK?!*
I HAVE *P-CHAN* TO PROTECT ME THROUGH THE NIGHT!
THAT'S RIGHT! *HEH HEH HEH!*
UM... OINK ?

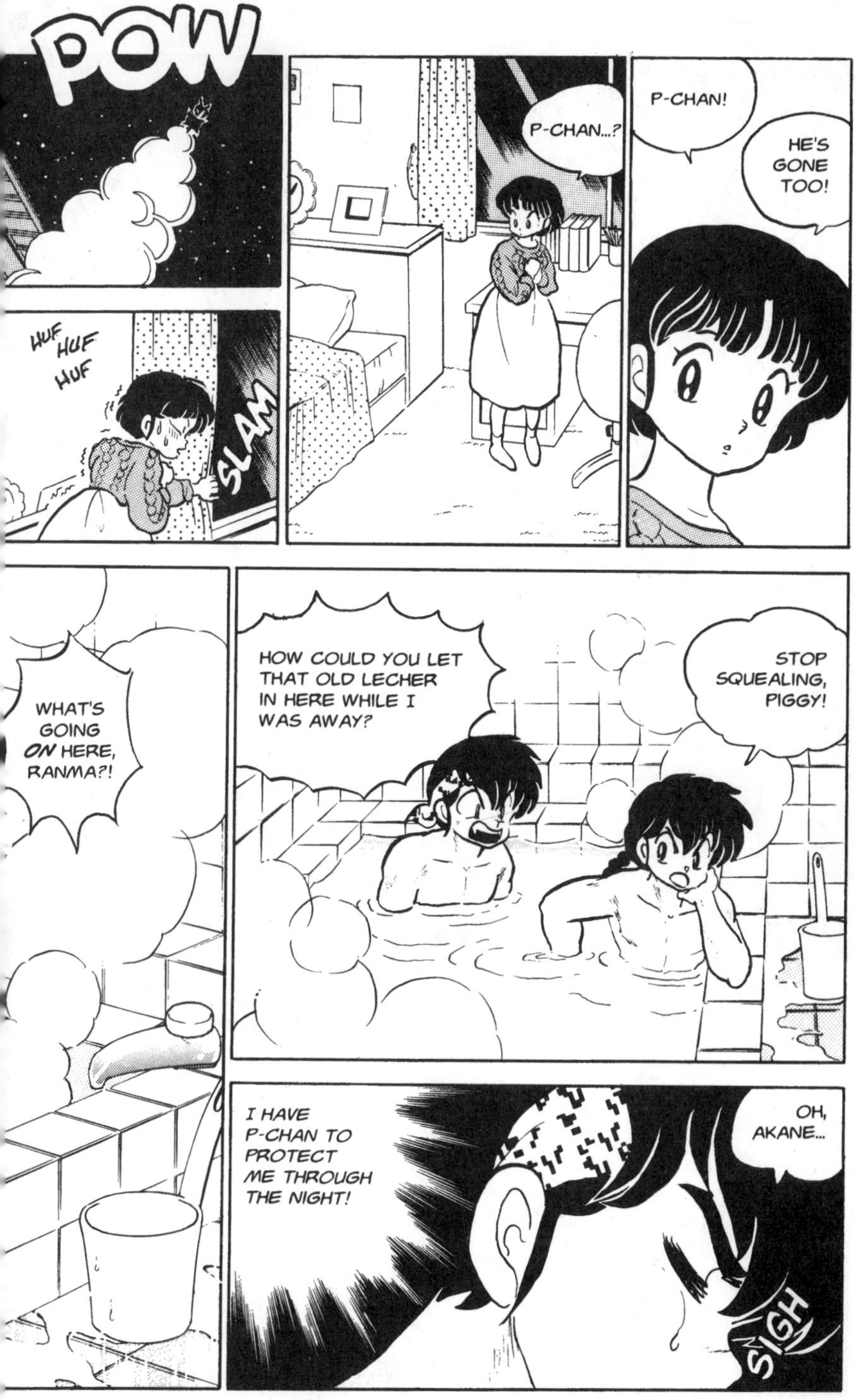
POW
HUF HUF HUF
SLAM
P-CHAN...?
P-CHAN!
HE'S GONE TOO!
WHAT'S GOING *ON* HERE, RANMA?!
HOW COULD YOU LET THAT OLD LECHER IN HERE WHILE I WAS AWAY?
STOP SQUEALING, PIGGY!
I HAVE P-CHAN TO PROTECT ME THROUGH THE NIGHT!
OH, AKANE...
SIGH

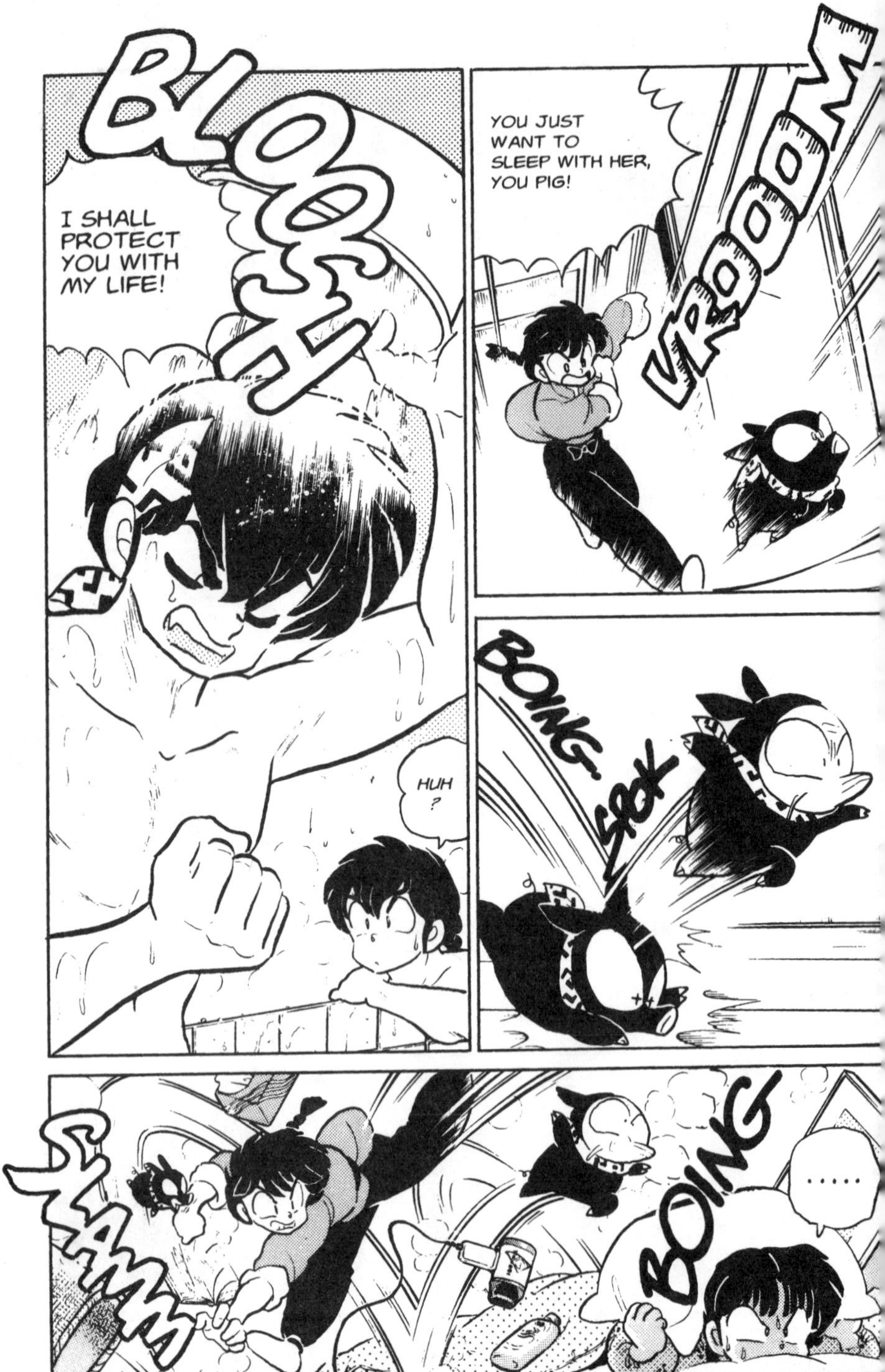
BLOOSH
I SHALL PROTECT YOU WITH MY LIFE!
HUH?
YOU JUST WANT TO SLEEP WITH HER, YOU PIG!
VROOOOM
BOING
SPOK
SLAMM
BOING
.....

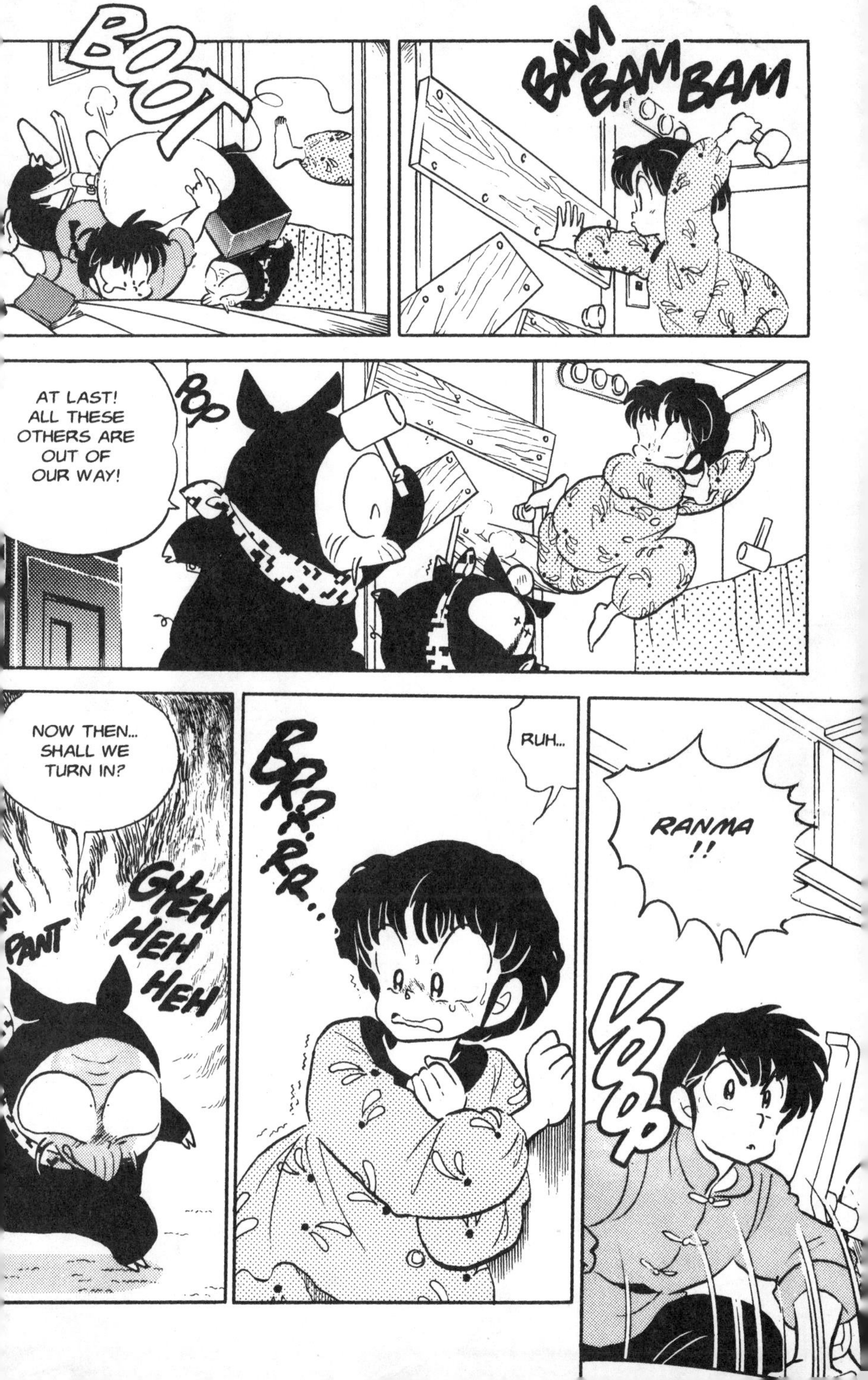
BOOT
BAM BAM BAM
POP
AT LAST! ALL THESE OTHERS ARE OUT OF OUR WAY!
NOW THEN... SHALL WE TURN IN?
PANT
GHEH HEH HEH
BRRRRR...
RUH...
RANMA !!
VOOP

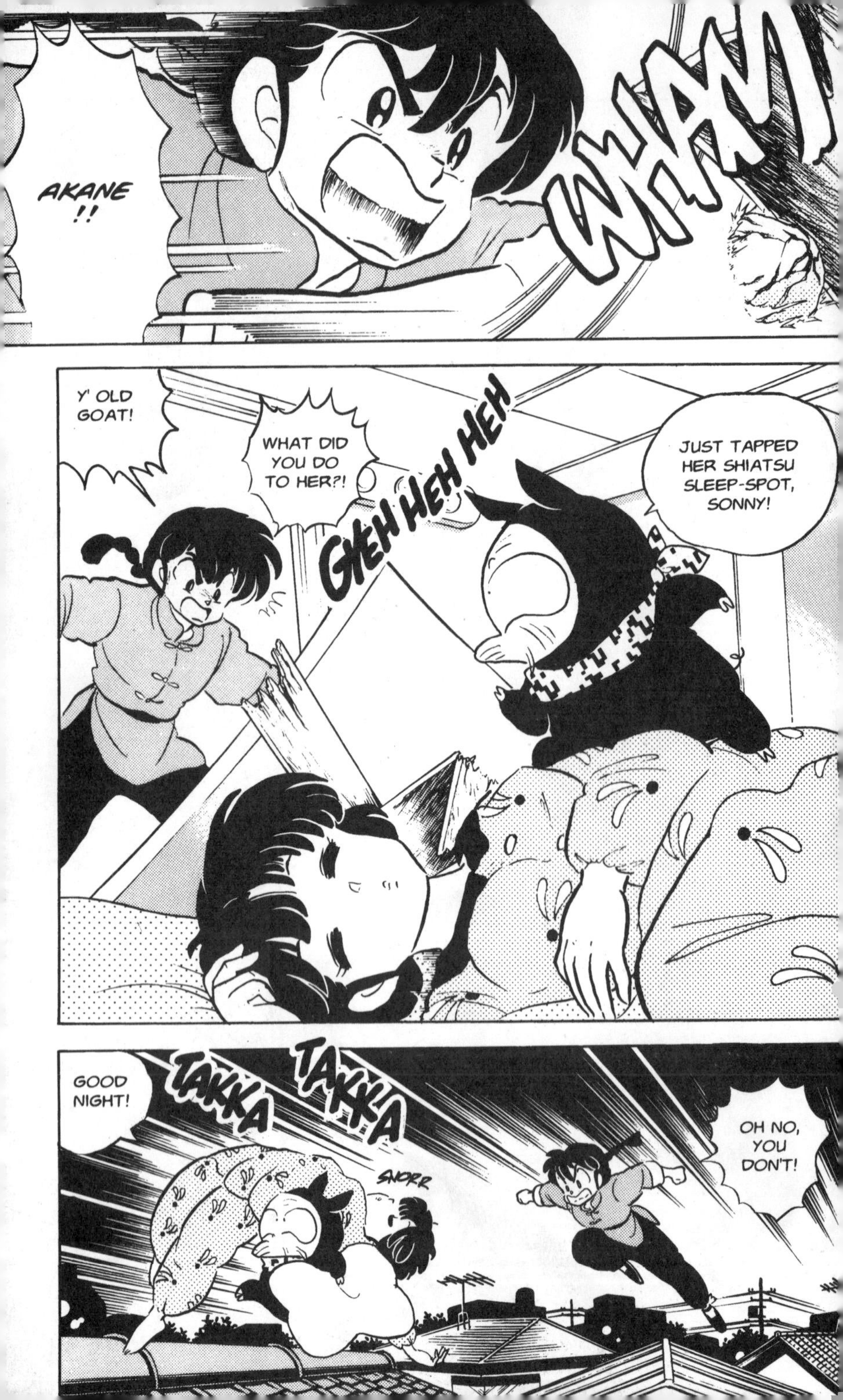
AKANE !!
WHAM!
Y' OLD GOAT!
WHAT DID YOU DO TO HER?!
GYEH HEH HEH
JUST TAPPED HER SHIATSU SLEEP-SPOT, SONNY!
GOOD NIGHT!
TAKKA
TAKKA
SNORR
OH NO, YOU DON'T!

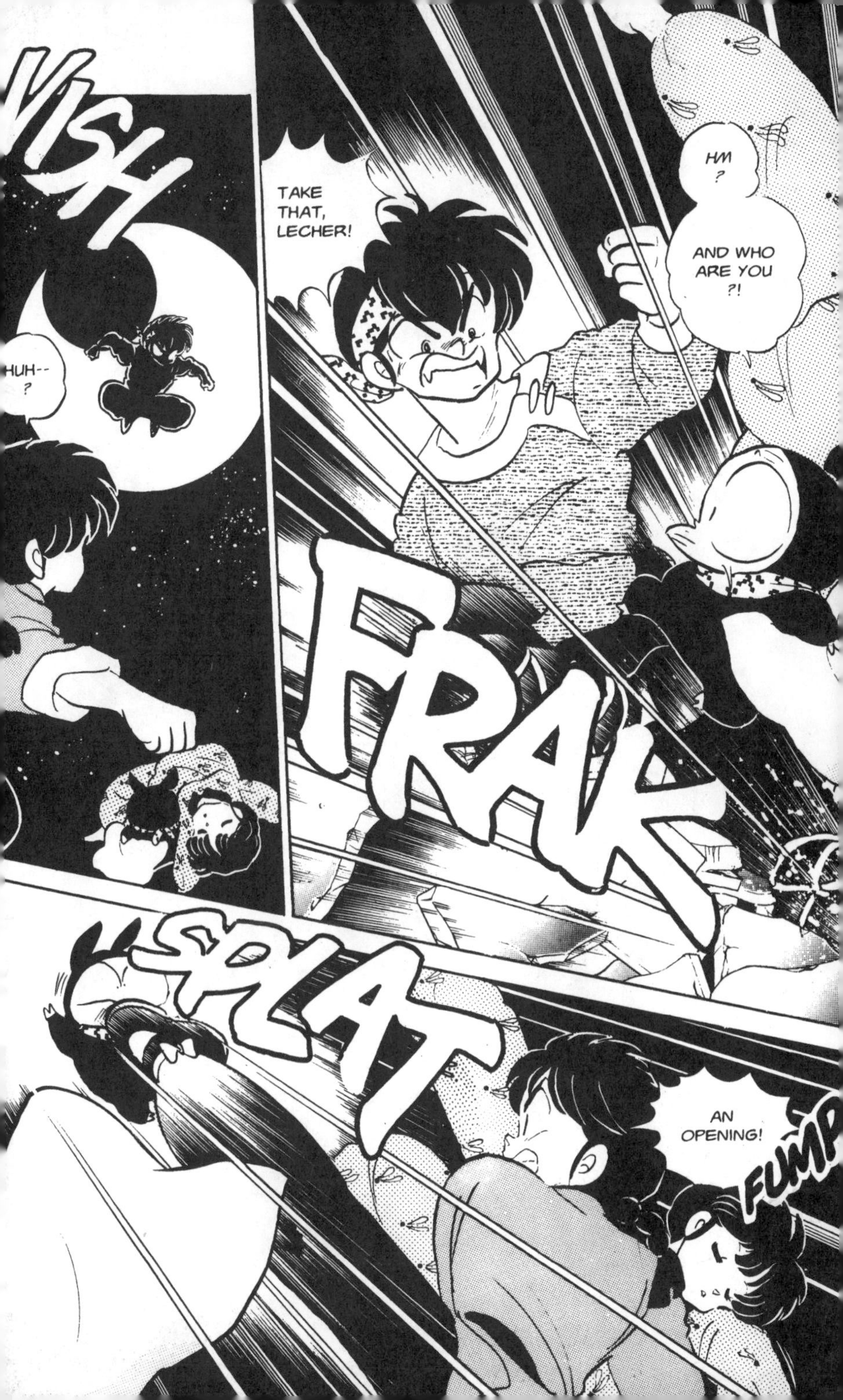

VISH
HUH-- ?
TAKE THAT, LECHER!
HM ?
AND WHO ARE YOU ?!
FRAK
SPLAT
AN OPENING!
FUMP

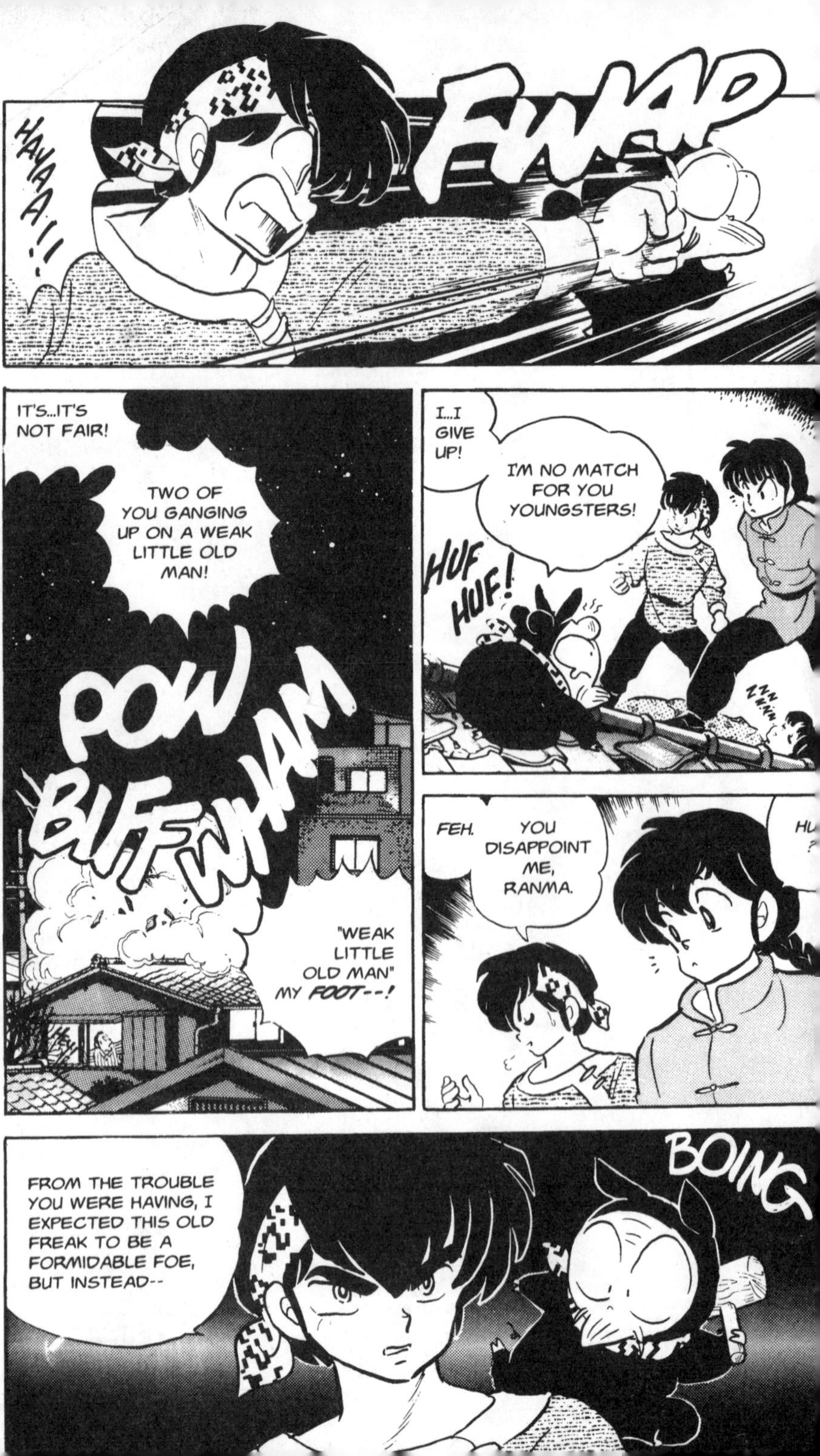
HAYAA!!!
FWAP
IT'S...IT'S NOT FAIR!
TWO OF YOU GANGING UP ON A WEAK LITTLE OLD MAN!
POW
BIF
WHAM
"WEAK LITTLE OLD MAN" MY FOOT--!
I...I GIVE UP!
I'M NO MATCH FOR YOU YOUNGSTERS!
HUF HUF!
FEH.
YOU DISAPPOINT ME, RANMA.
FROM THE TROUBLE YOU WERE HAVING, I EXPECTED THIS OLD FREAK TO BE A FORMIDABLE FOE, BUT INSTEAD--
BOING

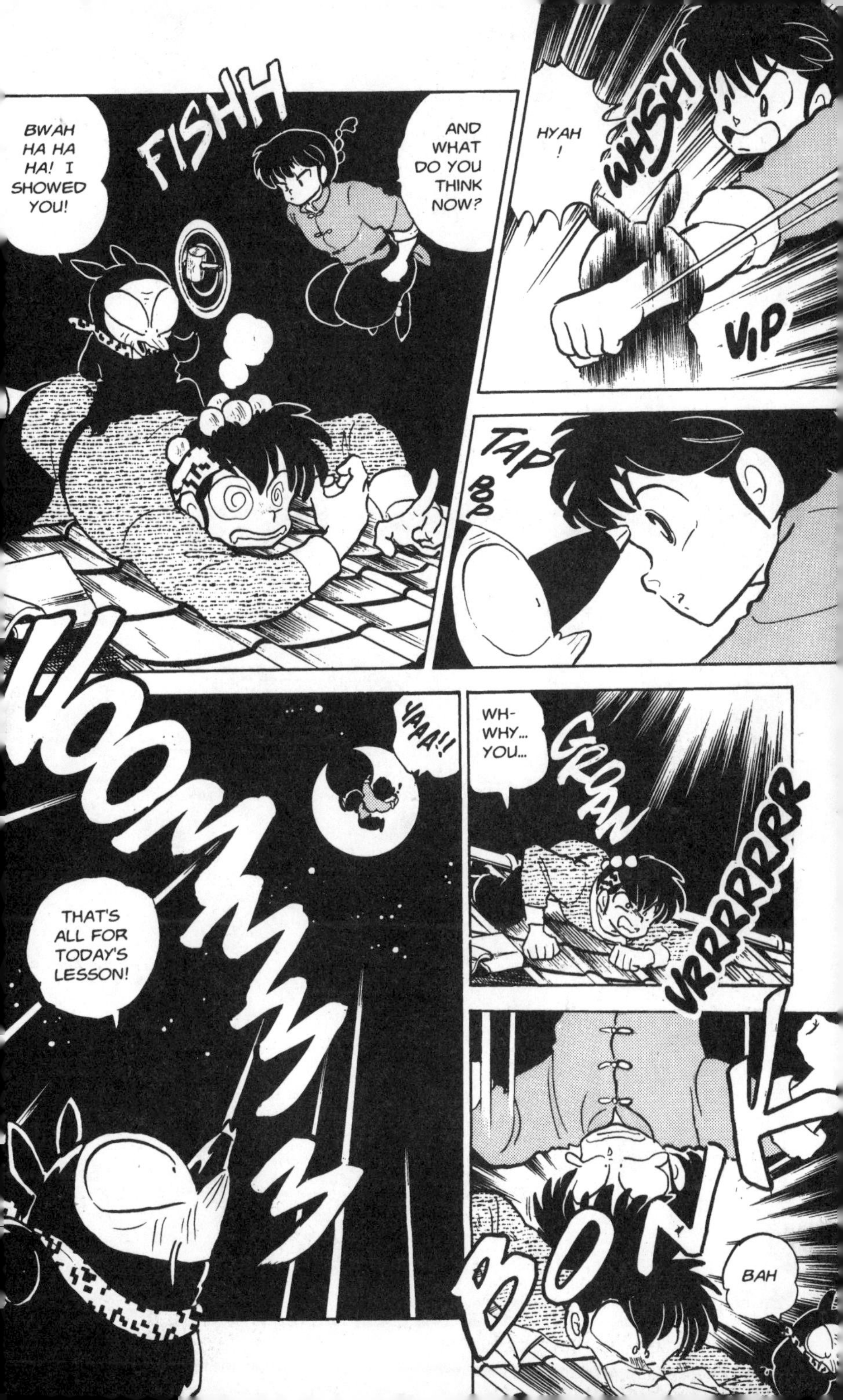
BWAH HA HA HA! I SHOWED YOU!
FISHH
AND WHAT DO YOU THINK NOW?
HYAH!
WHSH
VIP
TAP
BOP
VOOMMMMM
YAAA!!
THAT'S ALL FOR TODAY'S LESSON!
WH-WHY... YOU...
GROAN
VRRRRRRR
BONK
BAH

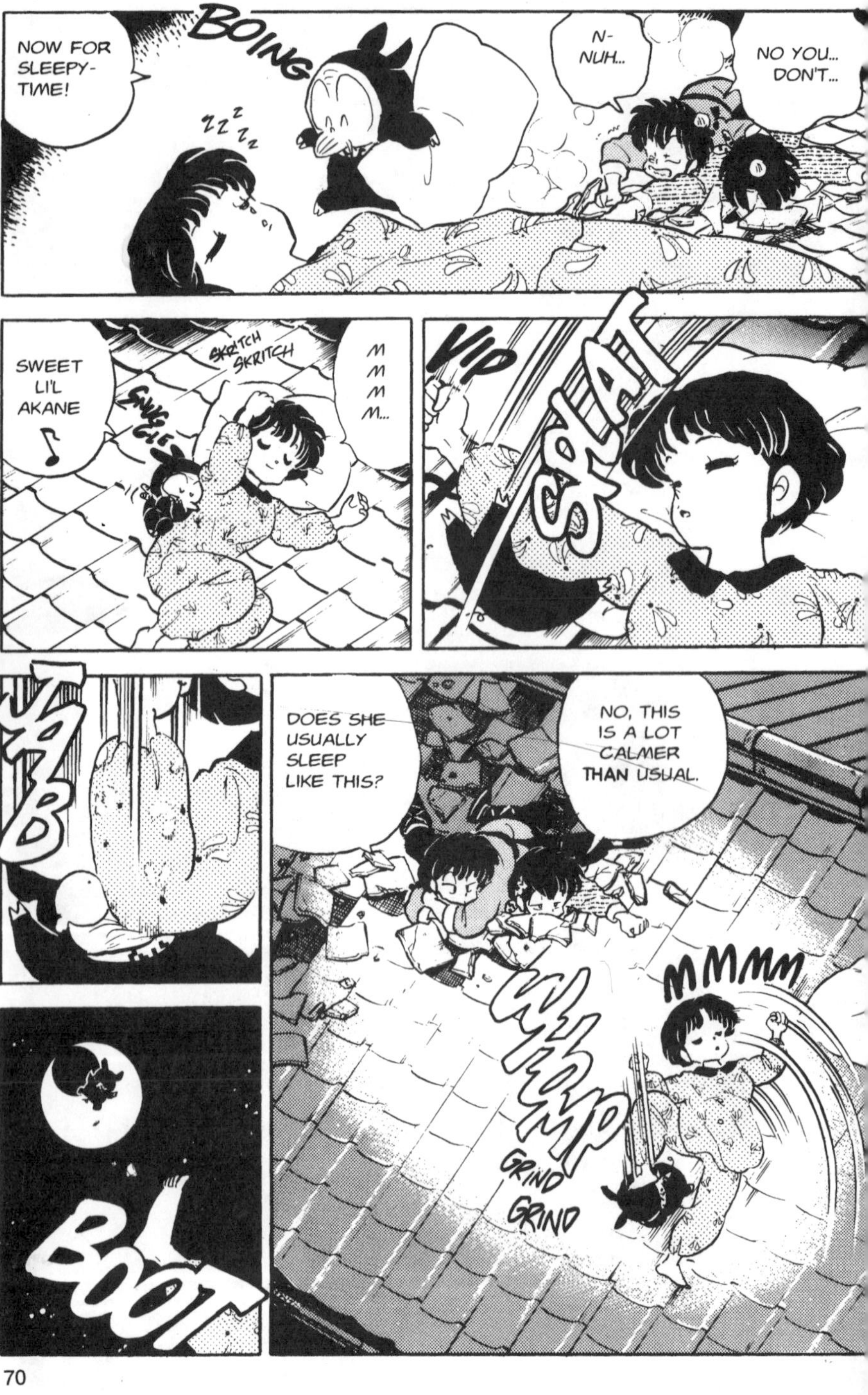
NOW FOR SLEEPY-TIME!
BOING
ZZZZZ
N-NUH...
NO YOU... DON'T...
SWEET LI'L AKANE ♪
SKRITCH SKRITCH
SNUGGLE
MMMM...
VIP
SPLAT
JAB
DOES SHE USUALLY SLEEP LIKE THIS?
NO, THIS IS A LOT CALMER THAN USUAL.
WHOMP
MMMMM
GRIND GRIND
BOOT

PART 5

THE WRATH OF HAPPOSAI

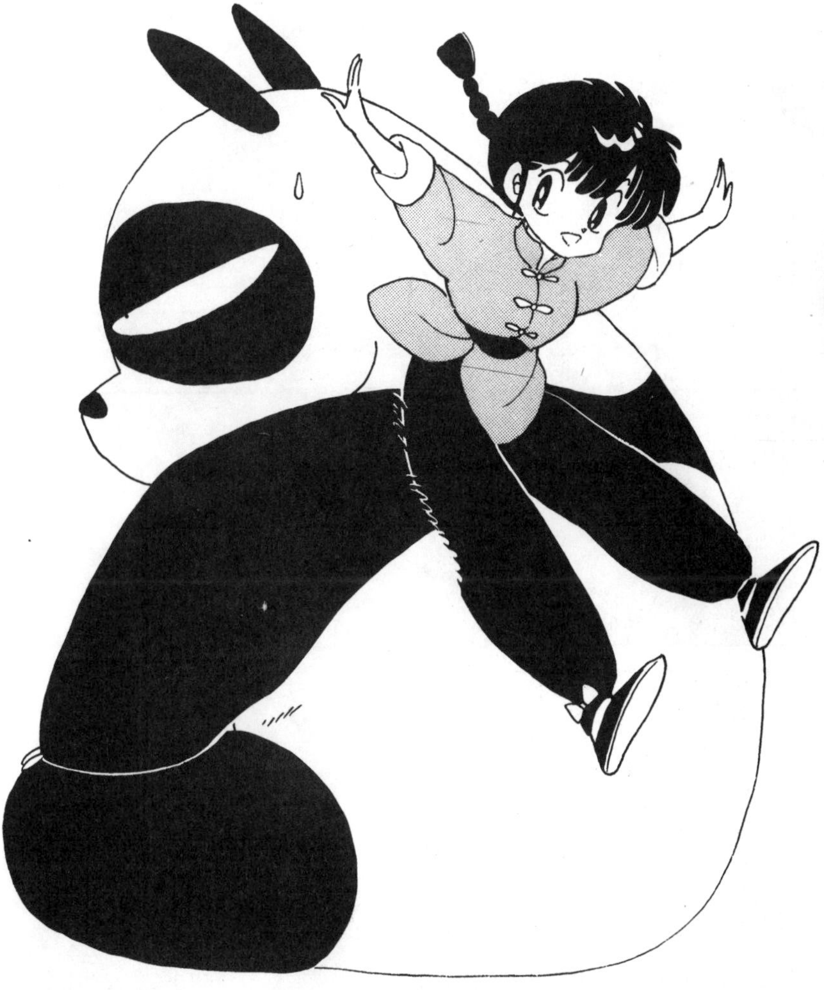

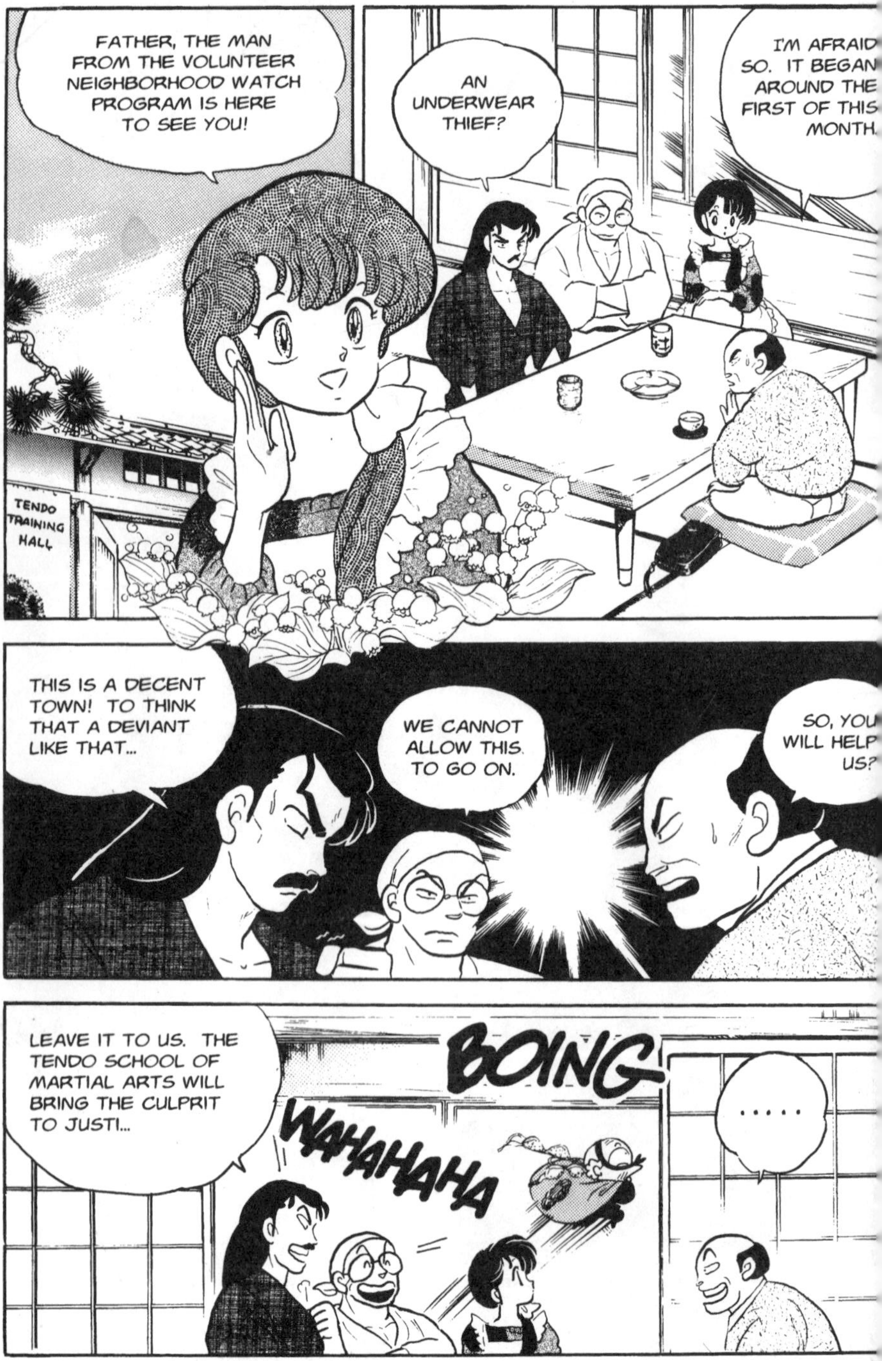

FATHER, THE MAN FROM THE VOLUNTEER NEIGHBORHOOD WATCH PROGRAM IS HERE TO SEE YOU!
TENDO TRAINING HALL
AN UNDERWEAR THIEF?
I'M AFRAID SO. IT BEGAN AROUND THE FIRST OF THIS MONTH.
THIS IS A DECENT TOWN! TO THINK THAT A DEVIANT LIKE THAT...
WE CANNOT ALLOW THIS TO GO ON.
SO, YOU WILL HELP US?
LEAVE IT TO US. THE TENDO SCHOOL OF MARTIAL ARTS WILL BRING THE CULPRIT TO JUSTI...
BOING
WAHAHAHA
.....

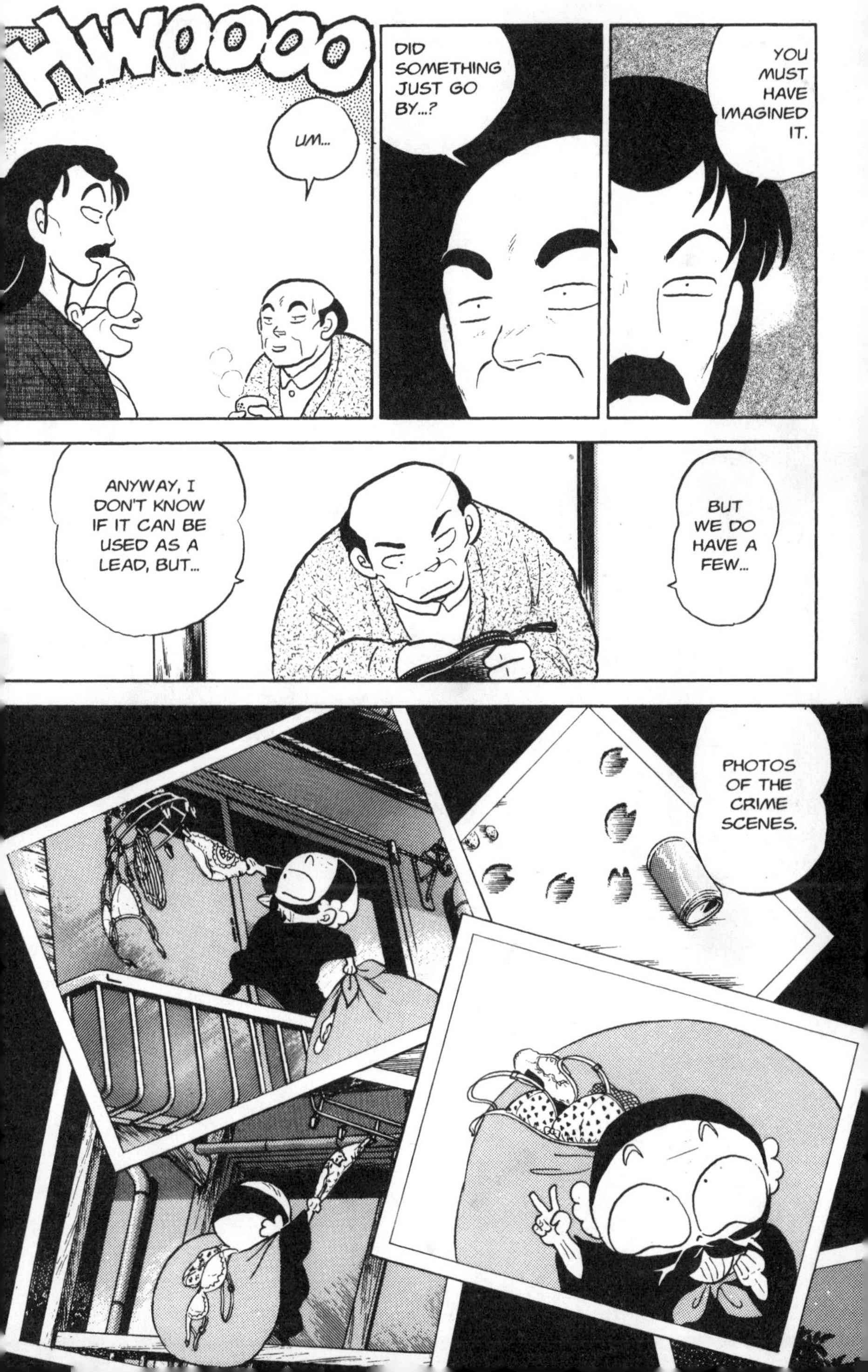
HWOOOO
UM...
DID SOMETHING JUST GO BY...?
YOU MUST HAVE IMAGINED IT.
ANYWAY, I DON'T KNOW IF IT CAN BE USED AS A LEAD, BUT...
BUT WE DO HAVE A FEW...
PHOTOS OF THE CRIME SCENES.

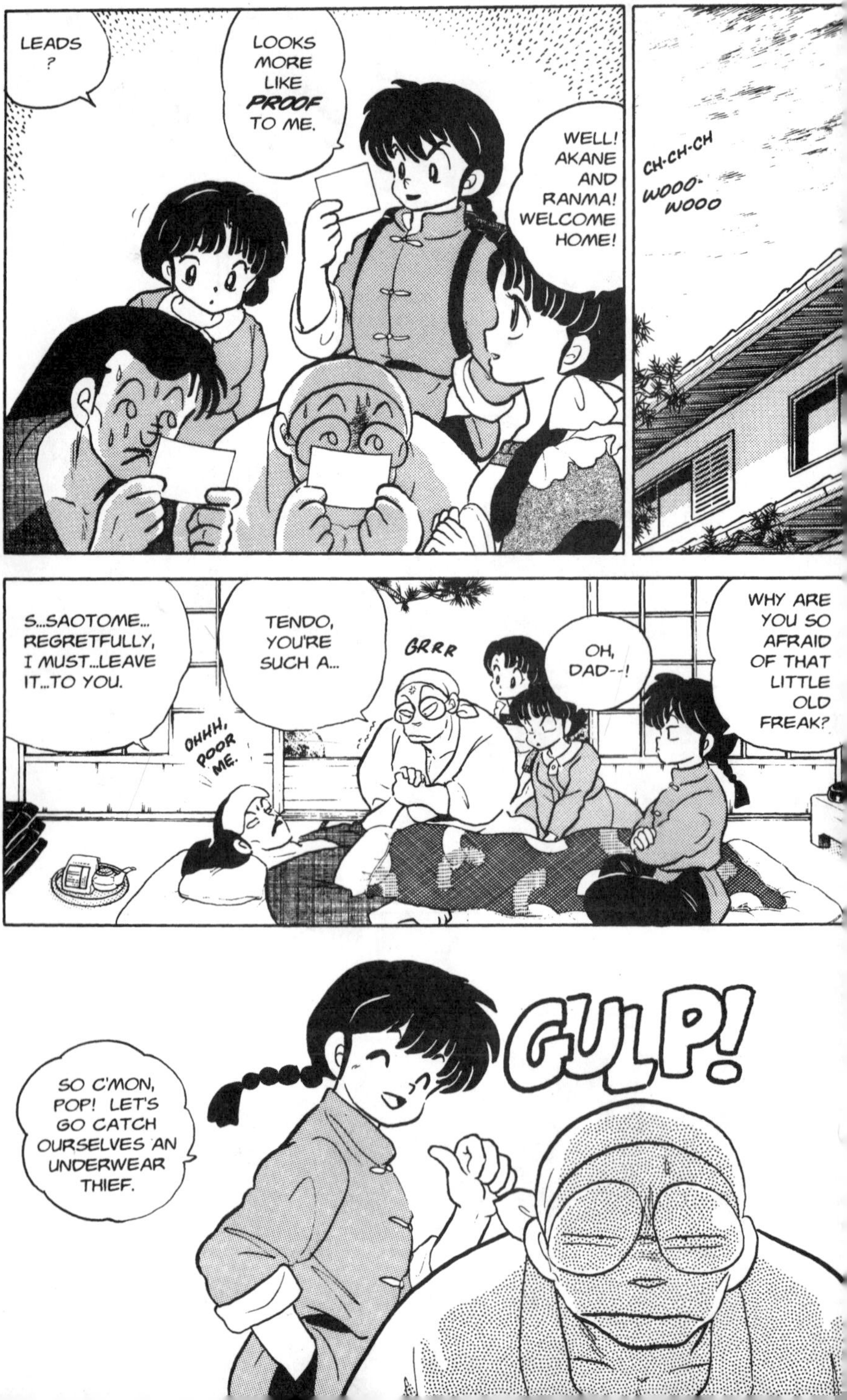

LEADS ?
LOOKS MORE LIKE PROOF TO ME.
WELL! AKANE AND RANMA! WELCOME HOME!
CH-CH-CH
WOOO-WOOO
S...SAOTOME... REGRETFULLY, I MUST...LEAVE IT...TO YOU.
TENDO, YOU'RE SUCH A...
OHHH, POOR ME.
GRRR
OH, DAD--!
WHY ARE YOU SO AFRAID OF THAT LITTLE OLD FREAK?
SO C'MON, POP! LET'S GO CATCH OURSELVES AN UNDERWEAR THIEF.
GULP!

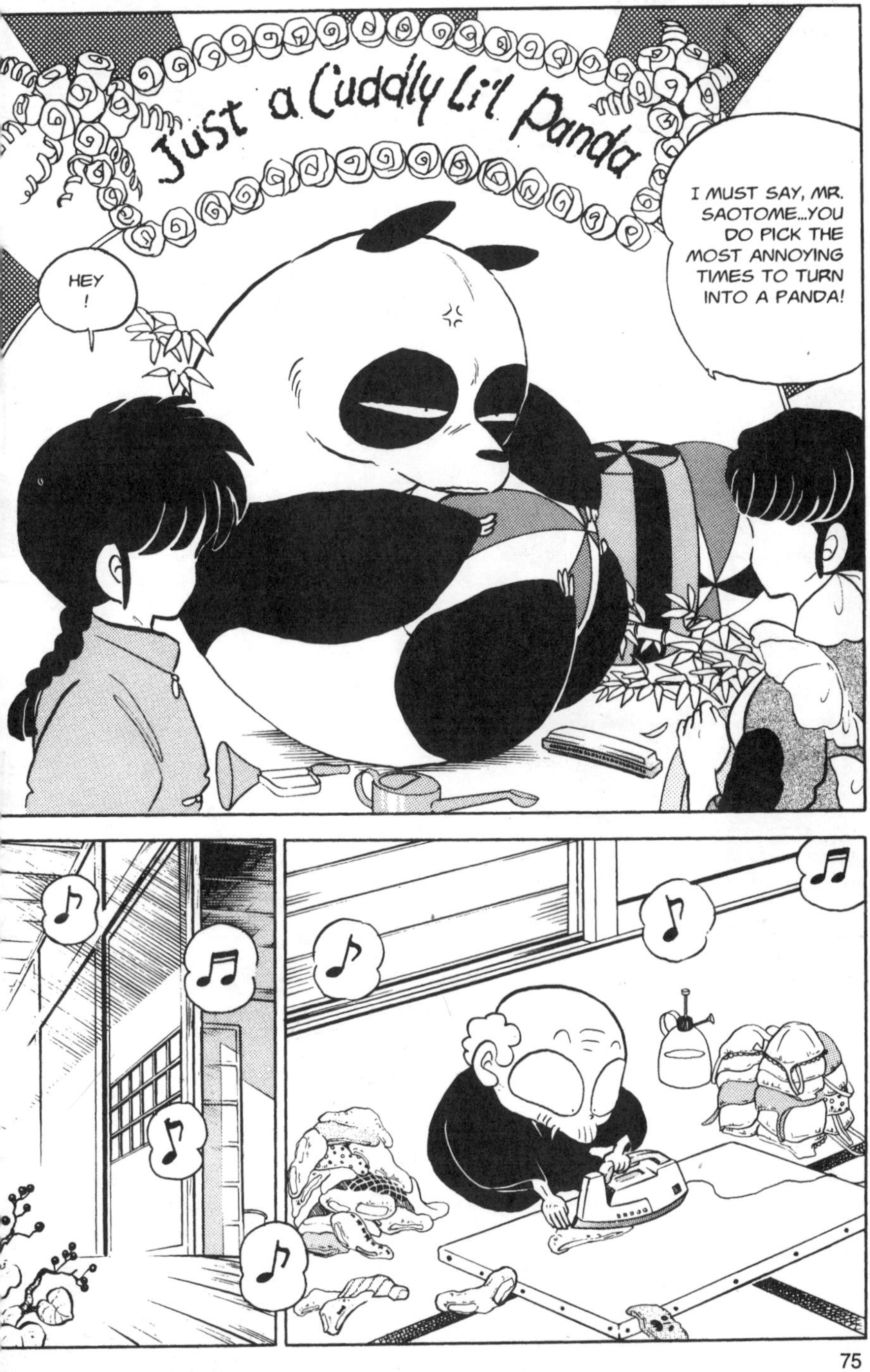
Just a Cuddly Li'l Panda
HEY !
I MUST SAY, MR. SAOTOME...YOU DO PICK THE MOST ANNOYING TIMES TO TURN INTO A PANDA!

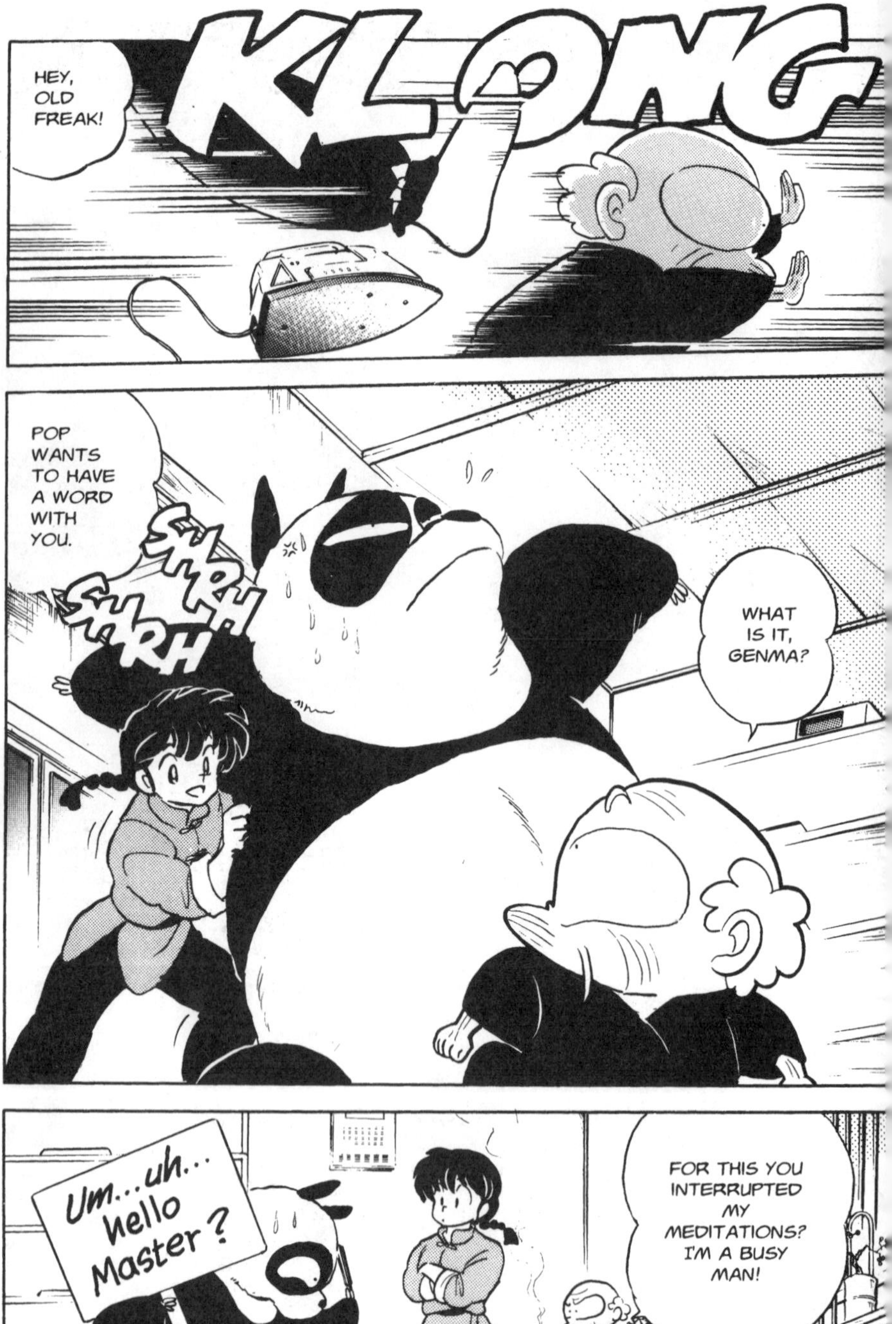
KLONG
HEY, OLD FREAK!
POP WANTS TO HAVE A WORD WITH YOU.
SHRRH SHRRH
WHAT IS IT, GENMA?
Um...uh... hello Master?
FOR THIS YOU INTERRUPTED MY MEDITATIONS? I'M A BUSY MAN!

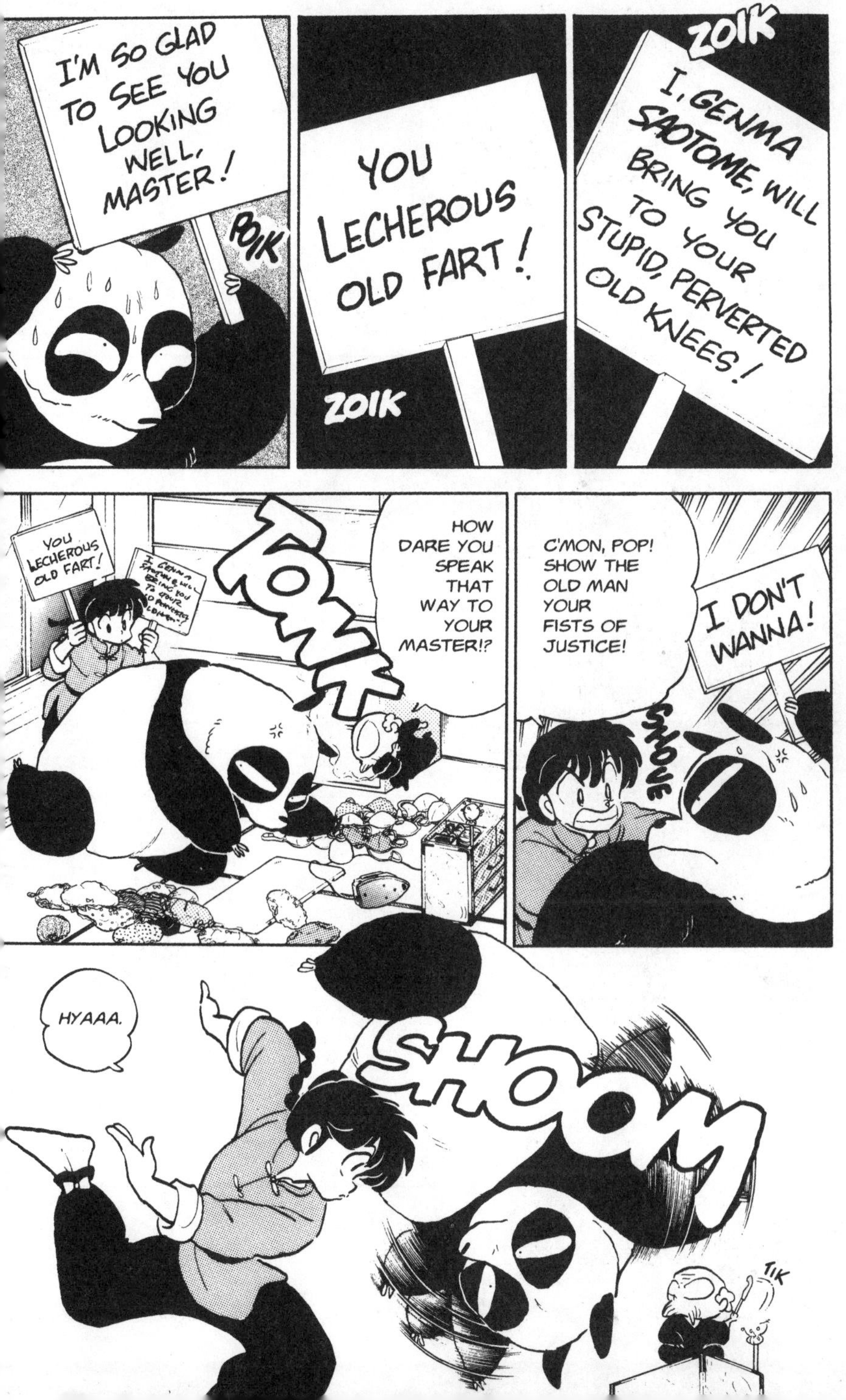
I'M SO GLAD TO SEE YOU LOOKING WELL, MASTER!
POIK
YOU LECHEROUS OLD FART!
ZOIK
ZOIK
I, GENMA SAOTOME, WILL BRING YOU TO YOUR STUPID, PERVERTED OLD KNEES!
YOU LECHEROUS OLD FART!
TONK
HOW DARE YOU SPEAK THAT WAY TO YOUR MASTER!?
C'MON, POP! SHOW THE OLD MAN YOUR FISTS OF JUSTICE!
I DON'T WANNA!
SHOVE
HYAAA.
SHOOM
TIK

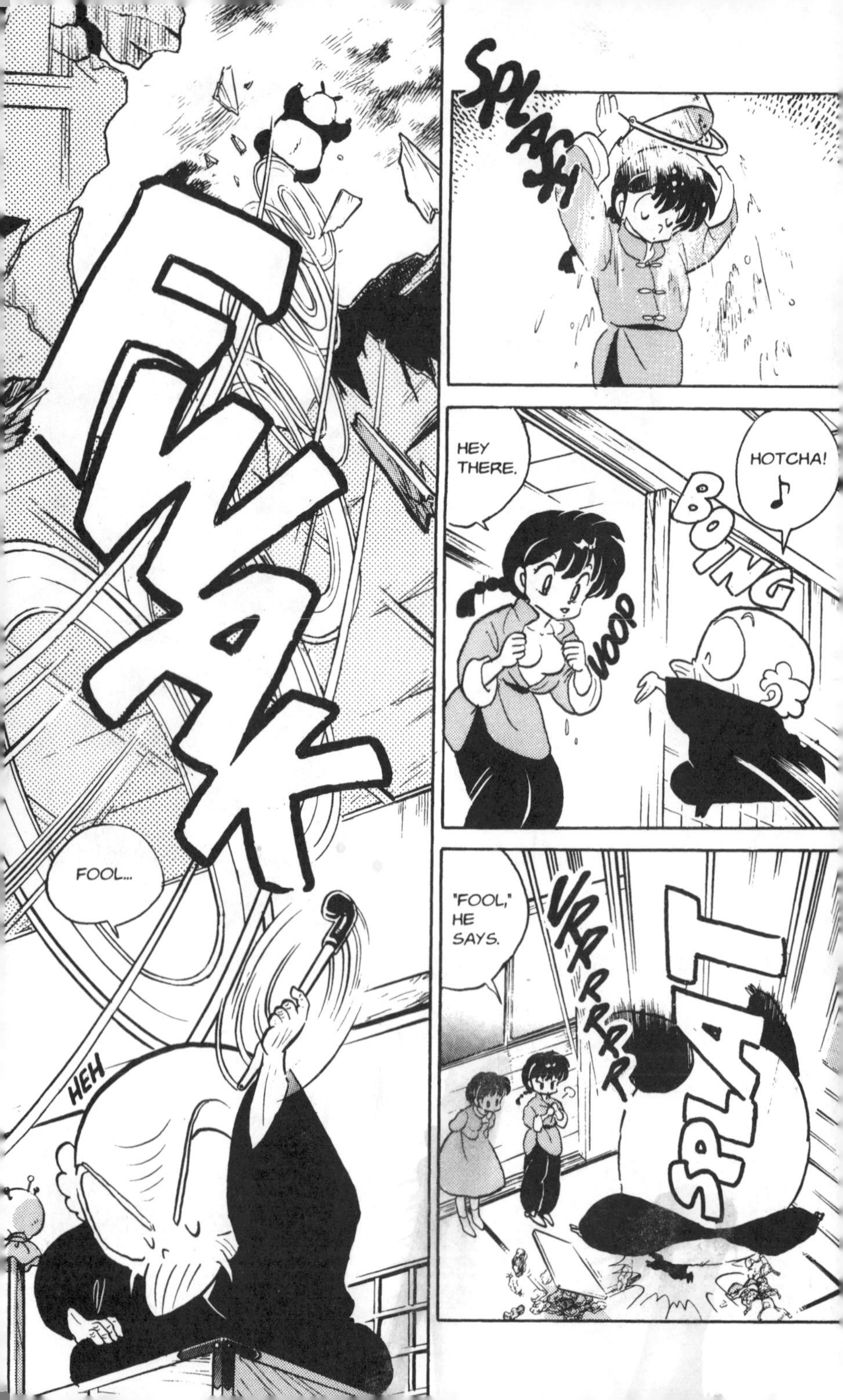
FZAK
FOOL...
HEH
SPLASH
HEY THERE.
HOTCHA! ♪
BOING
VOOP
"FOOL," HE SAYS.
VRRRRRRR
SPLAT

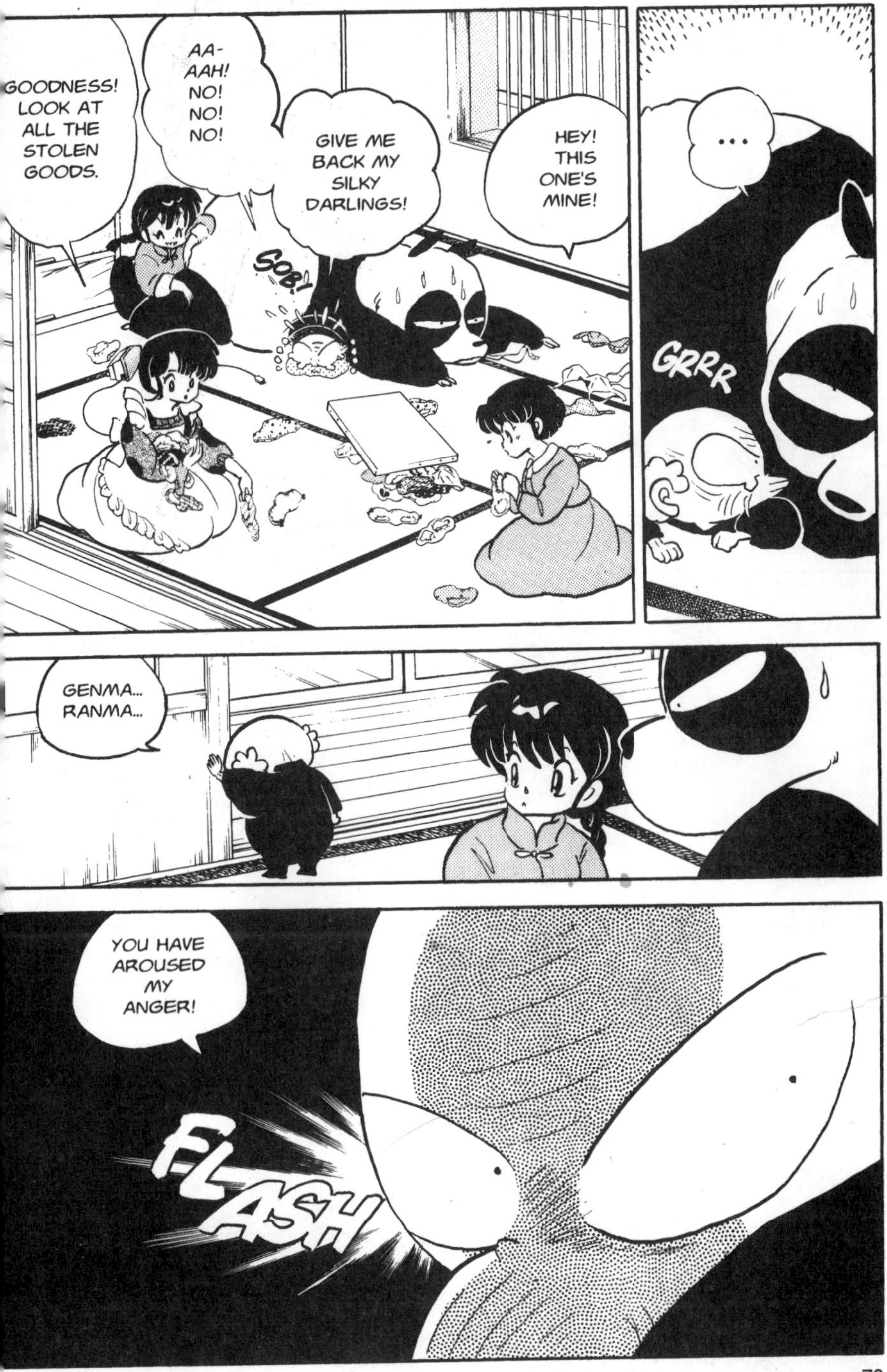
GOODNESS! LOOK AT ALL THE STOLEN GOODS.
AA-AAH! NO! NO! NO!
SOB!
GIVE ME BACK MY SILKY DARLINGS!
HEY! THIS ONE'S MINE!
...
GRRR
GENMA... RANMA...
YOU HAVE AROUSED MY ANGER!
FLASH

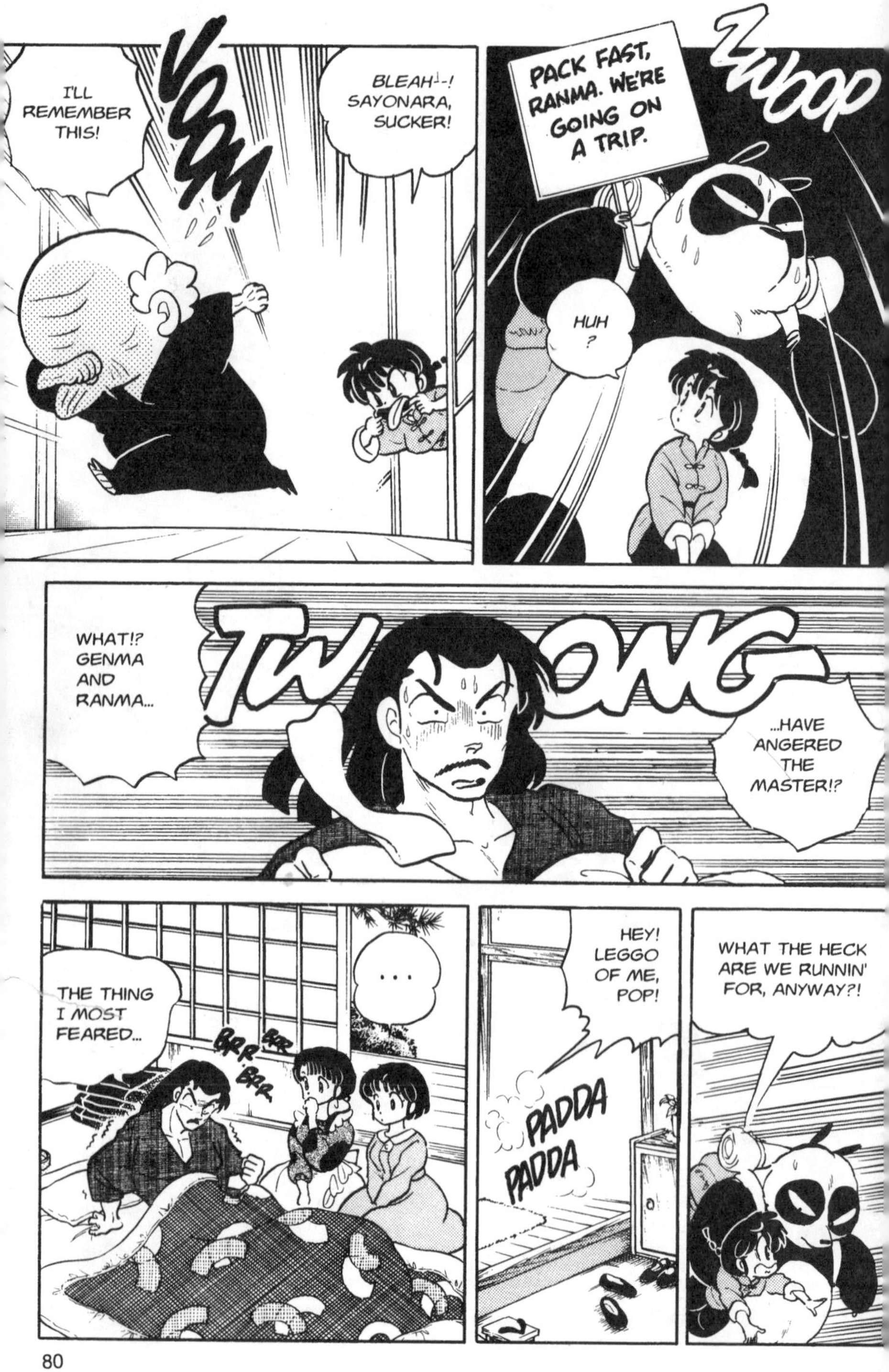
I'LL REMEMBER THIS!
VOOM
BLEAH--! SAYONARA, SUCKER!
PACK FAST, RANMA. WE'RE GOING ON A TRIP.
ZUBOOP
HUH ?
WHAT!? GENMA AND RANMA...
TW
ONG
...HAVE ANGERED THE MASTER!?
THE THING I MOST FEARED...
...
BRR BRR BRR
HEY! LEGGO OF ME, POP!
PADDA PADDA
WHAT THE HECK ARE WE RUNNIN' FOR, ANYWAY?!

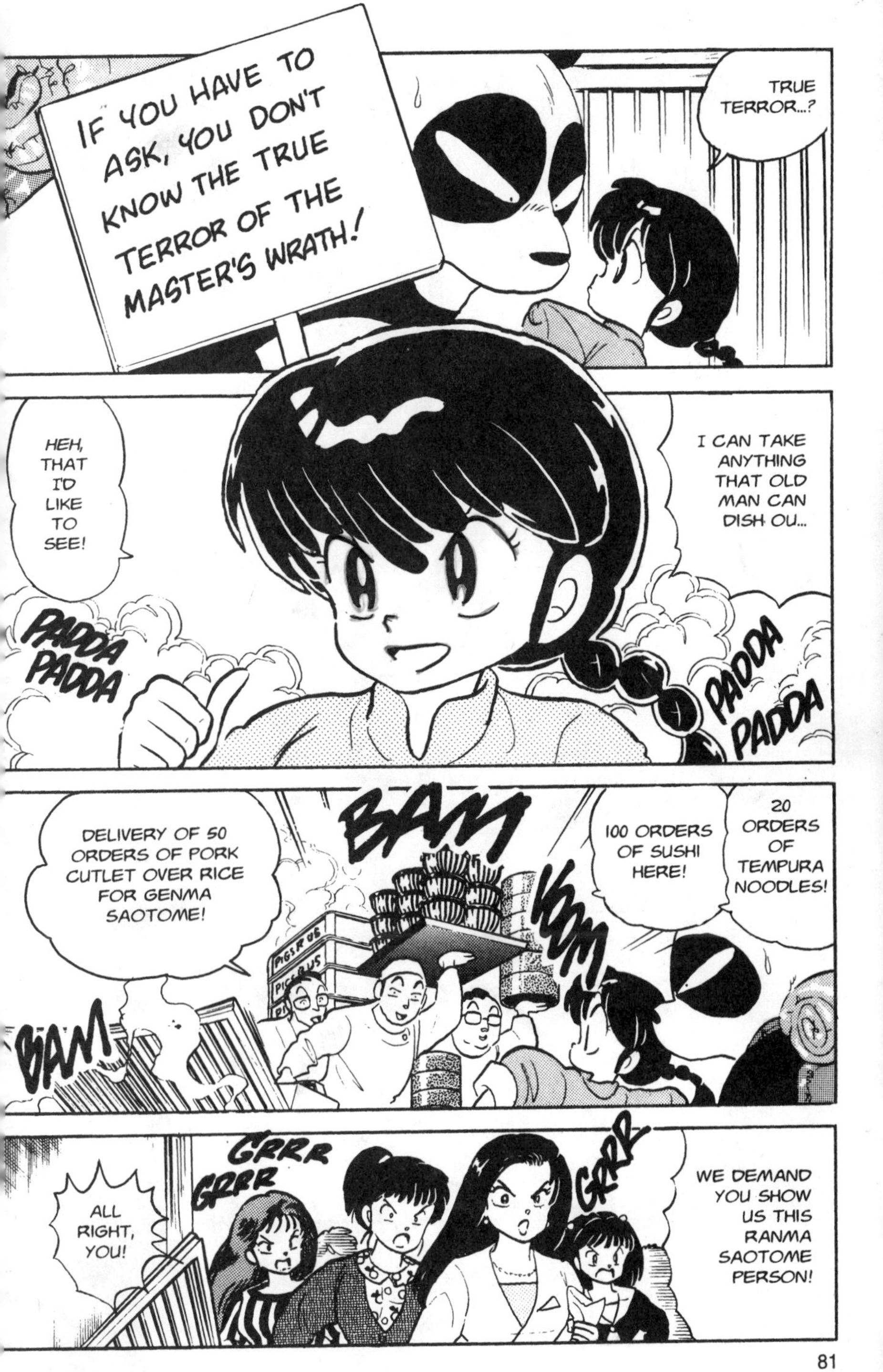
IF YOU HAVE TO ASK, YOU DON'T KNOW THE TRUE TERROR OF THE MASTER'S WRATH!
TRUE TERROR...?
HEH, THAT I'D LIKE TO SEE!
PADDA PADDA
I CAN TAKE ANYTHING THAT OLD MAN CAN DISH OU...
PADDA PADDA
DELIVERY OF 50 ORDERS OF PORK CUTLET OVER RICE FOR GENMA SAOTOME!
BAM
100 ORDERS OF SUSHI HERE!
20 ORDERS OF TEMPURA NOODLES!
VOOM
BAM
ALL RIGHT, YOU!
GRRR GRRR
GRRR
WE DEMAND YOU SHOW US THIS RANMA SAOTOME PERSON!

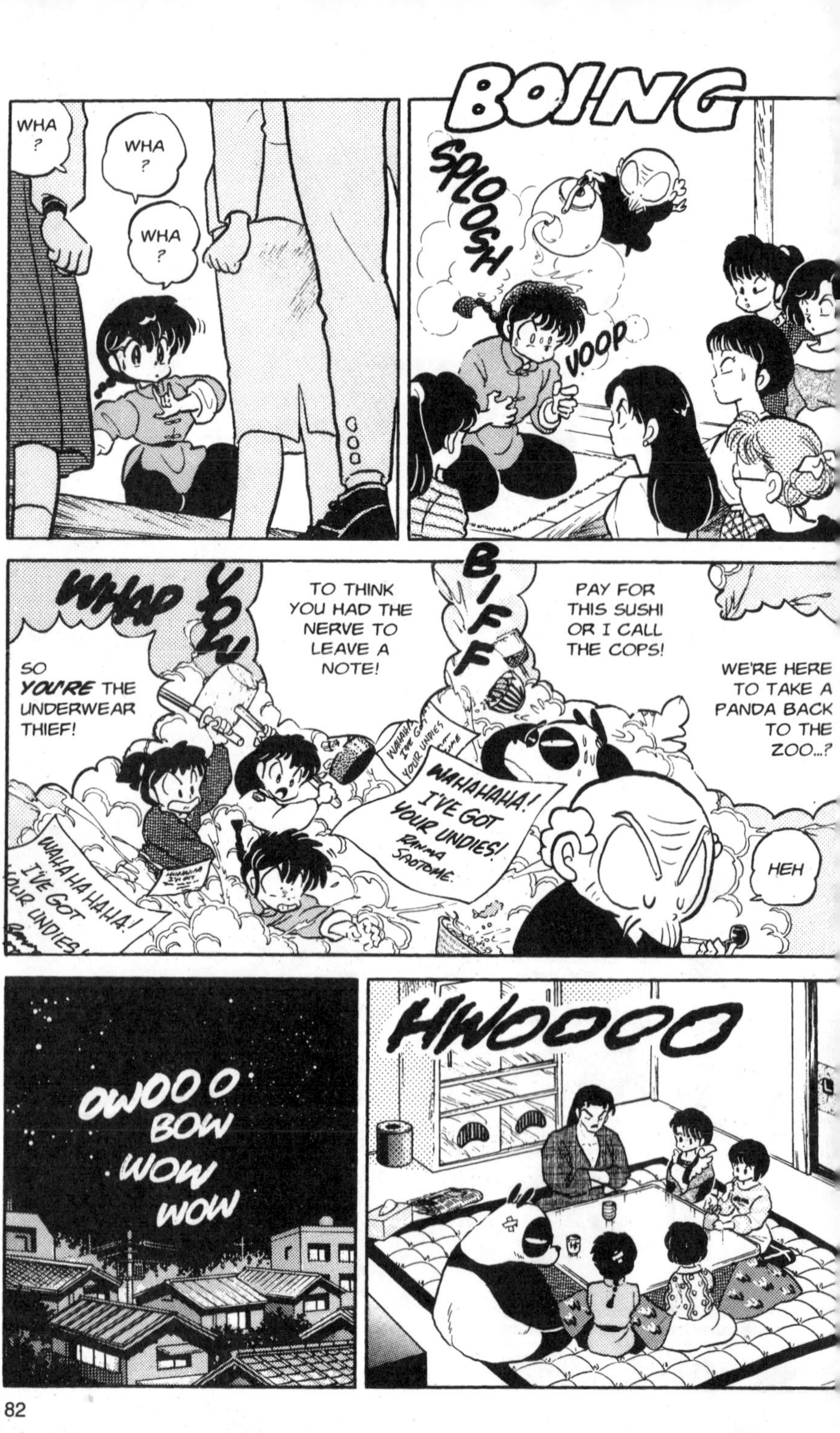
WHA ?
WHA ?
WHA ?
BOING
SPLOOSH
VOOP
WHAP
YOW
SO YOU'RE THE UNDERWEAR THIEF!
TO THINK YOU HAD THE NERVE TO LEAVE A NOTE!
BIFF
PAY FOR THIS SUSHI OR I CALL THE COPS!
WE'RE HERE TO TAKE A PANDA BACK TO THE ZOO...?
WAHAHAHA! I'VE GOT YOUR UNDIES! RANMA SAOTOME
HEH
OWOO O BOW WOW WOW
HWOOOO

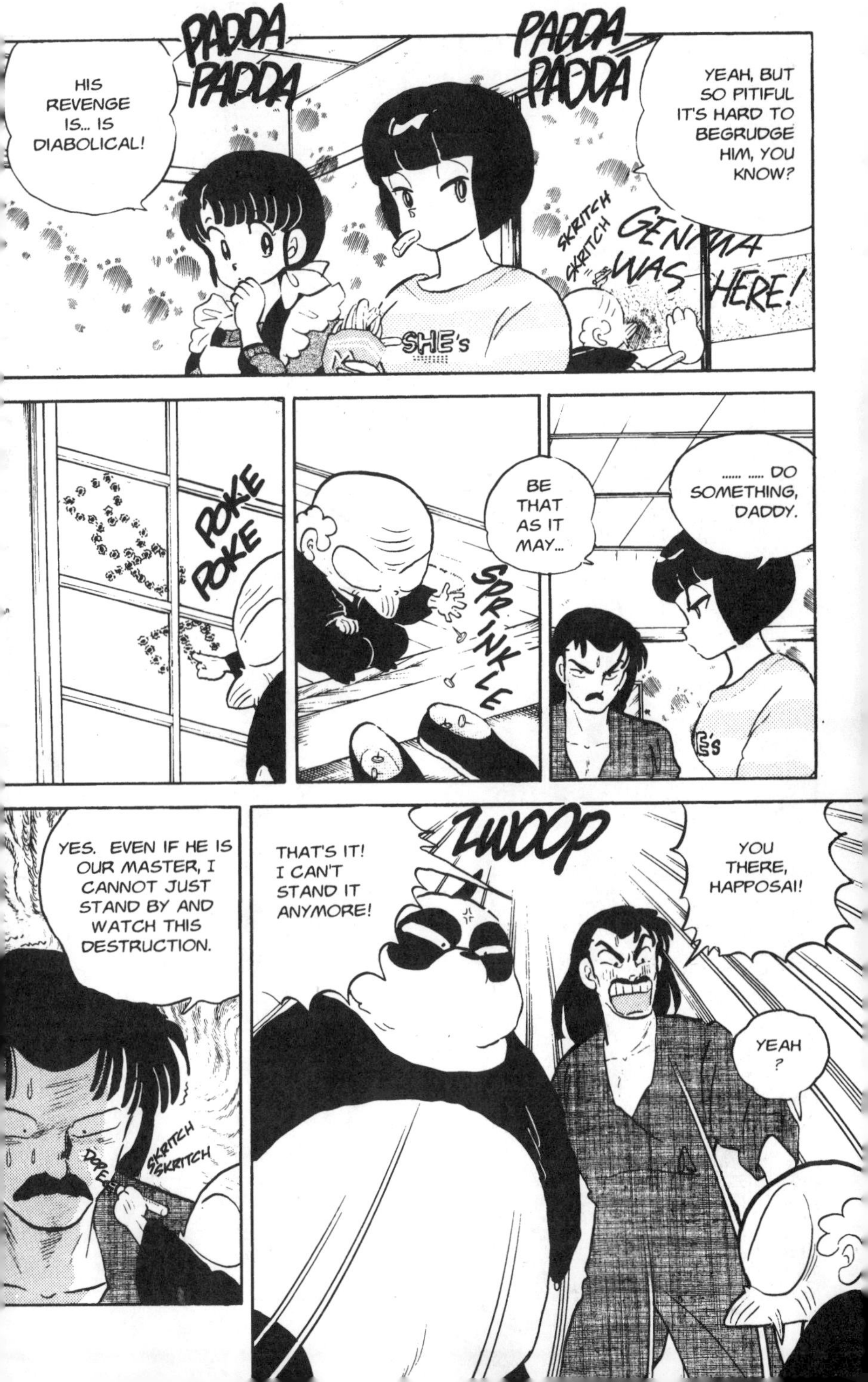
PADDA PADDA
HIS REVENGE IS... IS DIABOLICAL!
PADDA PADDA
YEAH, BUT SO PITIFUL IT'S HARD TO BEGRUDGE HIM, YOU KNOW?
SKRITCH SKRITCH
GENMA WAS HERE!
SHE's
POKE POKE
SPRINKLE
BE THAT AS IT MAY...
.... DO SOMETHING, DADDY.
E's
YES. EVEN IF HE IS OUR MASTER, I CANNOT JUST STAND BY AND WATCH THIS DESTRUCTION.
DOPE
SKRITCH SKRITCH
ZWOOP
THAT'S IT! I CAN'T STAND IT ANYMORE!
YOU THERE, HAPPOSAI!
YEAH ?

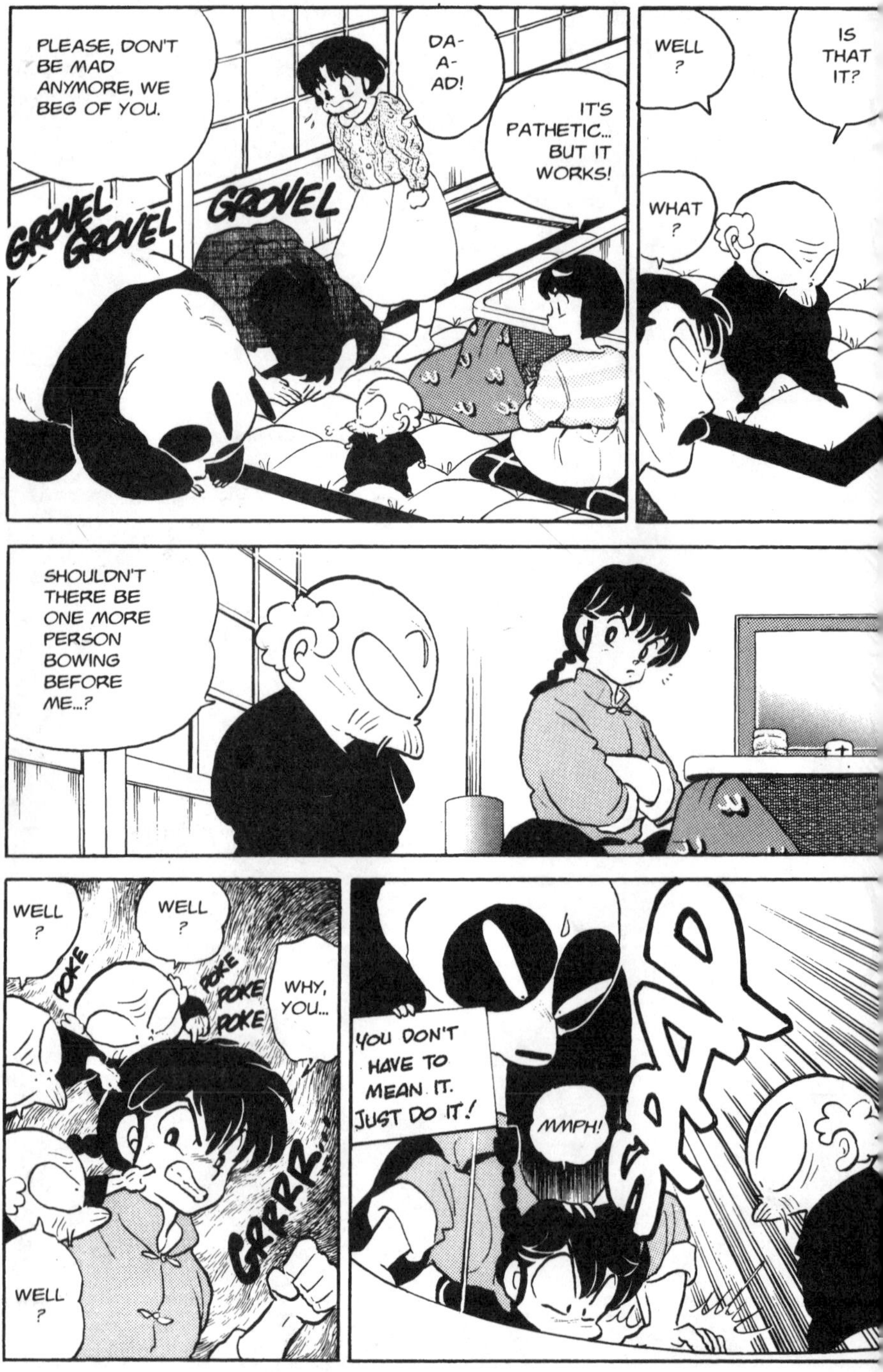

PLEASE, DON'T BE MAD ANYMORE, WE BEG OF YOU.
GROVEL GROVEL
GROVEL
DA-A-AD!
IT'S PATHETIC... BUT IT WORKS!
WELL?
IS THAT IT?
WHAT?
SHOULDN'T THERE BE ONE MORE PERSON BOWING BEFORE ME...?
WELL?
POKE
WELL?
POKE POKE POKE
WHY, YOU...
GRRRR...
WELL?
YOU DON'T HAVE TO MEAN IT. JUST DO IT!
MMPH!

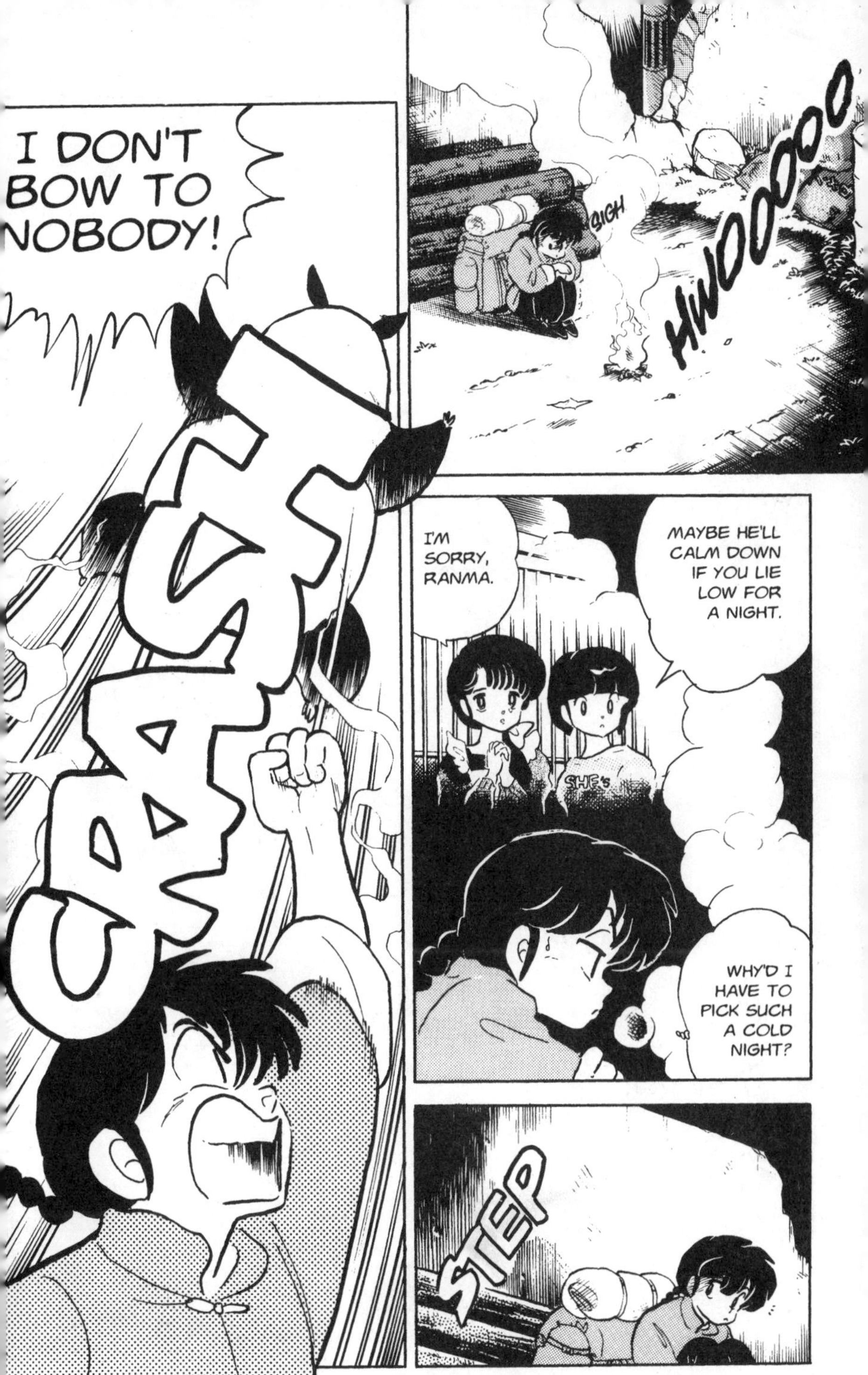
I DON'T BOW TO NOBODY!
CRASH
SIGH
HWOOOOOO
I'M SORRY, RANMA.
MAYBE HE'LL CALM DOWN IF YOU LIE LOW FOR A NIGHT.
SHE'S
WHY'D I HAVE TO PICK SUCH A COLD NIGHT?
STEP

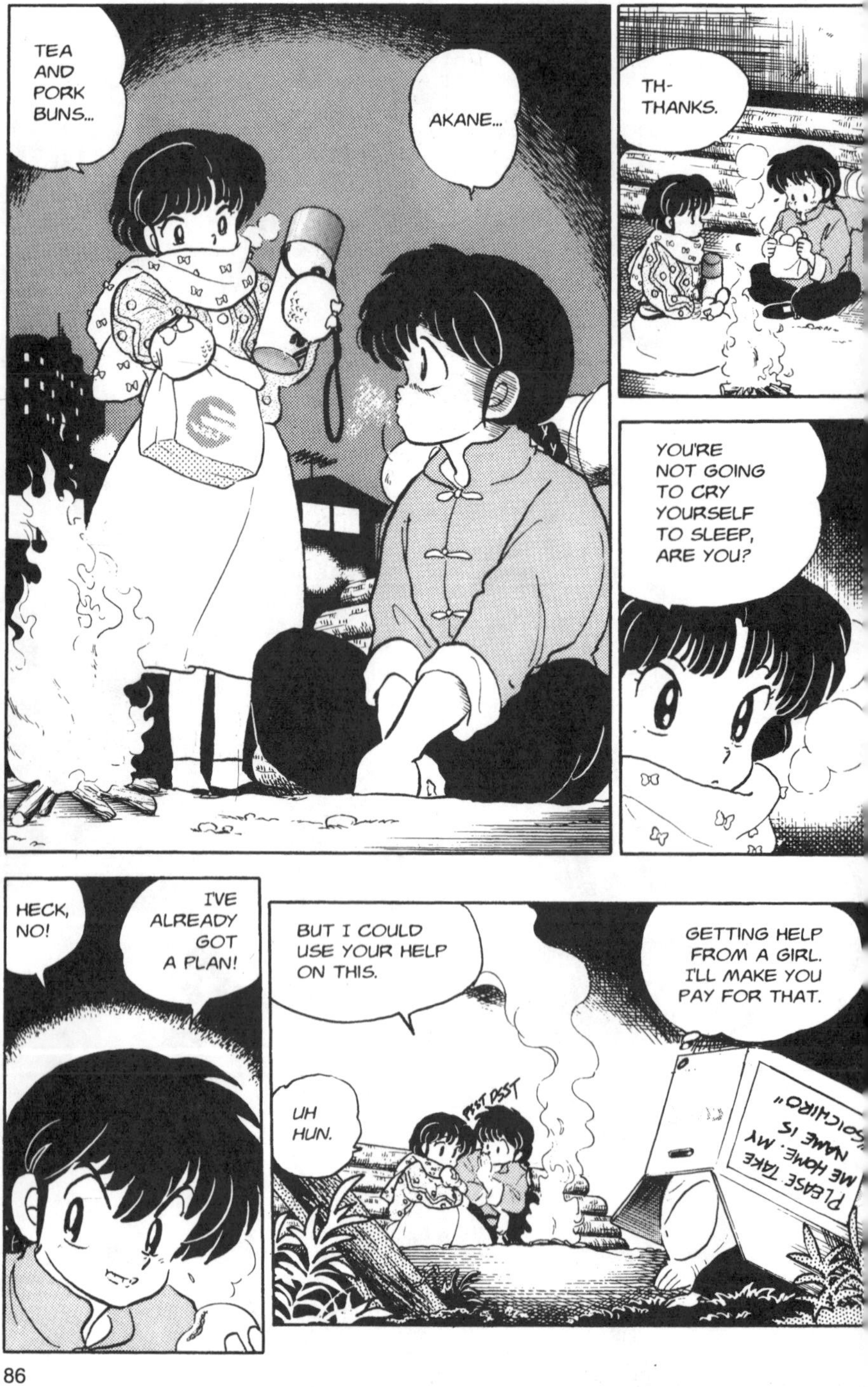
TEA AND PORK BUNS...
AKANE...
TH- THANKS.
YOU'RE NOT GOING TO CRY YOURSELF TO SLEEP, ARE YOU?
HECK, NO!
I'VE ALREADY GOT A PLAN!
BUT I COULD USE YOUR HELP ON THIS.
UH HUN.
PSST PSST
GETTING HELP FROM A GIRL. I'LL MAKE YOU PAY FOR THAT.
PLEASE TAKE ME HOME. MY NAME IS "SOICHIRO"

PART 6

THE SCENT OF A WOMAN

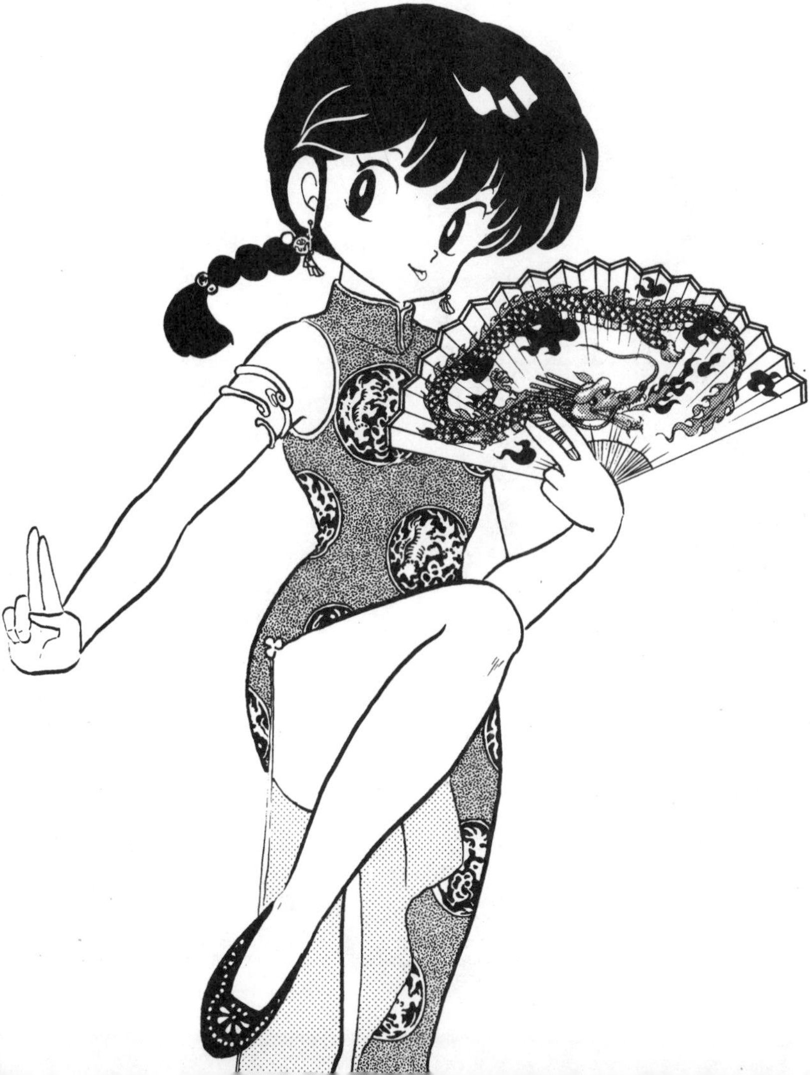

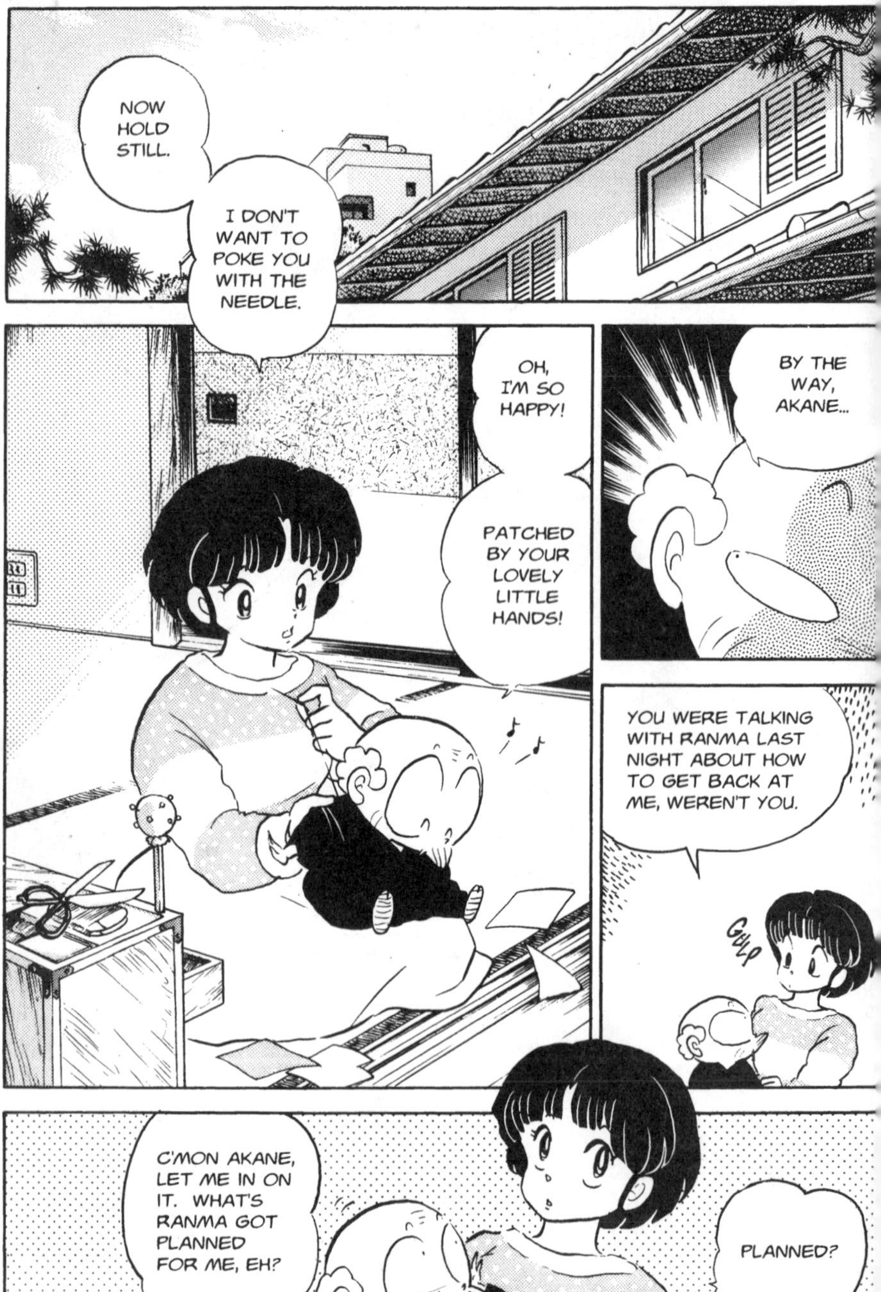

NOW HOLD STILL.
I DON'T WANT TO POKE YOU WITH THE NEEDLE.
OH, I'M SO HAPPY!
PATCHED BY YOUR LOVELY LITTLE HANDS!
BY THE WAY, AKANE...
YOU WERE TALKING WITH RANMA LAST NIGHT ABOUT HOW TO GET BACK AT ME, WEREN'T YOU.
GULP
C'MON AKANE, LET ME IN ON IT. WHAT'S RANMA GOT PLANNED FOR ME, EH?
PLANNED?

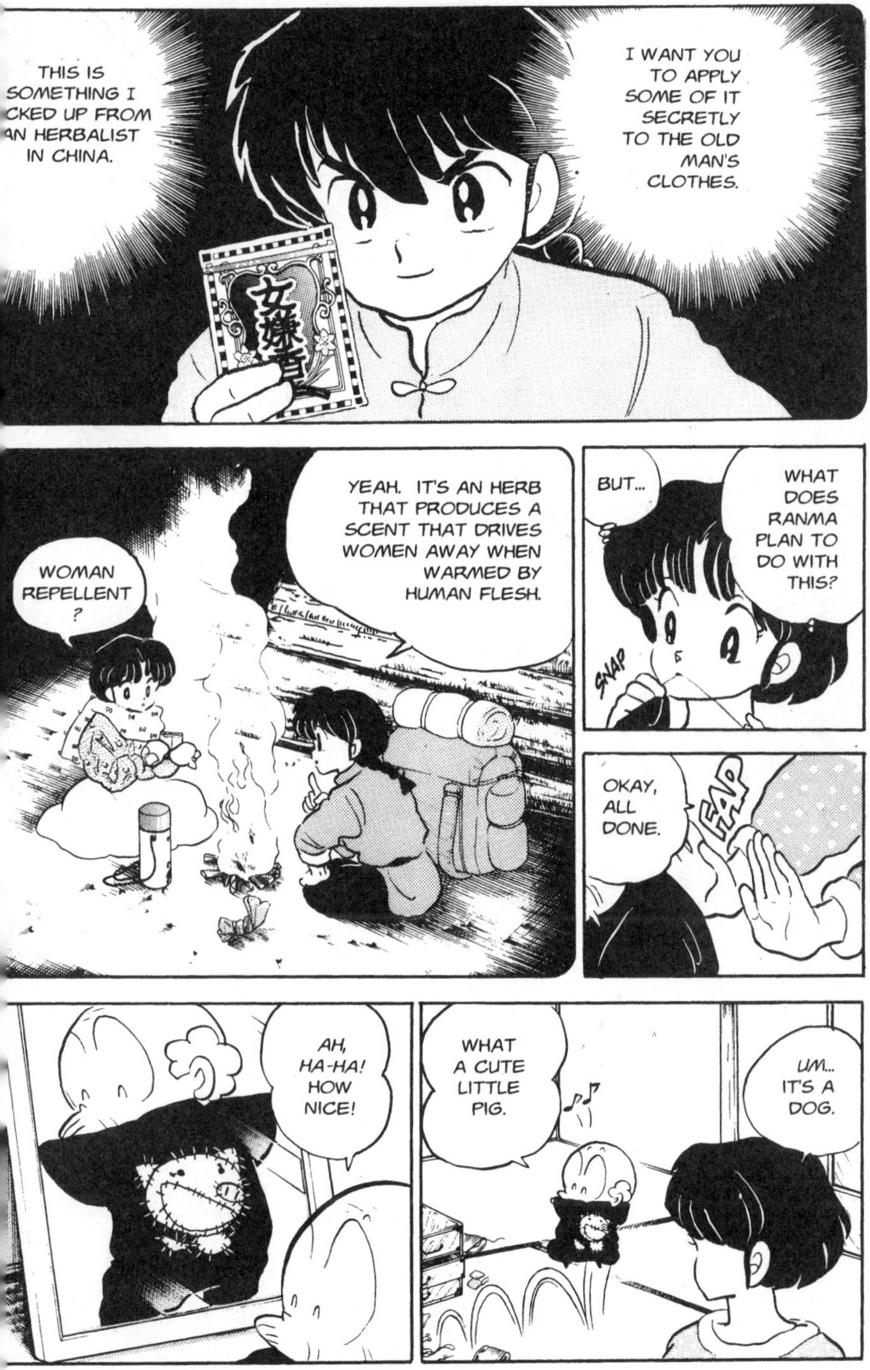
THIS IS SOMETHING I CKED UP FROM AN HERBALIST IN CHINA.
女嫌香
I WANT YOU TO APPLY SOME OF IT SECRETLY TO THE OLD MAN'S CLOTHES.
WOMAN REPELLENT ?
YEAH. IT'S AN HERB THAT PRODUCES A SCENT THAT DRIVES WOMEN AWAY WHEN WARMED BY HUMAN FLESH.
BUT...
WHAT DOES RANMA PLAN TO DO WITH THIS?
SNAP
OKAY, ALL DONE.
FAP
AH, HA-HA! HOW NICE!
WHAT A CUTE LITTLE PIG.
UM... IT'S A DOG.

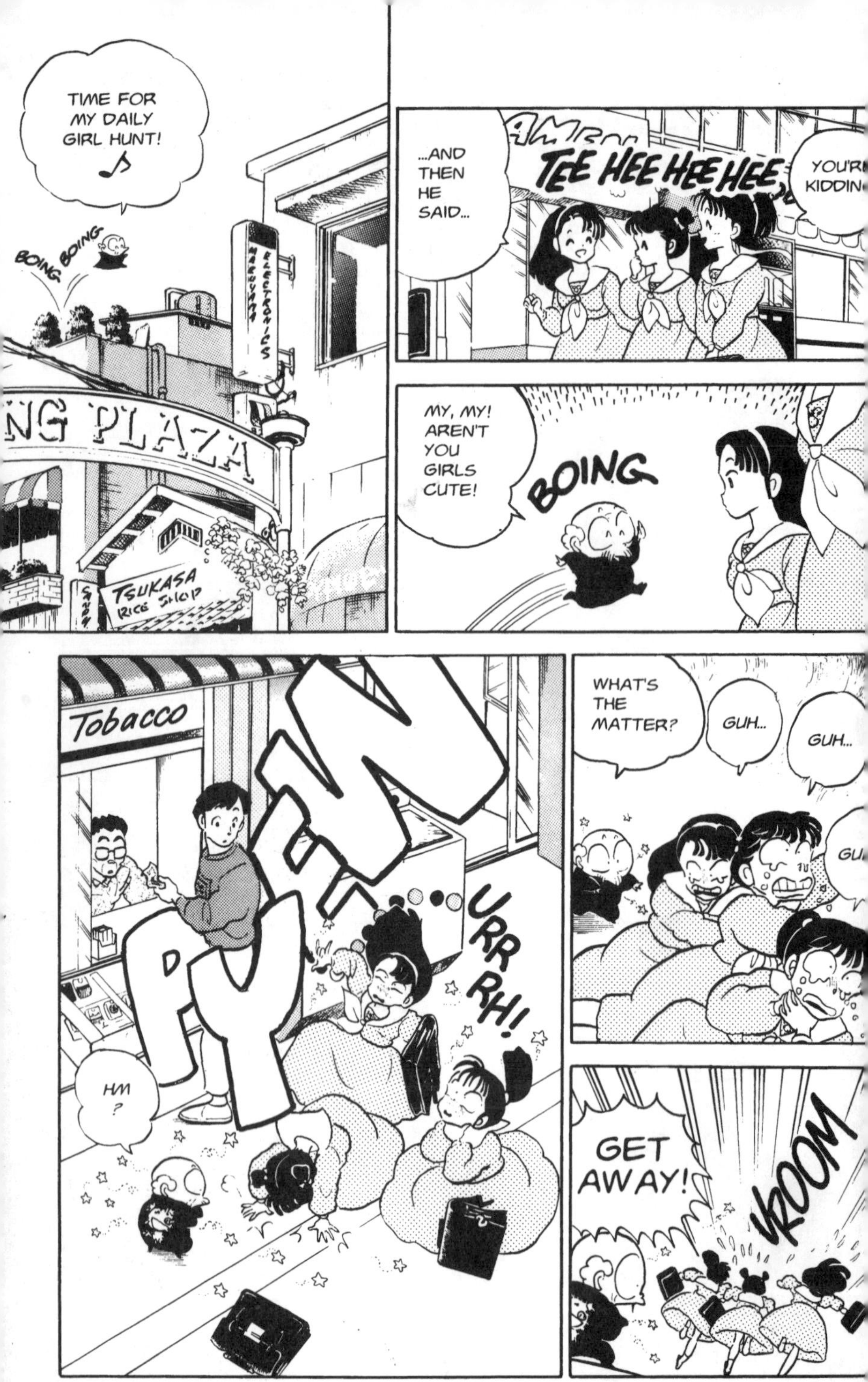
TIME FOR MY DAILY GIRL HUNT! ♪
BOING BOING
MARUYAMA ELECTRONICS
NG PLAZA
TSUKASA RICE SHOP
...AND THEN HE SAID...
TEE HEE HEE HEE
YOU'R KIDDIN
MY, MY! AREN'T YOU GIRLS CUTE!
BOING
Tobacco
PYUN
URRRH!
HM ?
WHAT'S THE MATTER?
GUH...
GUH...
GET AWAY!
VROOM

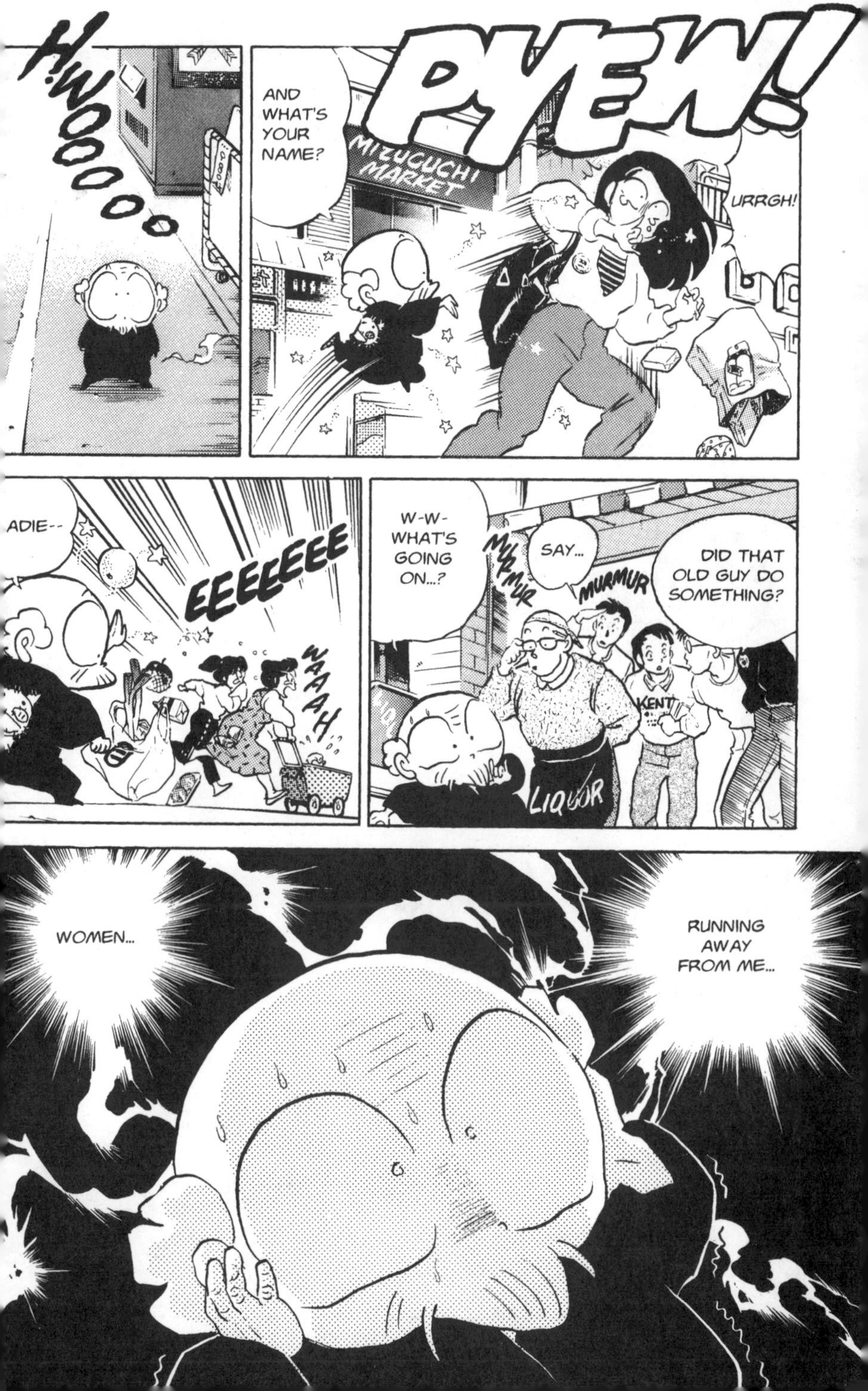
HWOOOOOO
AND WHAT'S YOUR NAME?
PYEW!
MIZUGUCHI MARKET
URRGH!
ADIE--
EEEEEEEE
WAAAH
W-W-WHAT'S GOING ON...?
MURMUR
SAY...
MURMUR
DID THAT OLD GUY DO SOMETHING?
KENT
LIQUOR
WOMEN...
RUNNING AWAY FROM ME...

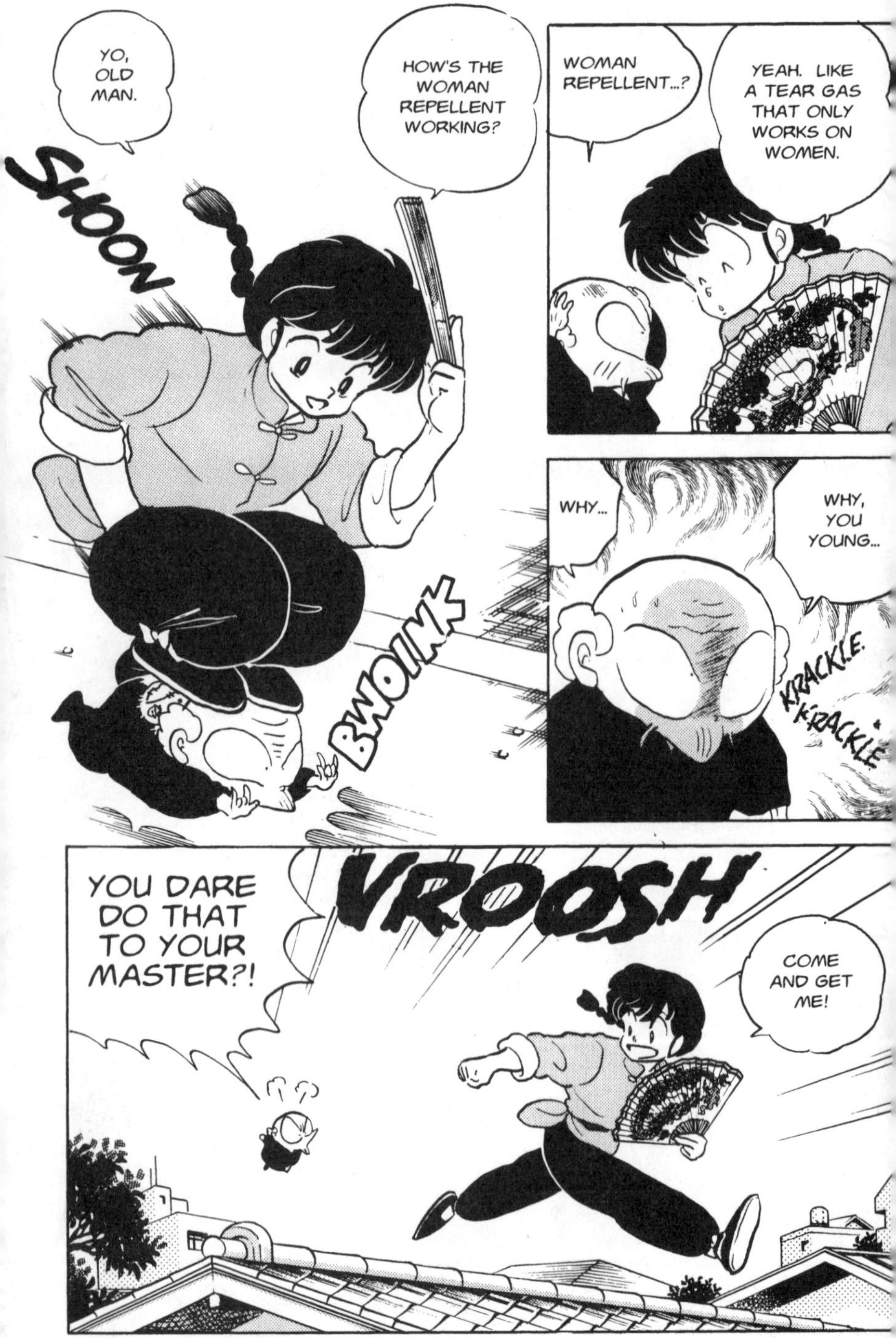
YO, OLD MAN.
HOW'S THE WOMAN REPELLENT WORKING?
SHOON
BWOIINK
WOMAN REPELLENT...?
YEAH. LIKE A TEAR GAS THAT ONLY WORKS ON WOMEN.
WHY...
WHY, YOU YOUNG...
KRACKLE
KRACKLE
YOU DARE DO THAT TO YOUR MASTER?!
VROOSH
COME AND GET ME!

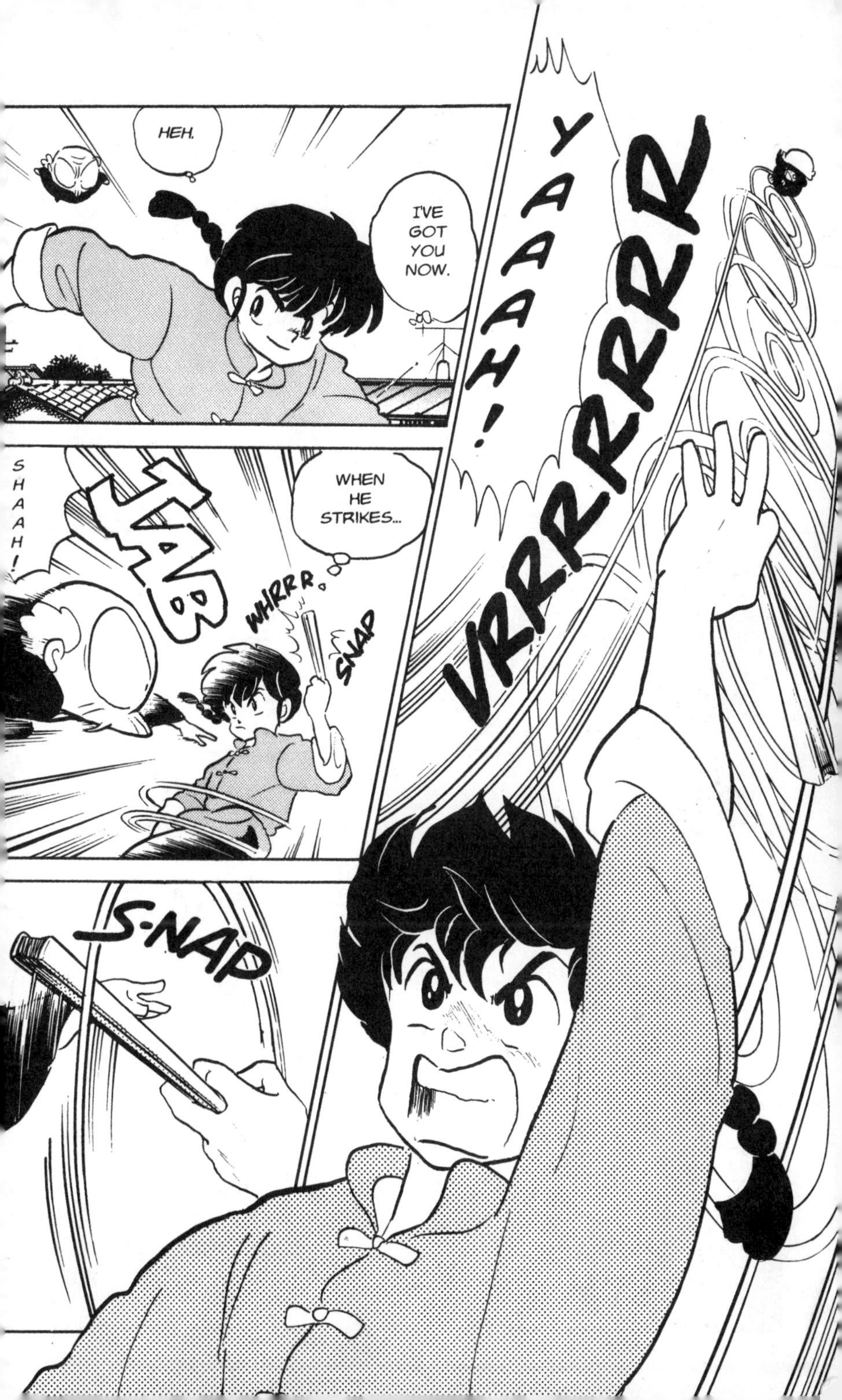
HEH.
I'VE GOT YOU NOW.
SHAAAH!
JAB
WHEN HE STRIKES...
WHRRR
SNAP
S-NAP
YAAAAH!
VRRRRRR

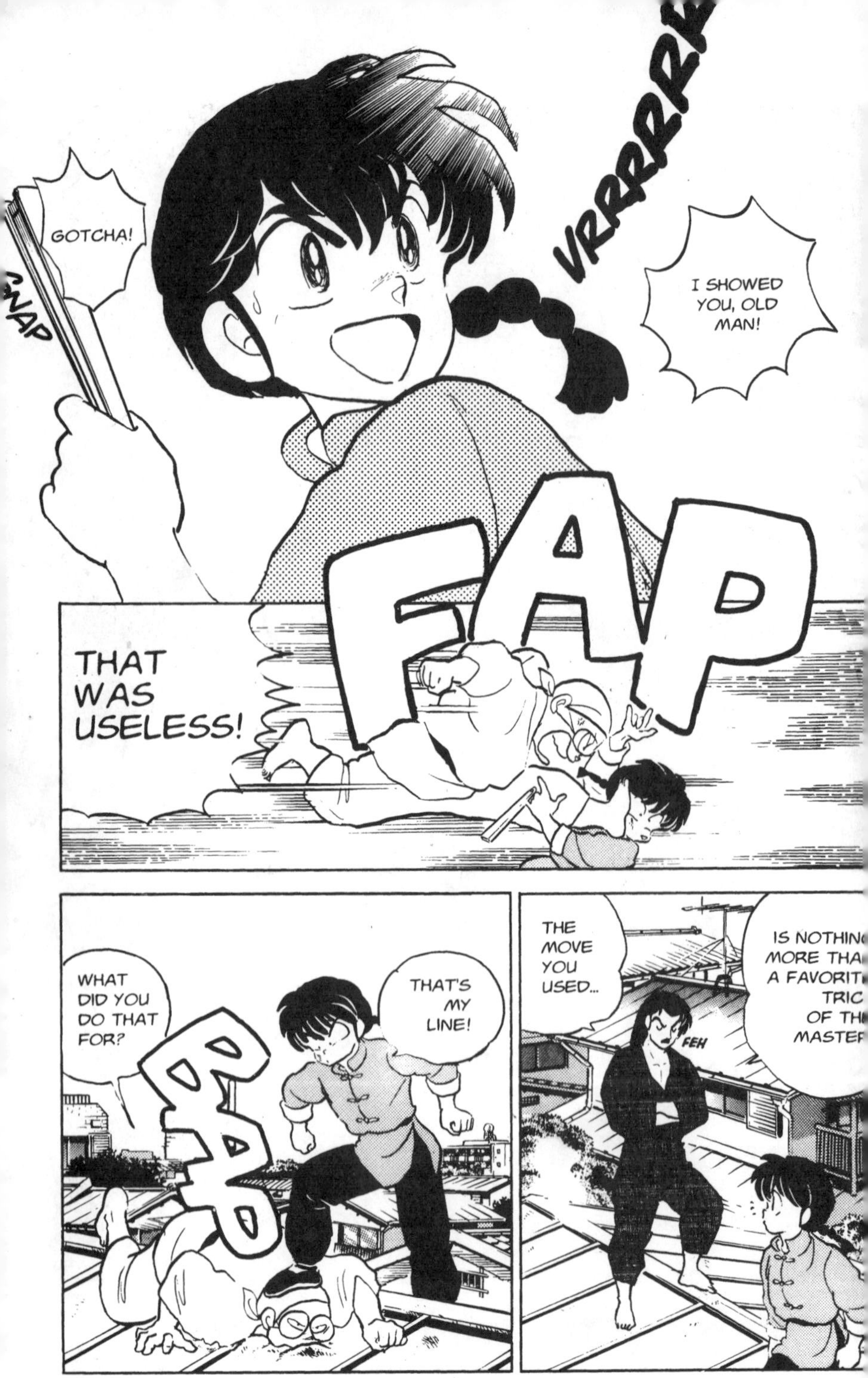
GOTCHA!
SNAP
VRRRRRR
I SHOWED YOU, OLD MAN!
FAP
THAT WAS USELESS!
WHAT DID YOU DO THAT FOR?
BAP
THAT'S MY LINE!
THE MOVE YOU USED...
FEH
IS NOTHIN MORE THA A FAVORIT TRIC OF TH MASTER

BY MAKING YOUR OPPONENT ANGRY ENOUGH TO ATTACK YOU, YOU USE HIS MOMENTUM...

...TO HURL HIM INTO THE AIR.

YOU PROBABLY THINK YOU GOT THE MASTER WITH HIS OWN TECHNIQUE...

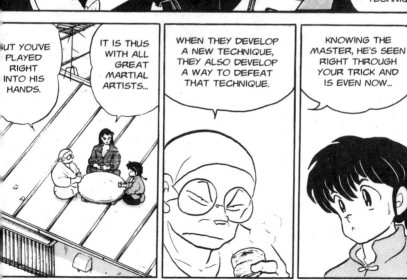

BUT YOU'VE PLAYED RIGHT INTO HIS HANDS.

IT IS THUS WITH ALL GREAT MARTIAL ARTISTS...

WHEN THEY DEVELOP A NEW TECHNIQUE, THEY ALSO DEVELOP A WAY TO DEFEAT THAT TECHNIQUE.

KNOWING THE MASTER, HE'S SEEN RIGHT THROUGH YOUR TRICK AND IS EVEN NOW...

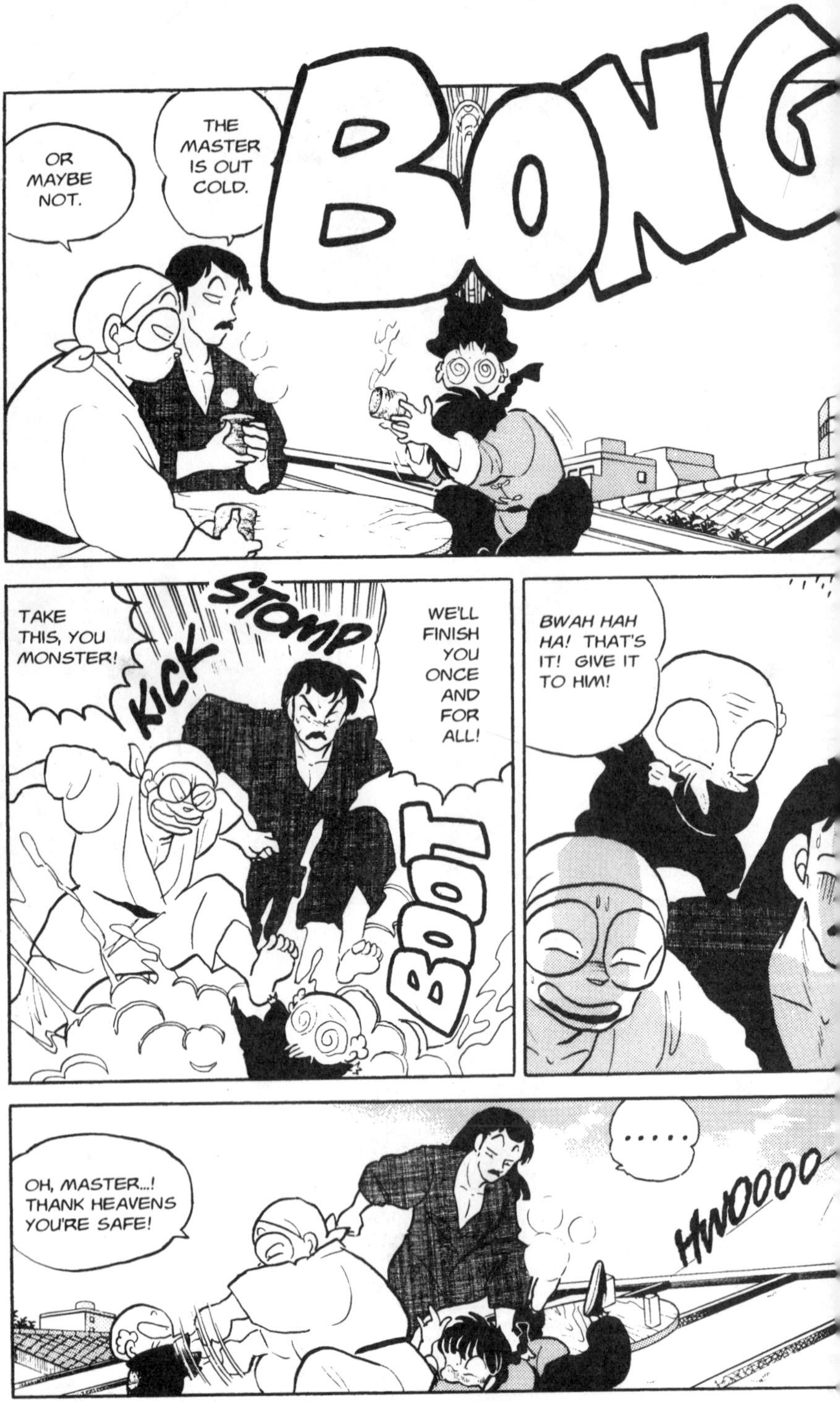
THE MASTER IS OUT COLD.
OR MAYBE NOT.
BONG
TAKE THIS, YOU MONSTER!
KICK
STOMP
WE'LL FINISH YOU ONCE AND FOR ALL!
BOOT
BWAH HAH HA! THAT'S IT! GIVE IT TO HIM!
OH, MASTER...! THANK HEAVENS YOU'RE SAFE!
.....
HWOOOO

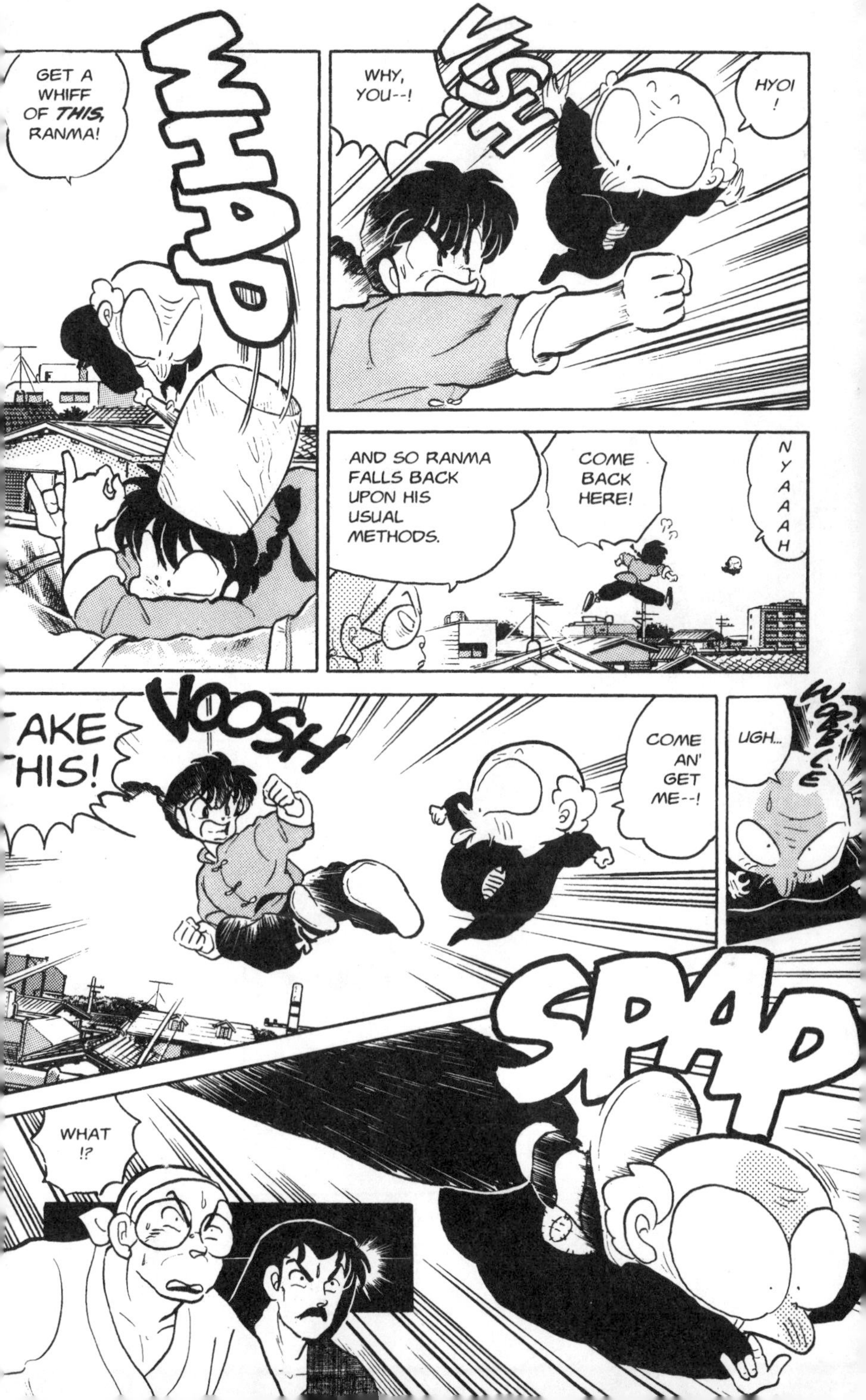
GET A WHIFF OF *THIS,* RANMA!
WHAP
WHY, YOU--!
VISH
HYOI!
AND SO RANMA FALLS BACK UPON HIS USUAL METHODS.
COME BACK HERE!
NYAAAAH
AKE HIS!
VOOSH
COME AN' GET ME--!
UGH...
WOBBLE
SPAP
WHAT !?

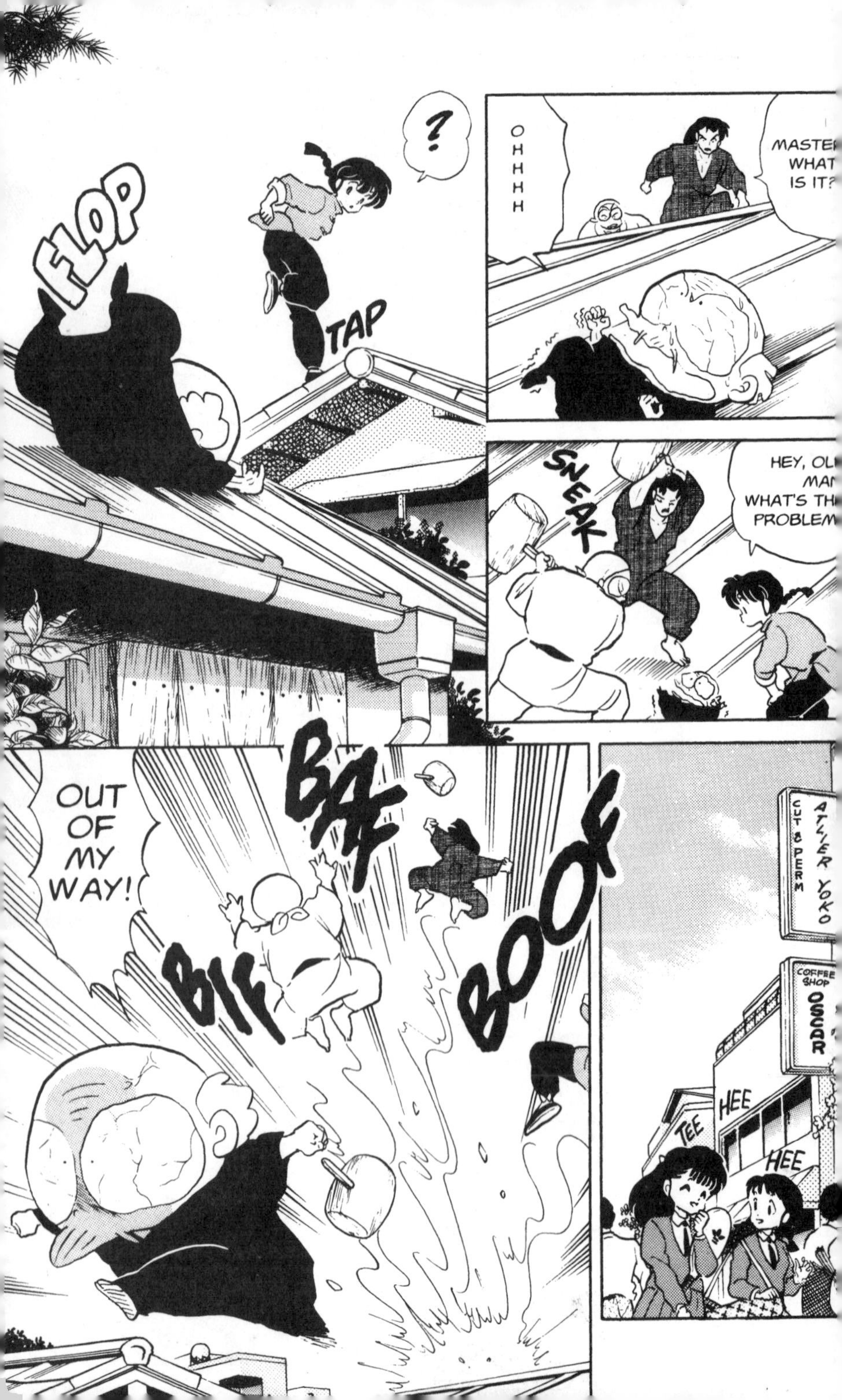
FLOP
?
TAP
OHHHH
MASTE
WHAT
IS IT?
SNEAK
HEY, OL
MAN
WHAT'S TH
PROBLEM
OUT OF MY WAY!
BA
BIF
BOOF
CUT & PERM
ATLIER YOKO
COFFEE SHOP
OSCAR
TEE HEE
HEE

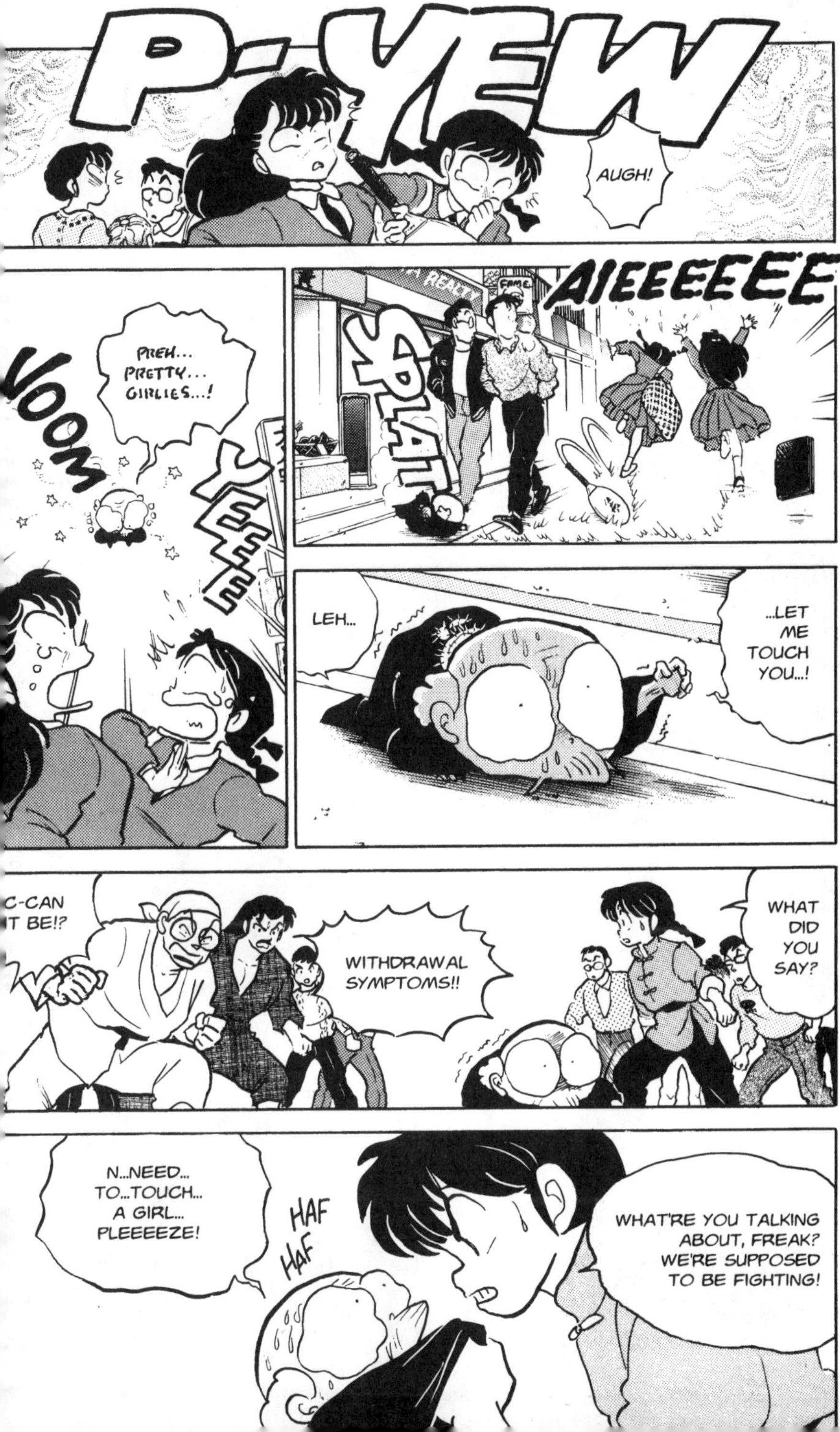
P-YEW
AUGH!
PREH... PRETTY... GIRLIES...!
VOOM
YEEEEE
SPLAT
AIEEEEEEE
LEH...
...LET ME TOUCH YOU...!
C-CAN IT BE!?
WITHDRAWAL SYMPTOMS!!
WHAT DID YOU SAY?
N...NEED... TO...TOUCH... A GIRL... PLEEEEZE!
HAF HAF
WHAT'RE YOU TALKING ABOUT, FREAK? WE'RE SUPPOSED TO BE FIGHTING!

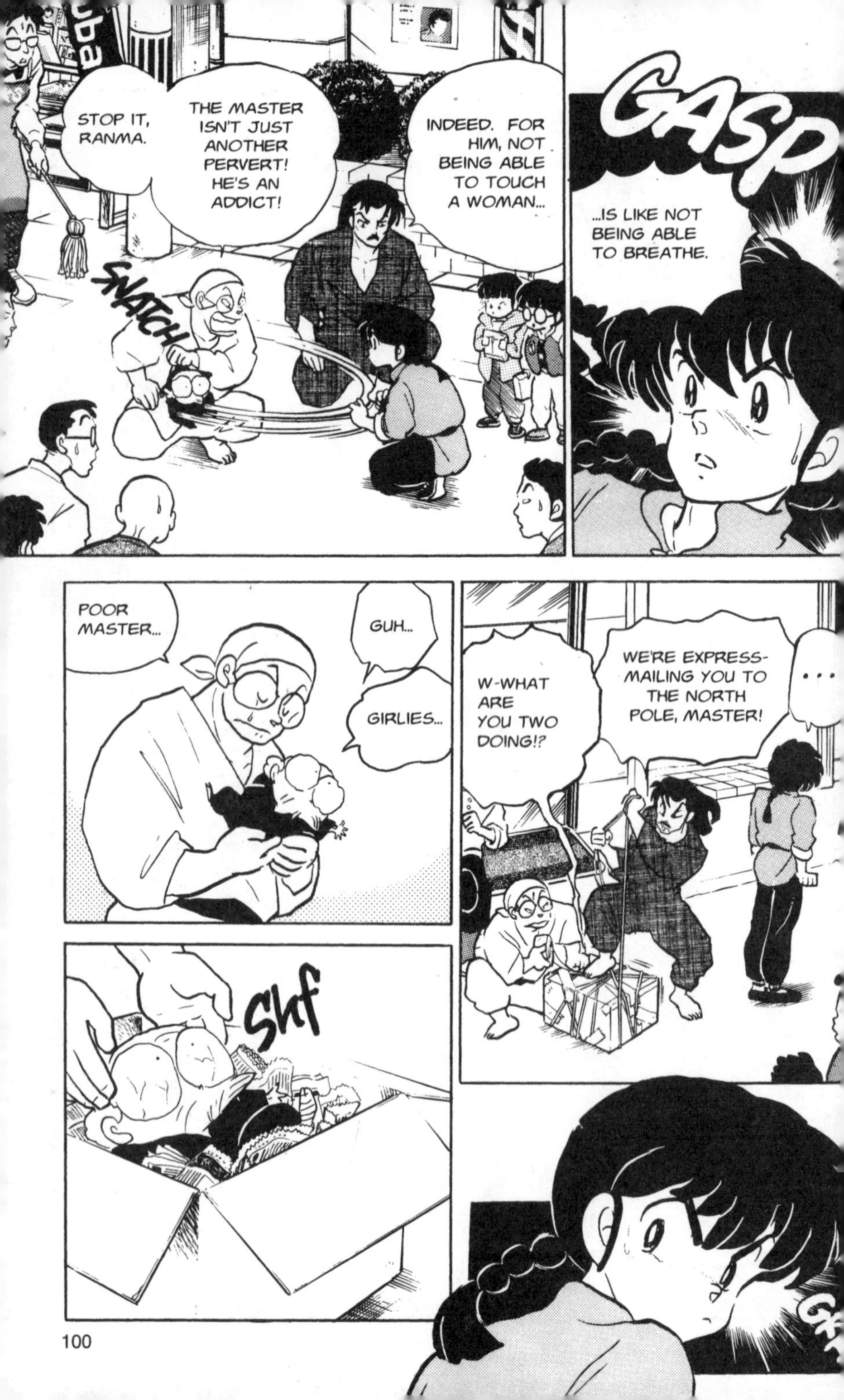
STOP IT, RANMA.
THE MASTER ISN'T JUST ANOTHER PERVERT! HE'S AN ADDICT!
INDEED. FOR HIM, NOT BEING ABLE TO TOUCH A WOMAN...
SNATCH
GASP
...IS LIKE NOT BEING ABLE TO BREATHE.
POOR MASTER...
GUH...
GIRLIES...
W-WHAT ARE YOU TWO DOING!?
WE'RE EXPRESS-MAILING YOU TO THE NORTH POLE, MASTER!
...
Shf

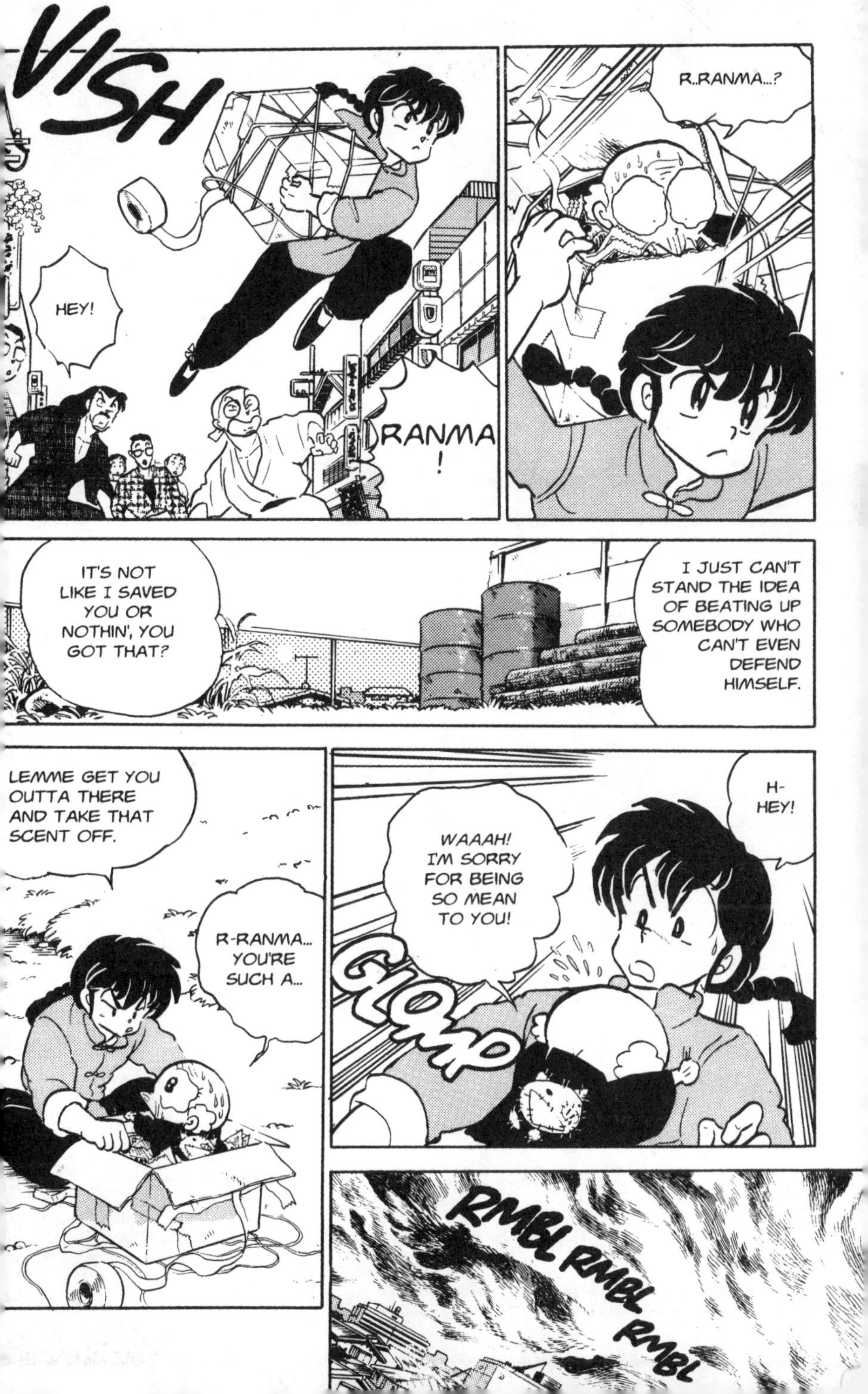
VISH
HEY!
RANMA!
R..RANMA...?
IT'S NOT LIKE I SAVED YOU OR NOTHIN', YOU GOT THAT?
I JUST CAN'T STAND THE IDEA OF BEATING UP SOMEBODY WHO CAN'T EVEN DEFEND HIMSELF.
LEMME GET YOU OUTTA THERE AND TAKE THAT SCENT OFF.
R-RANMA... YOU'RE SUCH A...
WAAAH! I'M SORRY FOR BEING SO MEAN TO YOU!
H- HEY!
GLOMP
RMBL RMBL RMBL RMBL

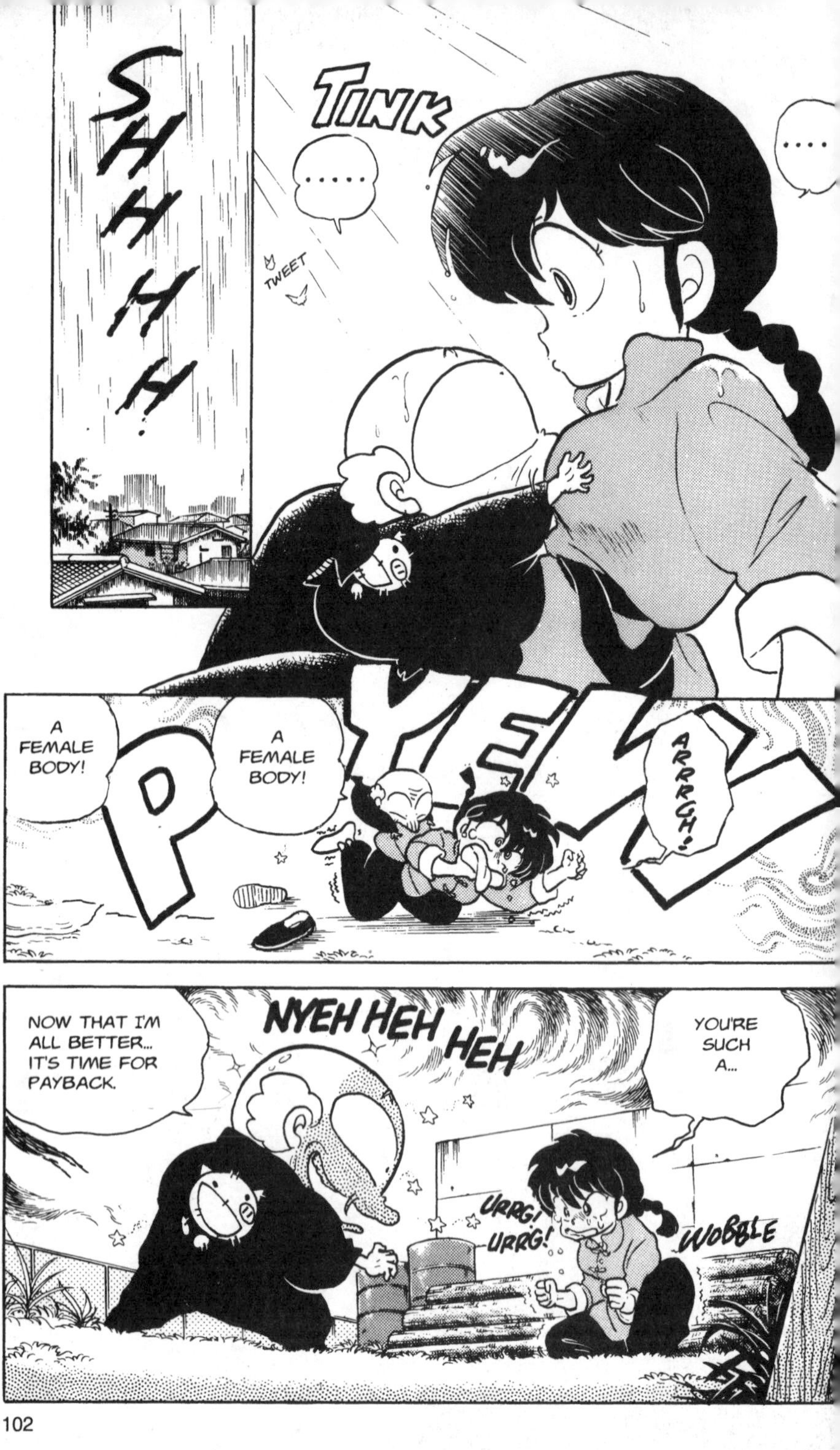
SHHHHH!
TINK
......
TWEET
....
A FEMALE BODY!
A FEMALE BODY!
ARRRGH!
NOW THAT I'M ALL BETTER... IT'S TIME FOR PAYBACK.
NYEH HEH HEH
YOU'RE SUCH A...
URRG! URRG!
WOBBLE

PART 7

FATHERS' KNOW BEST

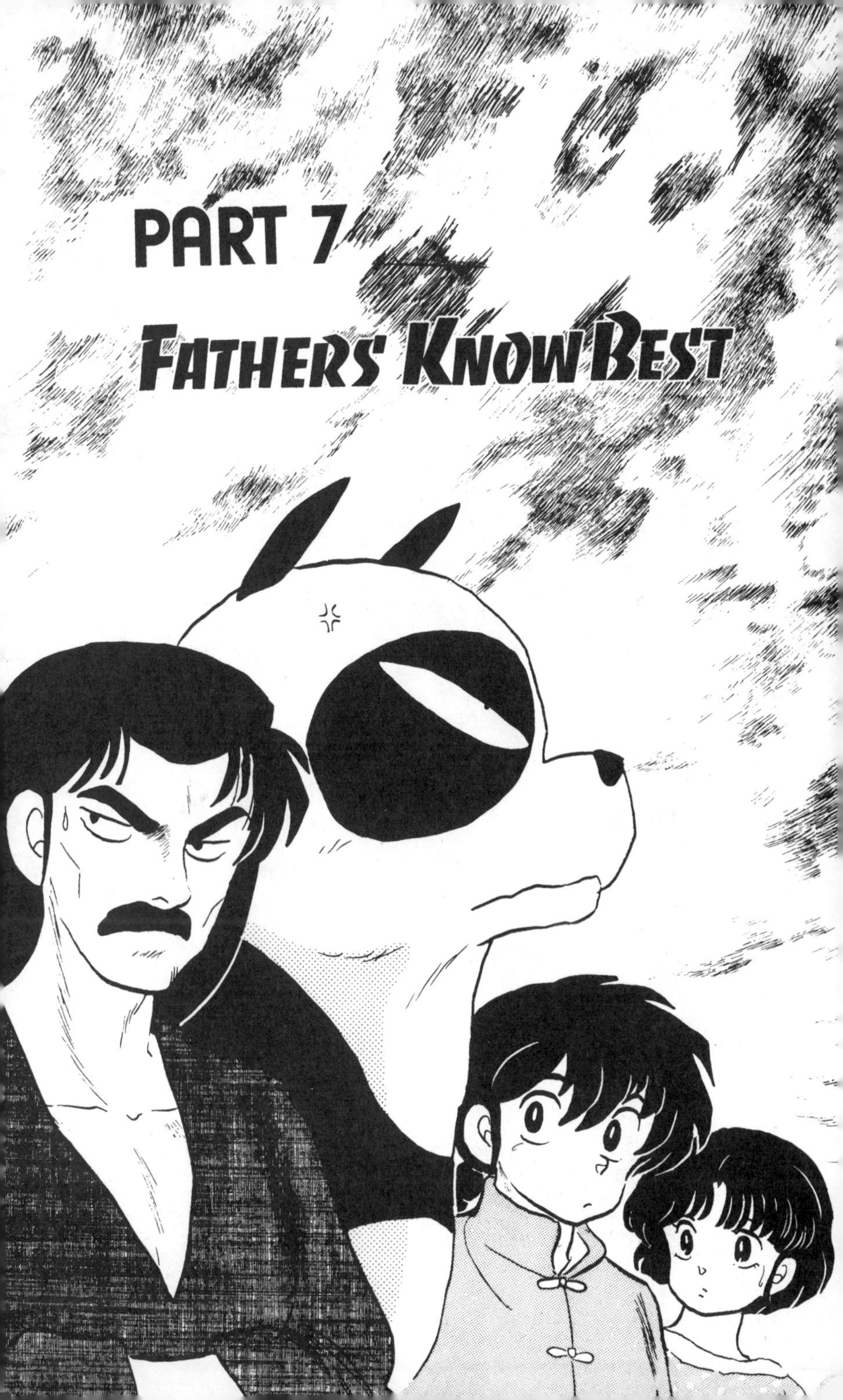

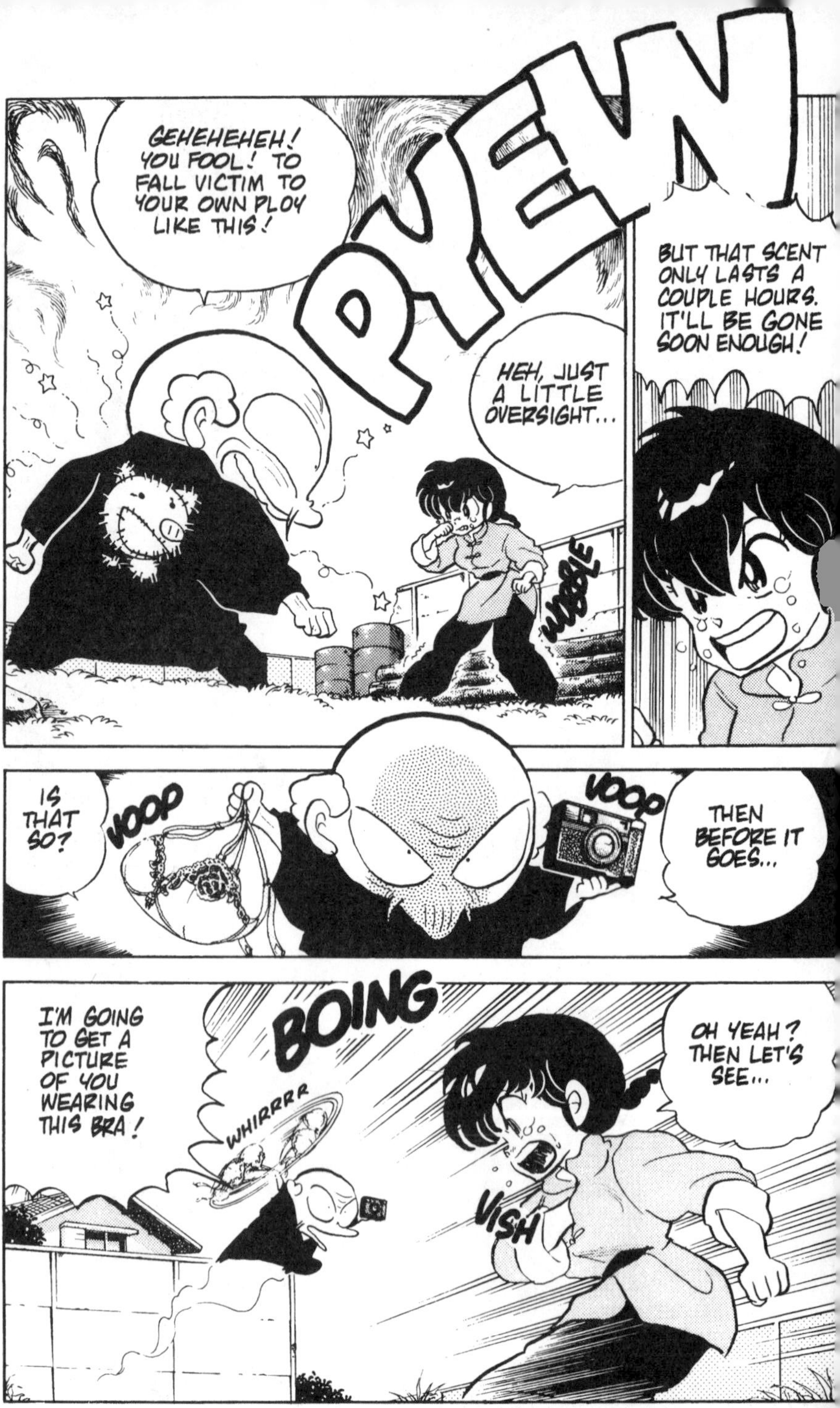
GEHEHEHEH! YOU FOOL! TO FALL VICTIM TO YOUR OWN PLOY LIKE THIS!
PYEW
HEH, JUST A LITTLE OVERSIGHT...
WOBBLE
BUT THAT SCENT ONLY LASTS A COUPLE HOURS. IT'LL BE GONE SOON ENOUGH!
IS THAT SO?
VOOP
VOOP
THEN BEFORE IT GOES...
I'M GOING TO GET A PICTURE OF YOU WEARING THIS BRA!
BOING
WHIRRRR
VISH
OH YEAH? THEN LET'S SEE...

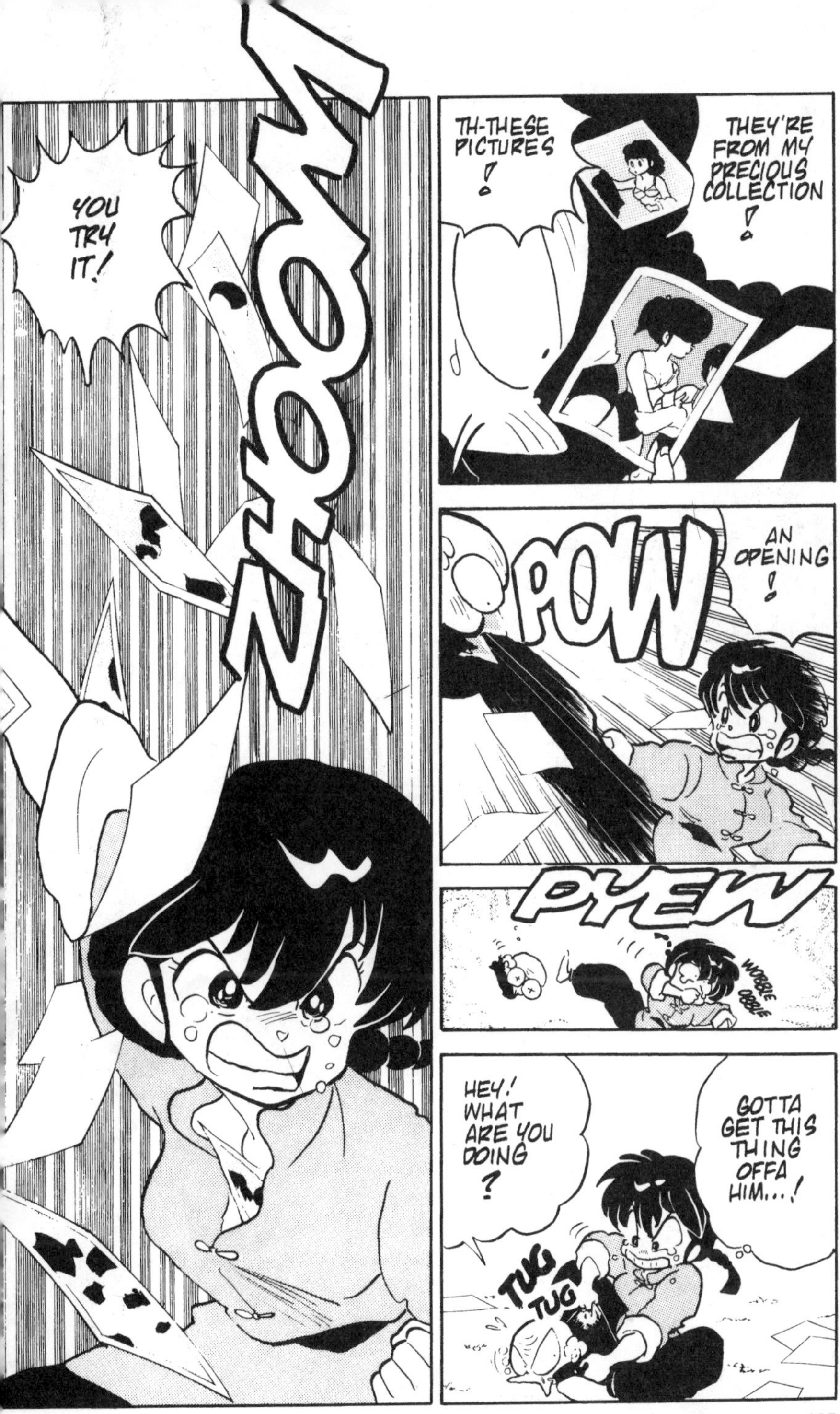
YOU TRY IT!
ZHOOM
TH-THESE PICTURES!
THEY'RE FROM MY PRECIOUS COLLECTION!
POW
AN OPENING!
PYEW
WOBBLE OBBLE
HEY! WHAT ARE YOU DOING?
GOTTA GET THIS THING OFFA HIM...!
TUG
TUG

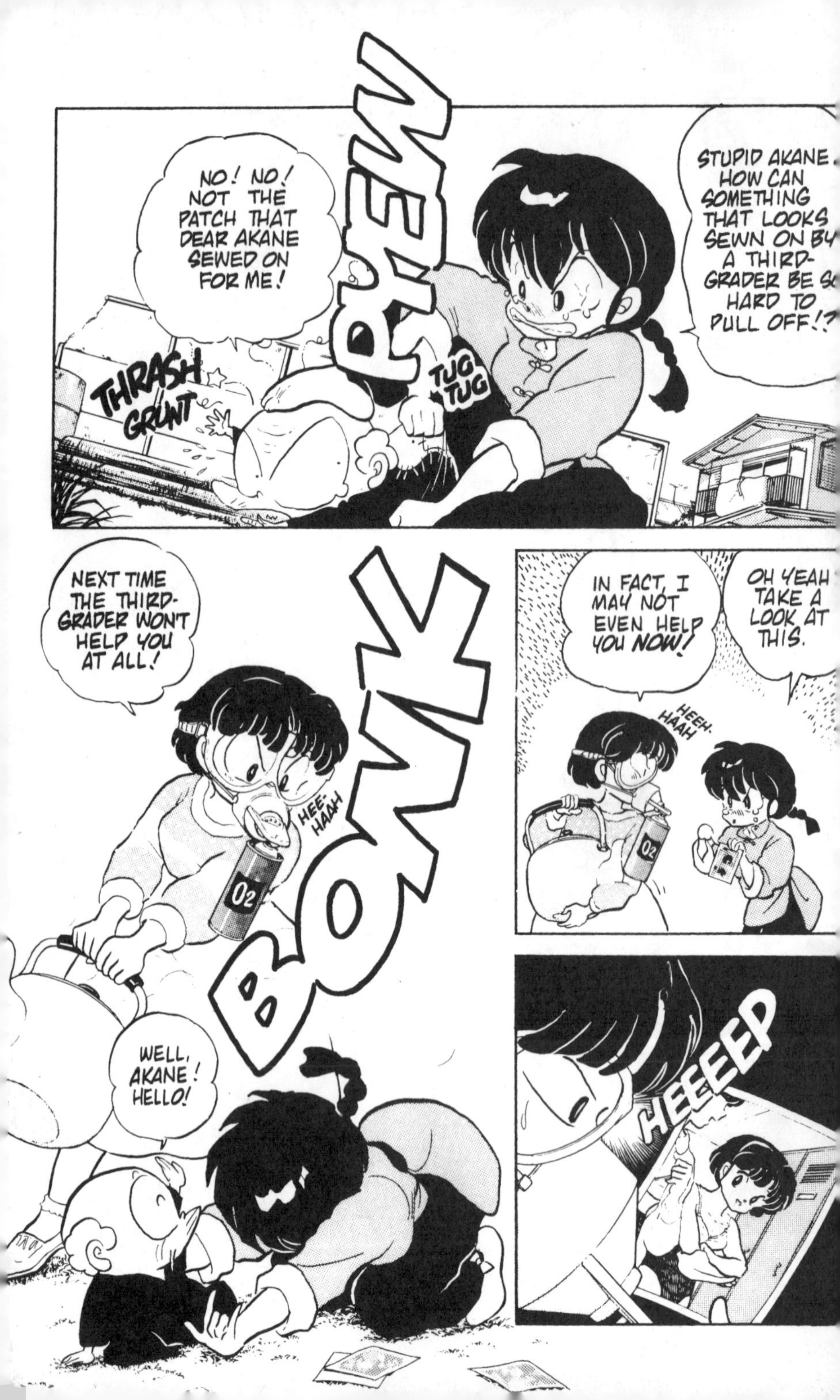
NO! NO! NOT THE PATCH THAT DEAR AKANE SEWED ON FOR ME!
PYEW
THRASH
GRUNT
TUG TUG
STUPID AKANE. HOW CAN SOMETHING THAT LOOKS SEWN ON BY A THIRD-GRADER BE SO HARD TO PULL OFF!?
NEXT TIME THE THIRD-GRADER WON'T HELP YOU AT ALL!
HEE-HAAH
BONK
WELL, AKANE! HELLO!
IN FACT, I MAY NOT EVEN HELP YOU NOW!
OH YEAH TAKE A LOOK AT THIS.
HEEH-HAAH
HEEEEP

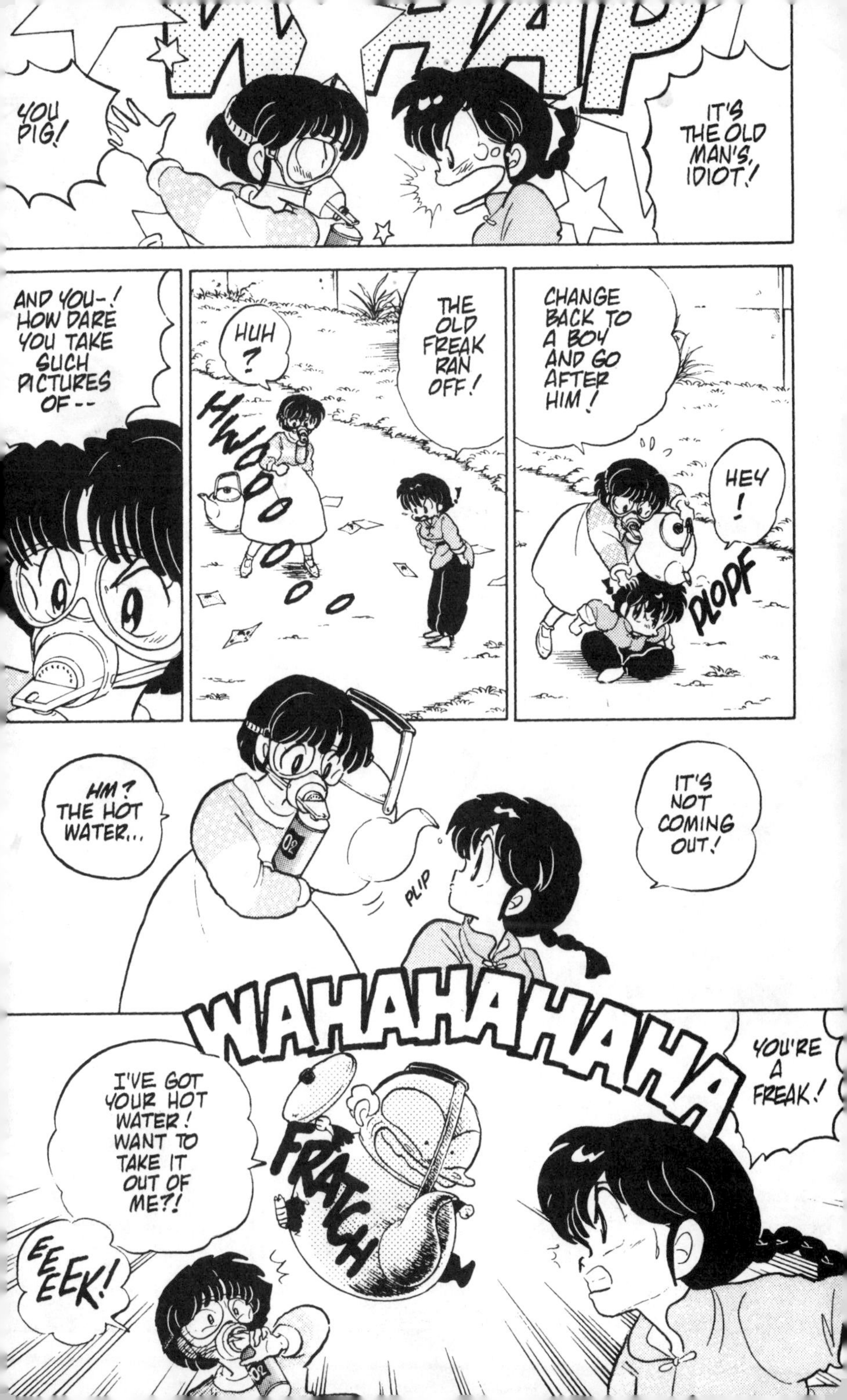
WHAP
YOU PIG!
IT'S THE OLD MAN'S, IDIOT!
AND YOU-! HOW DARE YOU TAKE SUCH PICTURES OF--
HUH?
HWOOOOOO
THE OLD FREAK RAN OFF!
CHANGE BACK TO A BOY AND GO AFTER HIM!
HEY!
PLOPF
HM? THE HOT WATER...
PLIP
IT'S NOT COMING OUT!
WAHAHAHAHAHA
I'VE GOT YOUR HOT WATER! WANT TO TAKE IT OUT OF ME?!
FRATCH
YOU'RE A FREAK!
EEEEK!

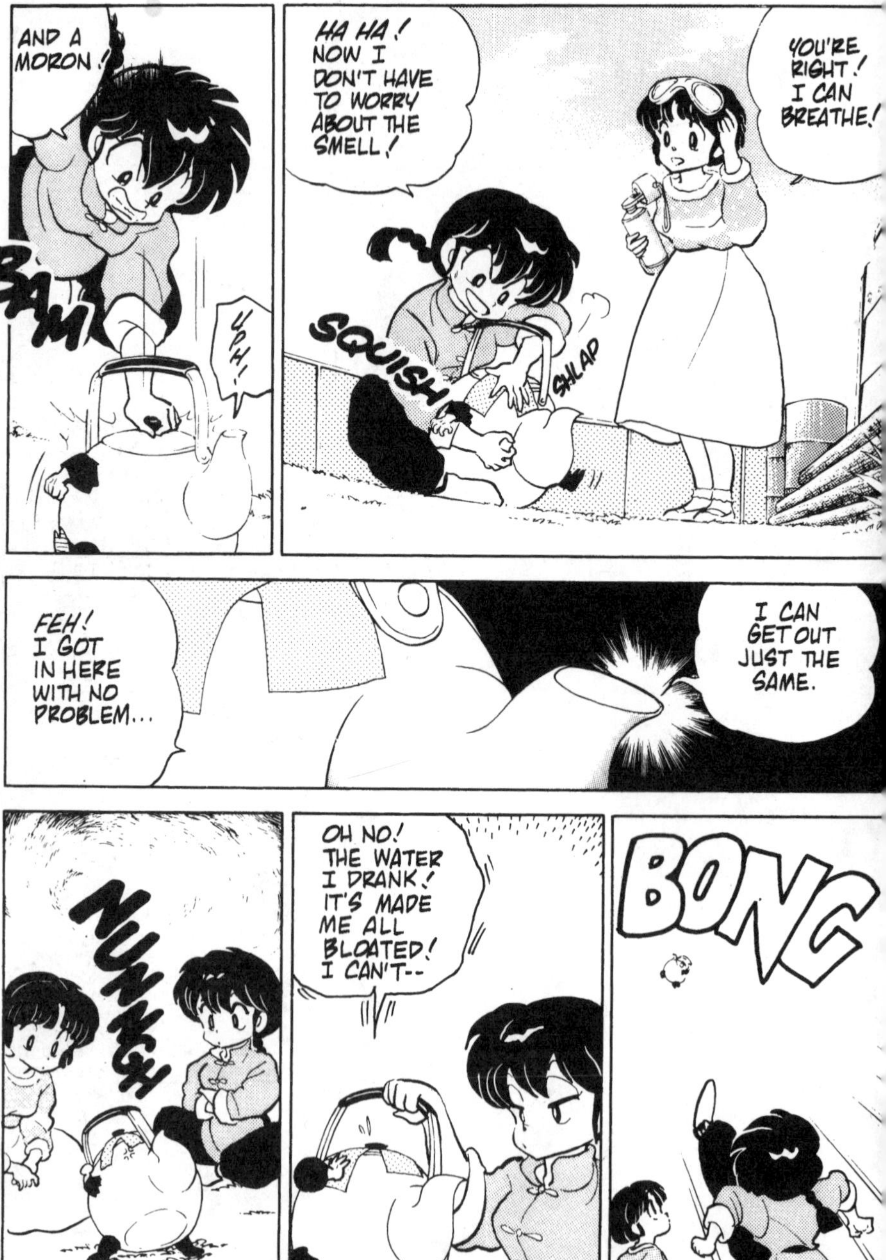

AND A MORON!
BAM
UPH!
HA HA! NOW I DON'T HAVE TO WORRY ABOUT THE SMELL!
SQUISH
SHLAP
YOU'RE RIGHT! I CAN BREATHE!
FEH! I GOT IN HERE WITH NO PROBLEM...
I CAN GET OUT JUST THE SAME.
NUNNGH
OH NO! THE WATER I DRANK! IT'S MADE ME ALL BLOATED! I CAN'T--
BONG

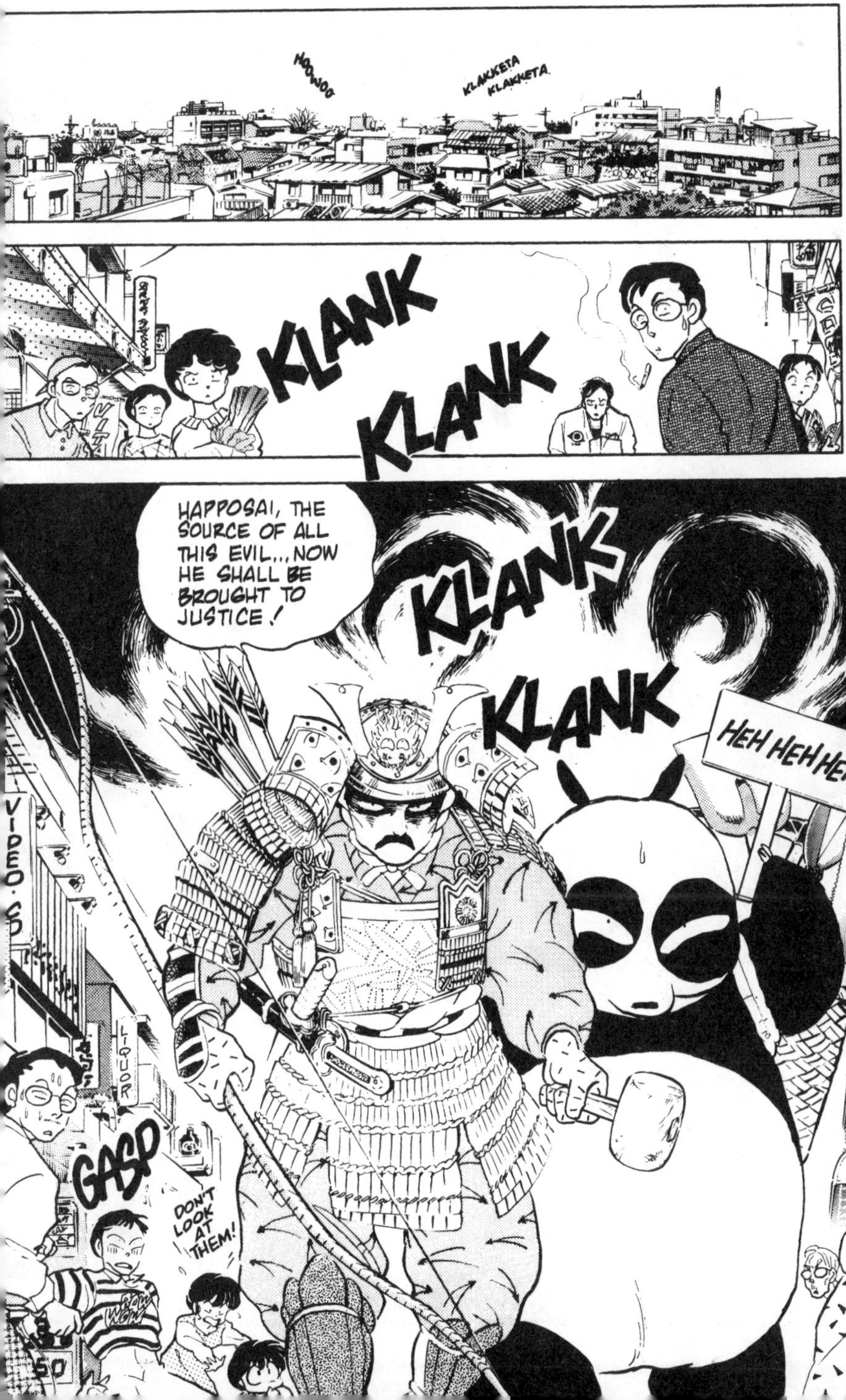
HOOWOO
KLAKKETA KLAKKETA
KLANK
KLANK
HAPPOSAI, THE SOURCE OF ALL THIS EVIL... NOW HE SHALL BE BROUGHT TO JUSTICE!
KLANK
KLANK
HEH HEH HEH!
VIDEO
LIQUOR
FUTONS
GASP
DON'T LOOK AT THEM!

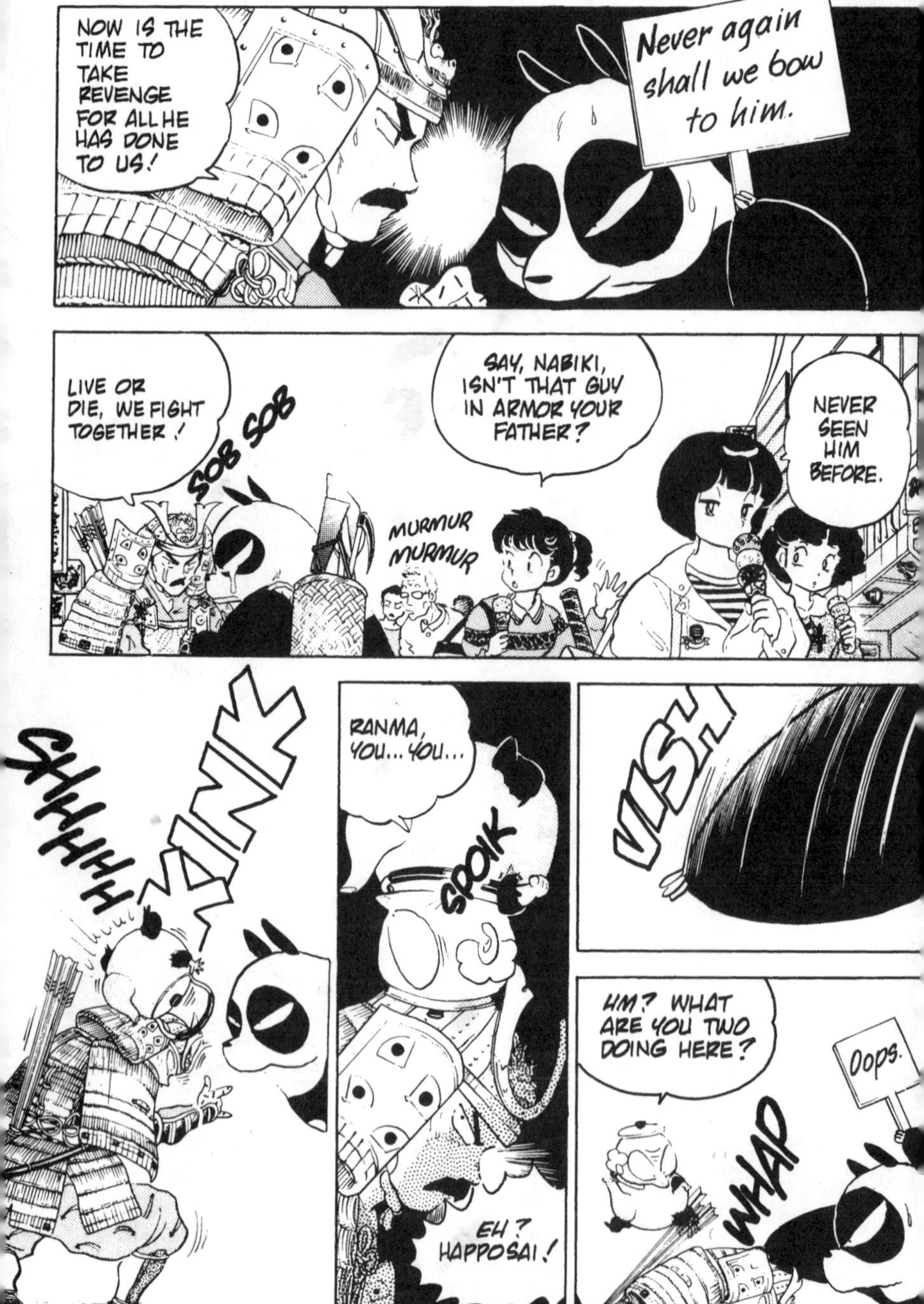
NOW IS THE TIME TO TAKE REVENGE FOR ALL HE HAS DONE TO US!
Never again shall we bow to him.
LIVE OR DIE, WE FIGHT TOGETHER!
SOB SOB
MURMUR MURMUR
SAY, NABIKI, ISN'T THAT GUY IN ARMOR YOUR FATHER?
NEVER SEEN HIM BEFORE.
GHHHHHH
YANK
RANMA, YOU... YOU...
SPOIK
EH? HAPPOSAI!
VISH
HM? WHAT ARE YOU TWO DOING HERE?
WHAP
Oops.

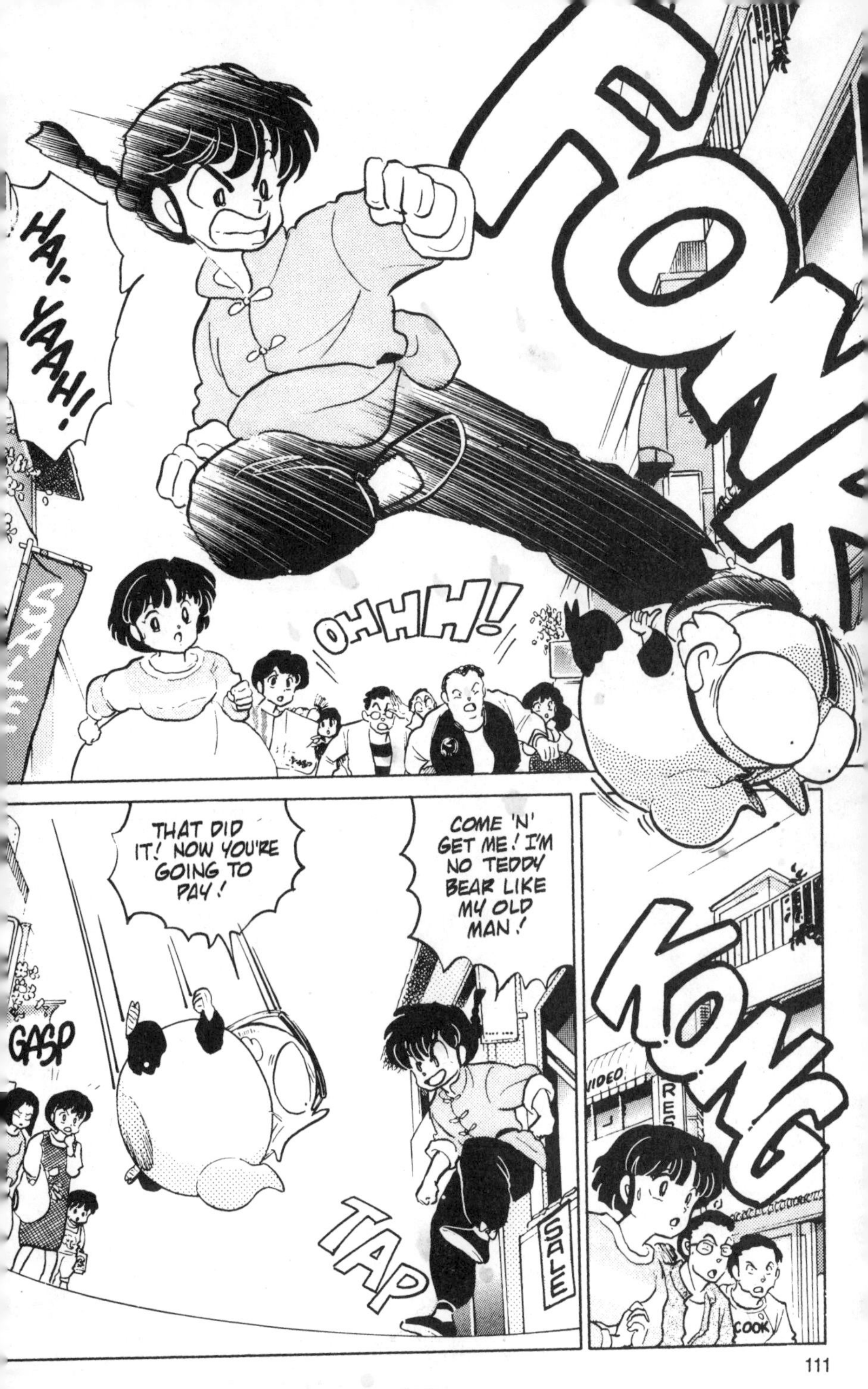
HAI-YAAH!
OHHHH!
THAT DID IT! NOW YOU'RE GOING TO PAY!
GASP
COME 'N' GET ME! I'M NO TEDDY BEAR LIKE MY OLD MAN!
TAP
SALE
KONG
VIDEO
COOK

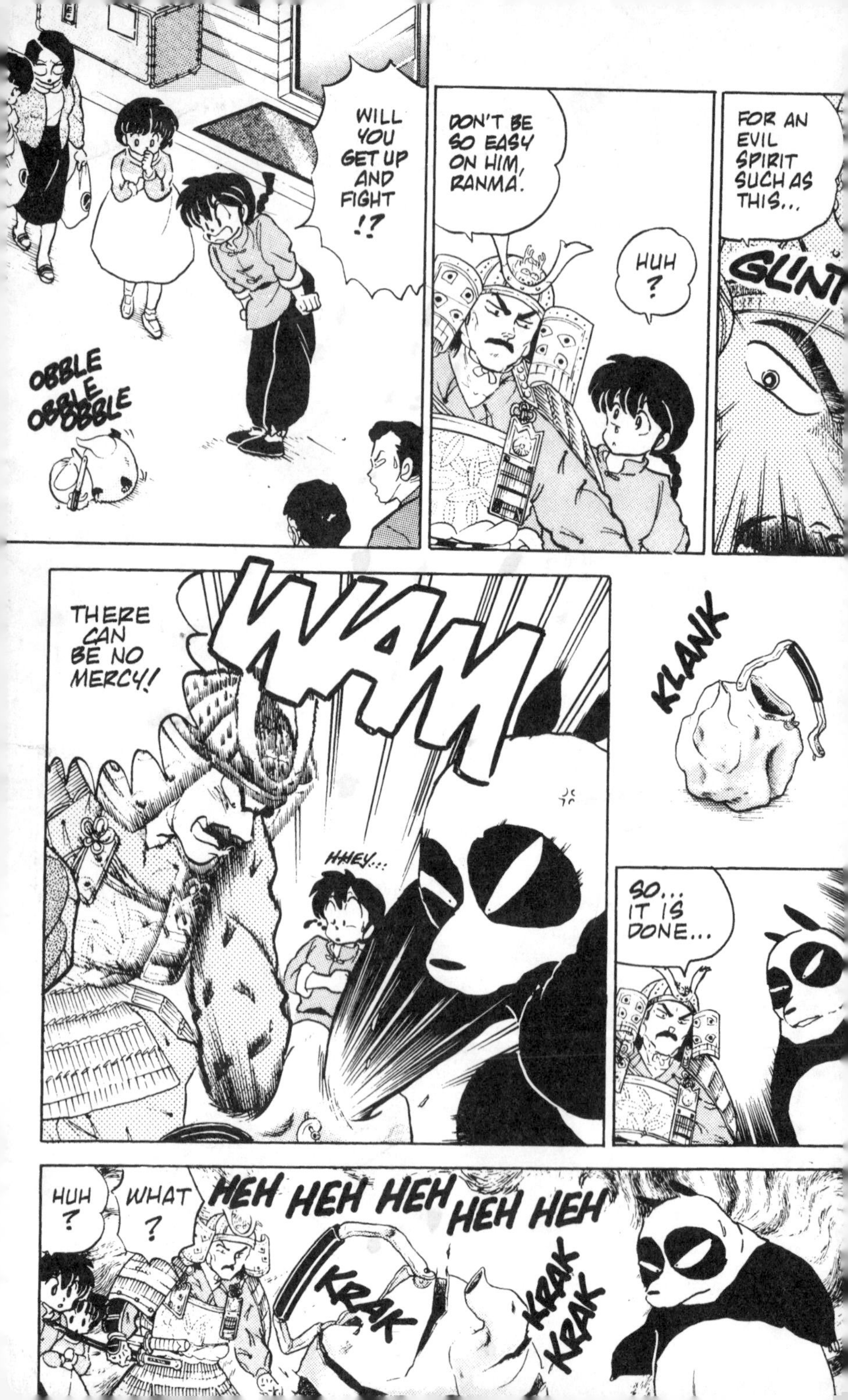
WILL YOU GET UP AND FIGHT !?
OBBLE OBBLE OBBLE OBBLE
DON'T BE SO EASY ON HIM, RANMA.
HUH ?
FOR AN EVIL SPIRIT SUCH AS THIS...
GLINT
THERE CAN BE NO MERCY!
WAM
HHEY...
KLANK
SO... IT IS DONE...
HUH ?
WHAT ?
HEH HEH HEH HEH HEH HEH
KRAK
KRAK KRAK

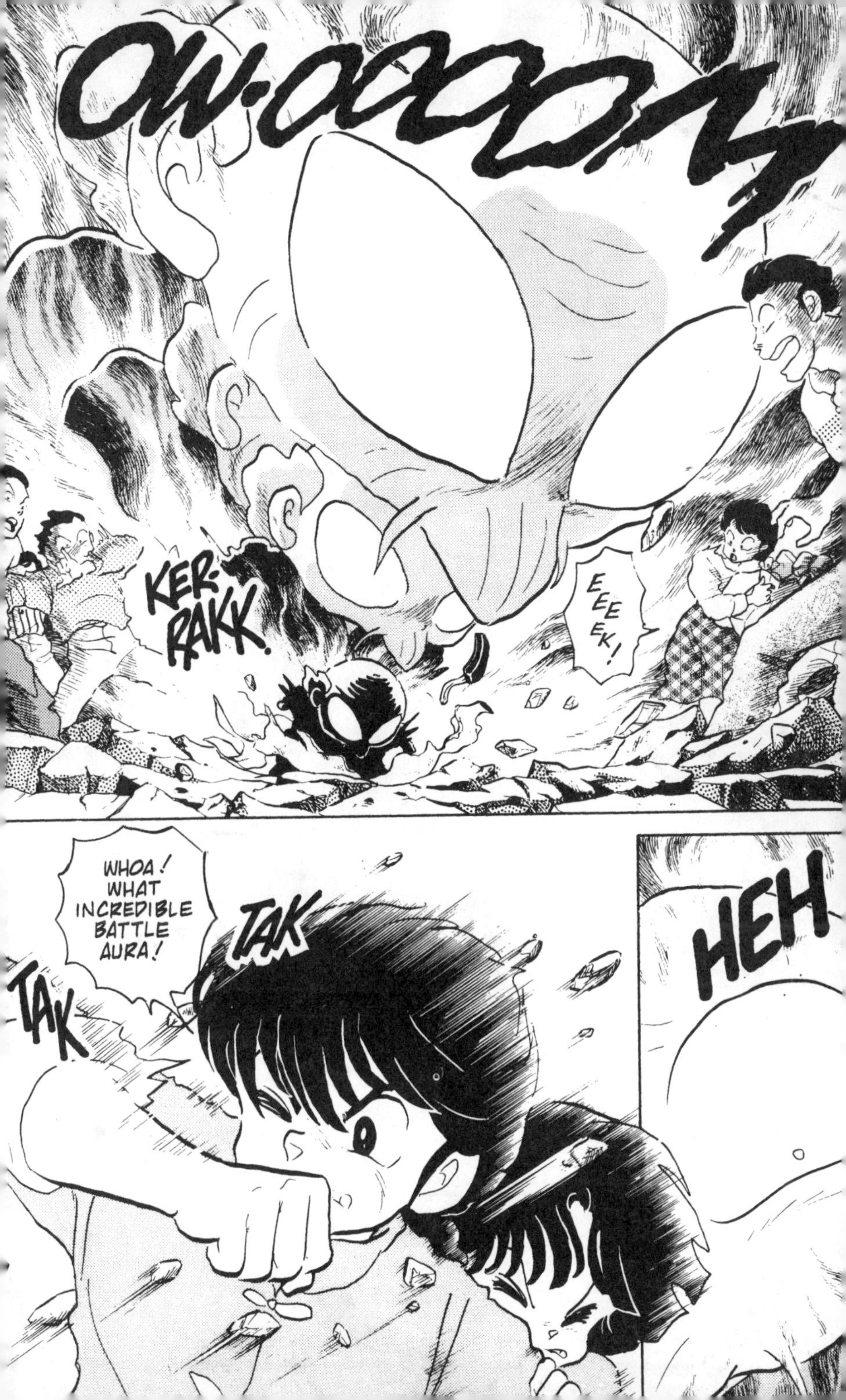
OW-OOOOOM
KER-RAKK!
EEEEK!
WHOA! WHAT INCREDIBLE BATTLE AURA!
TAK
TAK
HEH

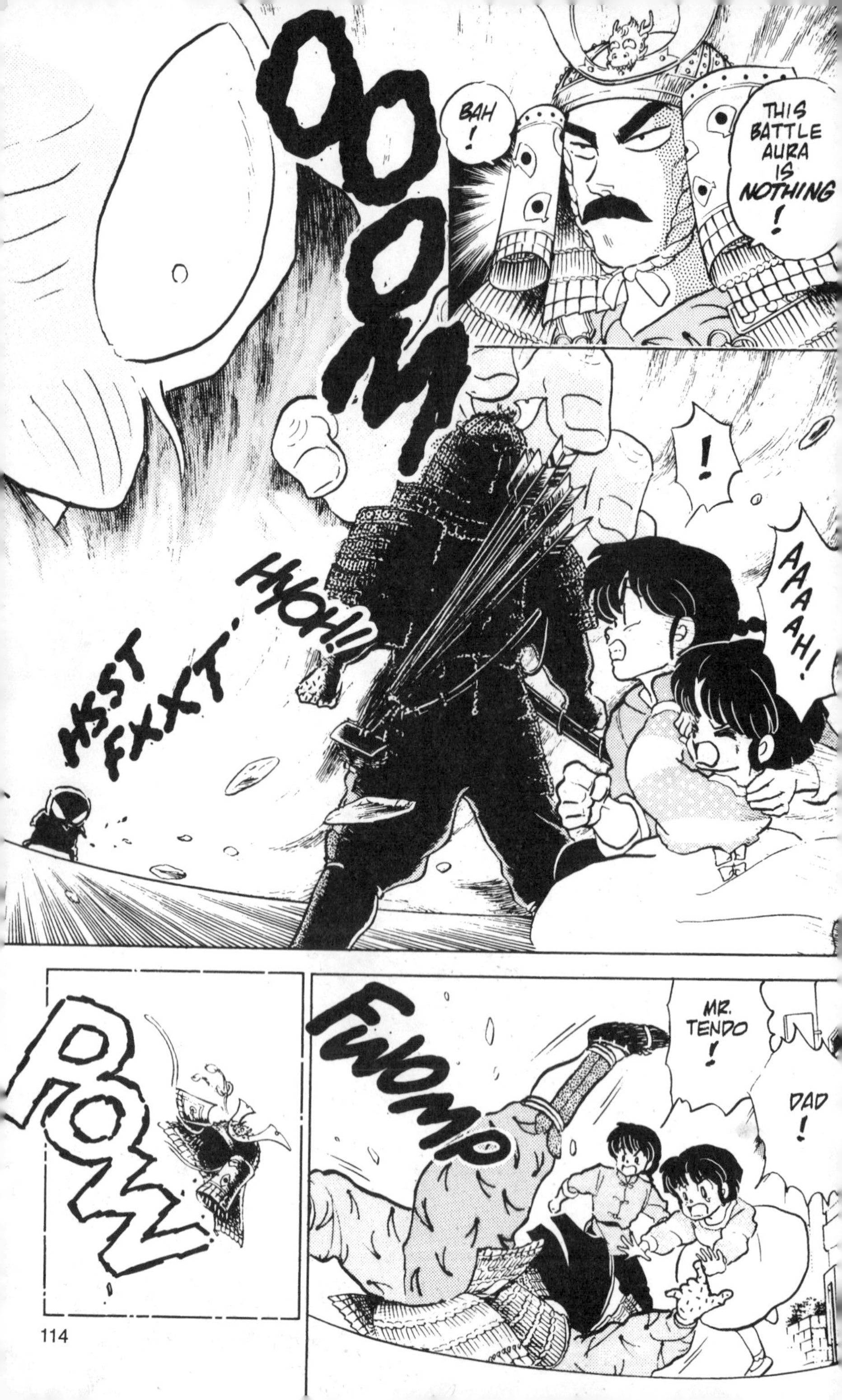

OOOM
BAH!
THIS BATTLE AURA IS NOTHING!
!
AAAAAH!
HYOH!!
HSST FXXT
POW
FWOMP
MR. TENDO!
DAD!

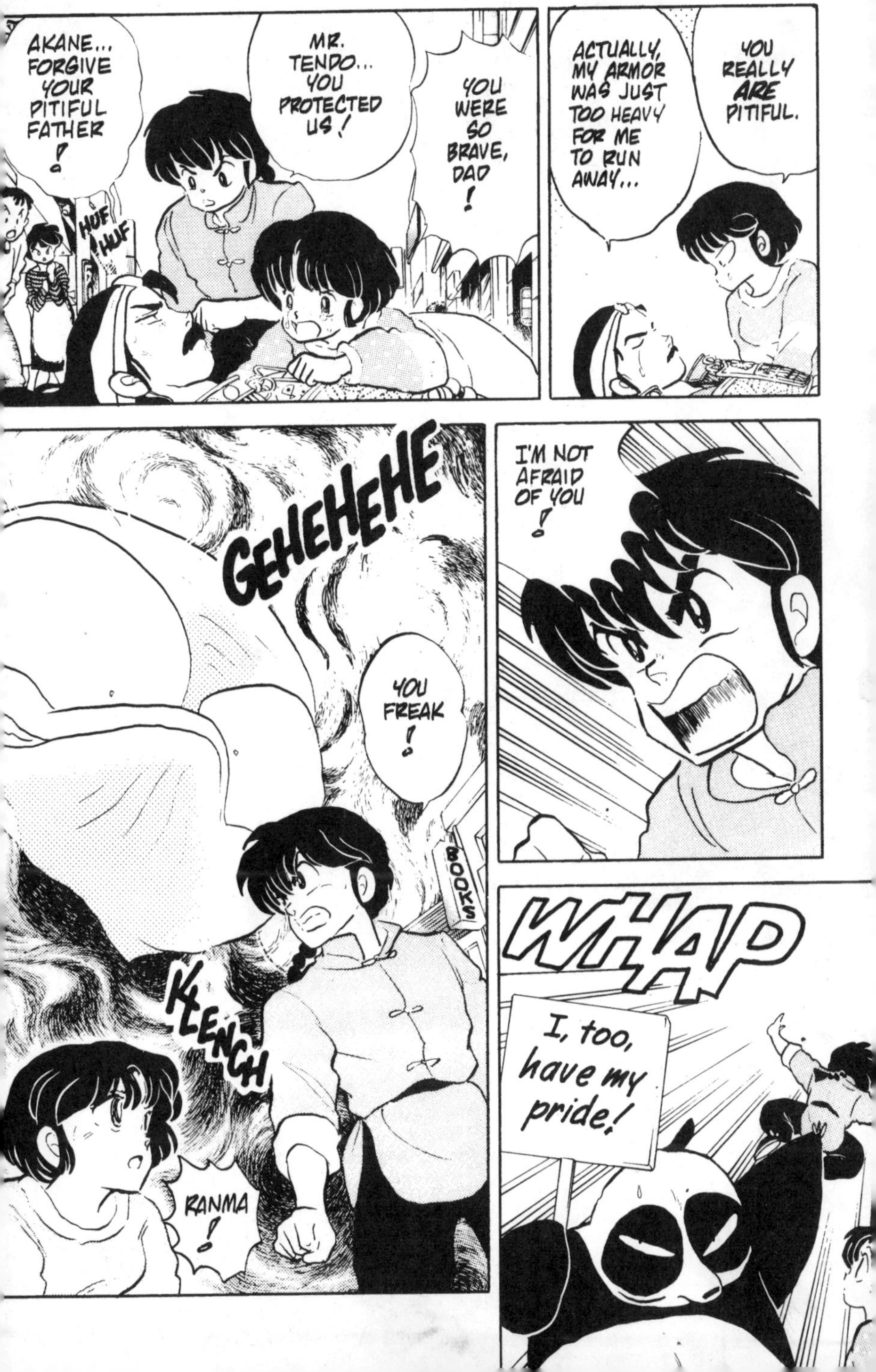
AKANE... FORGIVE YOUR PITIFUL FATHER!
MR. TENDO... YOU PROTECTED US!
YOU WERE SO BRAVE, DAD!
HUF HUF
ACTUALLY, MY ARMOR WAS JUST TOO HEAVY FOR ME TO RUN AWAY...
YOU REALLY ARE PITIFUL.
GEHEHEHE
YOU FREAK!
BOOKS
KLENCH
RANMA!
I'M NOT AFRAID OF YOU!
WHAP
I, too, have my pride!

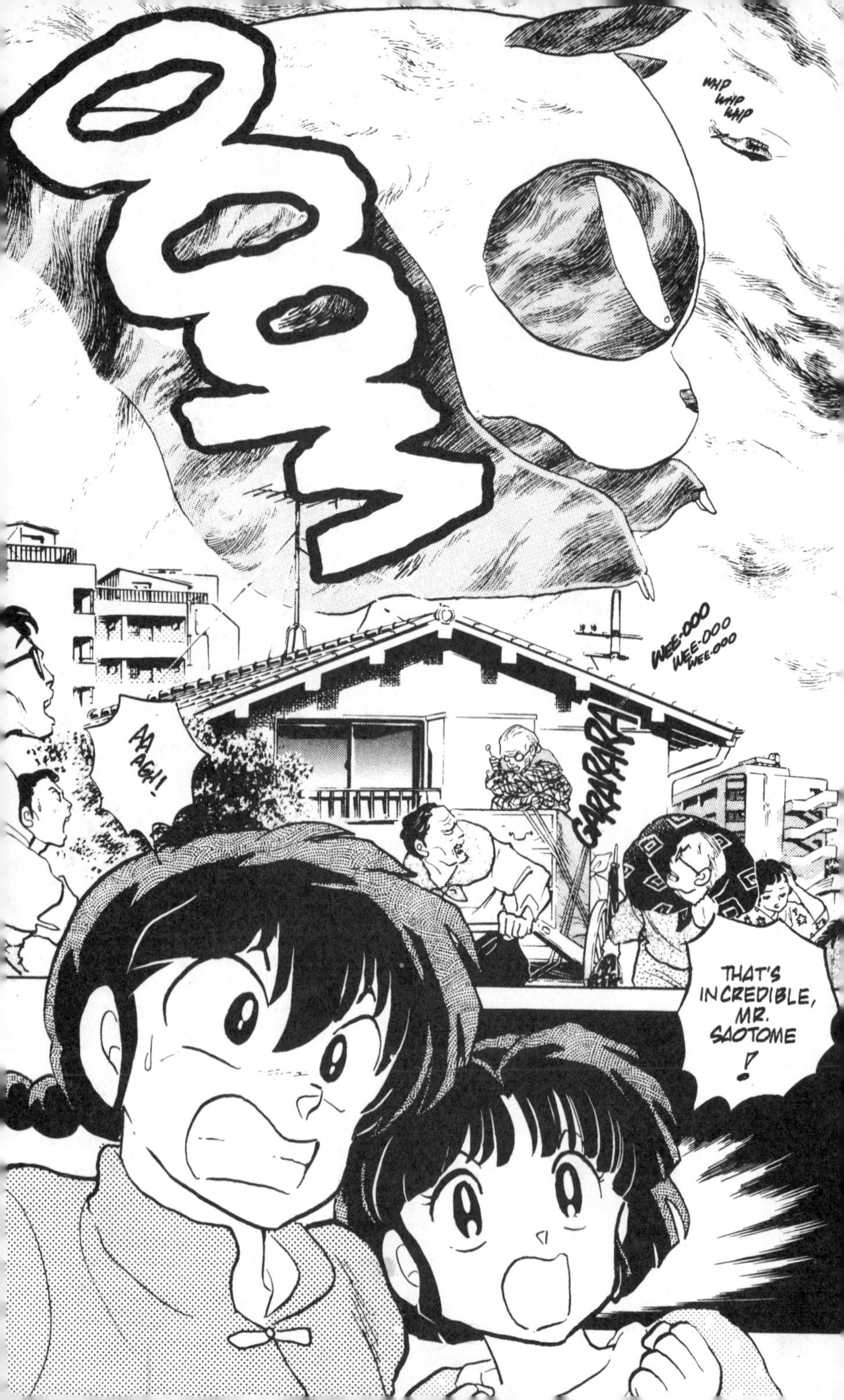
WHIP WHIP WHIP
WEE-OOO WEE-OOO WEE-OOO
AAAGH!!
GARARARA
THAT'S INCREDIBLE, MR. SAOTOME!

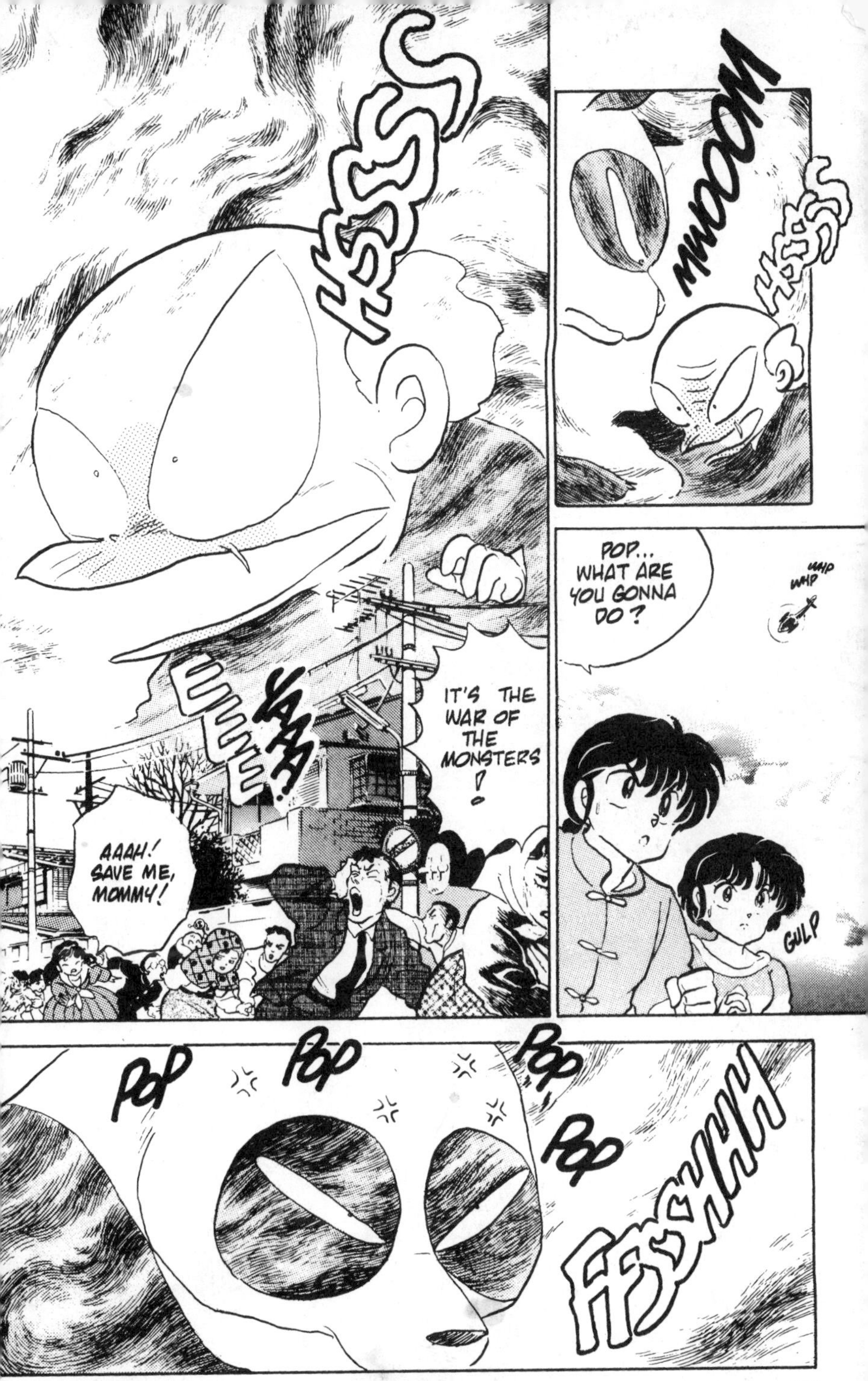
HSSSS
IT'S THE WAR OF THE MONSTERS!
AAAH! SAVE ME, MOMMY!
MWOOOM
HSSSS
POP... WHAT ARE YOU GONNA DO?
WHP WHP
GULP
POP POP POP POP
FFSSHHH

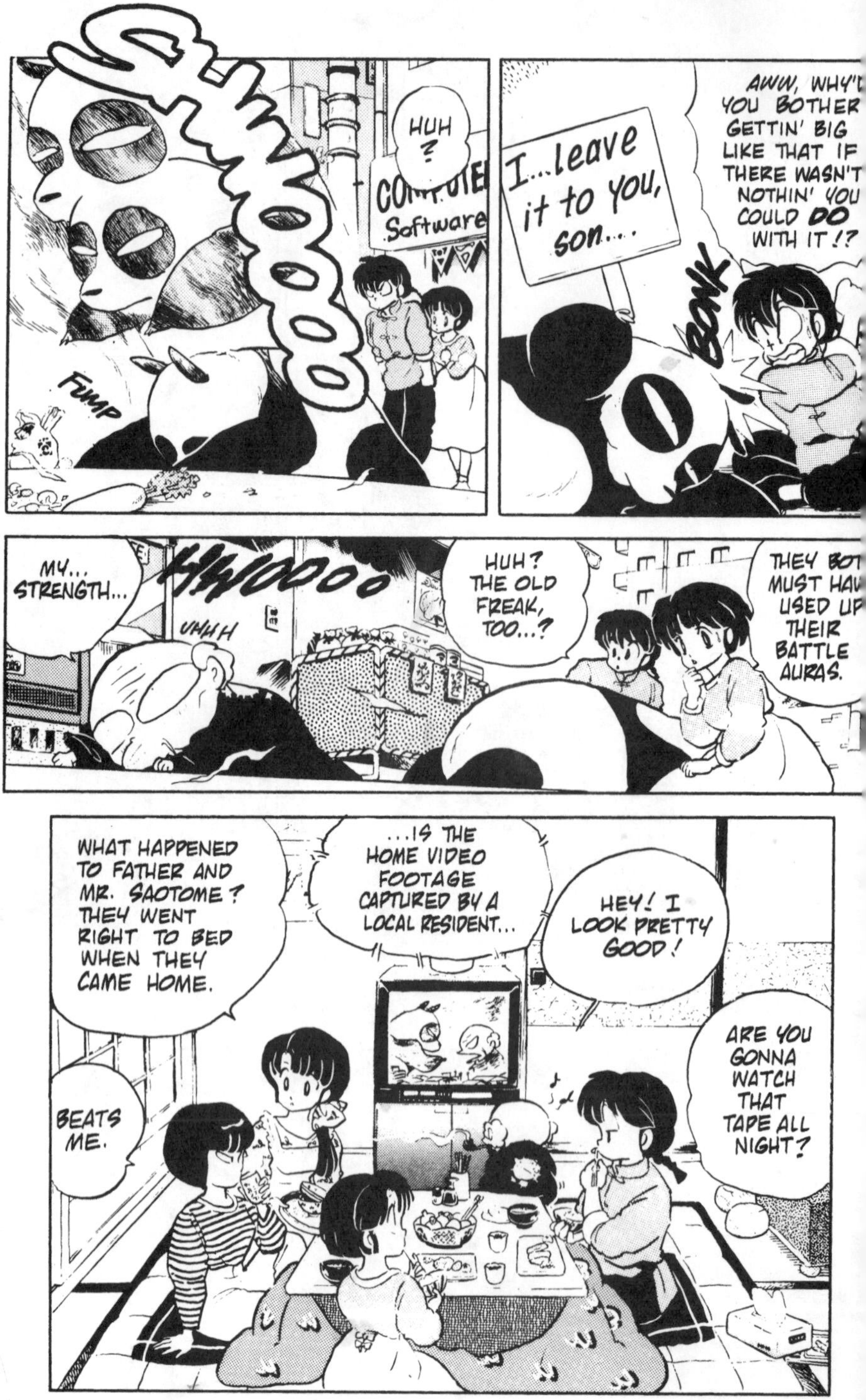
SHWOOOOOO
HUH ?
COMPUTER
Software
FUMP
I...leave it to you, son.....
AWW, WHY'D YOU BOTHER GETTIN' BIG LIKE THAT IF THERE WASN'T NOTHIN' YOU COULD DO WITH IT!?
BONK
MY... STRENGTH...
HWOOOOO
UHUH
HUH? THE OLD FREAK, TOO...?
THEY BOT MUST HAV USED UP THEIR BATTLE AURAS.
WHAT HAPPENED TO FATHER AND MR. SAOTOME? THEY WENT RIGHT TO BED WHEN THEY CAME HOME.
...IS THE HOME VIDEO FOOTAGE CAPTURED BY A LOCAL RESIDENT...
HEY! I LOOK PRETTY GOOD!
BEATS ME.
ARE YOU GONNA WATCH THAT TAPE ALL NIGHT?

PART 8

INSTANT SPRING

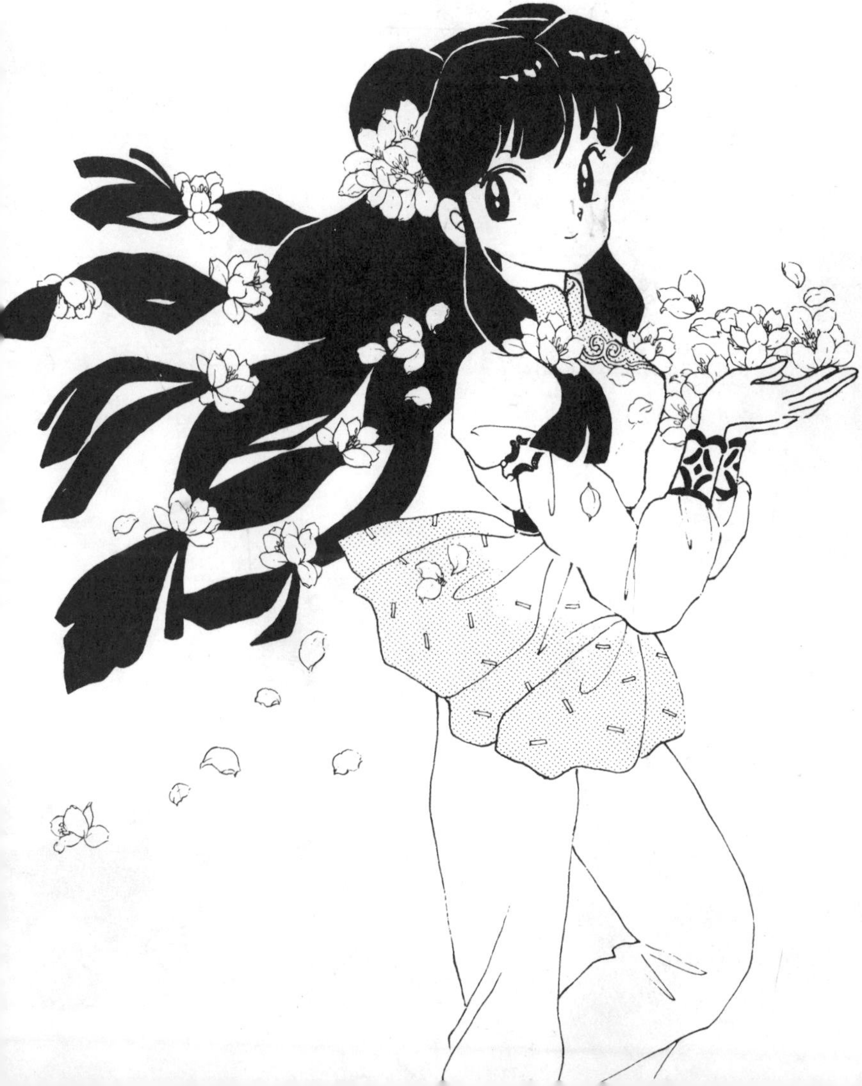

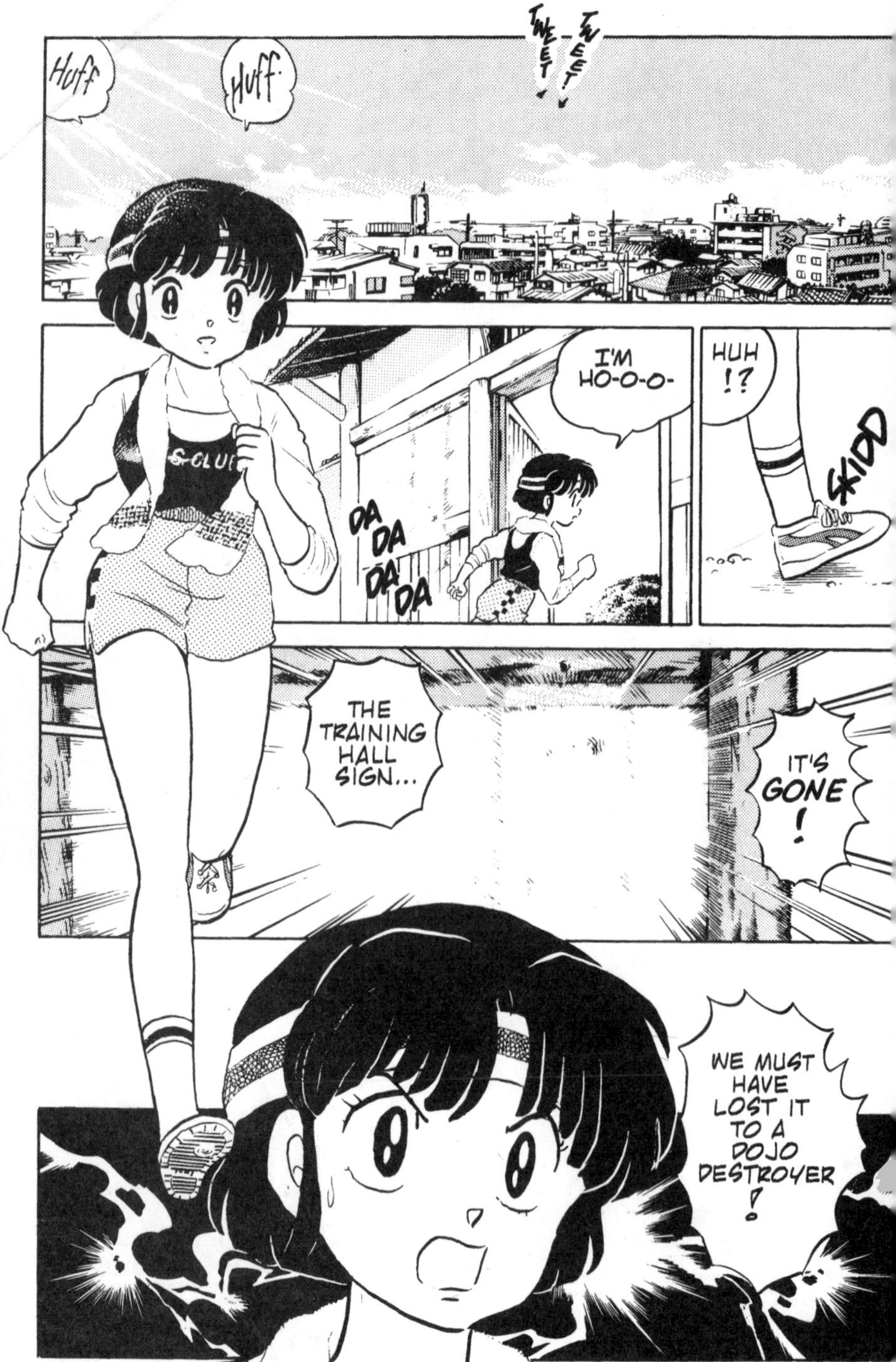

TWEET TWEET
Huff
Huff
I'M HO-O-O-
DA DA DA DA
HUH !?
SKIDD
THE TRAINING HALL SIGN...
IT'S GONE!
WE MUST HAVE LOST IT TO A DOJO DESTROYER!

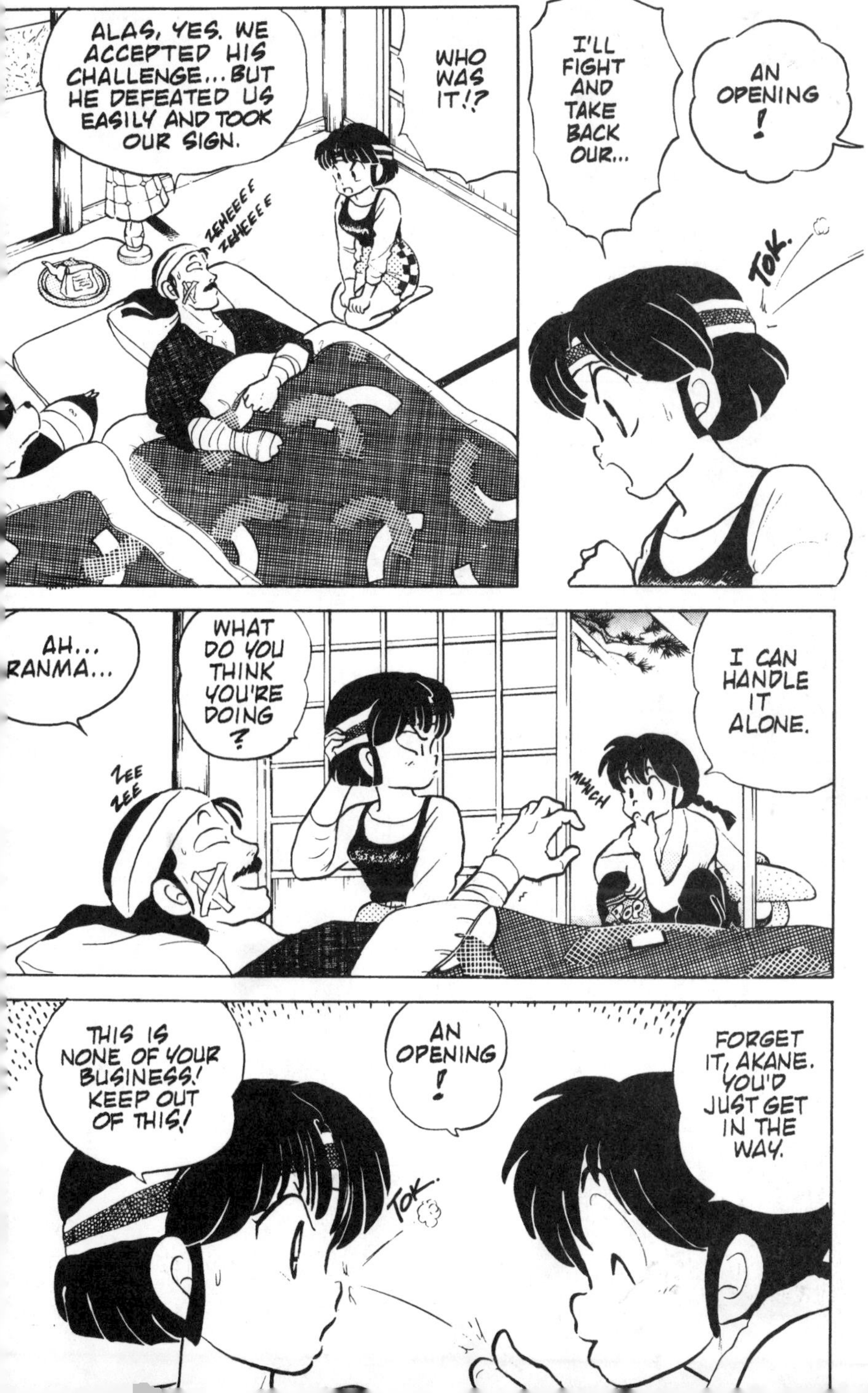
ALAS, YES. WE ACCEPTED HIS CHALLENGE...BUT HE DEFEATED US EASILY AND TOOK OUR SIGN.
ZEHEEEEE ZEHEEEEE
WHO WAS IT!?
I'LL FIGHT AND TAKE BACK OUR...
AN OPENING!
TOK.
AH... RANMA...
WHAT DO YOU THINK YOU'RE DOING?
ZEE ZEE
MUNCH
I CAN HANDLE IT ALONE.
THIS IS NONE OF YOUR BUSINESS! KEEP OUT OF THIS!
AN OPENING!
TOK.
FORGET IT, AKANE. YOU'D JUST GET IN THE WAY.

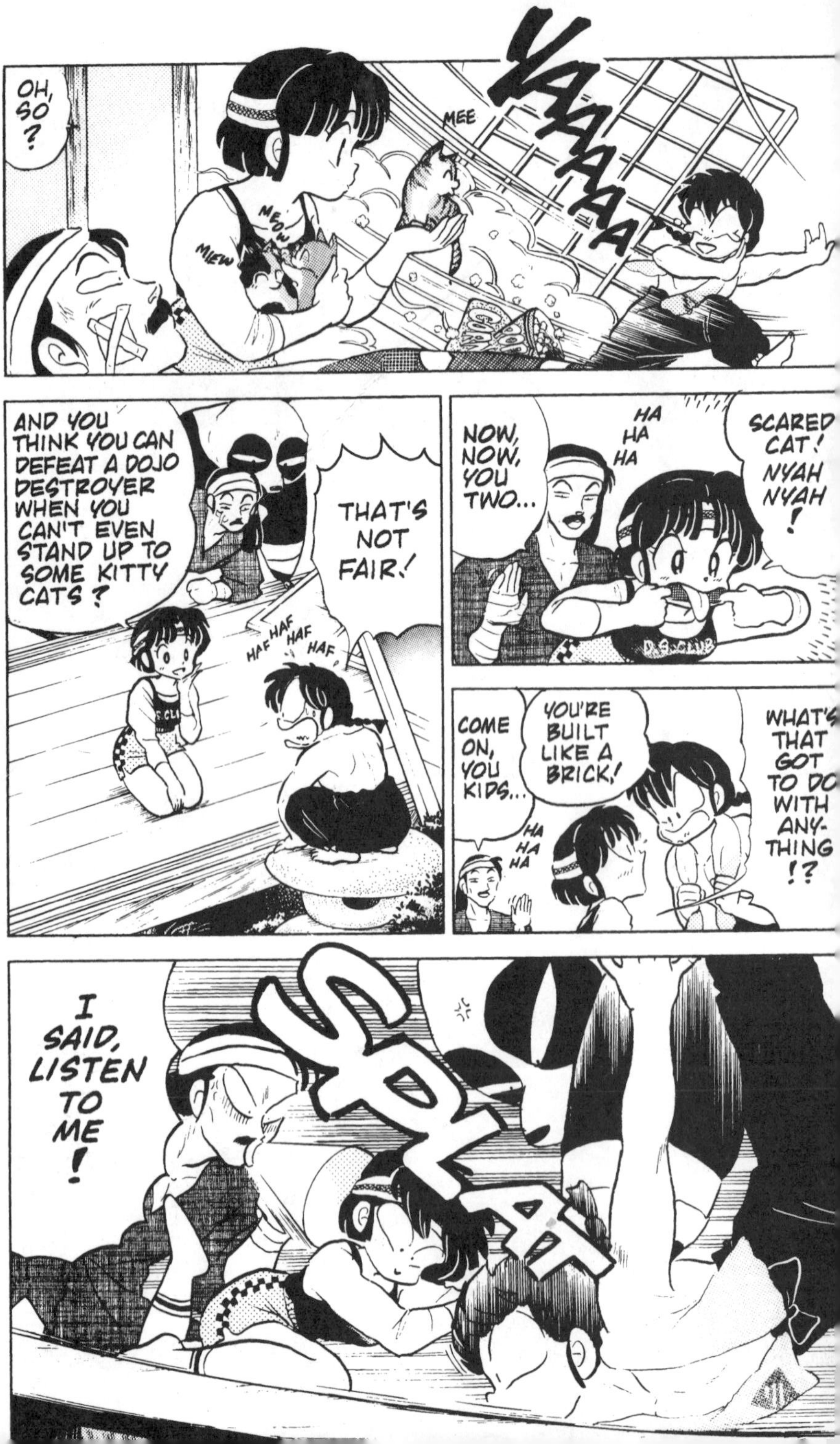
OH, SO?
MEE
MEOW
MIEW
YAAAAA
AND YOU THINK YOU CAN DEFEAT A DOJO DESTROYER WHEN YOU CAN'T EVEN STAND UP TO SOME KITTY CATS?
THAT'S NOT FAIR!
HAF HAF HAF HAF
NOW, NOW, YOU TWO...
HA HA HA
SCARED CAT! NYAH NYAH!
COME ON, YOU KIDS...
HA HA HA
YOU'RE BUILT LIKE A BRICK!
WHAT'S THAT GOT TO DO WITH ANYTHING!?
I SAID, LISTEN TO ME!
SPLAT

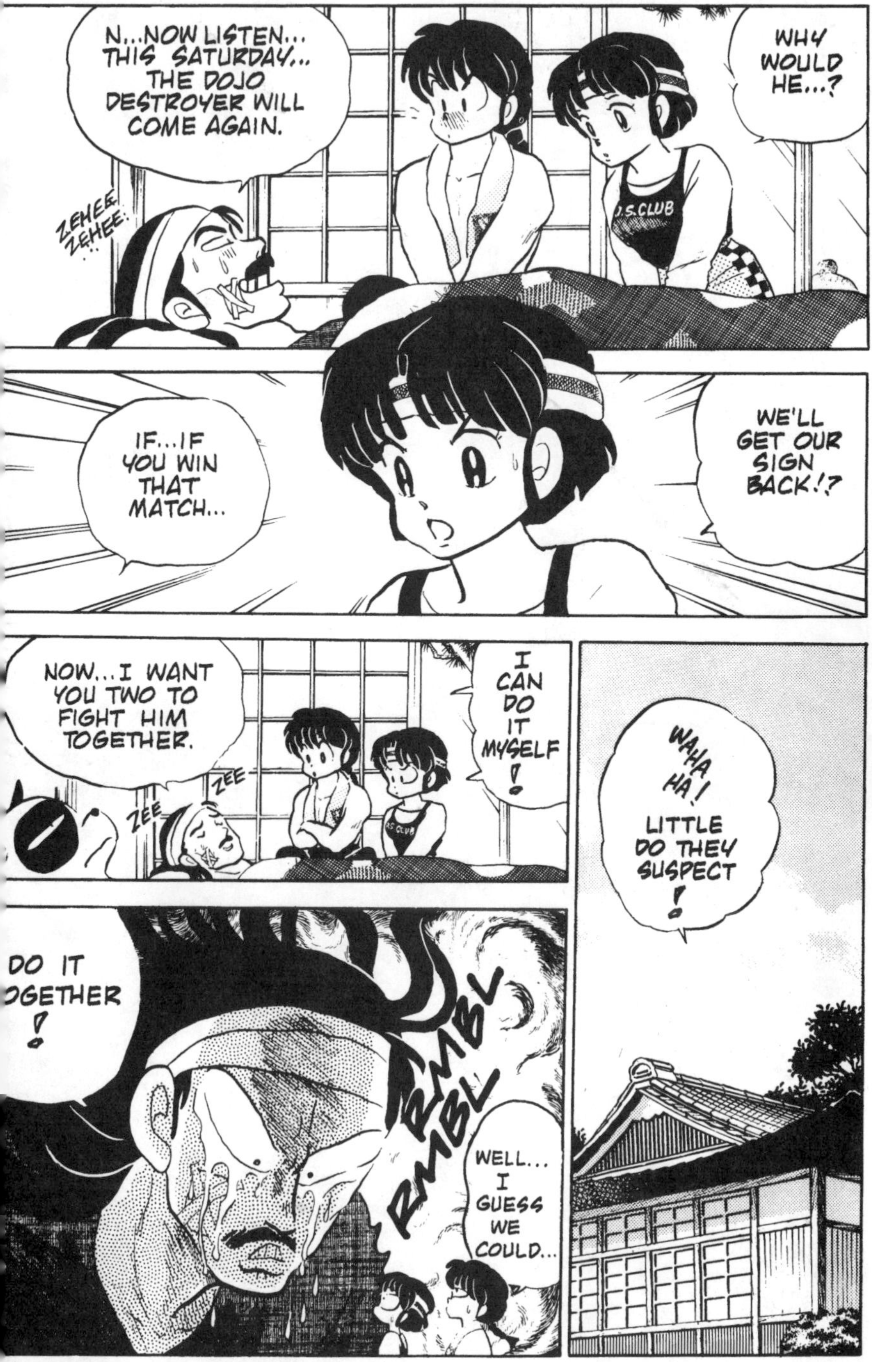
N...NOW LISTEN... THIS SATURDAY... THE DOJO DESTROYER WILL COME AGAIN.
ZEHEE ZEHEE...
WHY WOULD HE...?
IF...IF YOU WIN THAT MATCH...
WE'LL GET OUR SIGN BACK!?
NOW...I WANT YOU TWO TO FIGHT HIM TOGETHER.
ZEE ZEE
I CAN DO IT MYSELF!
DO IT OGETHER!
RMBL RMBL
WELL... I GUESS WE COULD...
WAHAHA! LITTLE DO THEY SUSPECT!

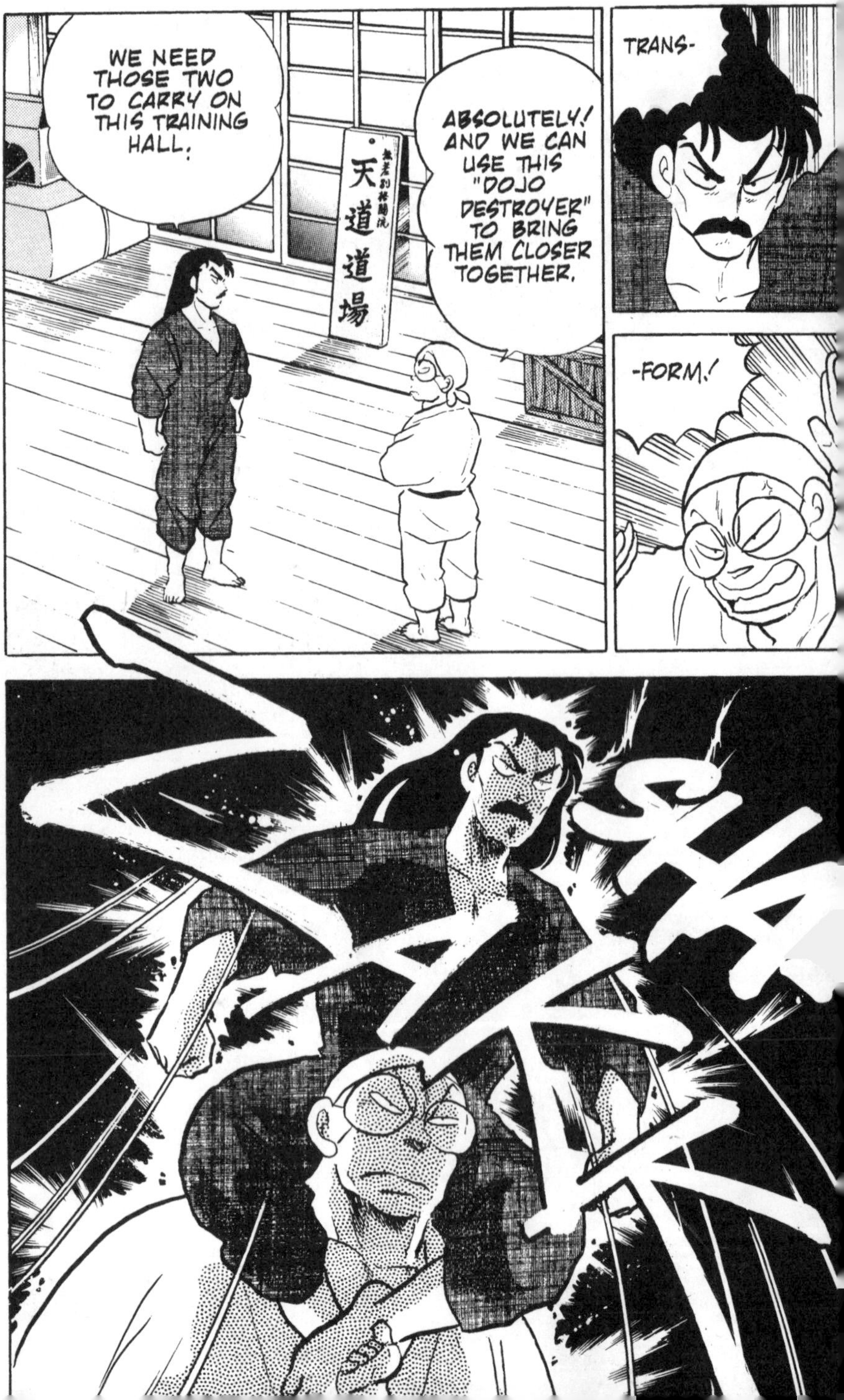
WE NEED THOSE TWO TO CARRY ON THIS TRAINING HALL.
天道道場
ABSOLUTELY! AND WE CAN USE THIS "DOJO DESTROYER" TO BRING THEM CLOSER TOGETHER.
TRANS-
-FORM!

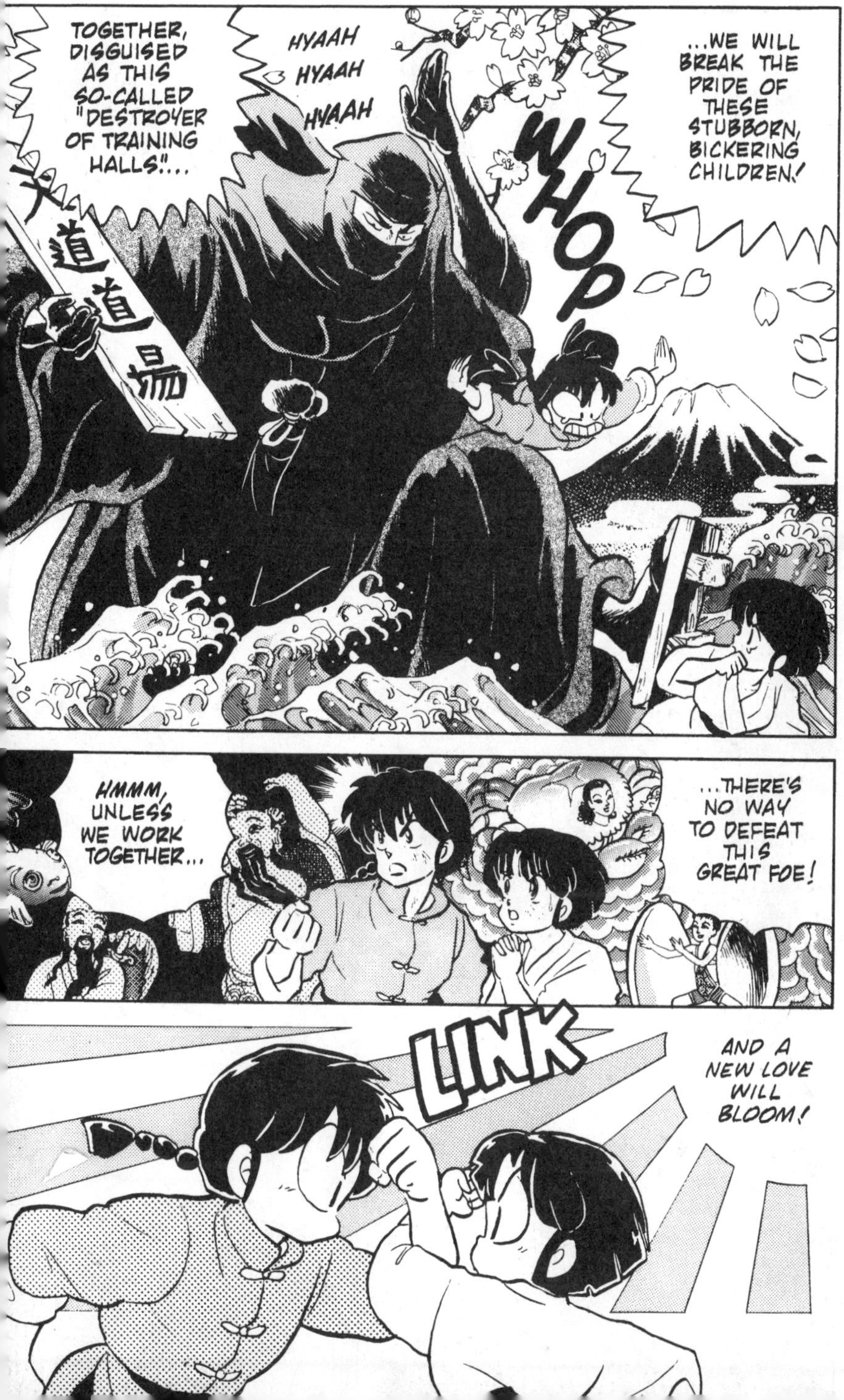
TOGETHER, DISGUISED AS THIS SO-CALLED "DESTROYER OF TRAINING HALLS"...
HYAAH HYAAH HYAAH
WHOP
...WE WILL BREAK THE PRIDE OF THESE STUBBORN, BICKERING CHILDREN!
道道場
HMMM, UNLESS WE WORK TOGETHER...
...THERE'S NO WAY TO DEFEAT THIS GREAT FOE!
LINK
AND A NEW LOVE WILL BLOOM!

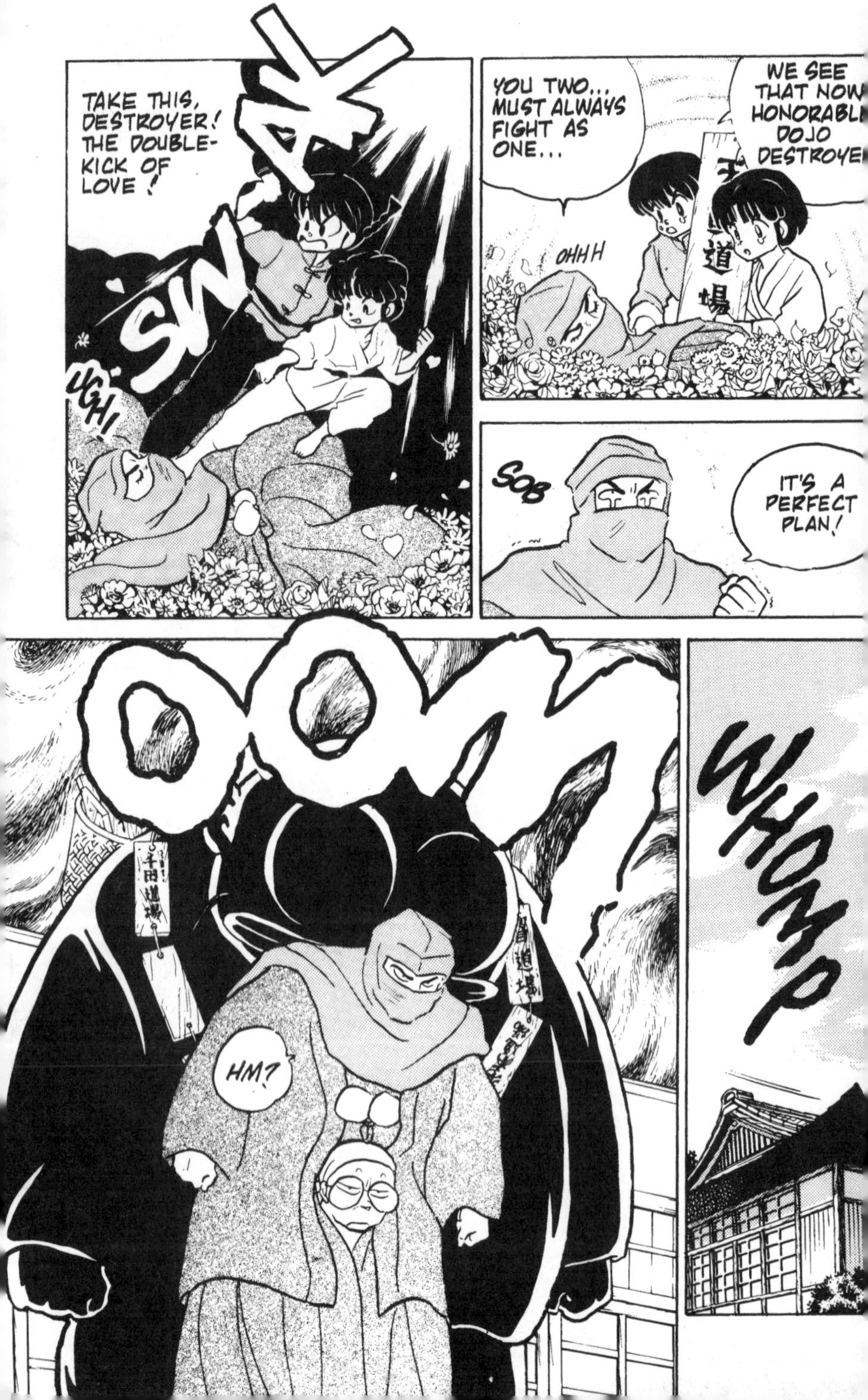
TAKE THIS, DESTROYER! THE DOUBLE-KICK OF LOVE!
UGH!
YOU TWO... MUST ALWAYS FIGHT AS ONE...
WE SEE THAT NOW HONORABL DOJO DESTROYE
OHHH
SOB
IT'S A PERFECT PLAN!
OOM
HM?
WHOMP

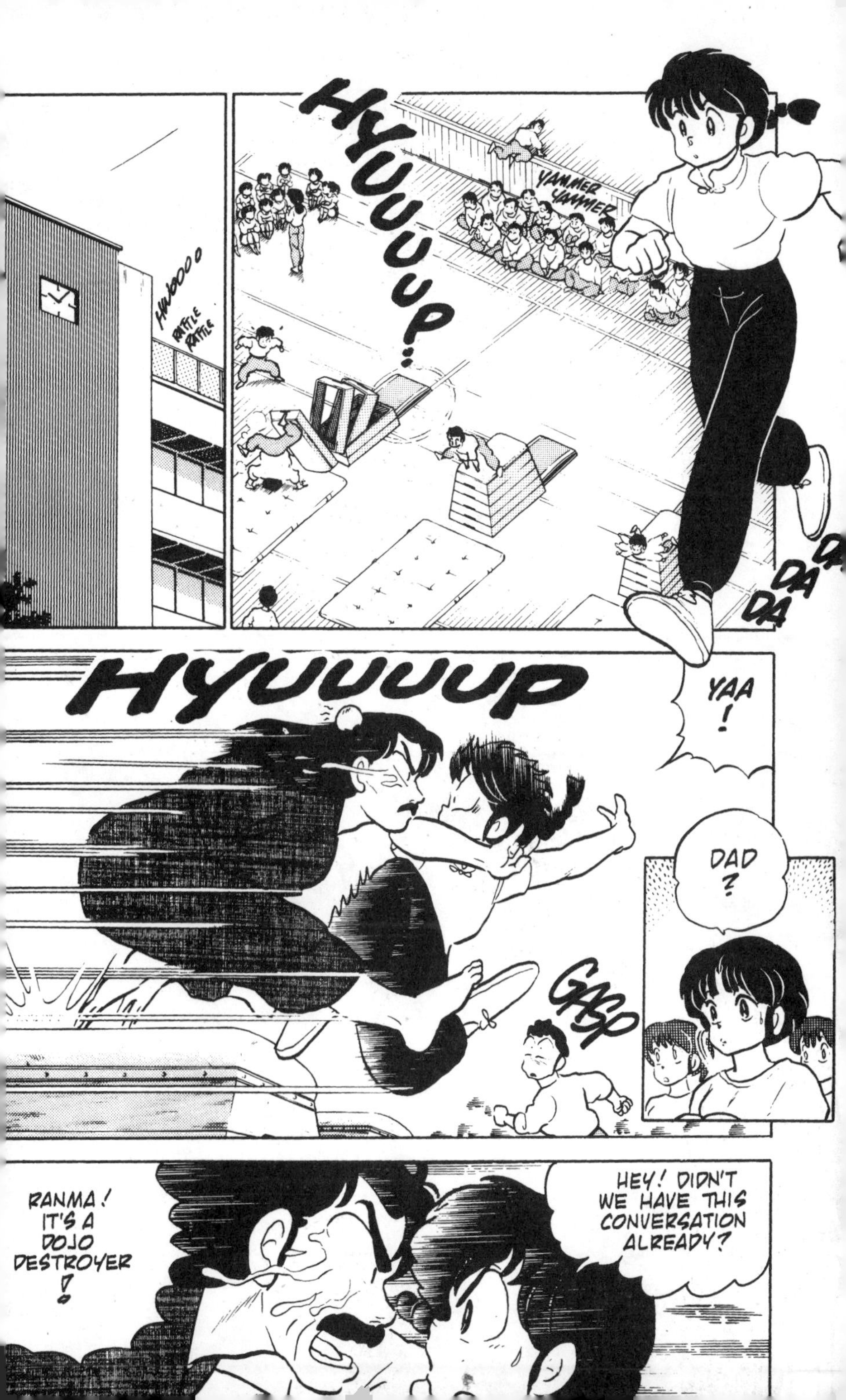
HWOOOO
RATTLE RATTLE
HYUUUUUP..
YAMMER YAMMER
DA DA DA
HYUUUUP
YAA!
DAD?
GASP
RANMA! IT'S A DOJO DESTROYER!
HEY! DIDN'T WE HAVE THIS CONVERSATION ALREADY?

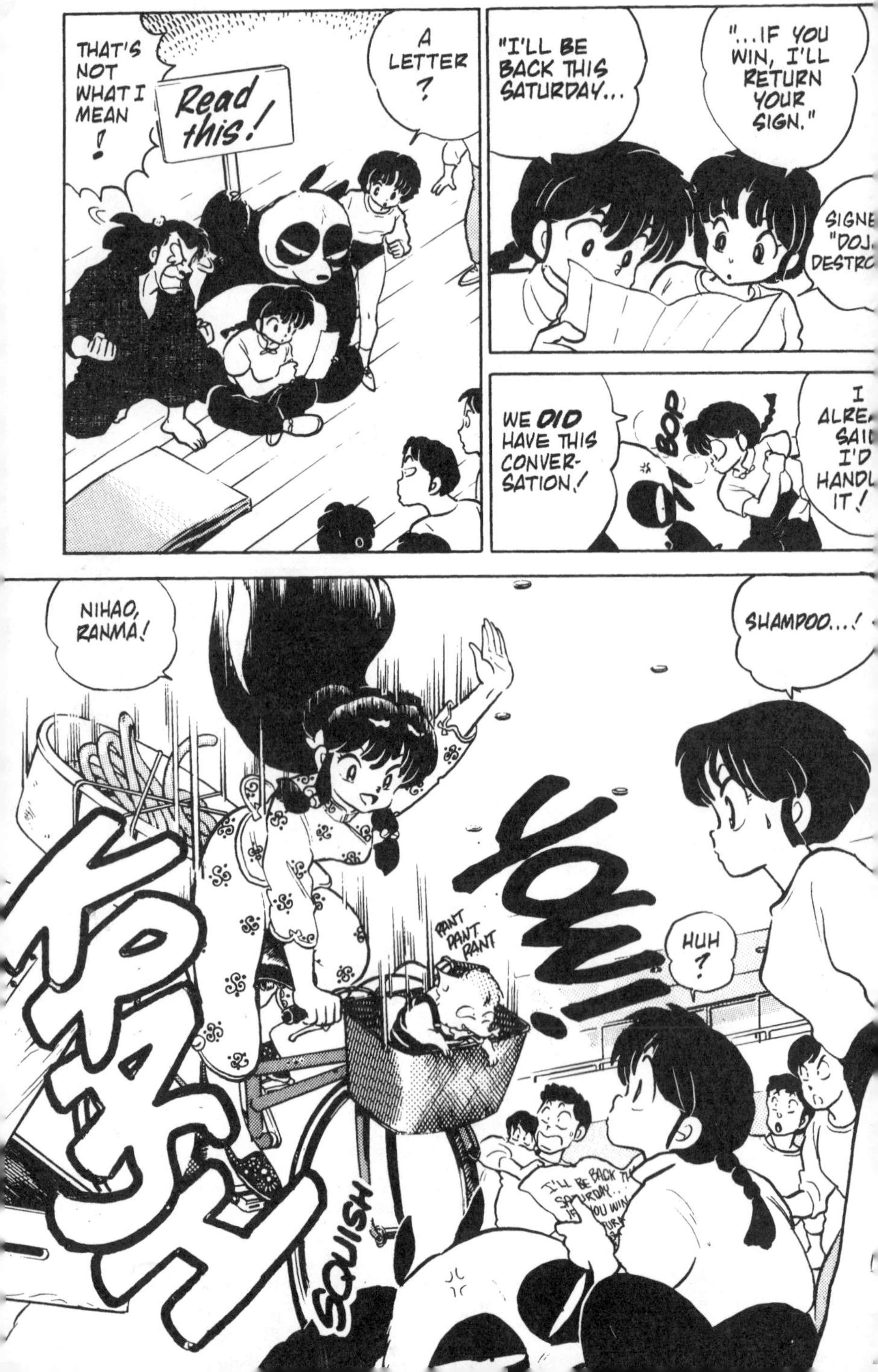
THAT'S NOT WHAT I MEAN!
Read this!
A LETTER?
"I'LL BE BACK THIS SATURDAY...
"...IF YOU WIN, I'LL RETURN YOUR SIGN."
SIGNE "DOJ DESTRO
WE DID HAVE THIS CONVER-SATION!
BOP
I ALRE SAI I'D HANDL IT!
NIHAO, RANMA!
SHAMPOO...!
KRASH
YOW!!
PANT PANT PANT
HUH?
SQUISH

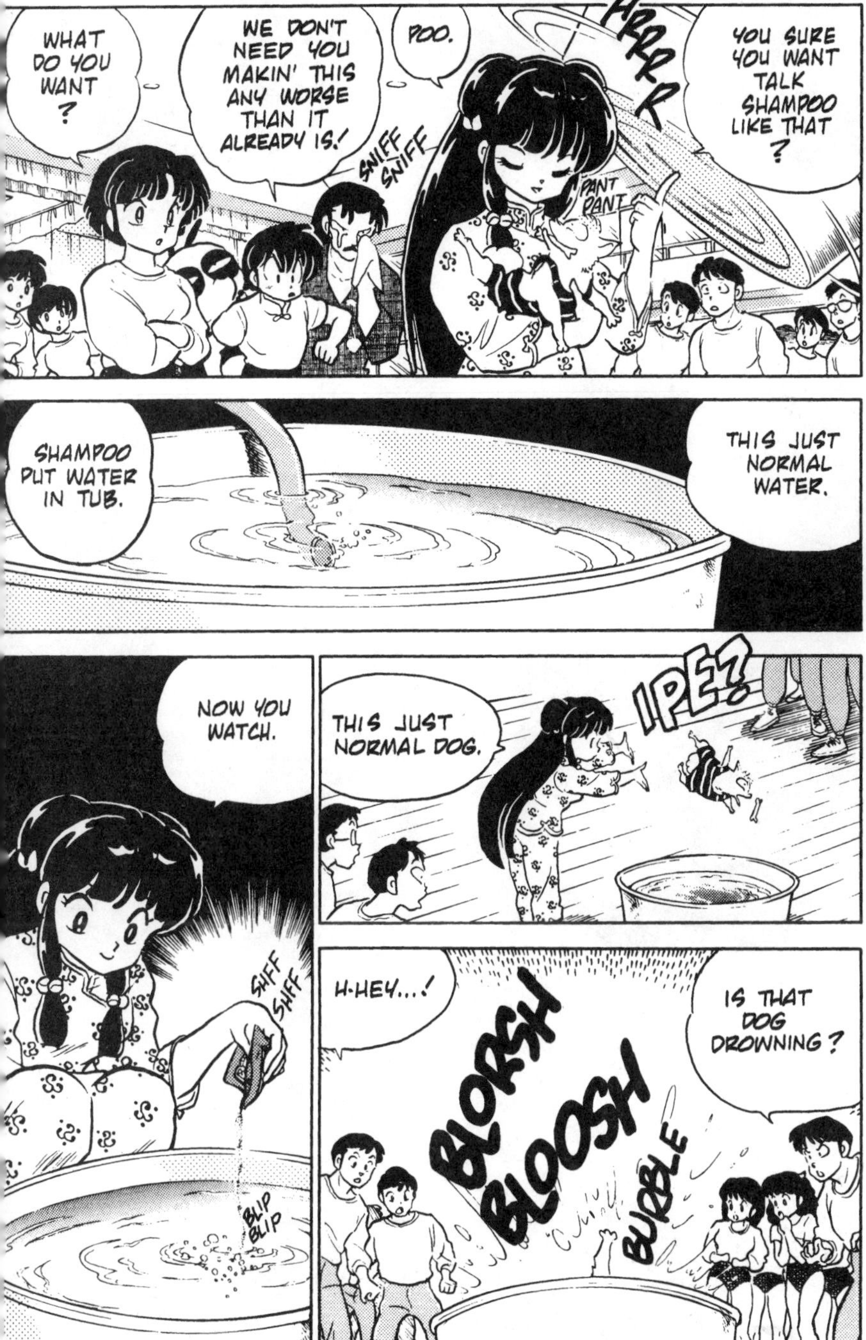
WHAT DO YOU WANT ?
WE DON'T NEED YOU MAKIN' THIS ANY WORSE THAN IT ALREADY IS!
SNIFF SNIFF
POO.
WHRRRR
PANT PANT
YOU SURE YOU WANT TALK SHAMPOO LIKE THAT ?
SHAMPOO PUT WATER IN TUB.
THIS JUST NORMAL WATER.
NOW YOU WATCH.
SHFF SHFF
BLIP BLIP
THIS JUST NORMAL DOG.
IPE?
H-HEY...!
BLORSH
BLOOSH
BUBBLE
IS THAT DOG DROWNING ?

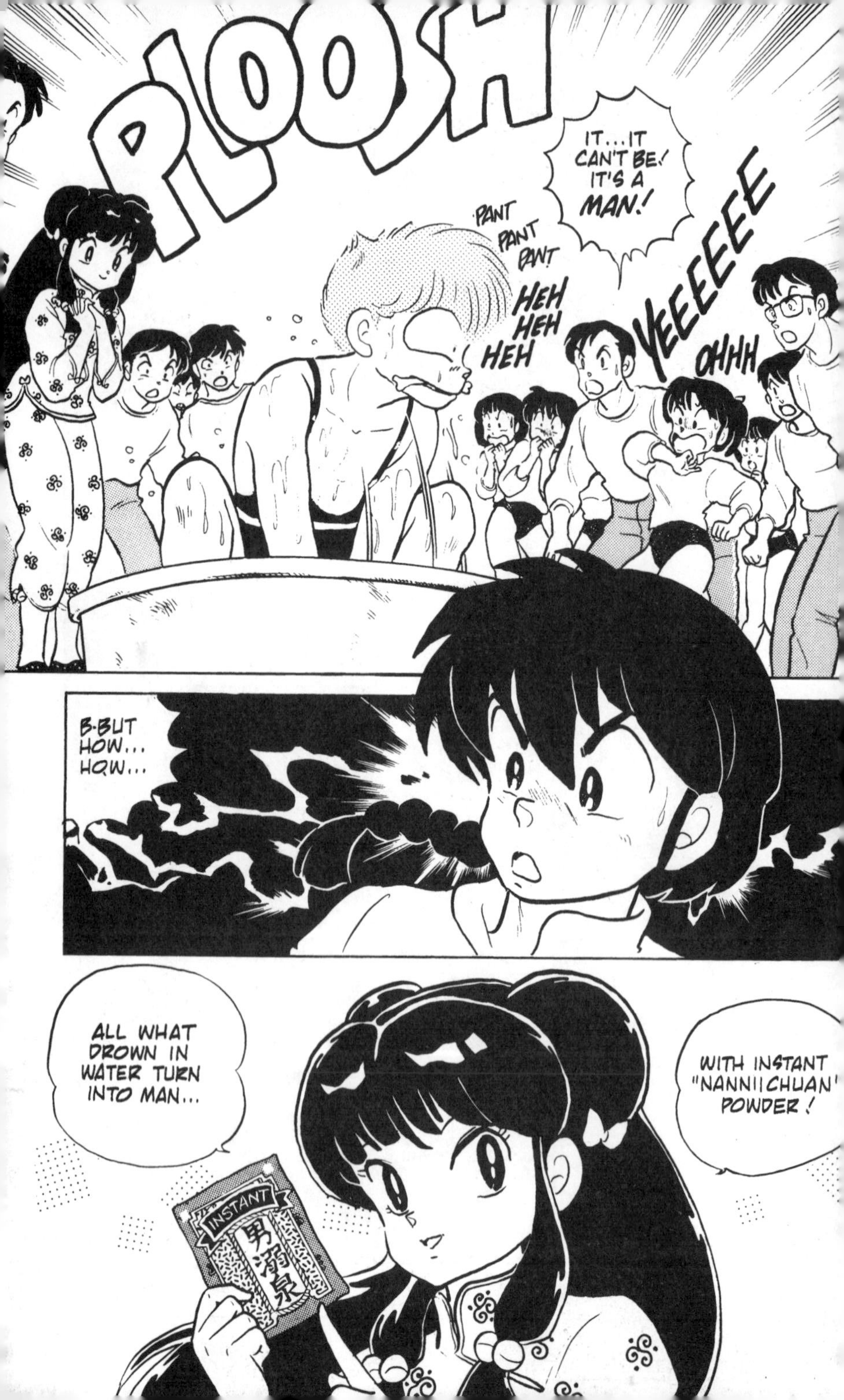
PLOOSH
IT... IT CAN'T BE! IT'S A MAN!
PANT PANT PANT
HEH HEH HEH
YEEEEEE
OHHH
B-BUT HOW... HOW...
ALL WHAT DROWN IN WATER TURN INTO MAN...
WITH INSTANT "NANNIICHUAN" POWDER!
INSTANT
男溺泉

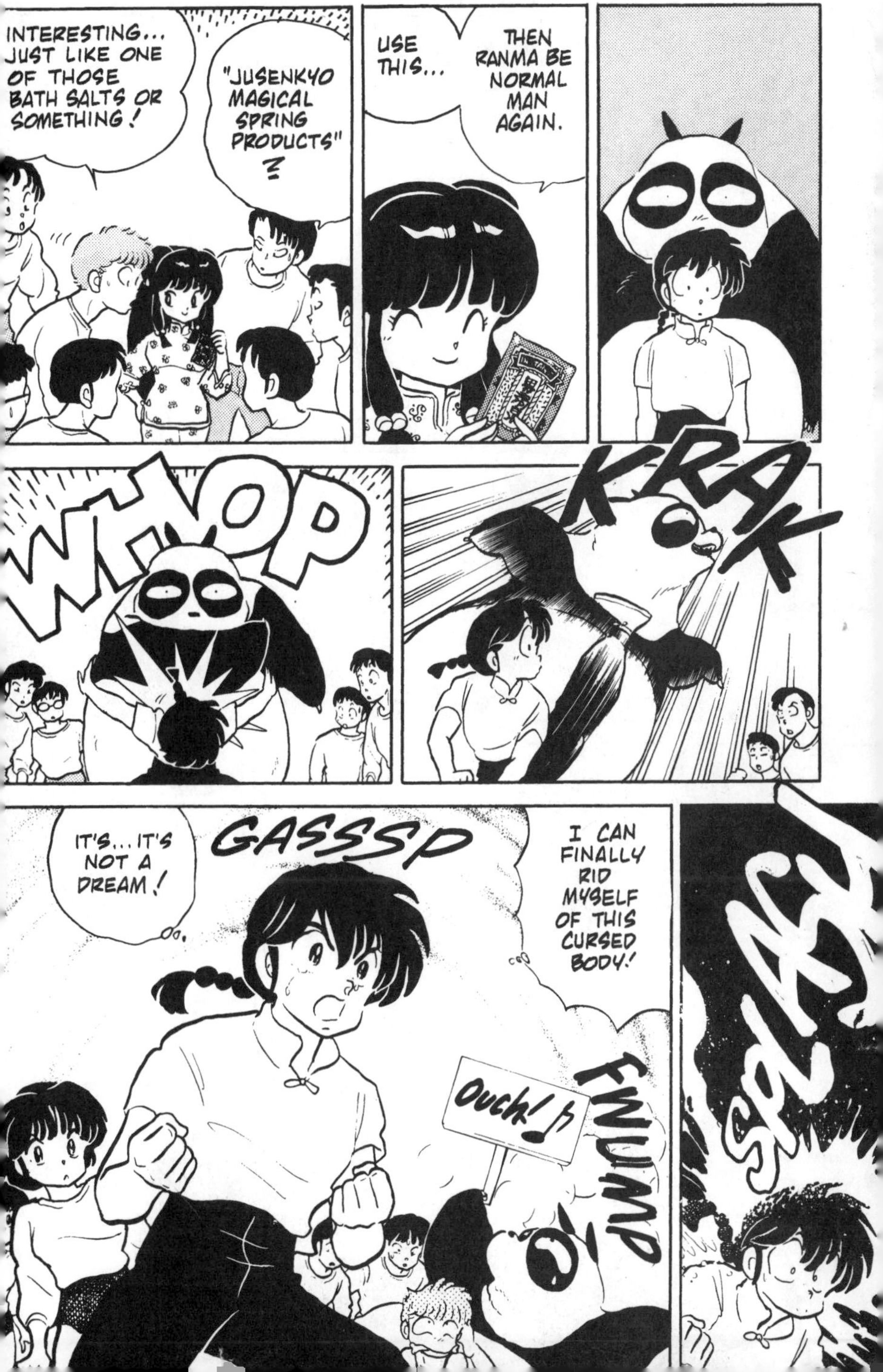
INTERESTING... JUST LIKE ONE OF THOSE BATH SALTS OR SOMETHING!
"JUSENKYO MAGICAL SPRING PRODUCTS"?
USE THIS...
THEN RANMA BE NORMAL MAN AGAIN.
WHOP
KRAK
IT'S... IT'S NOT A DREAM!
GASSSP
I CAN FINALLY RID MYSELF OF THIS CURSED BODY!
Ouch! ♪
FWUMP

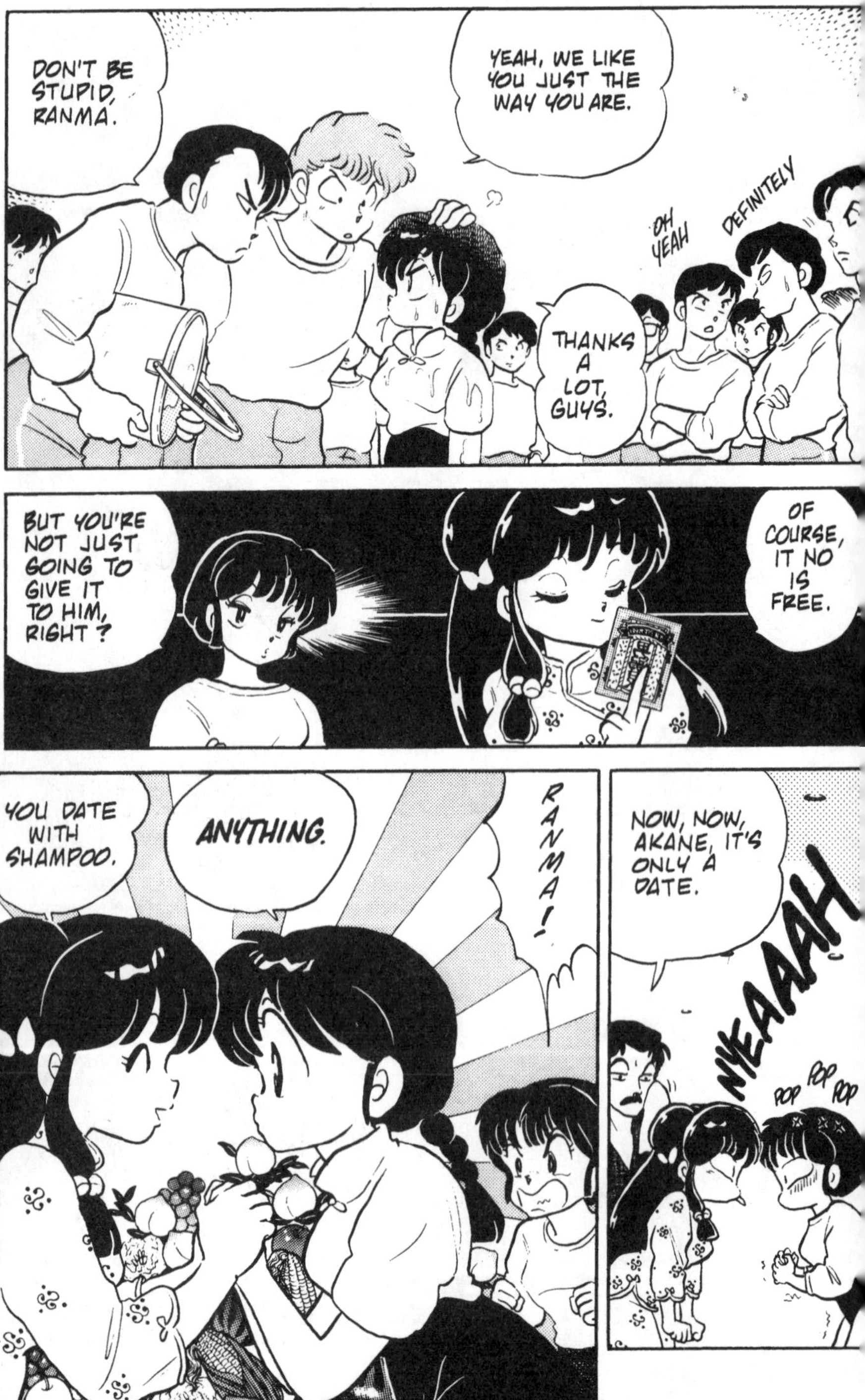
DON'T BE STUPID, RANMA.
YEAH, WE LIKE YOU JUST THE WAY YOU ARE.
OH YEAH
DEFINITELY
THANKS A LOT, GUYS.
BUT YOU'RE NOT JUST GOING TO GIVE IT TO HIM, RIGHT?
OF COURSE, IT NO IS FREE.
YOU DATE WITH SHAMPOO.
ANYTHING.
RANMA!
NOW, NOW, AKANE, IT'S ONLY A DATE.
NYEAAAH!
POP POP POP

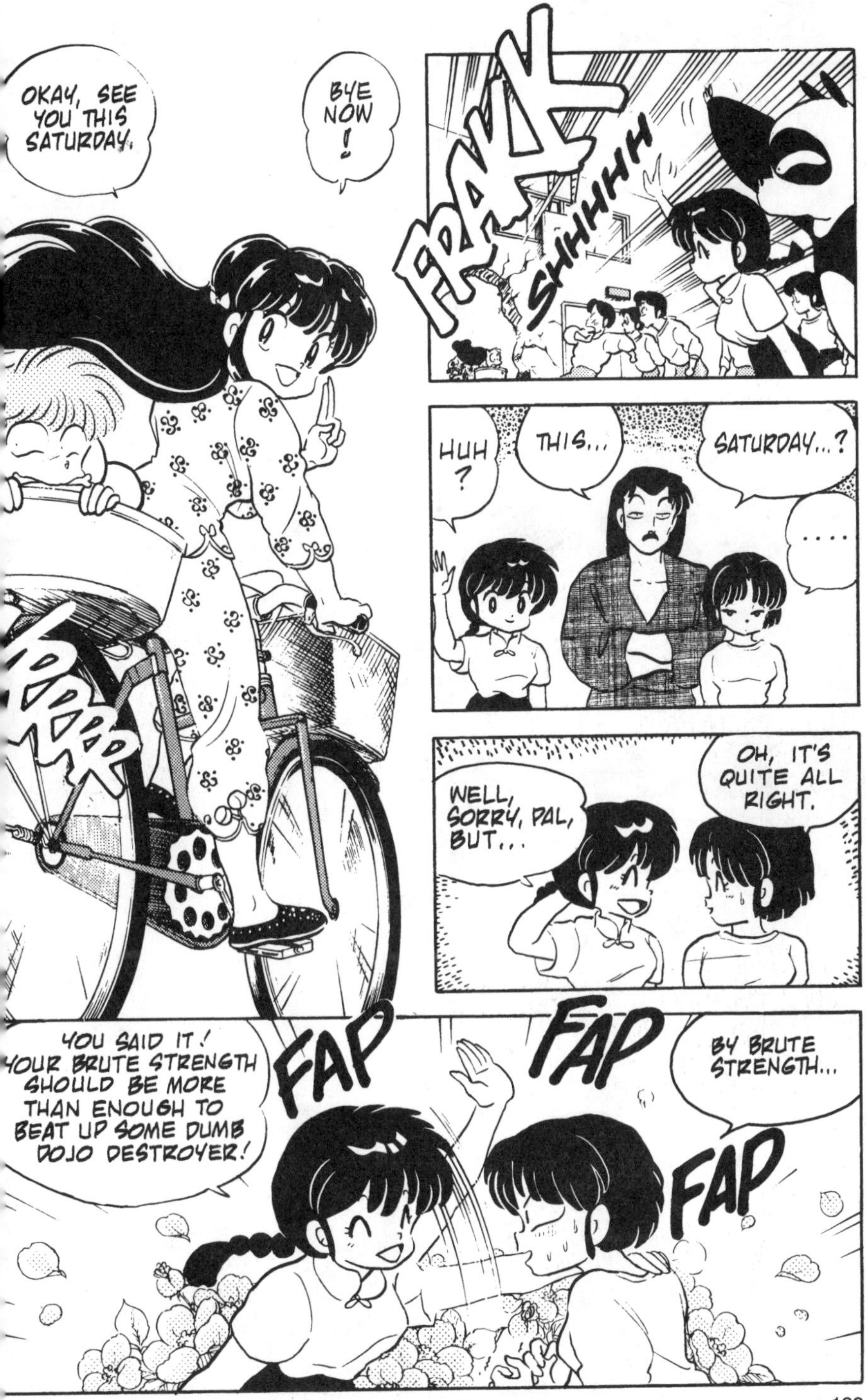
OKAY, SEE YOU THIS SATURDAY.
BYE NOW!
FRAAK
SHHHHH
HUH?
THIS...
SATURDAY...?
....
WELL, SORRY, PAL, BUT...
OH, IT'S QUITE ALL RIGHT.
YOU SAID IT! YOUR BRUTE STRENGTH SHOULD BE MORE THAN ENOUGH TO BEAT UP SOME DUMB DOJO DESTROYER!
FAP
FAP
BY BRUTE STRENGTH...
FAP

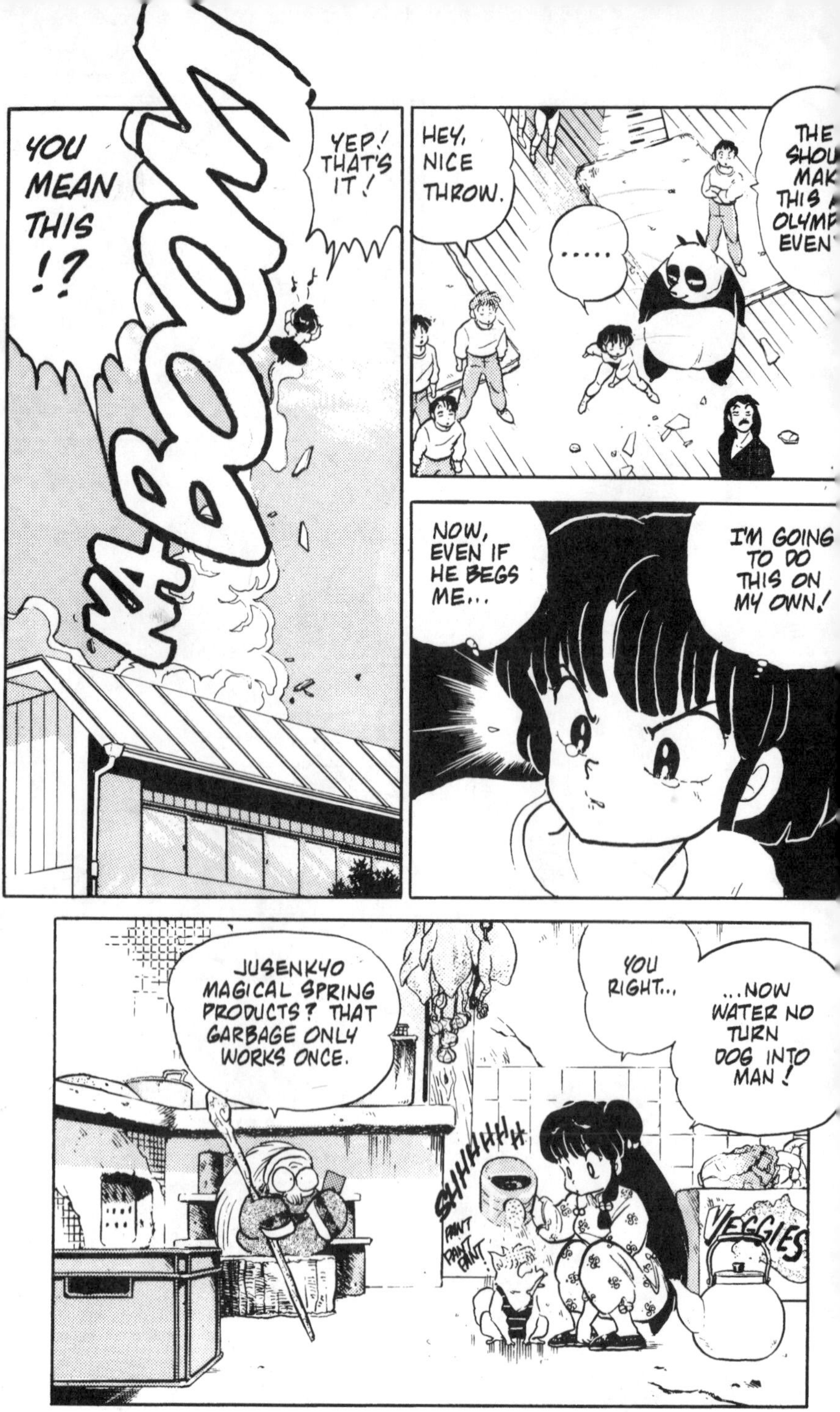
YOU MEAN THIS !?
KABOOM
YEP! THAT'S IT!
HEY, NICE THROW.
......
THE SHOU MAK THIS OLYMP EVEN
NOW, EVEN IF HE BEGS ME...
I'M GOING TO DO THIS ON MY OWN!
JUSENKYO MAGICAL SPRING PRODUCTS? THAT GARBAGE ONLY WORKS ONCE.
YOU RIGHT...
...NOW WATER NO TURN DOG INTO MAN!
SHHHHHH
PANT PANT PANT
VEGGIES

Part 9

NO NEED FOR RANMA

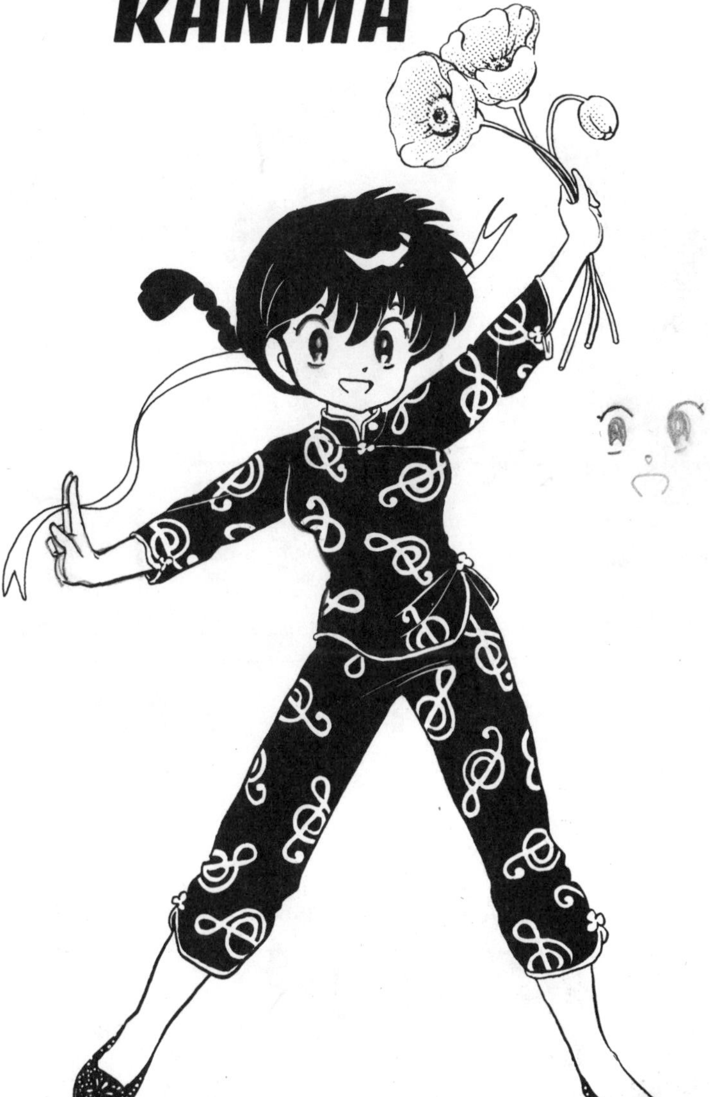

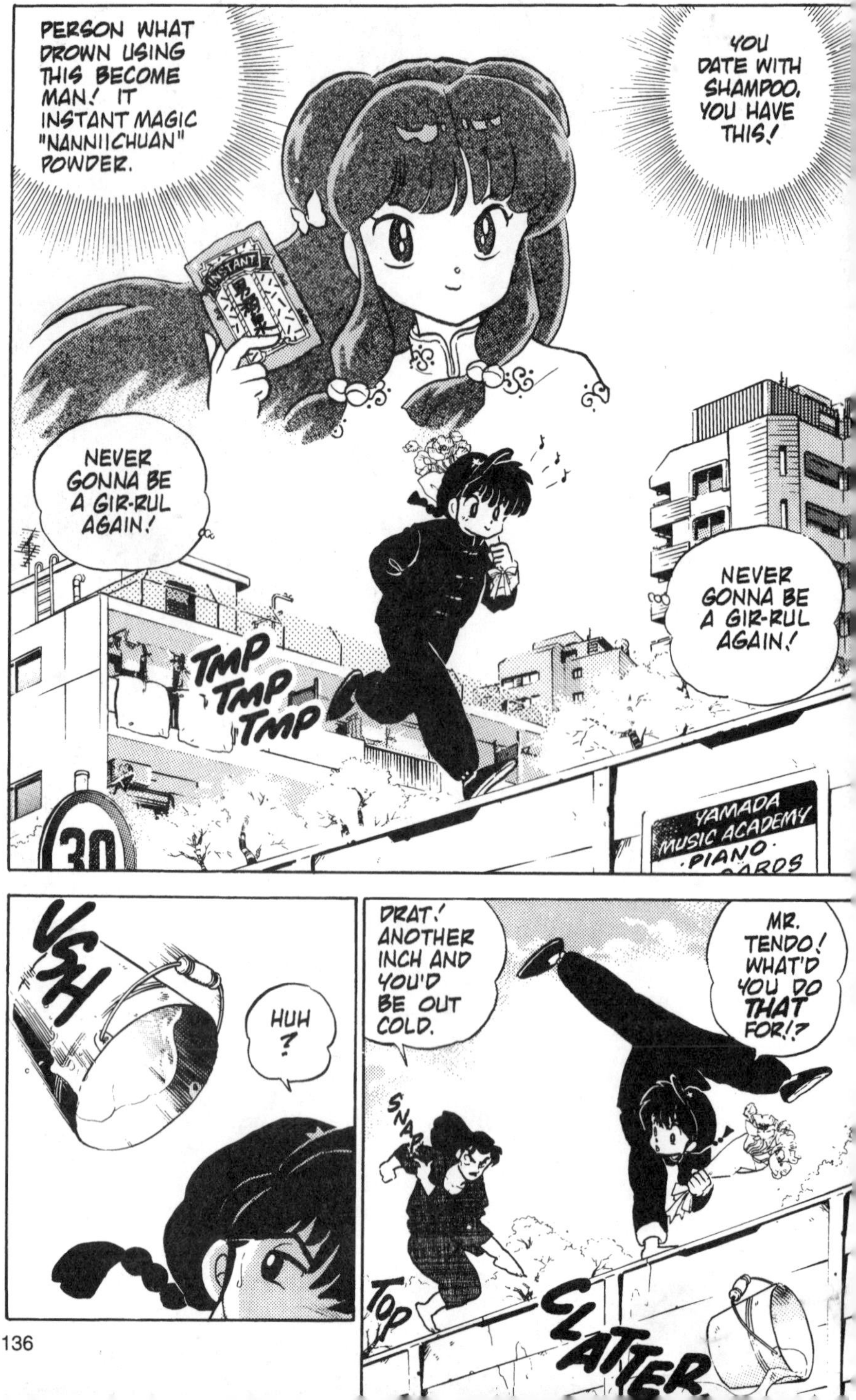
PERSON WHAT DROWN USING THIS BECOME MAN! IT INSTANT MAGIC "NANNIICHUAN" POWDER.
INSTANT
YOU DATE WITH SHAMPOO, YOU HAVE THIS!
NEVER GONNA BE A GIR-RUL AGAIN!
TMP TMP TMP
NEVER GONNA BE A GIR-RUL AGAIN!
30
YAMADA MUSIC ACADEMY
PIANO
USH
HUH ?
DRAT! ANOTHER INCH AND YOU'D BE OUT COLD.
MR. TENDO! WHAT'D YOU DO THAT FOR!?
SNAP
TOP
CLATTER

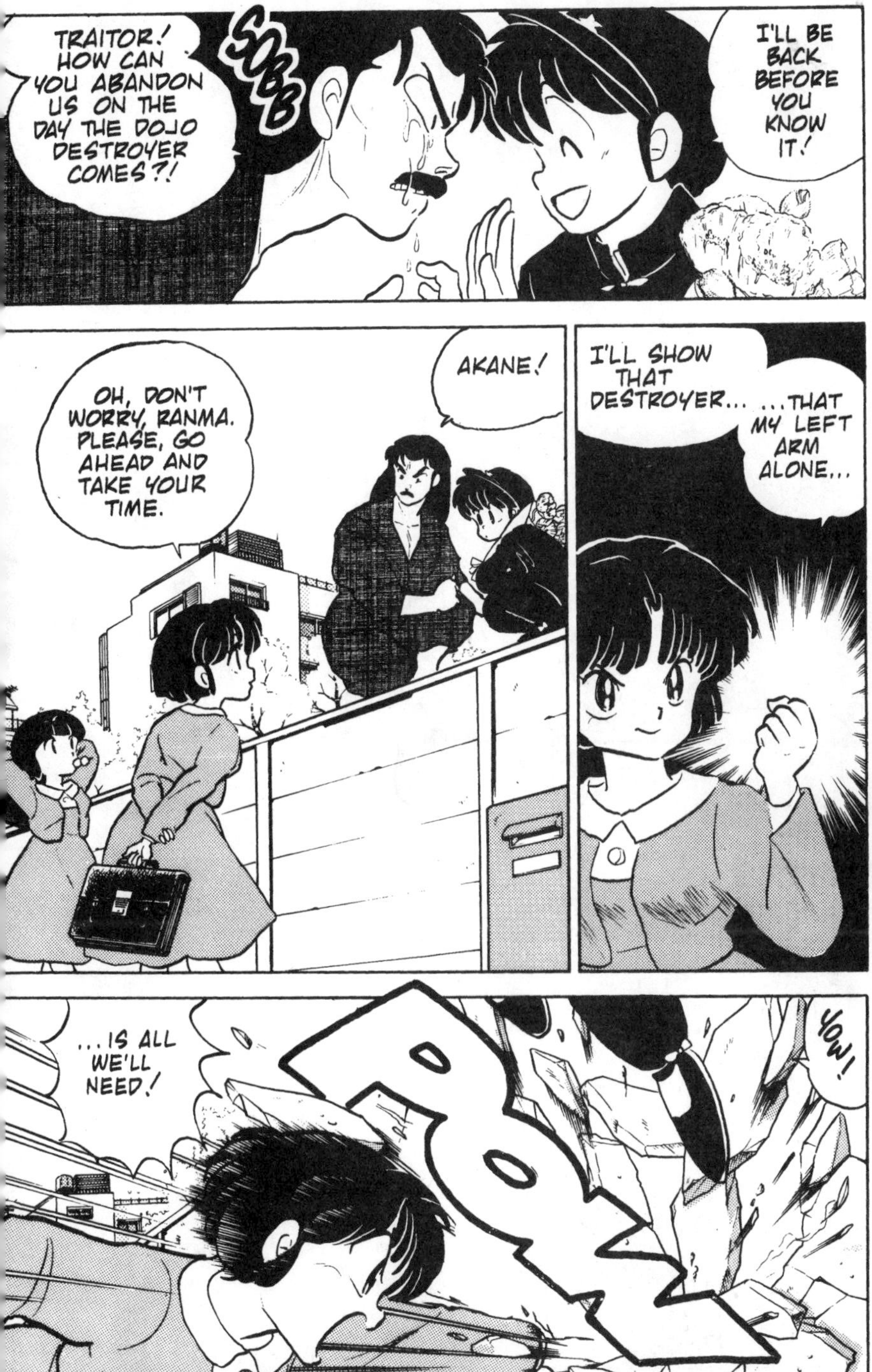

TRAITOR! HOW CAN YOU ABANDON US ON THE DAY THE DOJO DESTROYER COMES?!
SOBB
I'LL BE BACK BEFORE YOU KNOW IT!
OH, DON'T WORRY, RANMA. PLEASE, GO AHEAD AND TAKE YOUR TIME.
AKANE!
I'LL SHOW THAT DESTROYER...
...THAT MY LEFT ARM ALONE...
...IS ALL WE'LL NEED!
BOOM
YOW!

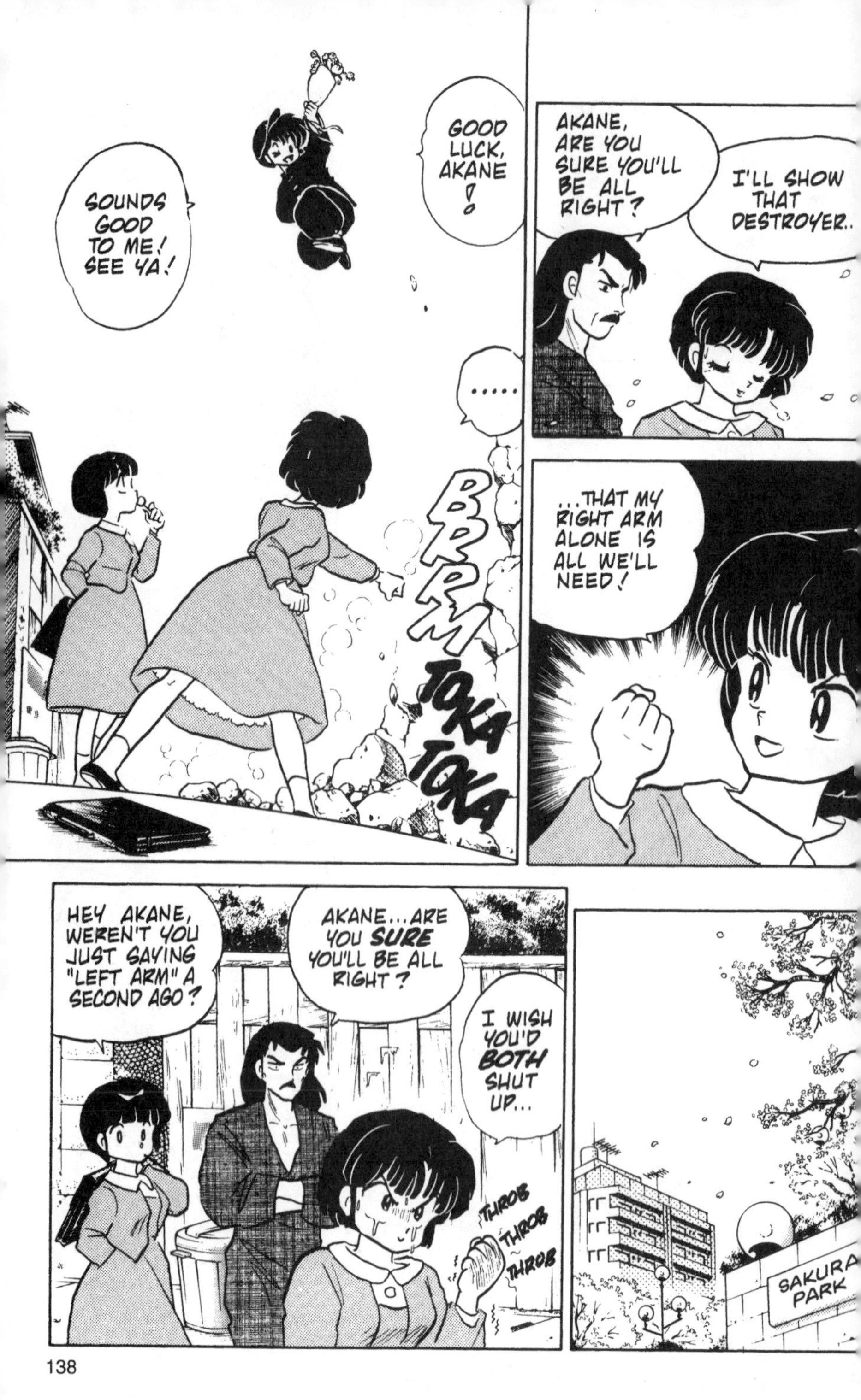
SOUNDS GOOD TO ME! SEE YA!
GOOD LUCK, AKANE!
AKANE, ARE YOU SURE YOU'LL BE ALL RIGHT?
I'LL SHOW THAT DESTROYER..
.....
BRRM
TOKA TOKA
...THAT MY RIGHT ARM ALONE IS ALL WE'LL NEED!
HEY AKANE, WEREN'T YOU JUST SAYING "LEFT ARM" A SECOND AGO?
AKANE...ARE YOU SURE YOU'LL BE ALL RIGHT?
I WISH YOU'D BOTH SHUT UP...
THROB THROB THROB
SAKURA PARK

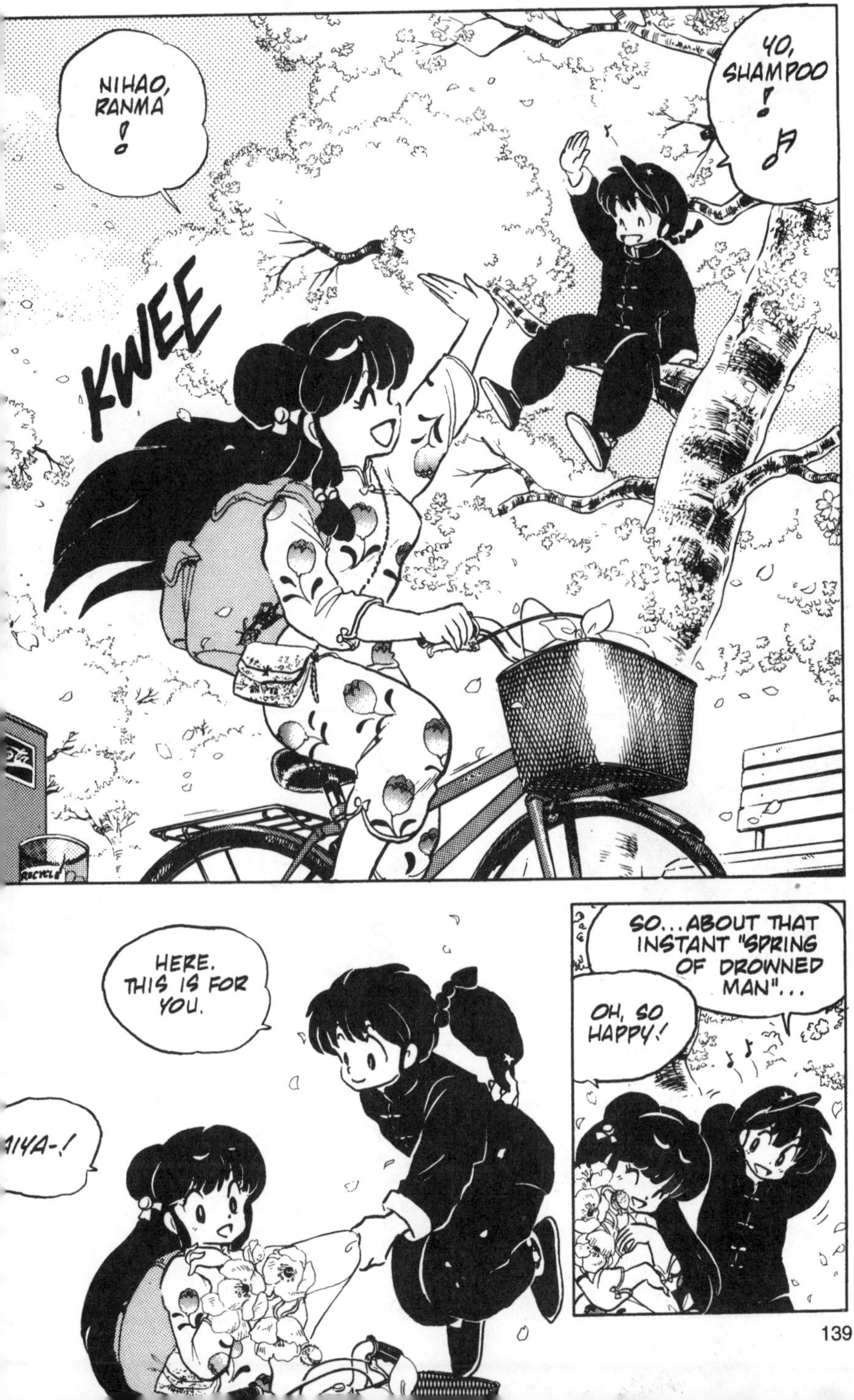
NIHAO, RANMA!
KWEE
YO, SHAMPOO!
HERE. THIS IS FOR YOU.
IYA-!
SO...ABOUT THAT INSTANT "SPRING OF DROWNED MAN"...
OH, SO HAPPY!

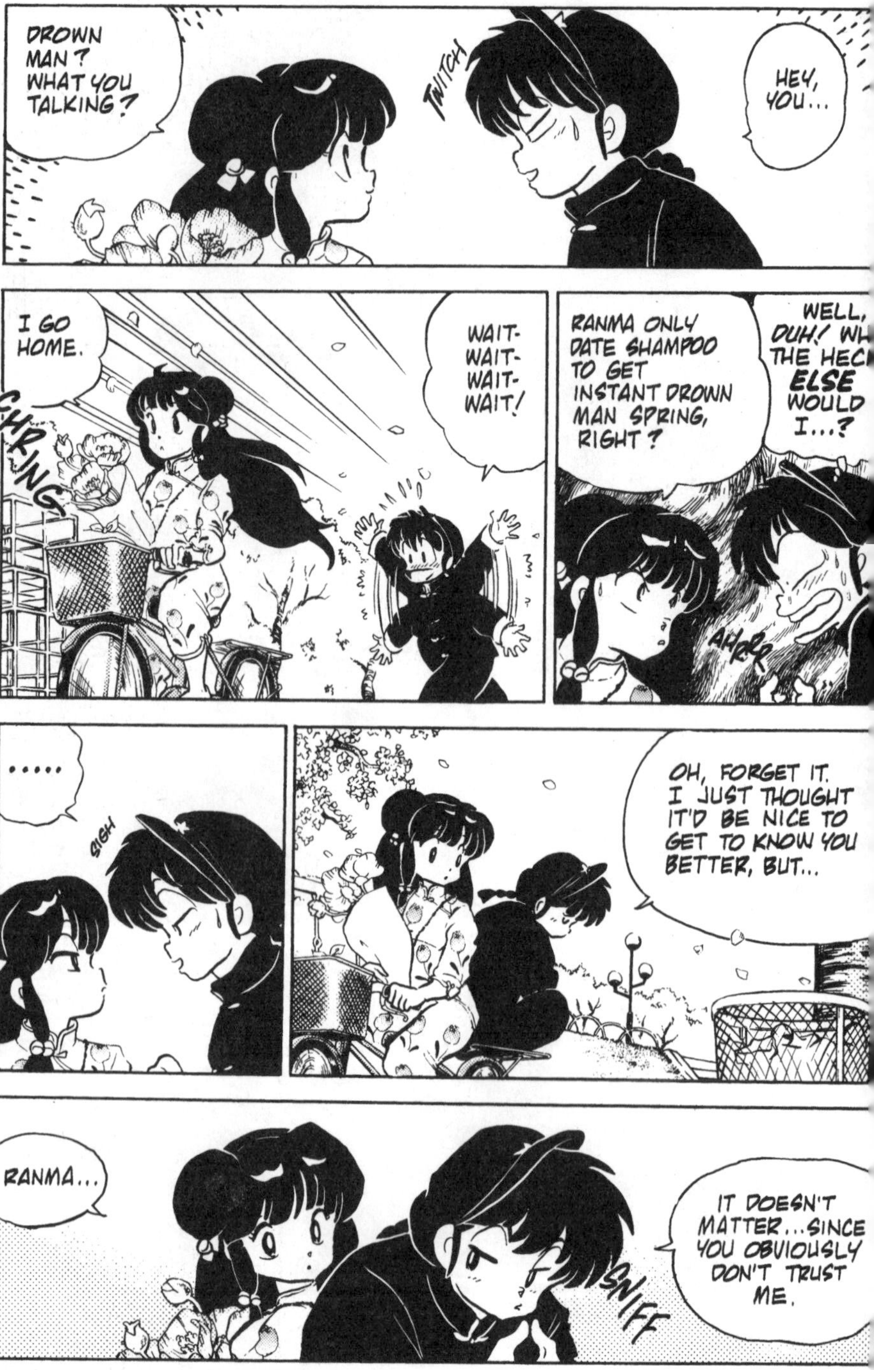
DROWN MAN? WHAT YOU TALKING?
TWITCH
HEY, YOU...
I GO HOME.
CHRING
WAIT-WAIT-WAIT-WAIT!
RANMA ONLY DATE SHAMPOO TO GET INSTANT DROWN MAN SPRING, RIGHT?
WELL, DUH! WH THE HEC ELSE WOULD I...?
AHRRR
.....
SIGH
OH, FORGET IT. I JUST THOUGHT IT'D BE NICE TO GET TO KNOW YOU BETTER, BUT...
RANMA...
IT DOESN'T MATTER...SINCE YOU OBVIOUSLY DON'T TRUST ME.
SNIFF

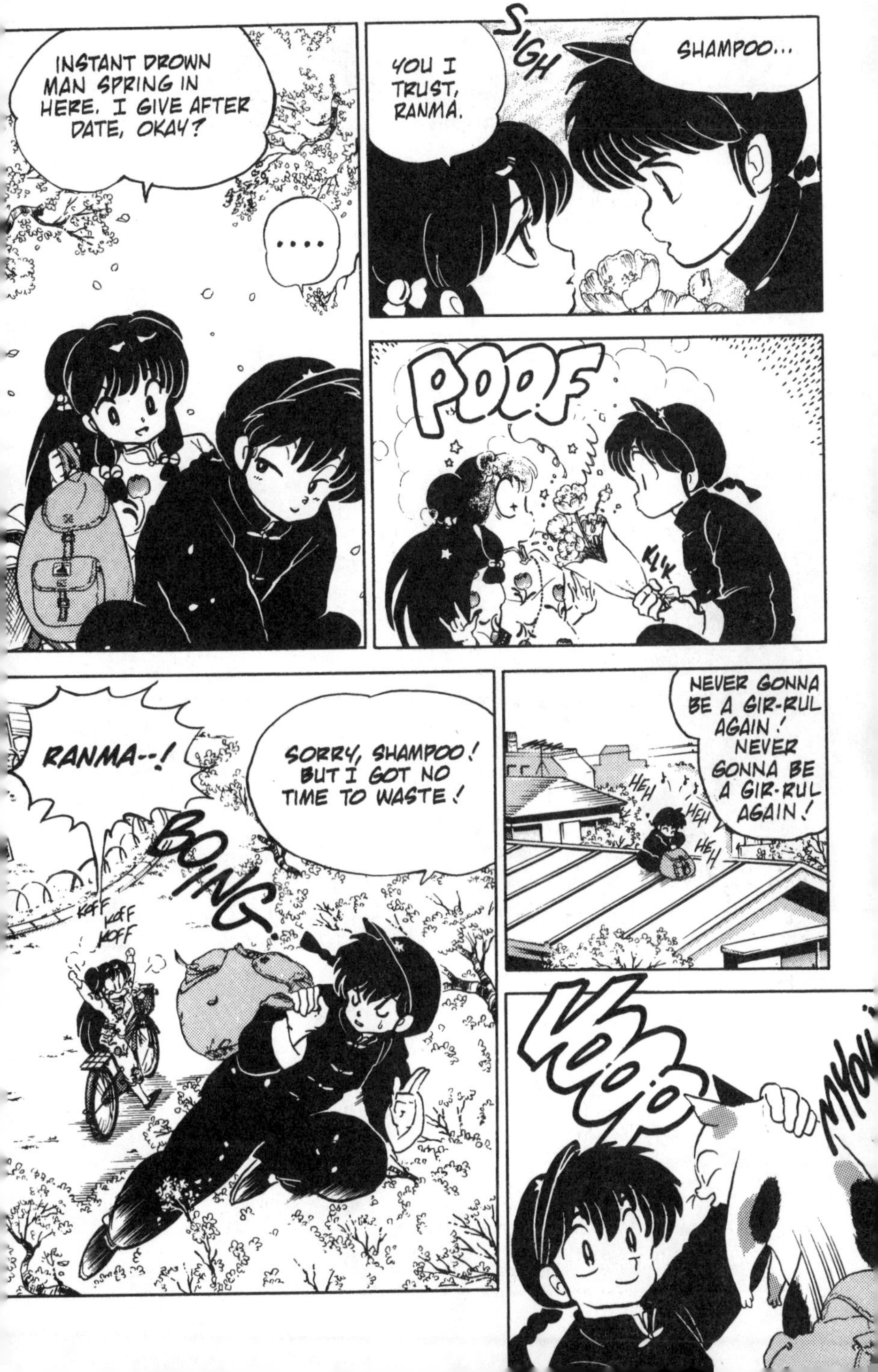

INSTANT DROWN MAN SPRING IN HERE. I GIVE AFTER DATE, OKAY?
....
SIGH
SHAMPOO...
YOU I TRUST, RANMA.
POOF
KLIK
RANMA--!
SORRY, SHAMPOO! BUT I GOT NO TIME TO WASTE!
BOING
KOFF KOFF KOFF
NEVER GONNA BE A GIR-RUL AGAIN! NEVER GONNA BE A GIR-RUL AGAIN!
HEH HEH HEH
MYOW

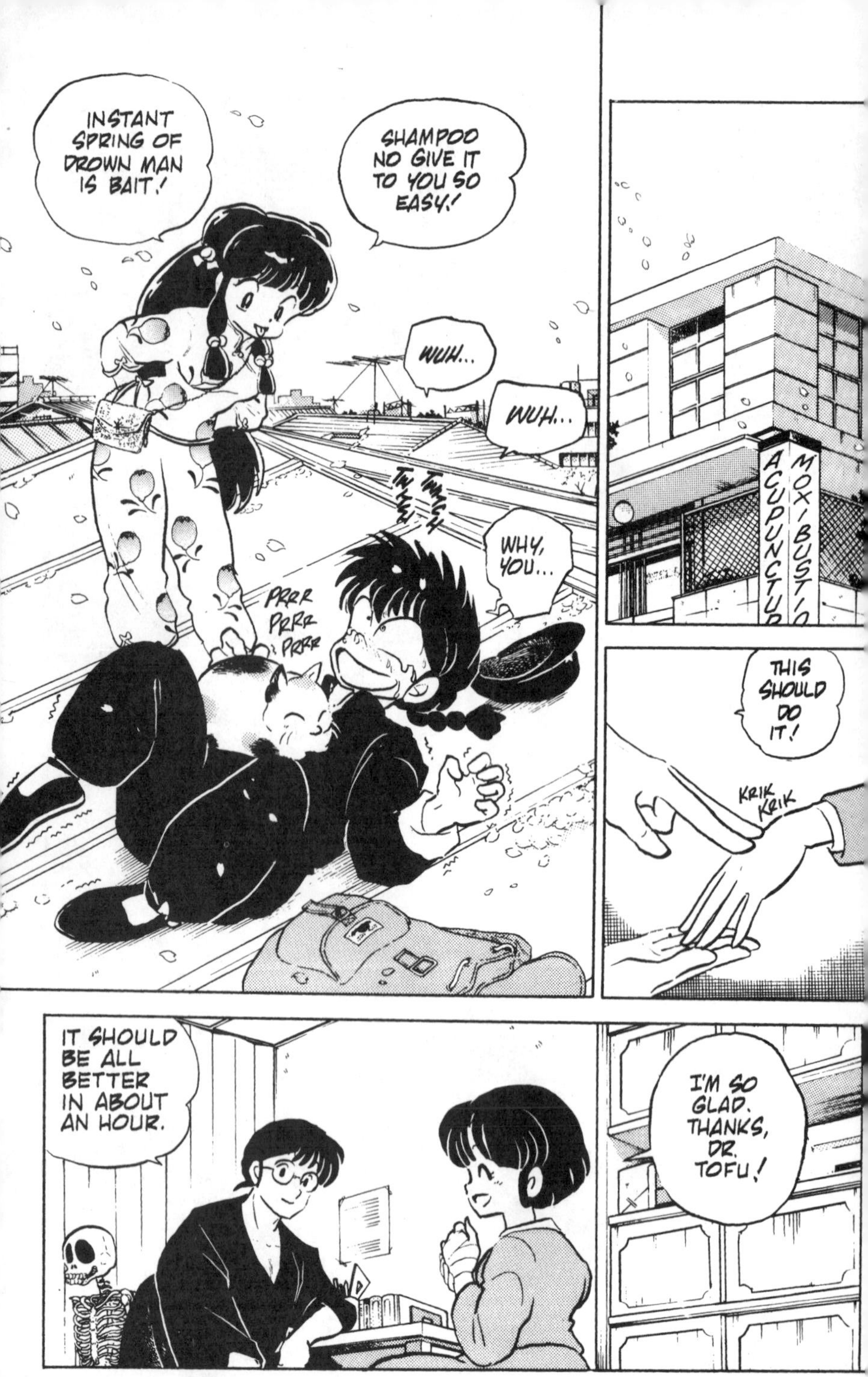
INSTANT SPRING OF DROWN MAN IS BAIT!
SHAMPOO NO GIVE IT TO YOU SO EASY!
WUH...
WUH...
WHY, YOU...
PRRR PRRR PRRR
MOXIBUSTIO
ACUPUNCTUR
THIS SHOULD DO IT!
KRIK KRIK
IT SHOULD BE ALL BETTER IN ABOUT AN HOUR.
I'M SO GLAD. THANKS, DR. TOFU!

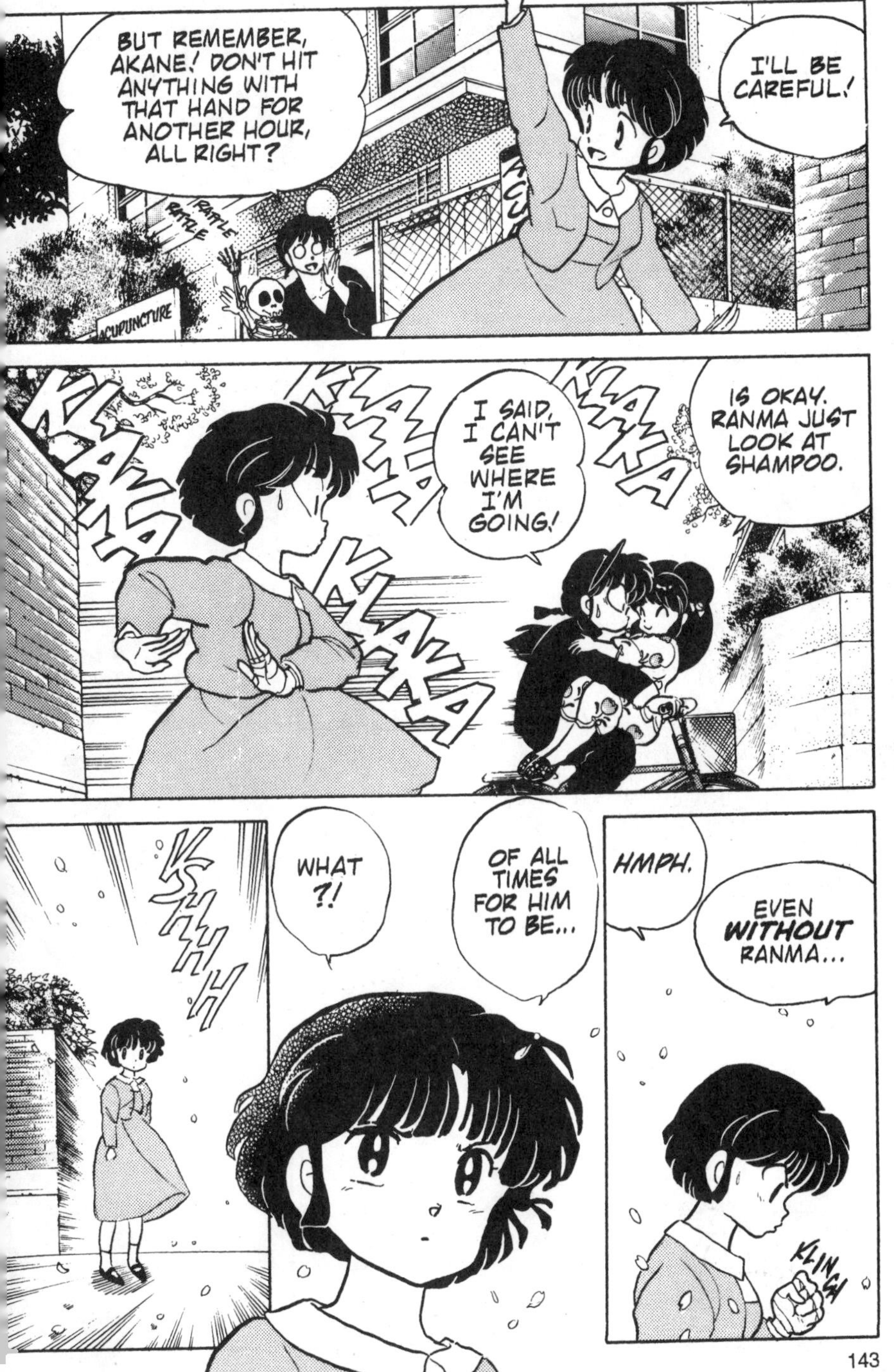
BUT REMEMBER, AKANE! DON'T HIT ANYTHING WITH THAT HAND FOR ANOTHER HOUR, ALL RIGHT?
RATTLE RATTLE
ACUPUNCTURE
I'LL BE CAREFUL!
KLAKA
KLAKA
I SAID, I CAN'T SEE WHERE I'M GOING!
KLAKA
KLAKA
IS OKAY. RANMA JUST LOOK AT SHAMPOO.
KSHHHH
WHAT ?!
OF ALL TIMES FOR HIM TO BE...
HMPH.
EVEN WITHOUT RANMA...
KLINCH

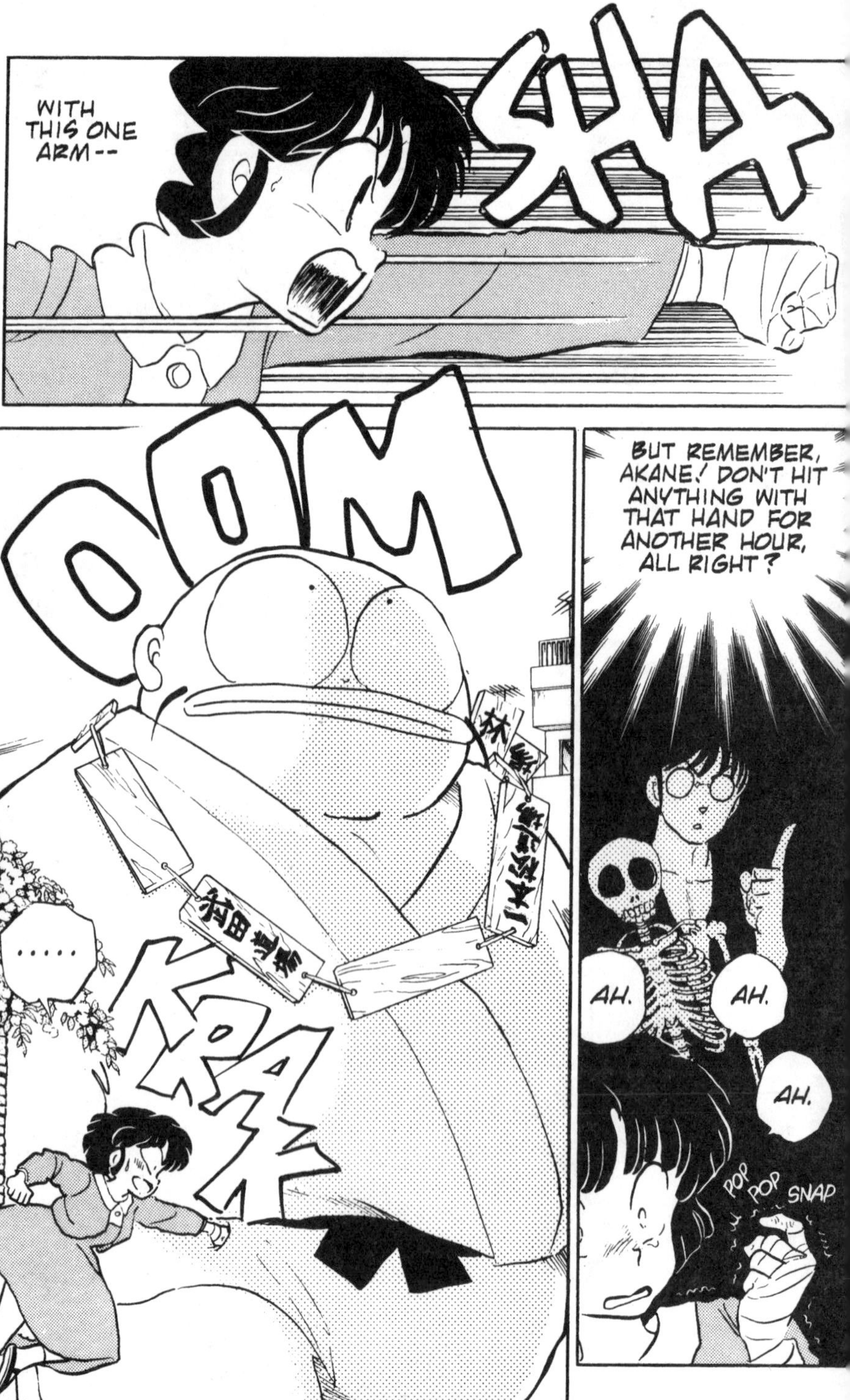
WITH THIS ONE ARM--
SHA
DOM
.....
KRA
BUT REMEMBER, AKANE! DON'T HIT ANYTHING WITH THAT HAND FOR ANOTHER HOUR, ALL RIGHT?
AH.
AH.
AH.
POP POP SNAP

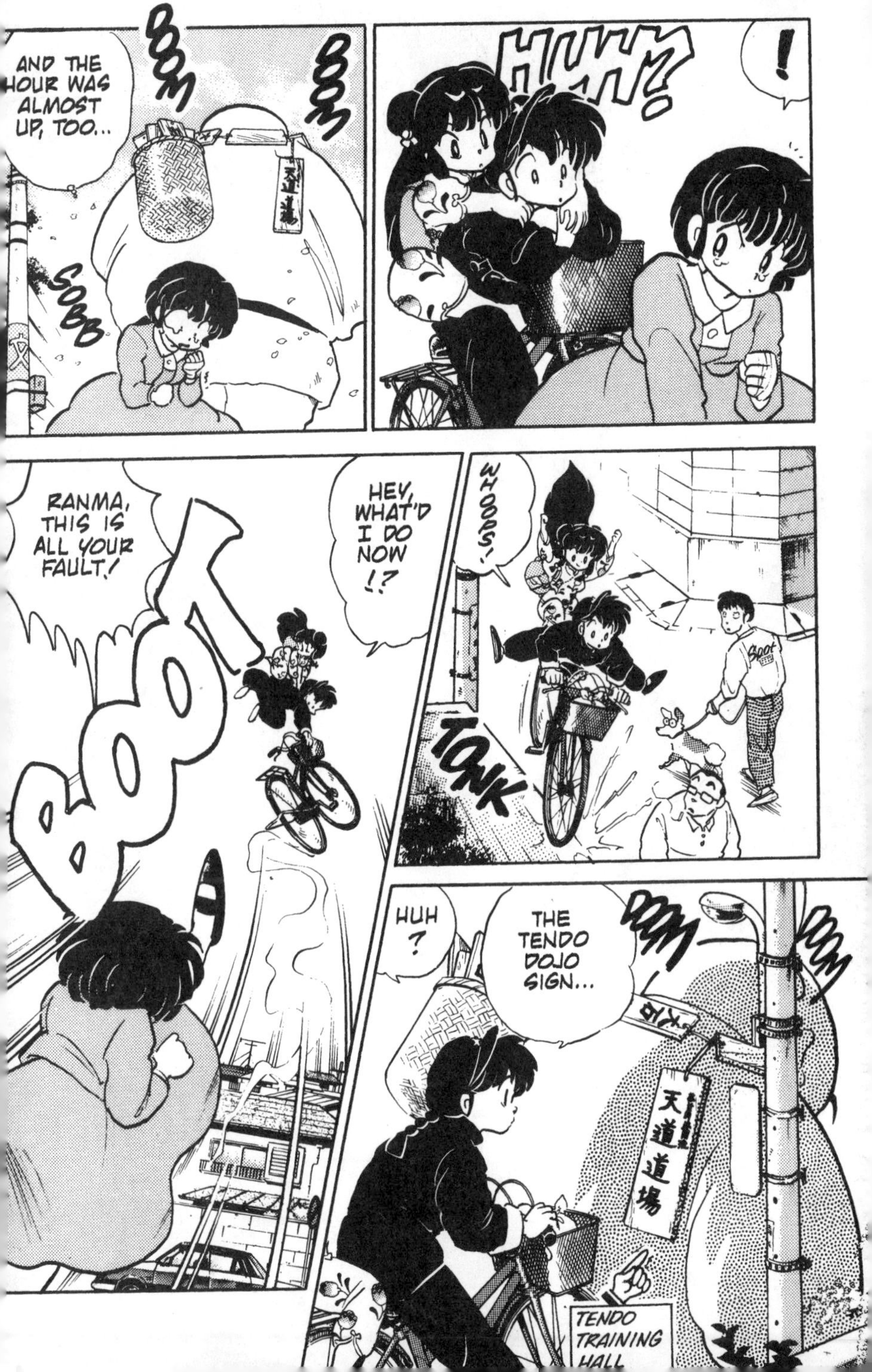

AND THE HOUR WAS ALMOST UP, TOO...
ZOOM
ZOOM
SOBB
HUH?
!
RANMA, THIS IS ALL YOUR FAULT!
BOOT
HEY, WHAT'D I DO NOW !?
WHOOPS!
TONK
HUH ?
THE TENDO DOJO SIGN...
DOOM
DOOM
天道道場
TENDO TRAINING HALL

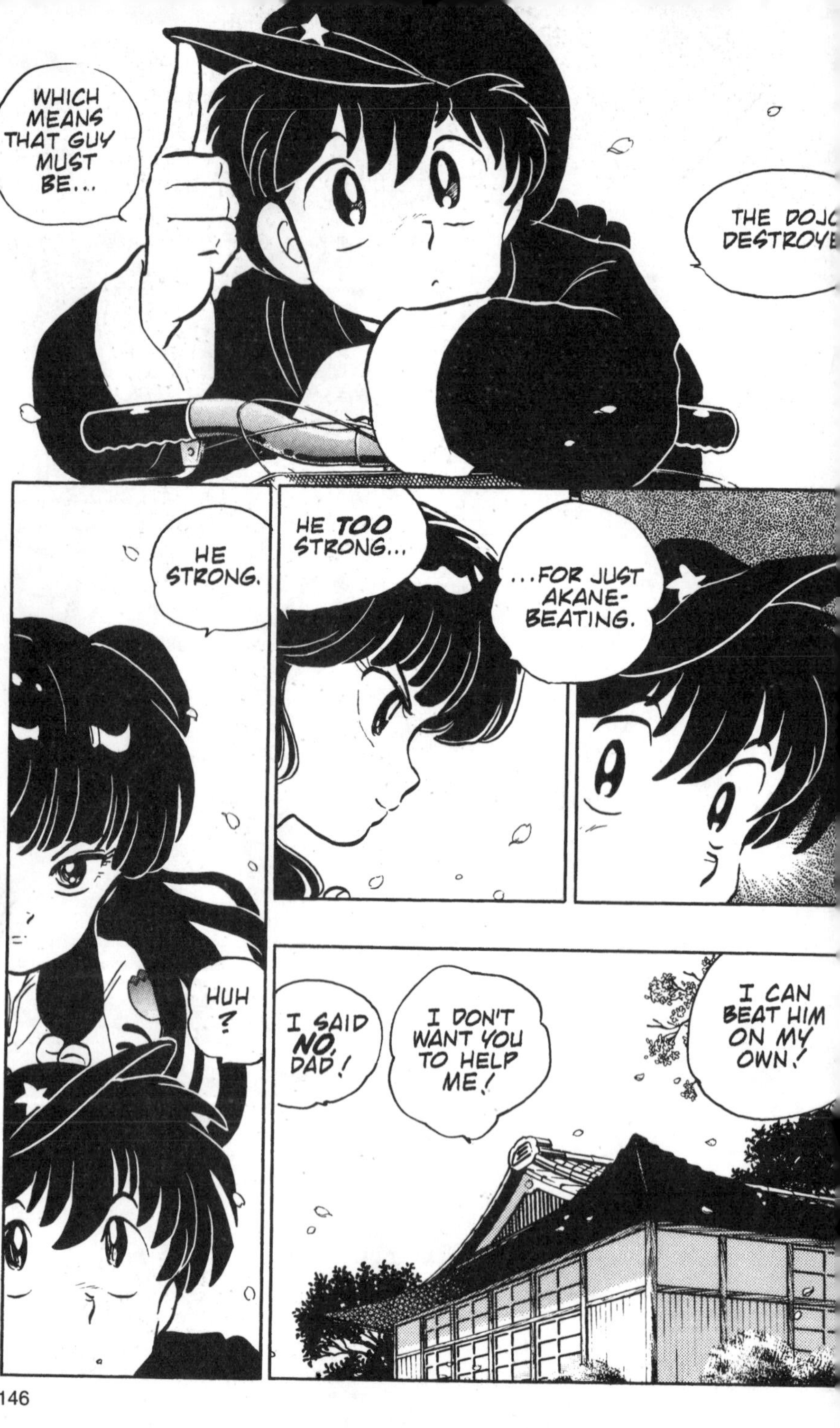
WHICH MEANS THAT GUY MUST BE...
THE DOJ DESTROYE
HE STRONG.
HUH ?
HE **TOO** STRONG...
...FOR JUST AKANE-BEATING.
I SAID **NO**, DAD!
I DON'T WANT YOU TO HELP ME!
I CAN BEAT HIM ON MY OWN!

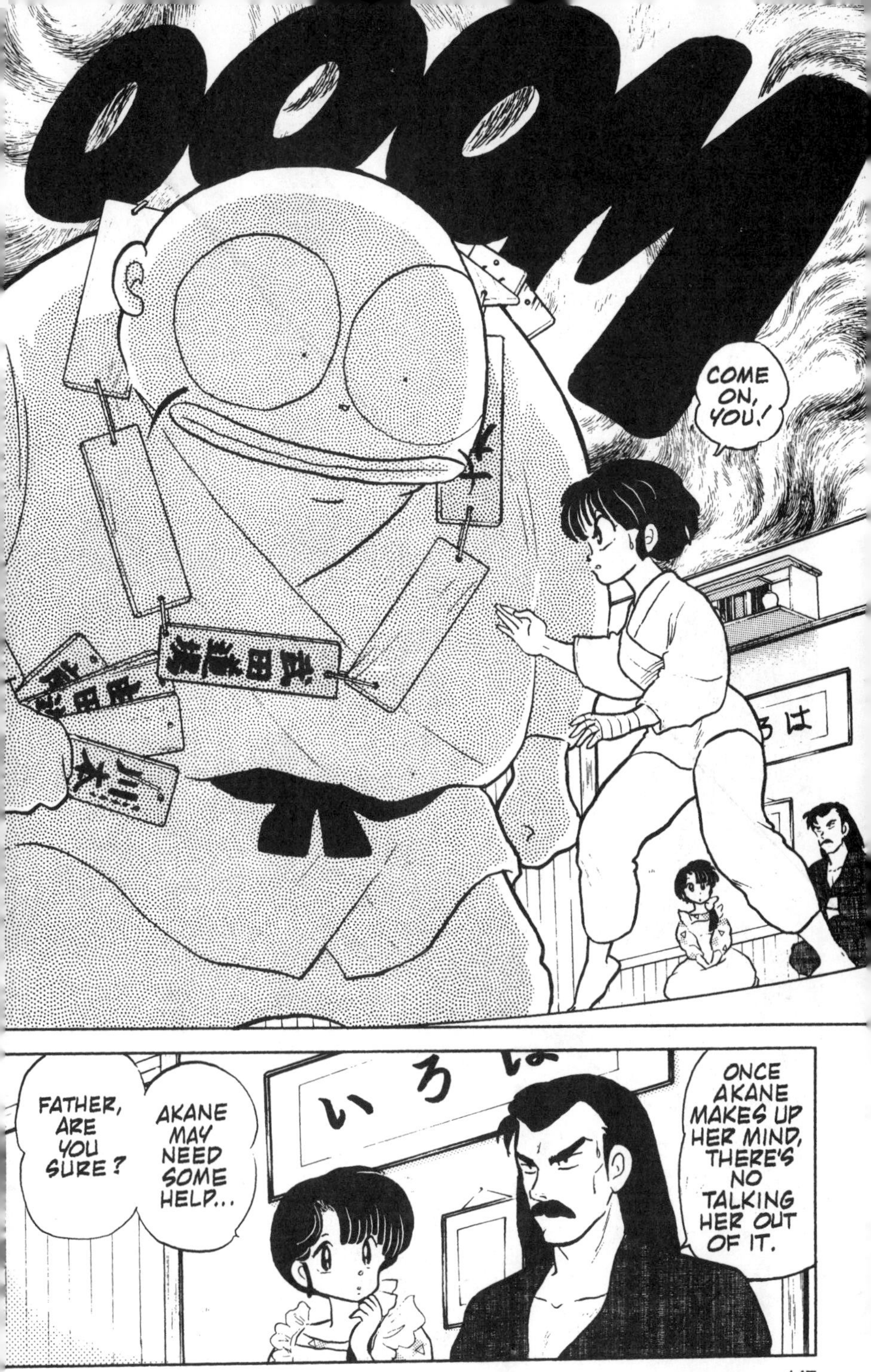
COME ON, YOU!
FATHER, ARE YOU SURE?
AKANE MAY NEED SOME HELP...
いろは
ONCE AKANE MAKES UP HER MIND, THERE'S NO TALKING HER OUT OF IT.

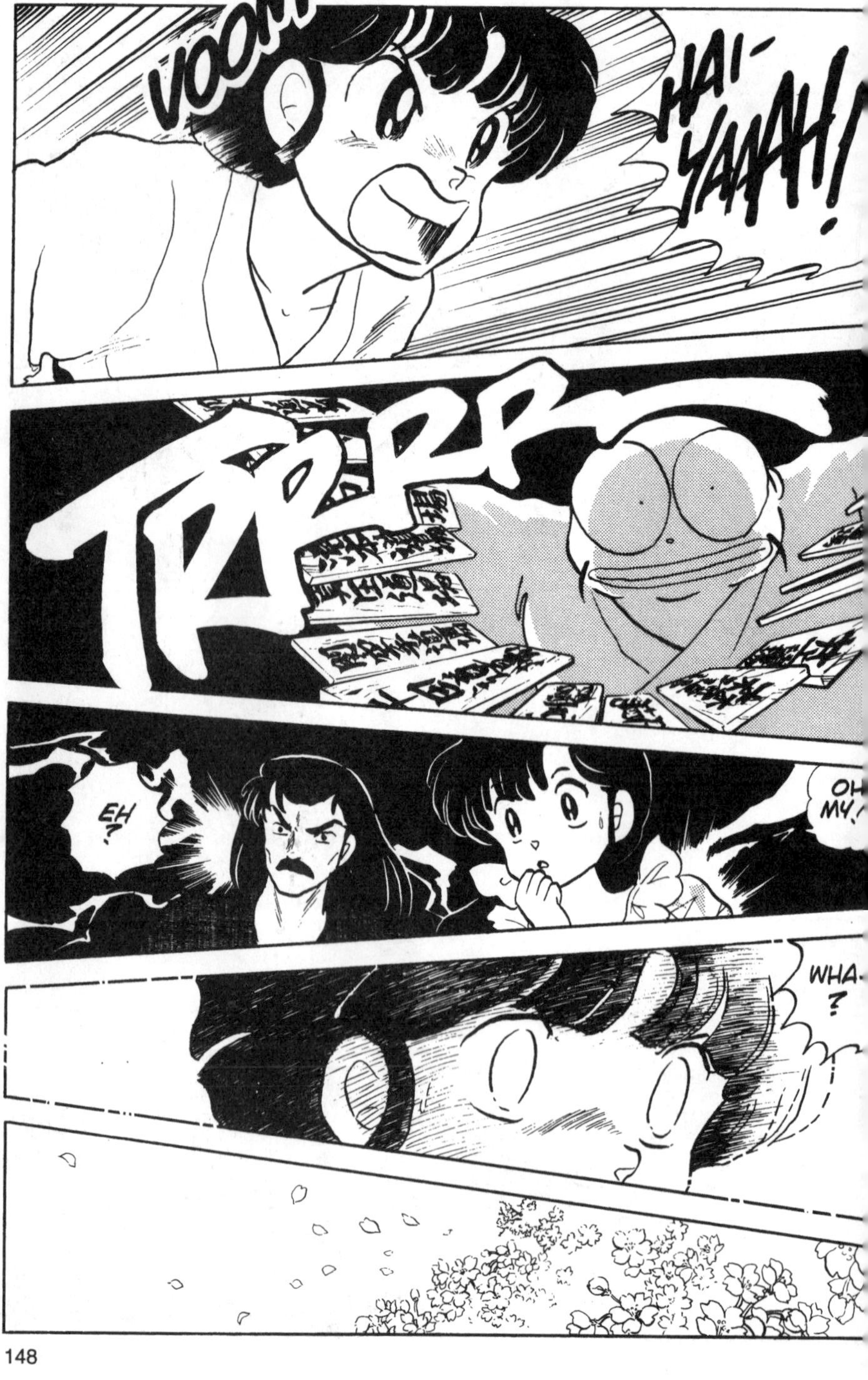
VOOM
HAI-YAAAH!
TRRR
EH?
OH MY!
WHA-?

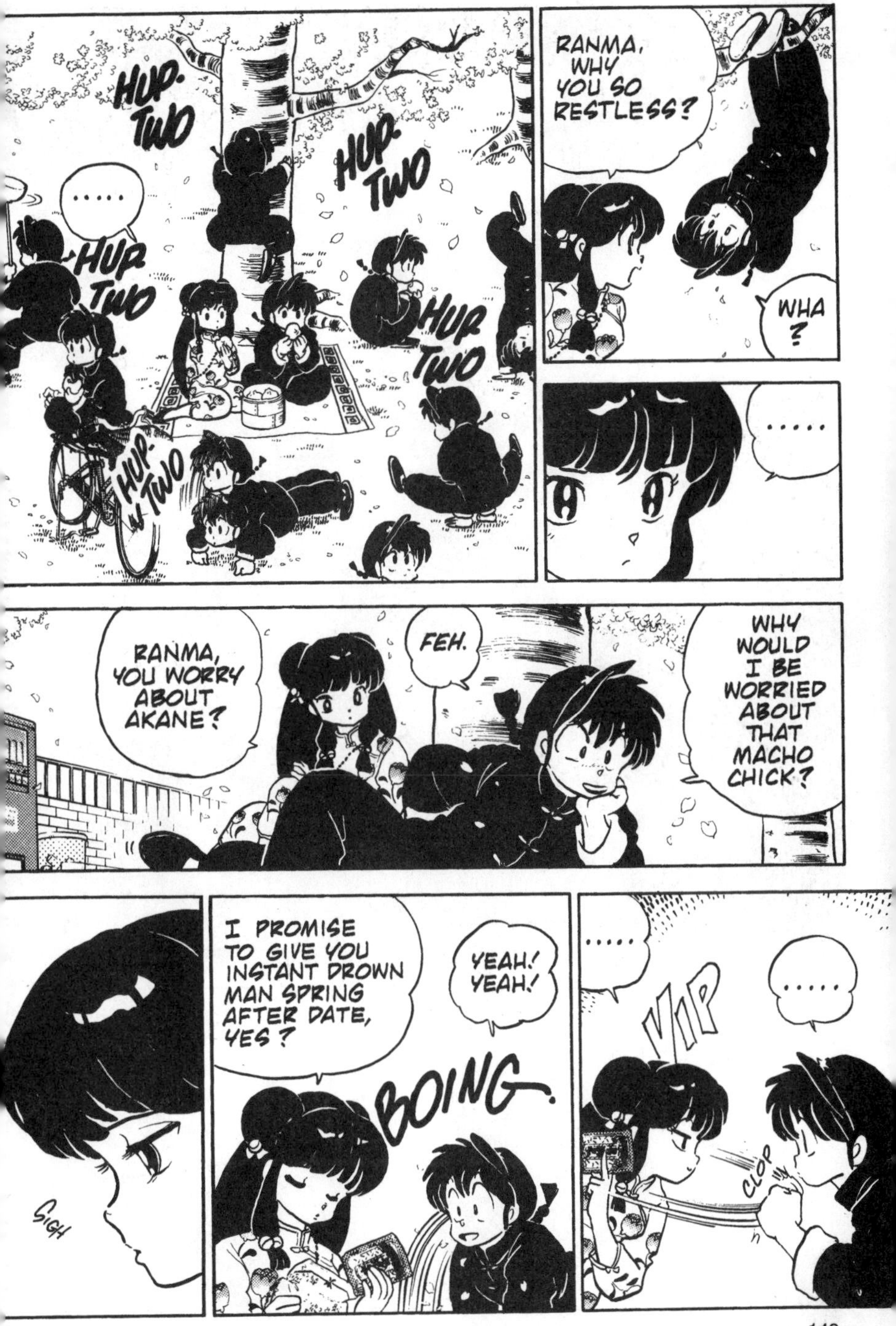
HUP. TWO
HUP. TWO
......
HUP TWO
HUP TWO
HUP. TWO
RANMA, WHY YOU SO RESTLESS?
WHA?
......
RANMA, YOU WORRY ABOUT AKANE?
FEH.
WHY WOULD I BE WORRIED ABOUT THAT MACHO CHICK?
SIGH
I PROMISE TO GIVE YOU INSTANT DROWN MAN SPRING AFTER DATE, YES?
YEAH! YEAH!
BOING
......
......
YIP
CLOP

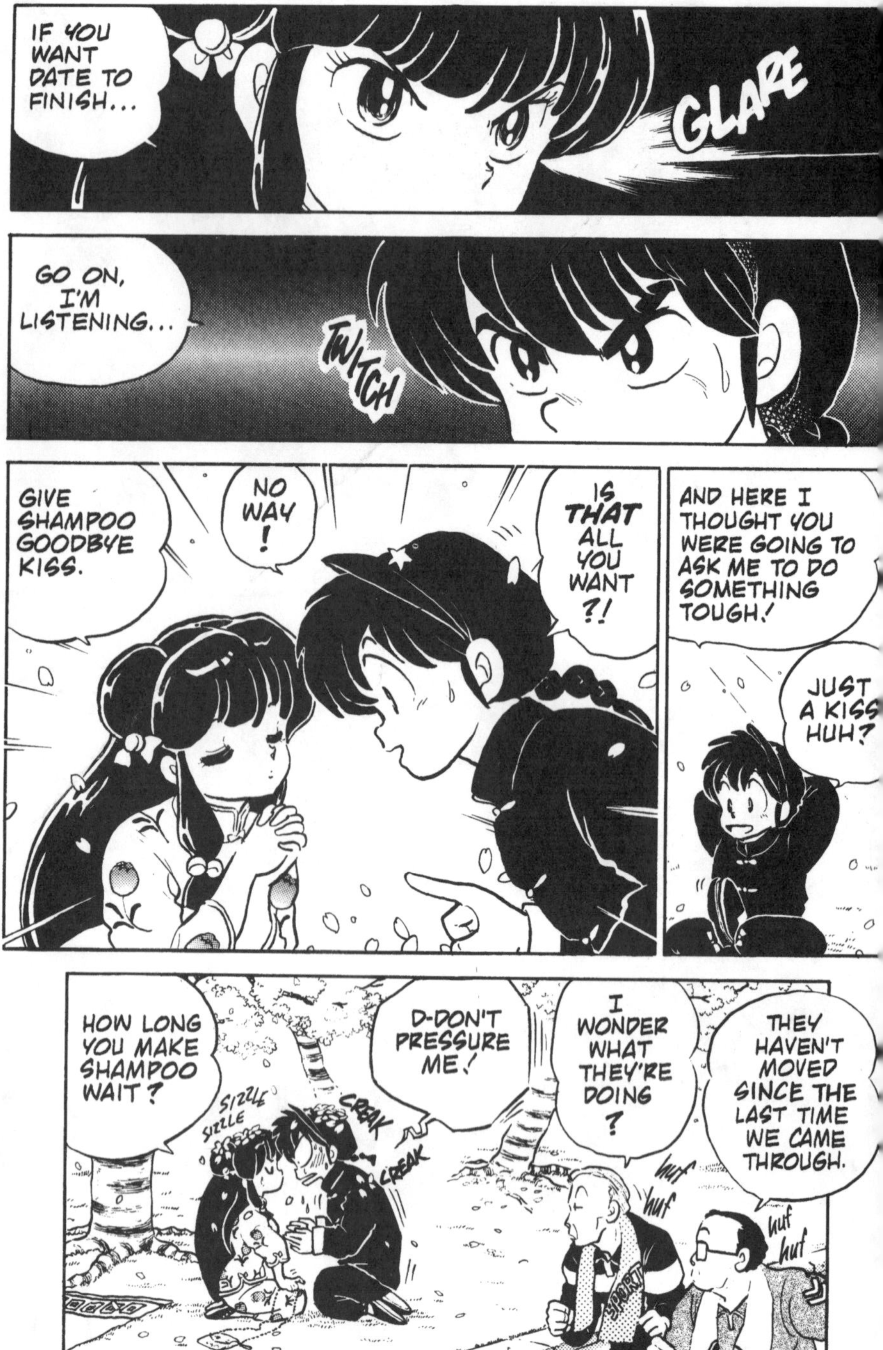
IF YOU WANT DATE TO FINISH...
GLARE
GO ON, I'M LISTENING...
TWITCH
GIVE SHAMPOO GOODBYE KISS.
NO WAY!
IS THAT ALL YOU WANT?!
AND HERE I THOUGHT YOU WERE GOING TO ASK ME TO DO SOMETHING TOUGH!
JUST A KISS HUH?
HOW LONG YOU MAKE SHAMPOO WAIT?
SIZZLE SIZZLE
CREAK CREAK
D-DON'T PRESSURE ME!
I WONDER WHAT THEY'RE DOING?
THEY HAVEN'T MOVED SINCE THE LAST TIME WE CAME THROUGH.
huf huf
huf huf

Part 10
THE DESTROYER STRIKES

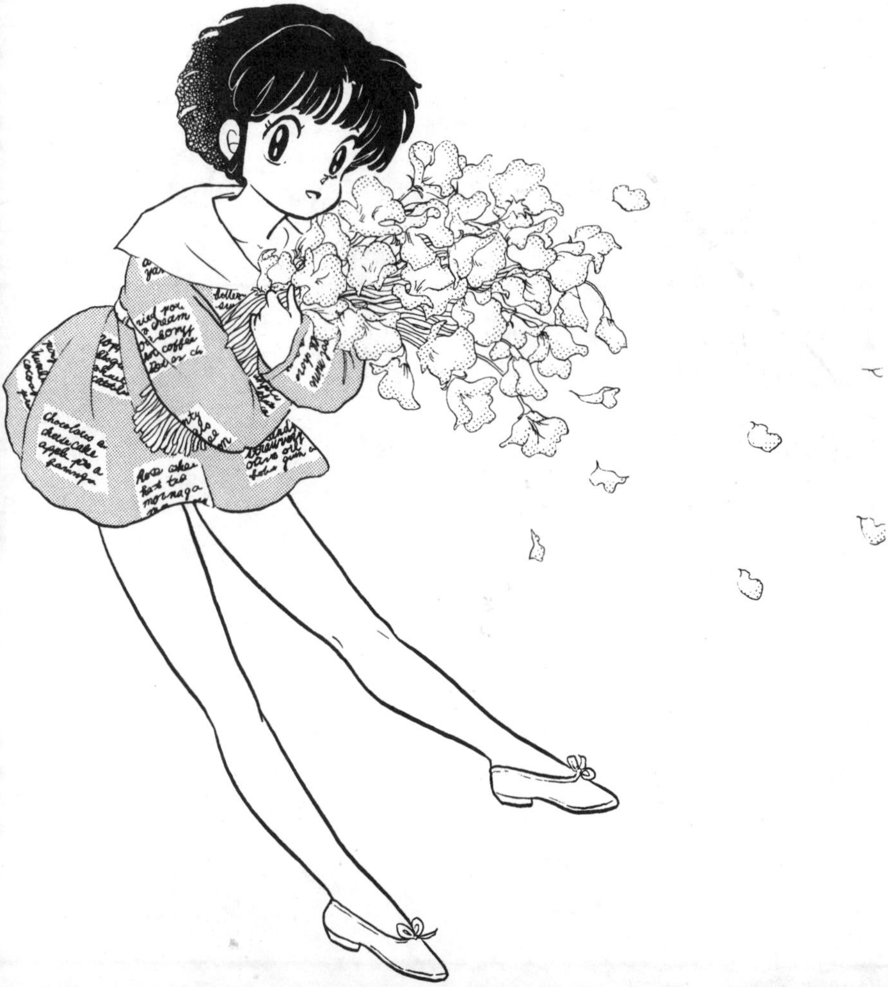

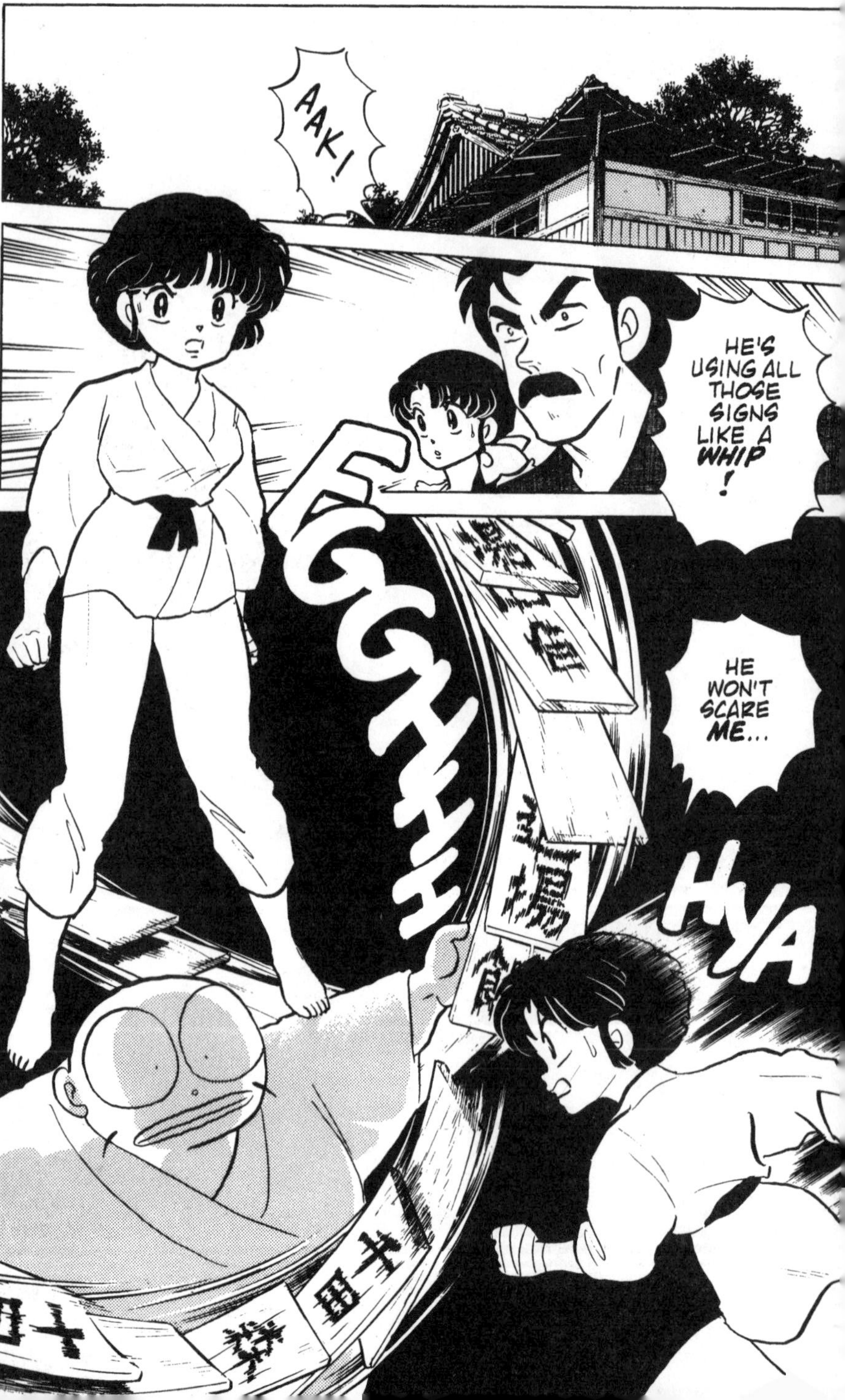
AAK!
HE'S USING ALL THOSE SIGNS LIKE A WHIP!
EGGHHH
HE WON'T SCARE ME...
HYA

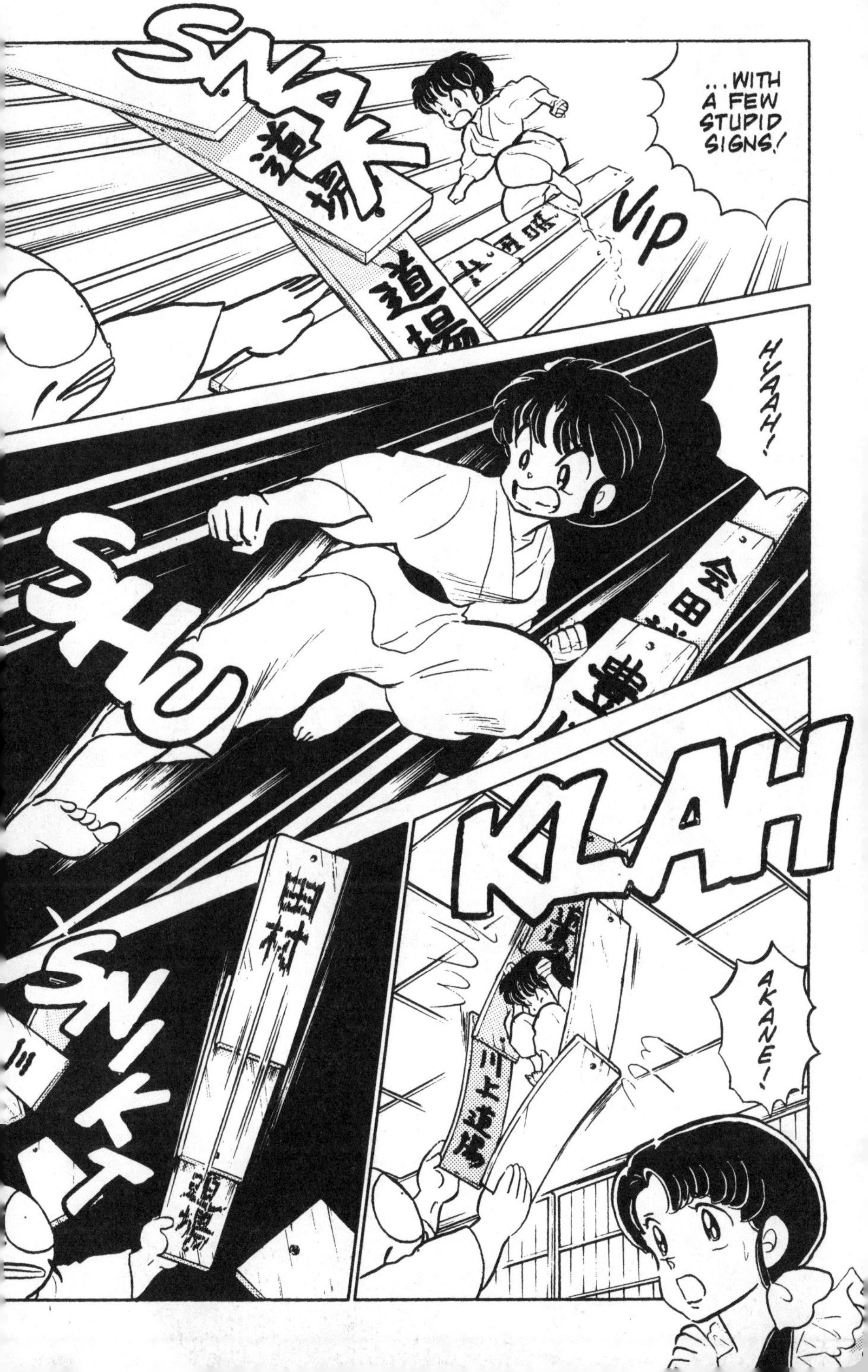

SNA
道場
道場
...WITH A FEW STUPID SIGNS!
VIP
SHU
HYAAH!
会田
SNIKT
KLAH
川上道場
AKANE!

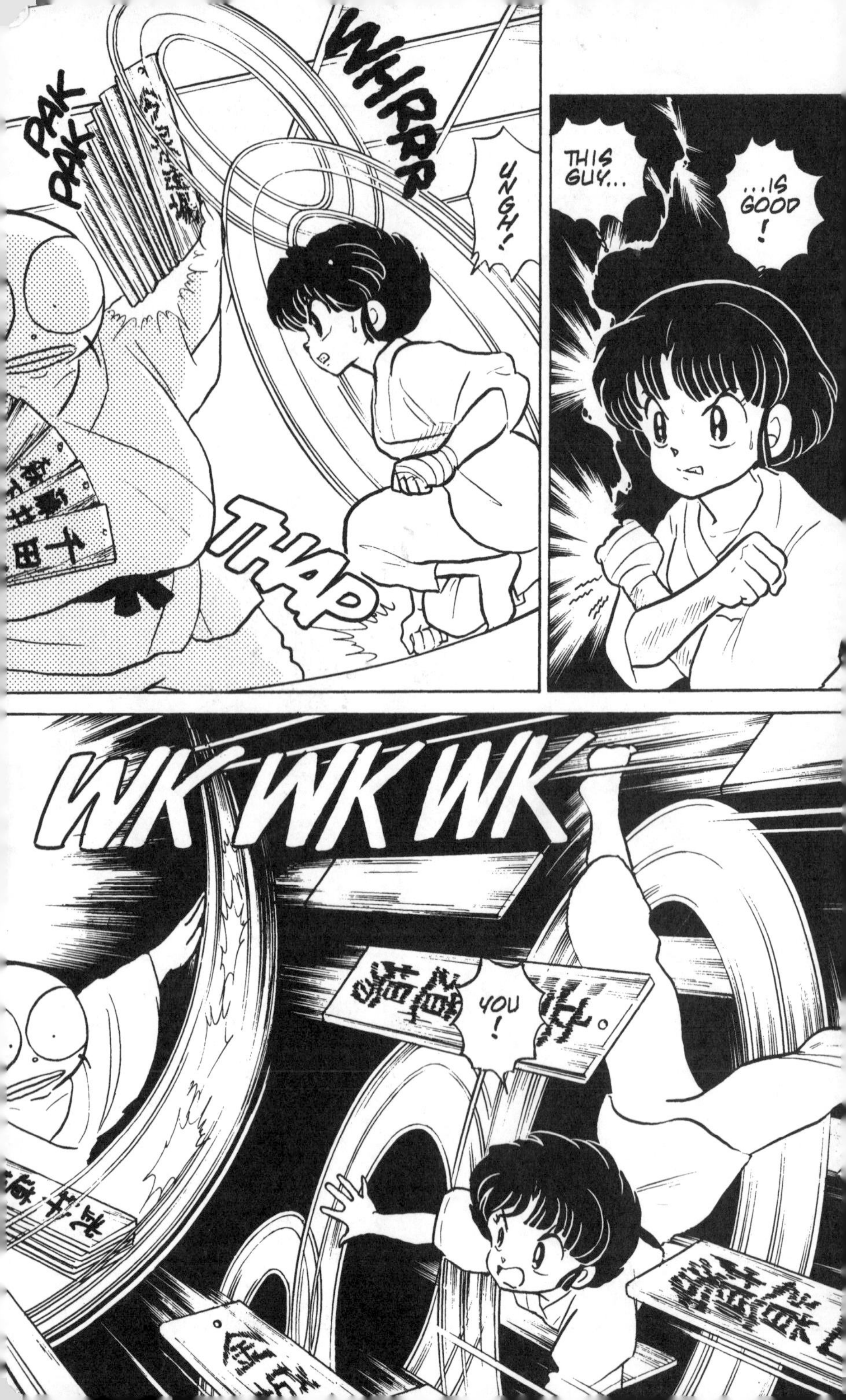
PAK PAK
WHIRRR
UNGH!
THAP
THIS GUY...
...IS GOOD!
WK WK WK
YOU!

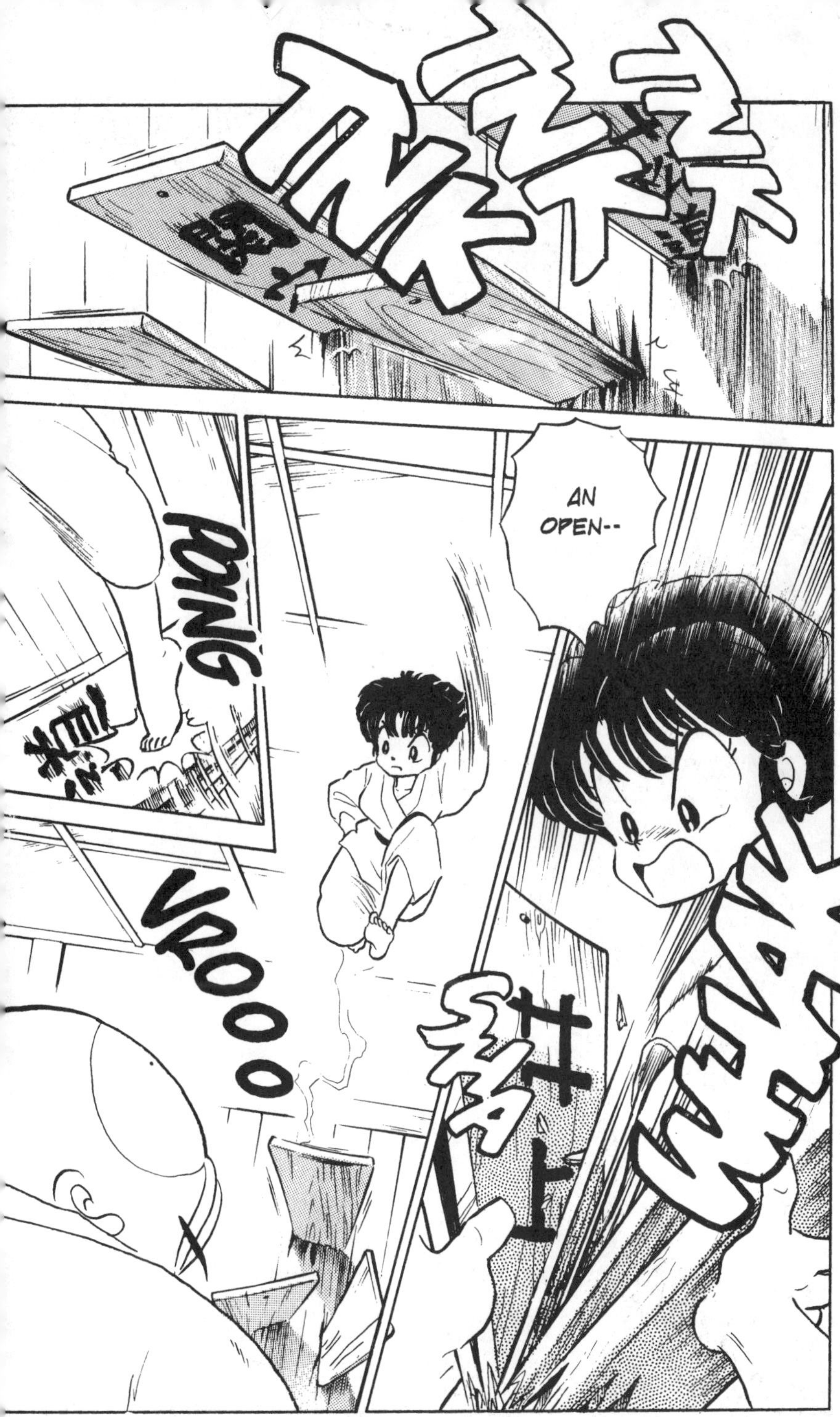
POING
VROOOO
AN OPEN--
WHAK

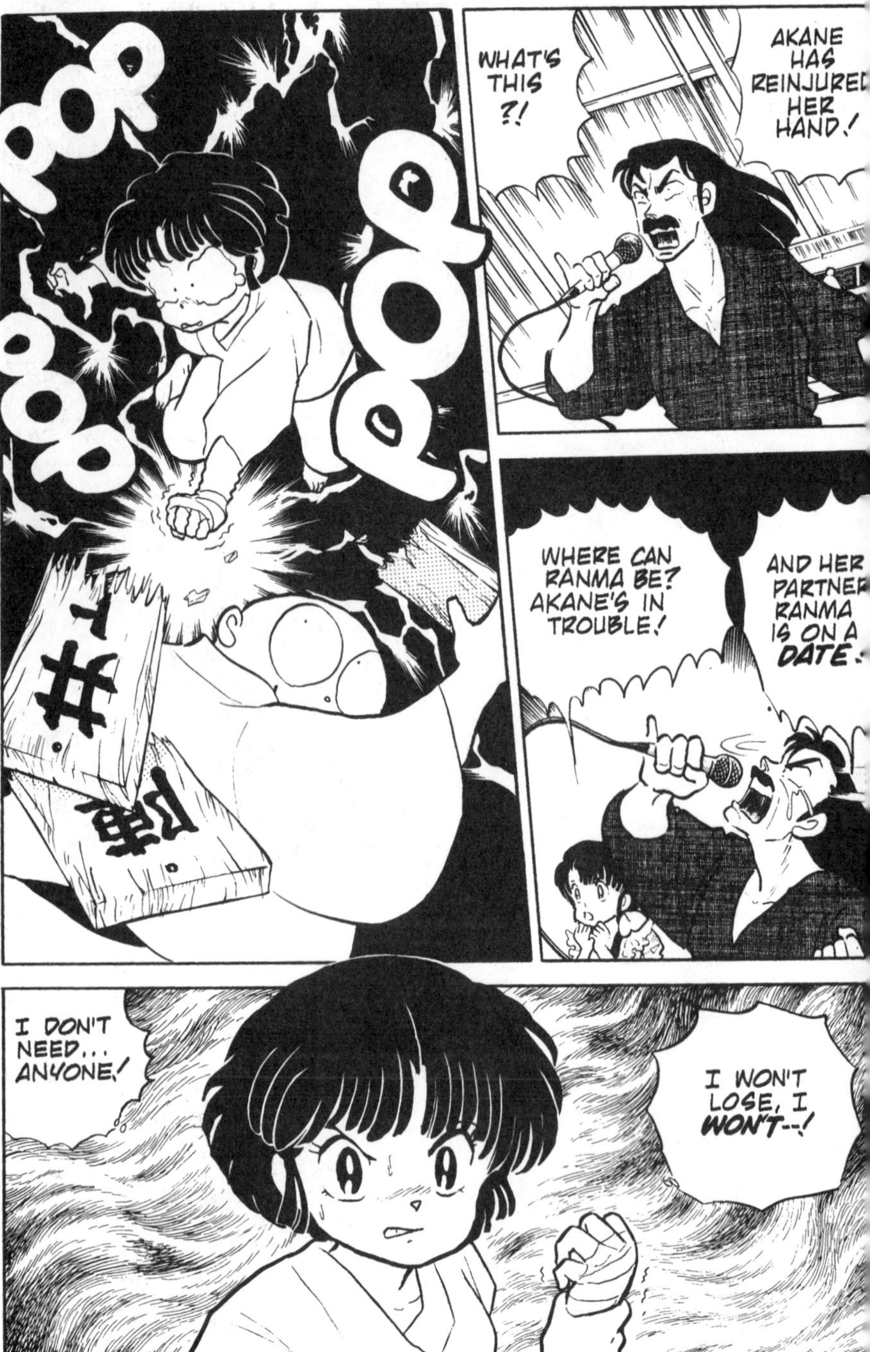
POP
POP
POP
WHAT'S THIS ?!
AKANE HAS REINJURED HER HAND!
WHERE CAN RANMA BE? AKANE'S IN TROUBLE!
AND HER PARTNER RANMA IS ON A DATE...
I DON'T NEED... ANYONE!
I WON'T LOSE, I WON'T--!

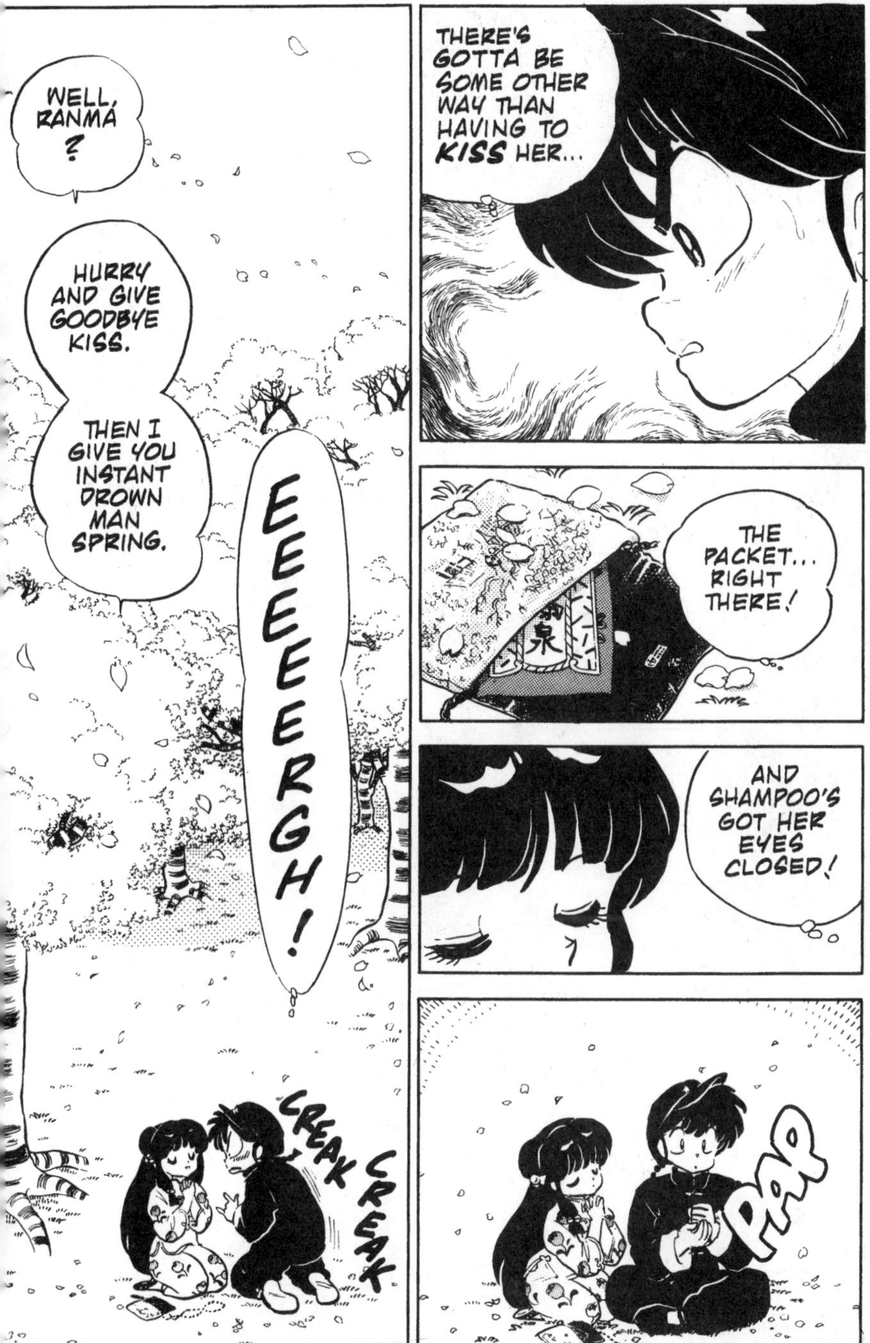
WELL, RANMA?
HURRY AND GIVE GOODBYE KISS.
THEN I GIVE YOU INSTANT DROWN MAN SPRING.
EEEEERGH!
CREAK CREAK
THERE'S GOTTA BE SOME OTHER WAY THAN HAVING TO **KISS** HER...
THE PACKET... RIGHT THERE!
AND SHAMPOO'S GOT HER EYES CLOSED!
PAP

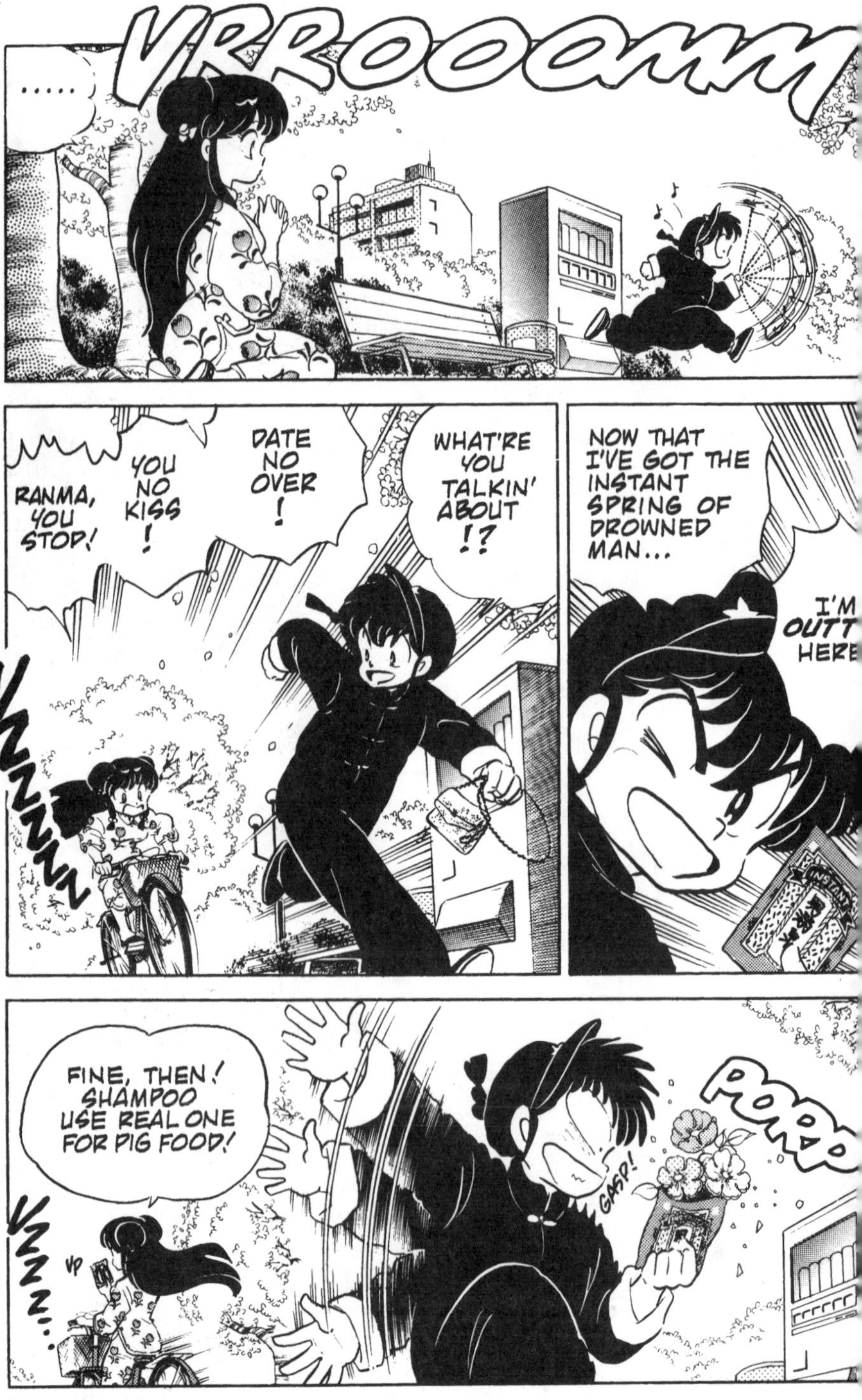
.....
VRROOMM
RANMA, YOU STOP!
YOU NO KISS!
DATE NO OVER!
WHAT'RE YOU TALKIN' ABOUT!?
VNNNNNN
NOW THAT I'VE GOT THE INSTANT SPRING OF DROWNED MAN...
I'M OUTT HERE
INSTANT
FINE, THEN! SHAMPOO USE REAL ONE FOR PIG FOOD!
VNNNN...
VP
GASP!
POPP

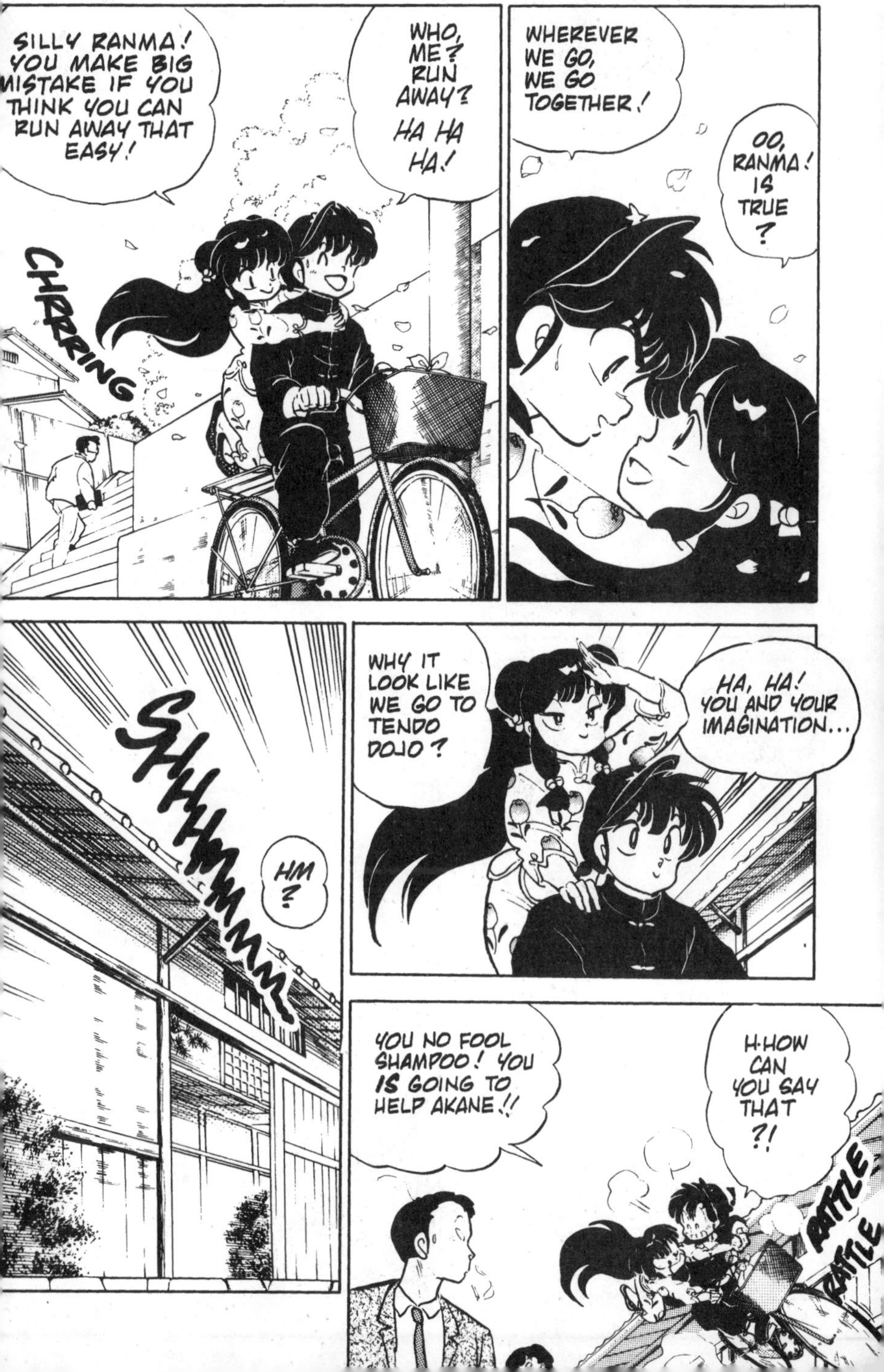
SILLY RANMA! YOU MAKE BIG MISTAKE IF YOU THINK YOU CAN RUN AWAY THAT EASY!
WHO, ME? RUN AWAY?
HA HA HA!
CHRRRING
WHEREVER WE GO, WE GO TOGETHER!
OO, RANMA! IS TRUE?
SHHHMMMM
HM?
WHY IT LOOK LIKE WE GO TO TENDO DOJO?
HA, HA! YOU AND YOUR IMAGINATION...
YOU NO FOOL SHAMPOO! YOU **IS** GOING TO HELP AKANE!!
H-HOW CAN YOU SAY THAT?!
RATTLE RATTLE

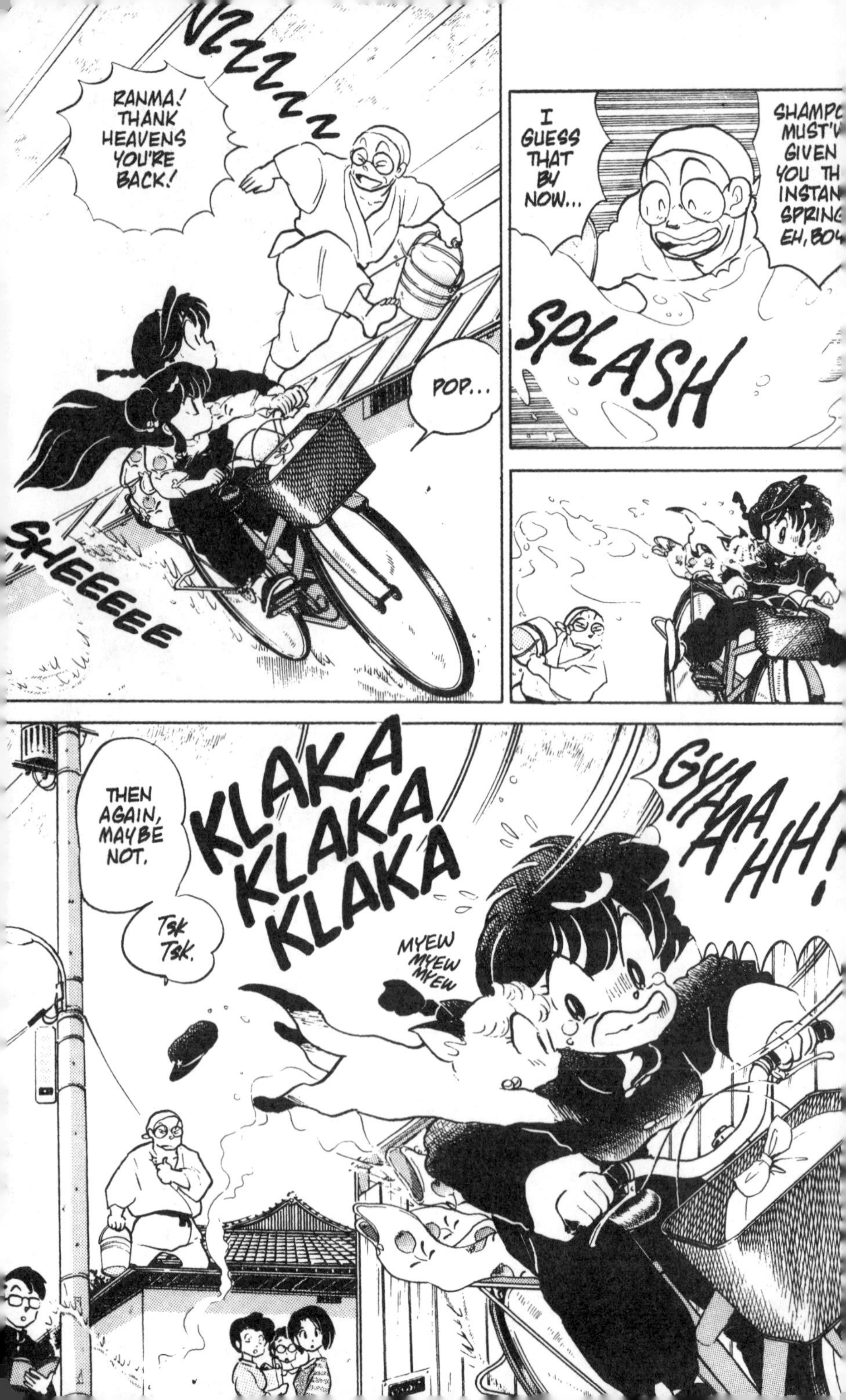

VZZZZZ
RANMA! THANK HEAVENS YOU'RE BACK!
POP...
SHEEEEEE
I GUESS THAT BY NOW...
SHAMPO MUST'V GIVEN YOU TH INSTAN SPRING EH, BOY
SPLASH
THEN AGAIN, MAYBE NOT.
TSK TSK.
KLAKA KLAKA KLAKA
MYEW MYEW MYEW
GYAAAAHH!

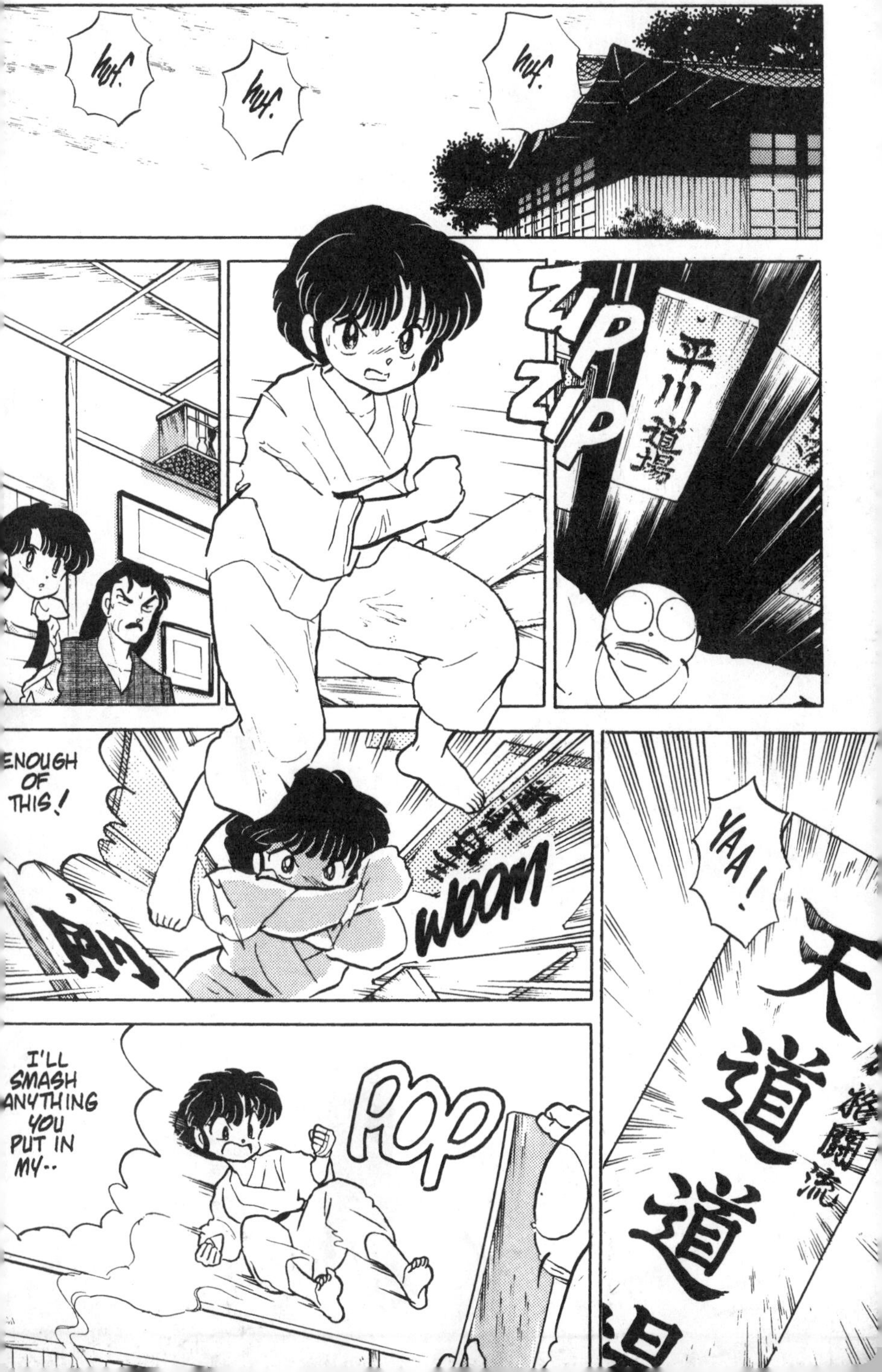

huf.
huf.
huf.
ZIP ZIP
平川道場
ENOUGH OF THIS!
WOOM
I'LL SMASH ANYTHING YOU PUT IN MY--
POP
YAA!
天道
格闘流

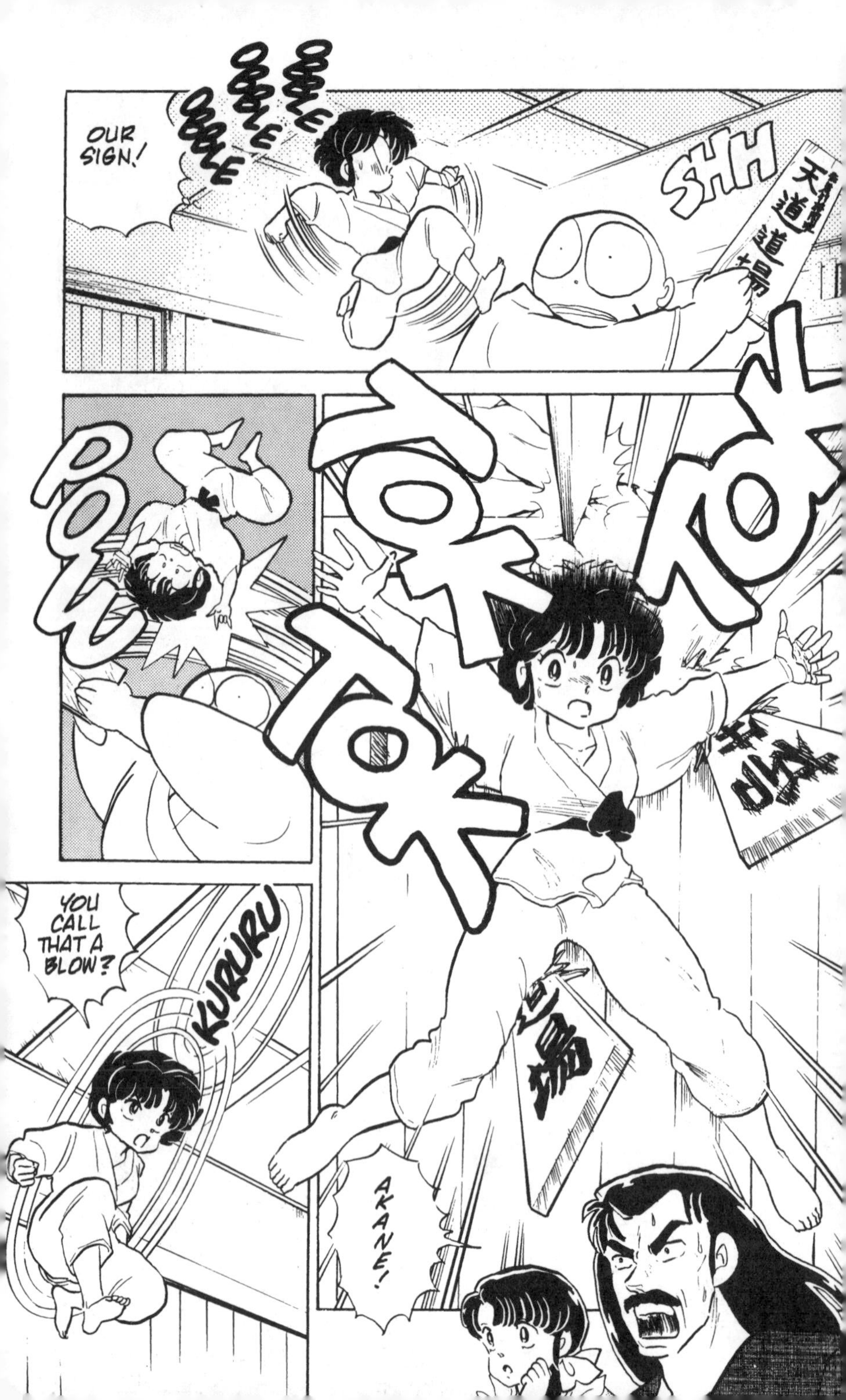
OOGLE
OOGLE
OOGLE
OUR SIGN!
SHH
POW
YOU CALL THAT A BLOW?
KURURU
TOK TOK
AKANE!

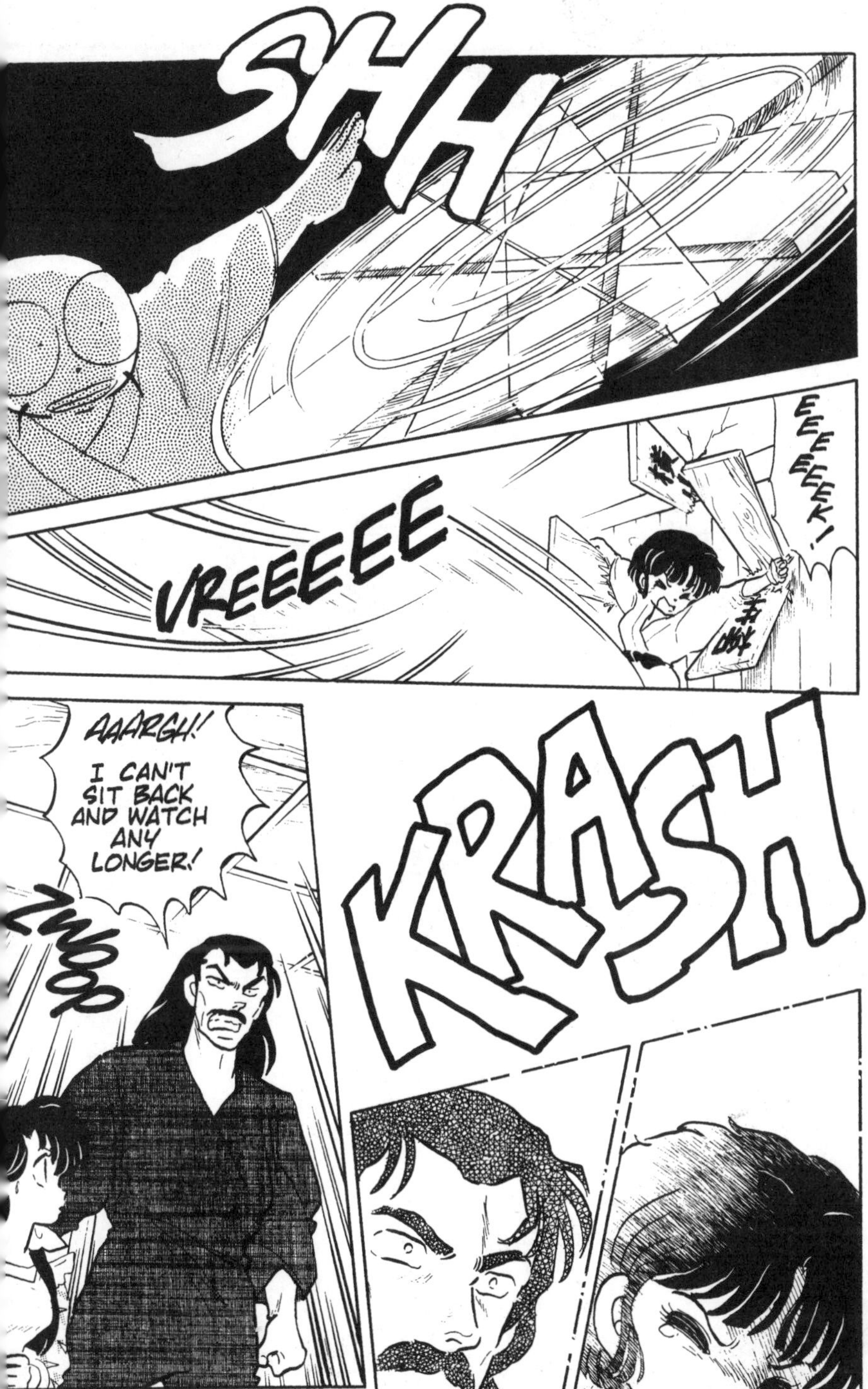
SHH
VREEEEE
EEEEEEK!
AAARGH!
I CAN'T SIT BACK AND WATCH ANY LONGER!
ZWOOP
KRASH

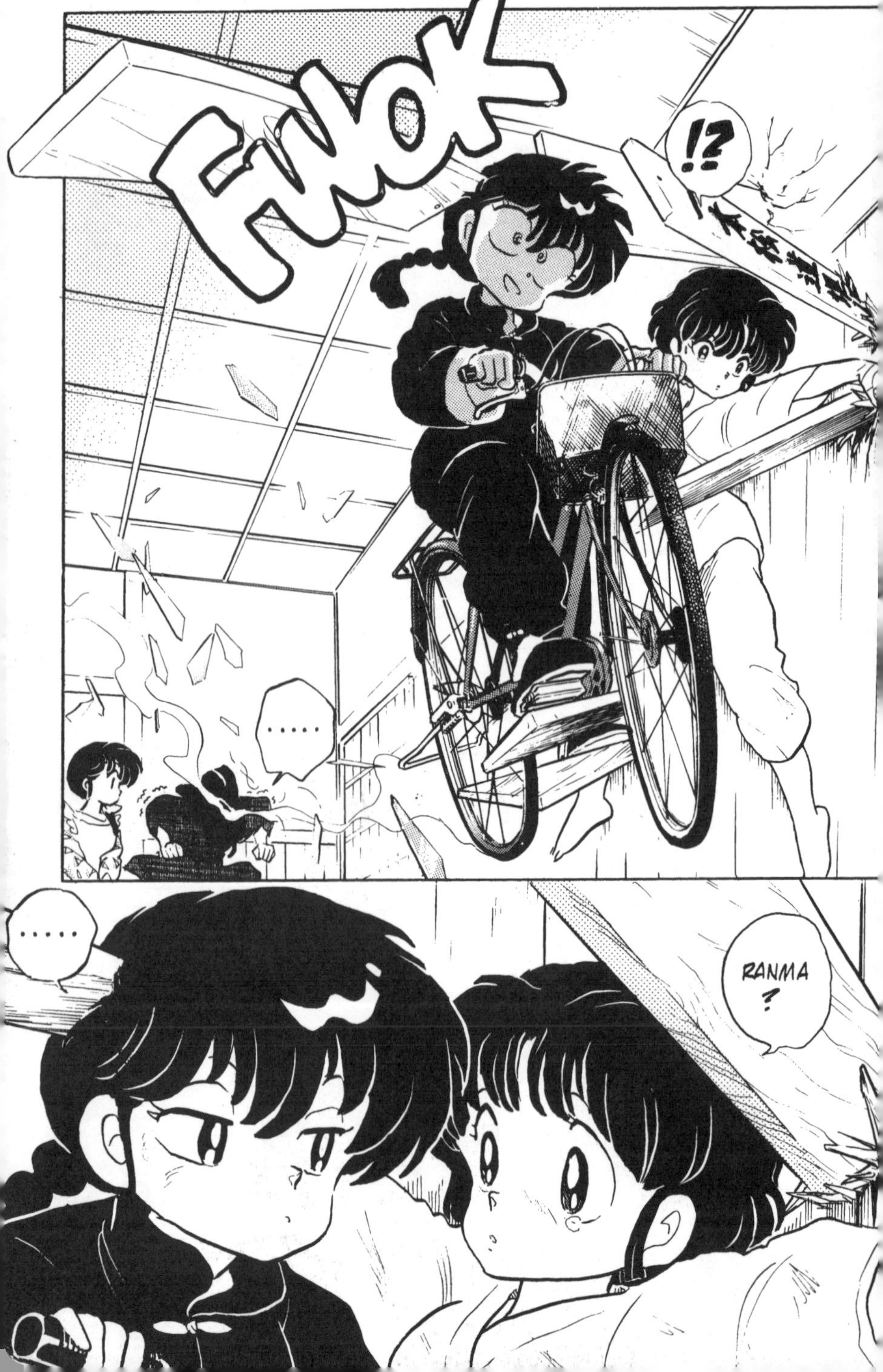
FWOK
!?
.....
......
RANMA
?

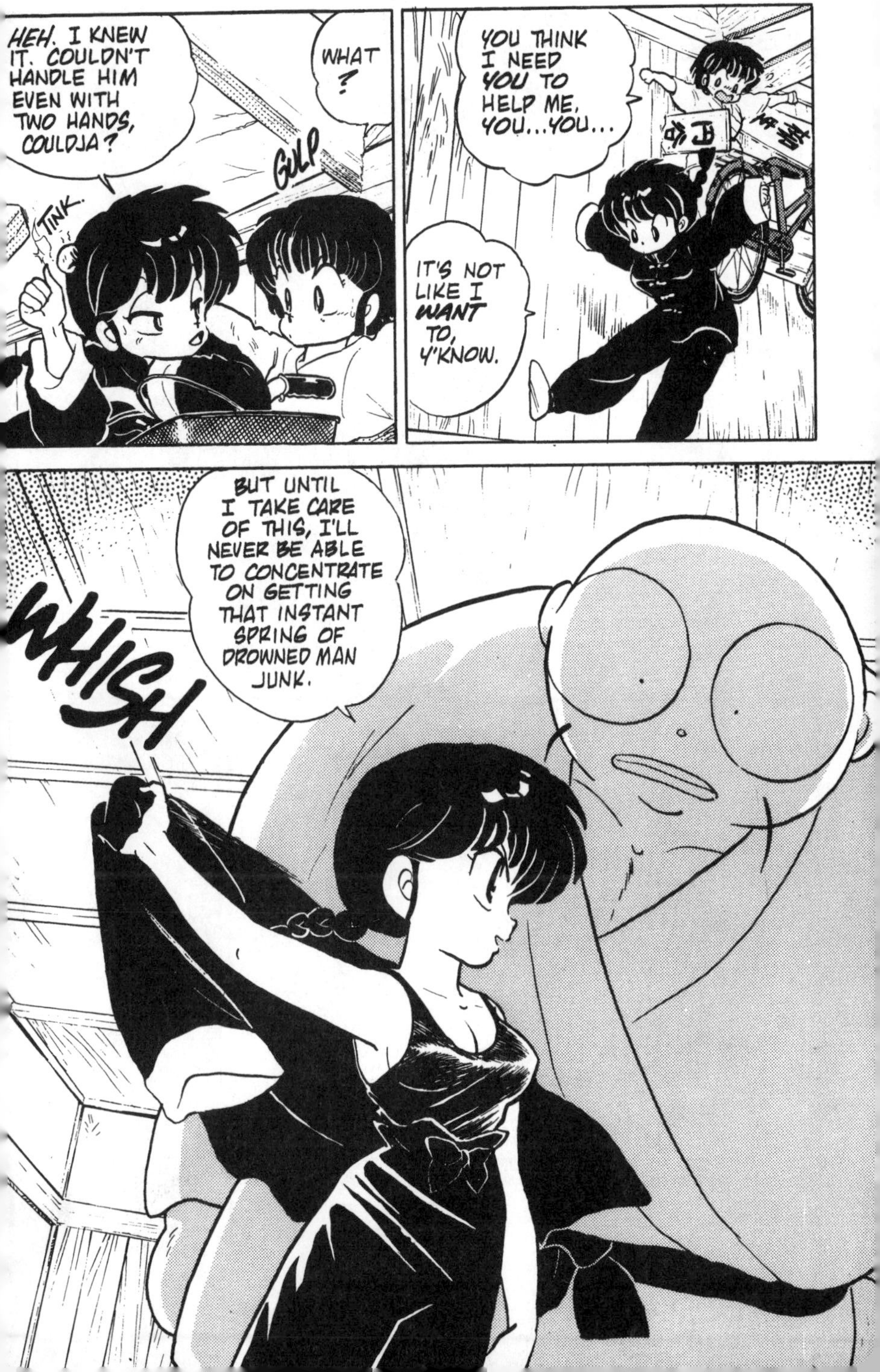
HEH. I KNEW IT. COULDN'T HANDLE HIM EVEN WITH TWO HANDS, COULDJA?
WHAT?
GULP
TINK.
YOU THINK I NEED YOU TO HELP ME, YOU...YOU...
IT'S NOT LIKE I WANT TO, Y'KNOW.
WHISH
BUT UNTIL I TAKE CARE OF THIS, I'LL NEVER BE ABLE TO CONCENTRATE ON GETTING THAT INSTANT SPRING OF DROWNED MAN JUNK.

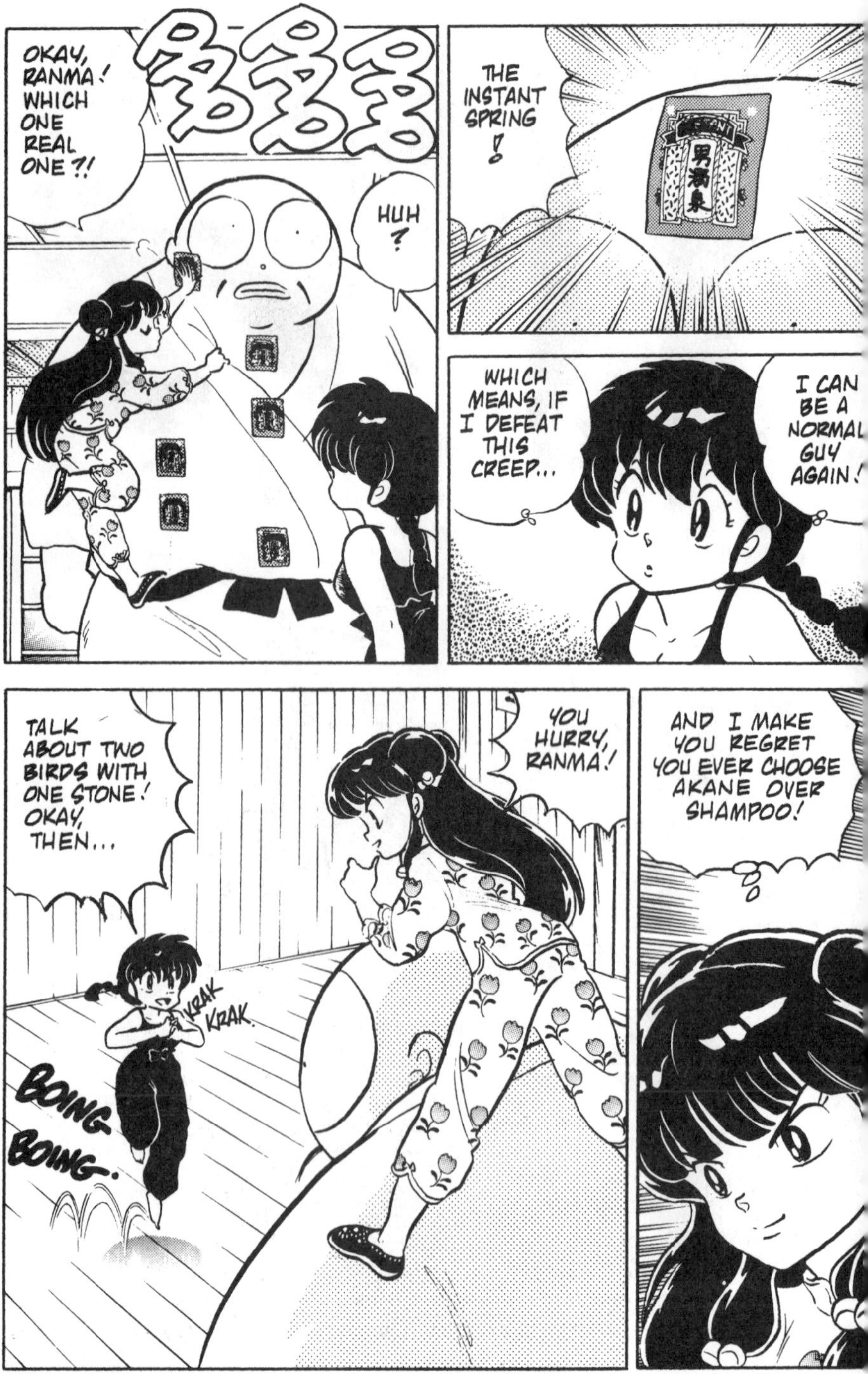
OKAY, RANMA! WHICH ONE REAL ONE?!
HUH?
THE INSTANT SPRING!
WHICH MEANS, IF I DEFEAT THIS CREEP...
I CAN BE A NORMAL GUY AGAIN!
TALK ABOUT TWO BIRDS WITH ONE STONE! OKAY, THEN...
KRAK KRAK
BOING BOING
YOU HURRY, RANMA!
AND I MAKE YOU REGRET YOU EVER CHOOSE AKANE OVER SHAMPOO!

PART 11

JUST ONE MORE KISS

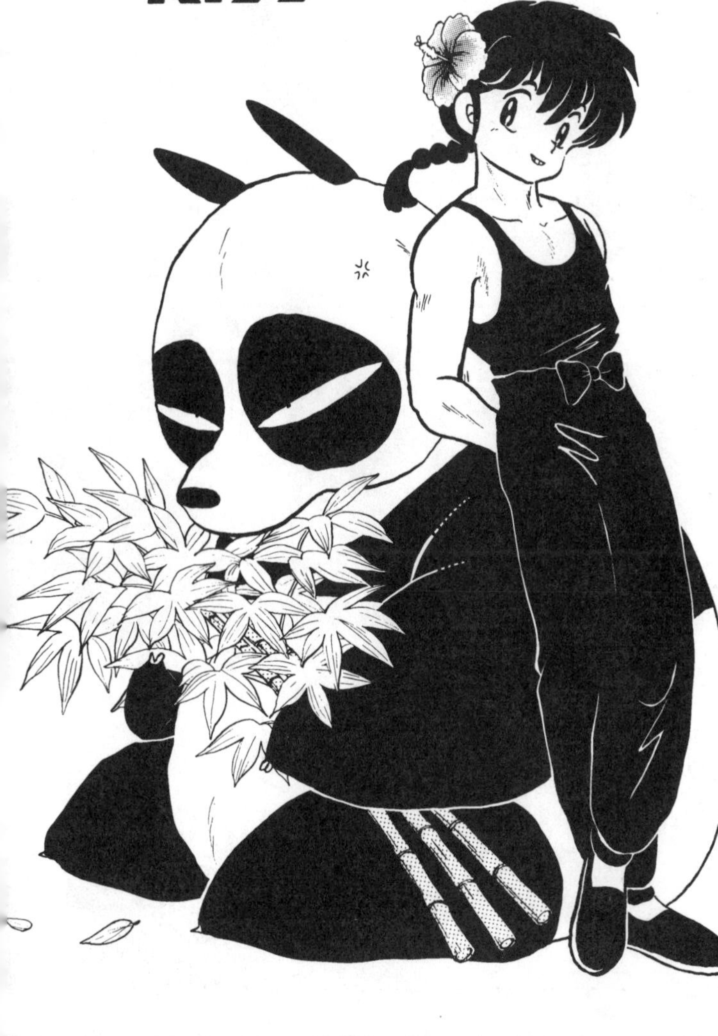

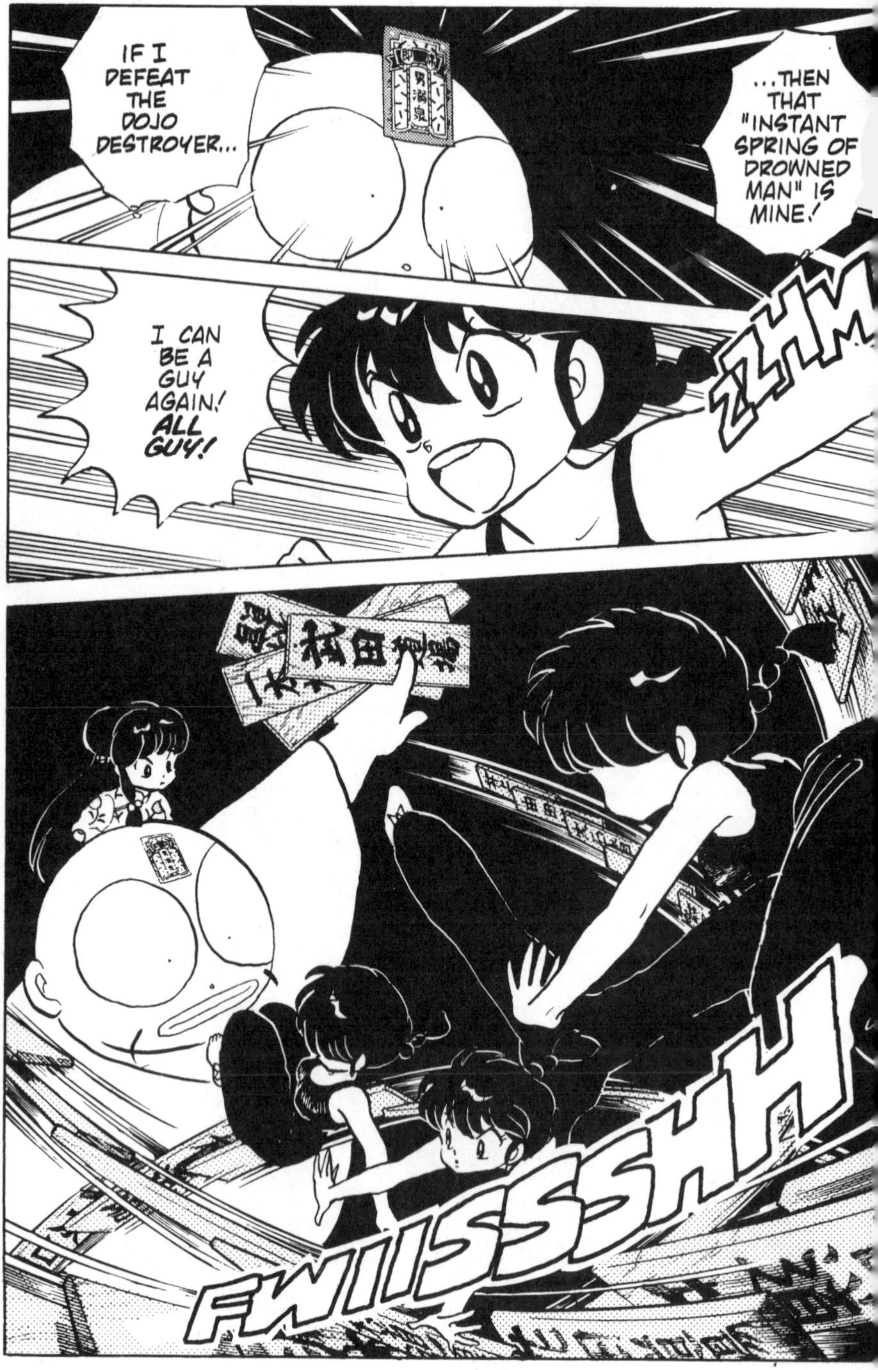

IF I DEFEAT THE DOJO DESTROYER...
...THEN THAT "INSTANT SPRING OF DROWNED MAN" IS MINE!
I CAN BE A GUY AGAIN! ALL GUY!
ZHM
FWIISSSHH

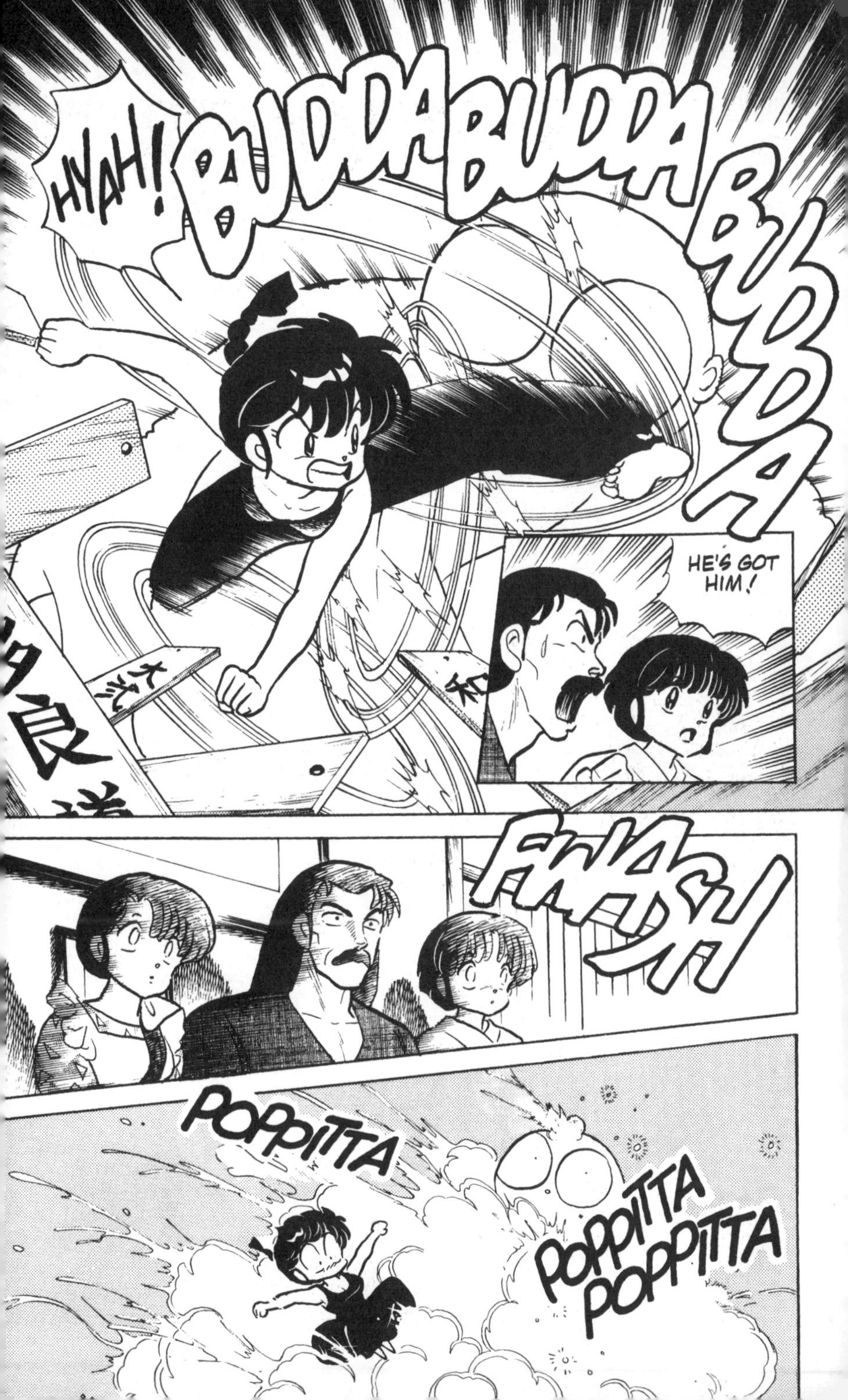
HYAH!
BUDDABUDDABUDDA
HE'S GOT HIM!
FWASH
POPPITTA
POPPITTA
POPPITTA

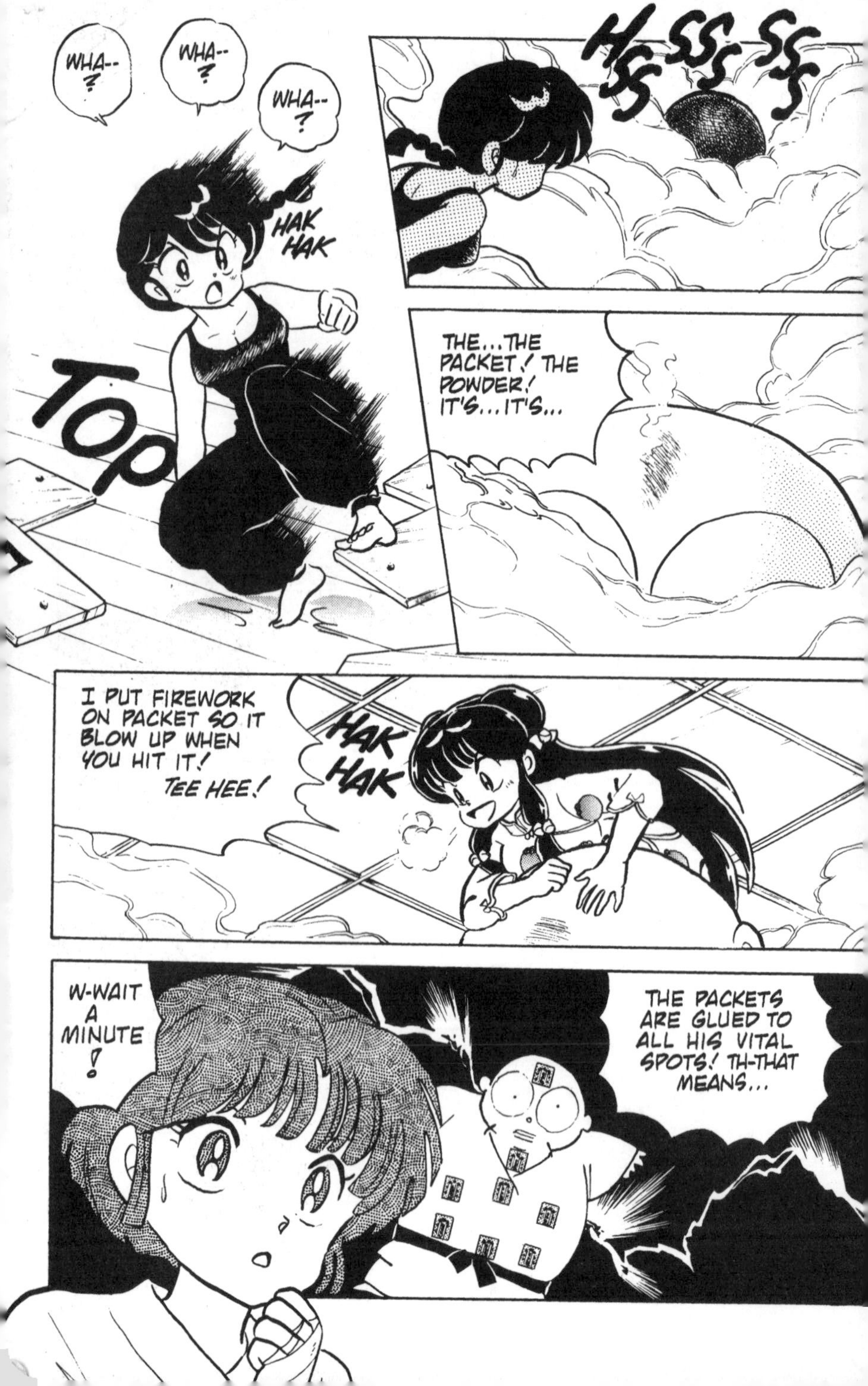
WHA--?
WHA--?
WHA--?
HAK HAK
TOP
HSSS SSS
THE...THE PACKET! THE POWDER! IT'S...IT'S...
I PUT FIREWORK ON PACKET SO IT BLOW UP WHEN YOU HIT IT! TEE HEE!
HAK HAK
W-WAIT A MINUTE!
THE PACKETS ARE GLUED TO ALL HIS VITAL SPOTS! TH-THAT MEANS...

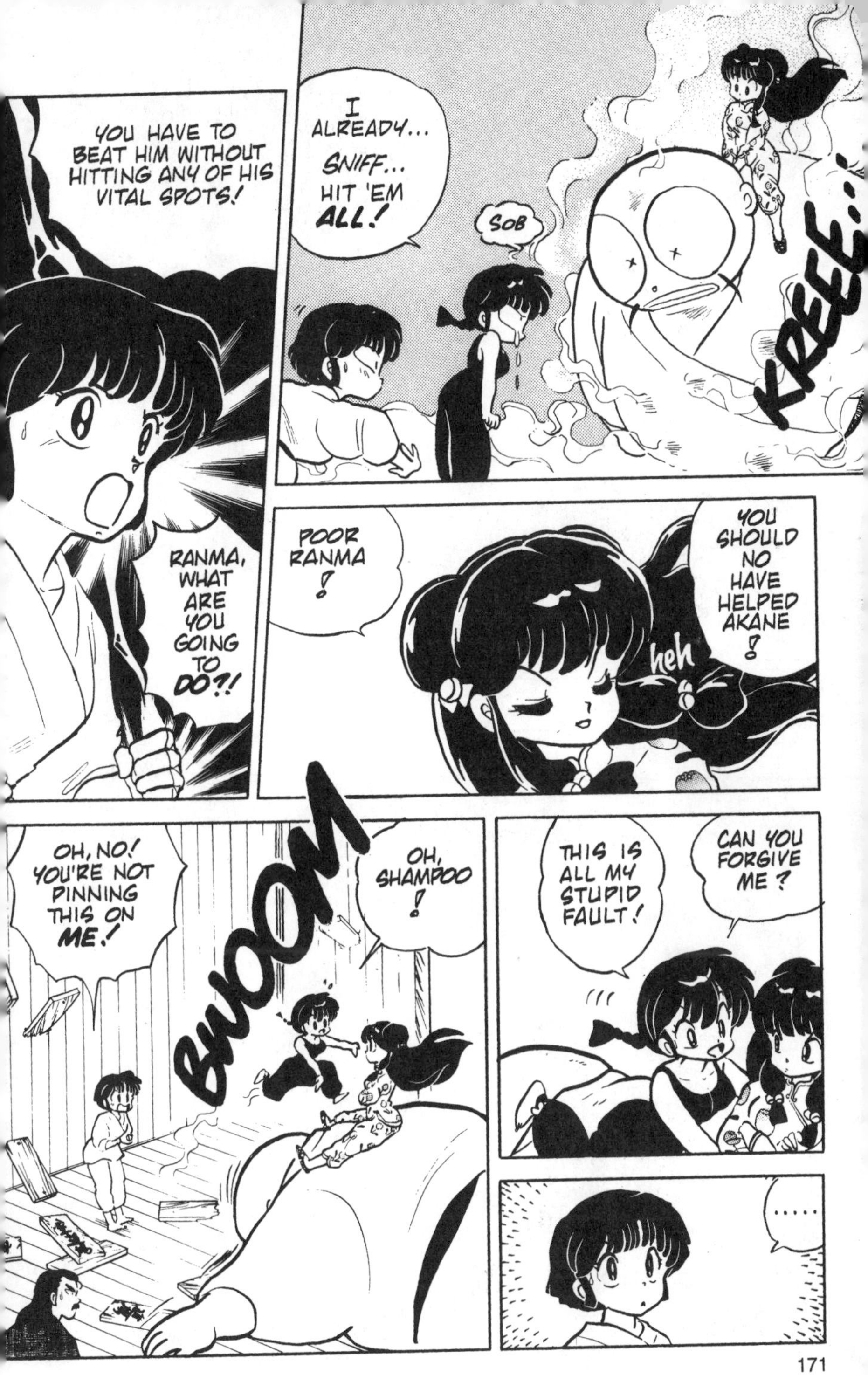

YOU HAVE TO BEAT HIM WITHOUT HITTING ANY OF HIS VITAL SPOTS!
RANMA, WHAT ARE YOU GOING TO DO?!
I ALREADY... SNIFF... HIT 'EM ALL!
SOB
KREEE...
POOR RANMA!
heh
YOU SHOULD NO HAVE HELPED AKANE!
OH, NO! YOU'RE NOT PINNING THIS ON ME!
BWOOM
OH, SHAMPOO!
THIS IS ALL MY STUPID FAULT!
CAN YOU FORGIVE ME?
......

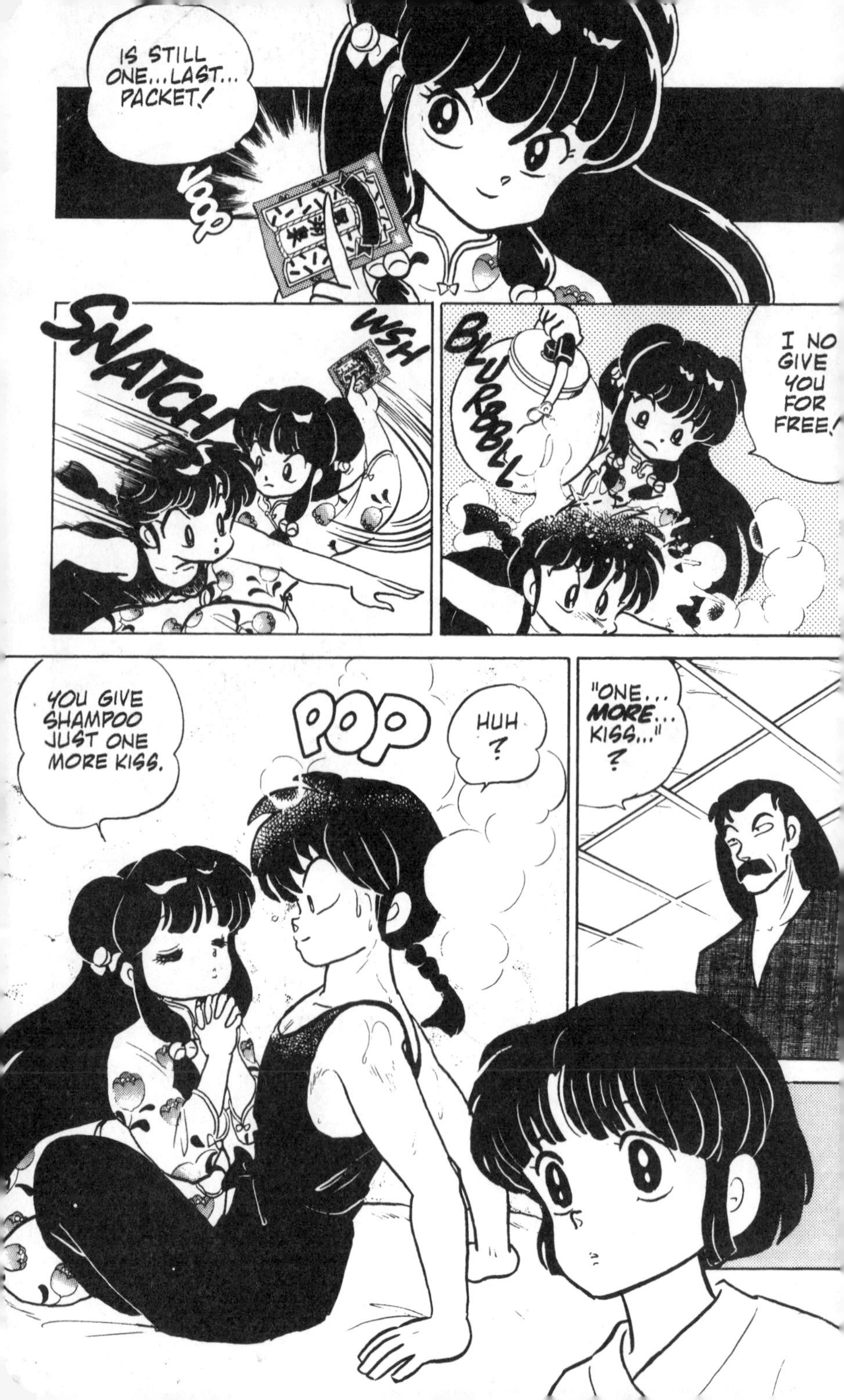
IS STILL ONE... LAST... PACKET!
VOOP
SNATCH
WSH
BLURBBLL
I NO GIVE YOU FOR FREE!
YOU GIVE SHAMPOO JUST ONE MORE KISS.
POP
HUH ?
"ONE... MORE... KISS..." ?

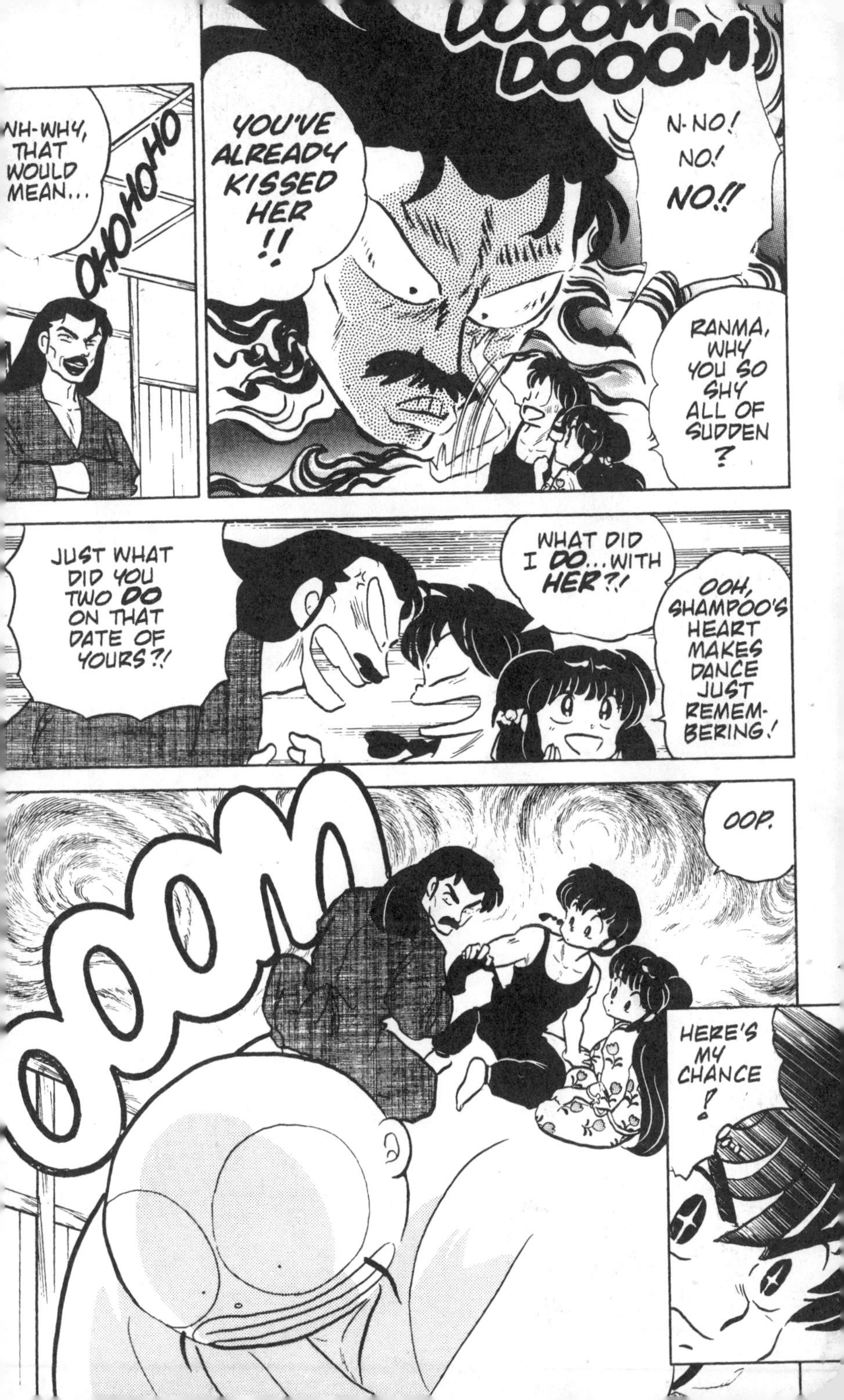

WH-WHY, THAT WOULD MEAN...
OHOHOHO
DOOOM
DOOOM
YOU'VE ALREADY KISSED HER!!
N-NO! NO! NO!!
RANMA, WHY YOU SO SHY ALL OF SUDDEN?
JUST WHAT DID YOU TWO DO ON THAT DATE OF YOURS?!
WHAT DID I DO...WITH HER?!
OOH, SHAMPOO'S HEART MAKES DANCE JUST REMEMBERING!
OOOM
OOP.
HERE'S MY CHANCE!

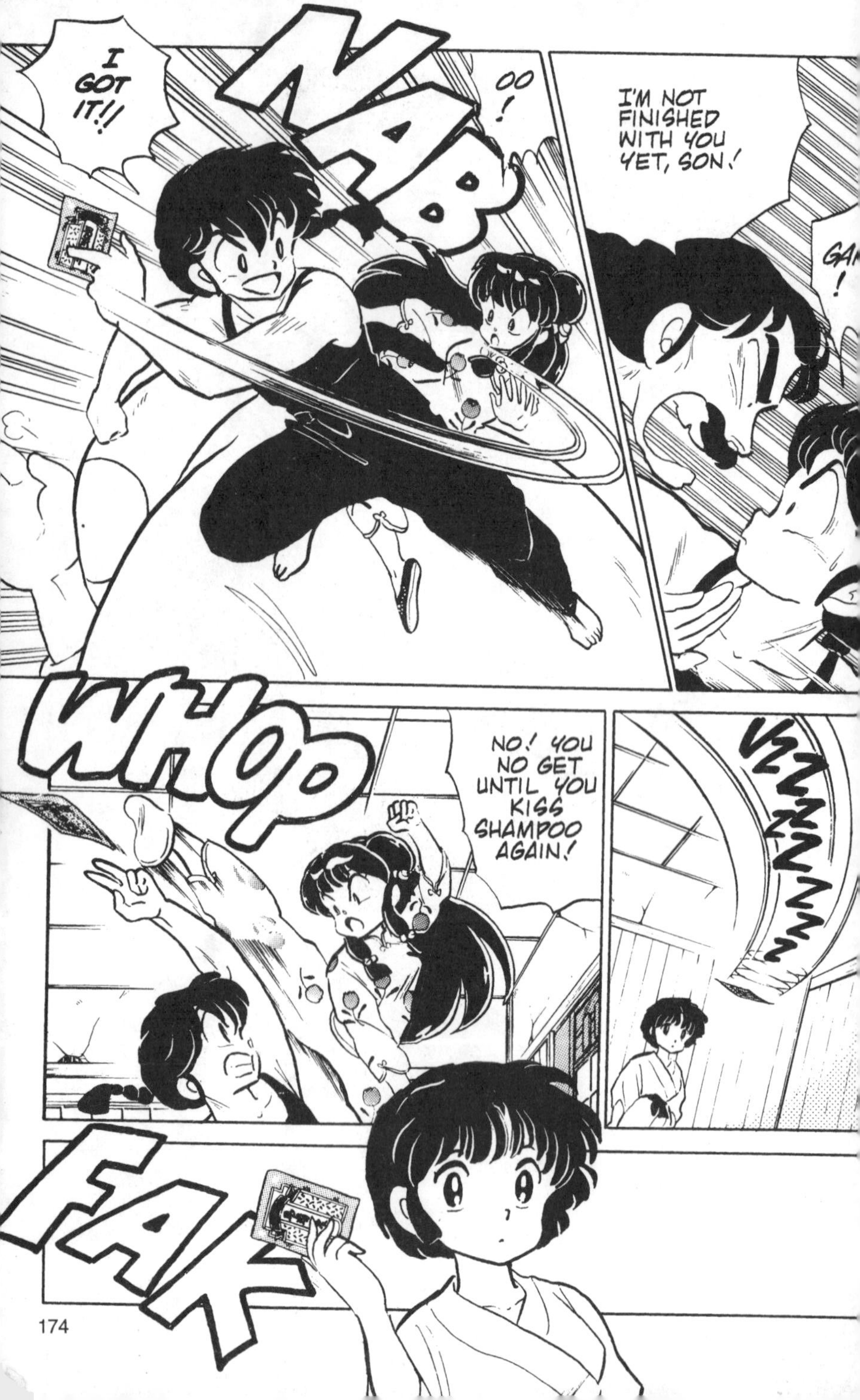
I GOT IT!!
NAB
OO!
I'M NOT FINISHED WITH YOU YET, SON!
GA!
WHOP
NO! YOU NO GET UNTIL YOU KISS SHAMPOO AGAIN!
VZZZZZZZZZ
FAK

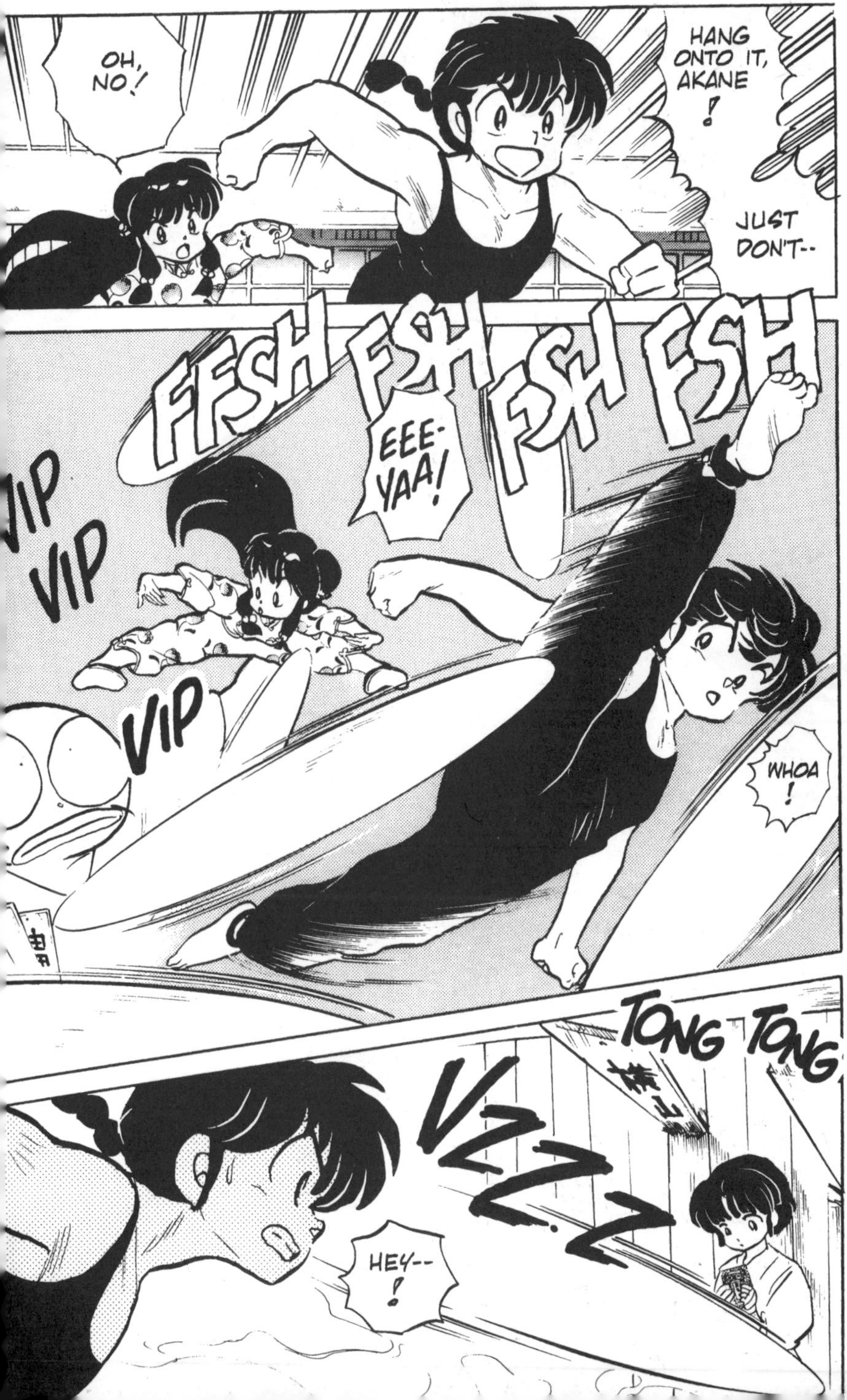
OH, NO!
HANG ONTO IT, AKANE!
JUST DON'T--
FFSH FSH FSH FSH
EEE-YAA!
VIP VIP
VIP
WHOA!
TONG TONG
HEY--!

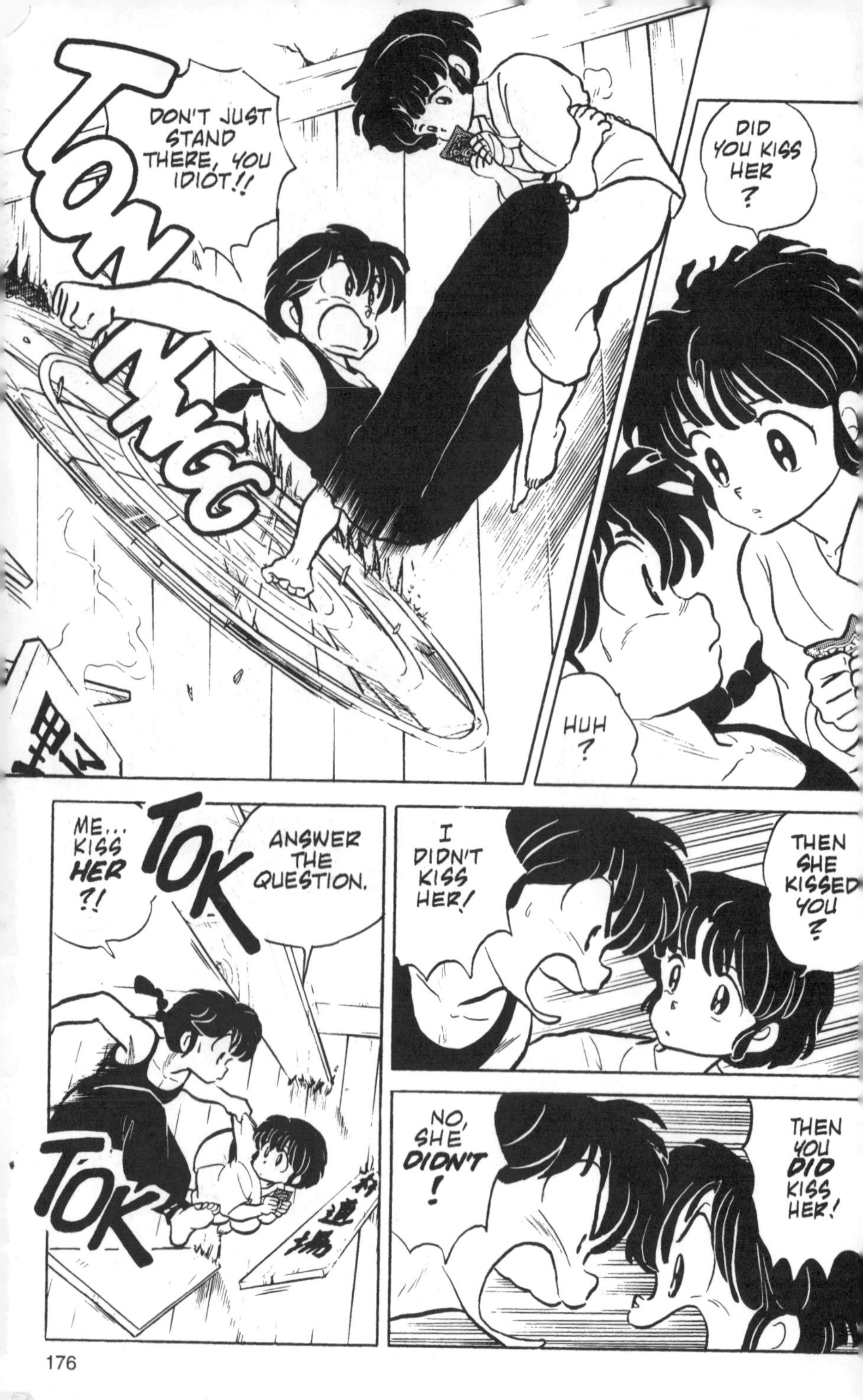
TONNNGG
DON'T JUST STAND THERE, YOU IDIOT!!
DID YOU KISS HER?
HUH?
ME... KISS HER?!
TOK
ANSWER THE QUESTION.
TOK
I DIDN'T KISS HER!
THEN SHE KISSED YOU?
NO, SHE DIDN'T!
THEN YOU DID KISS HER!

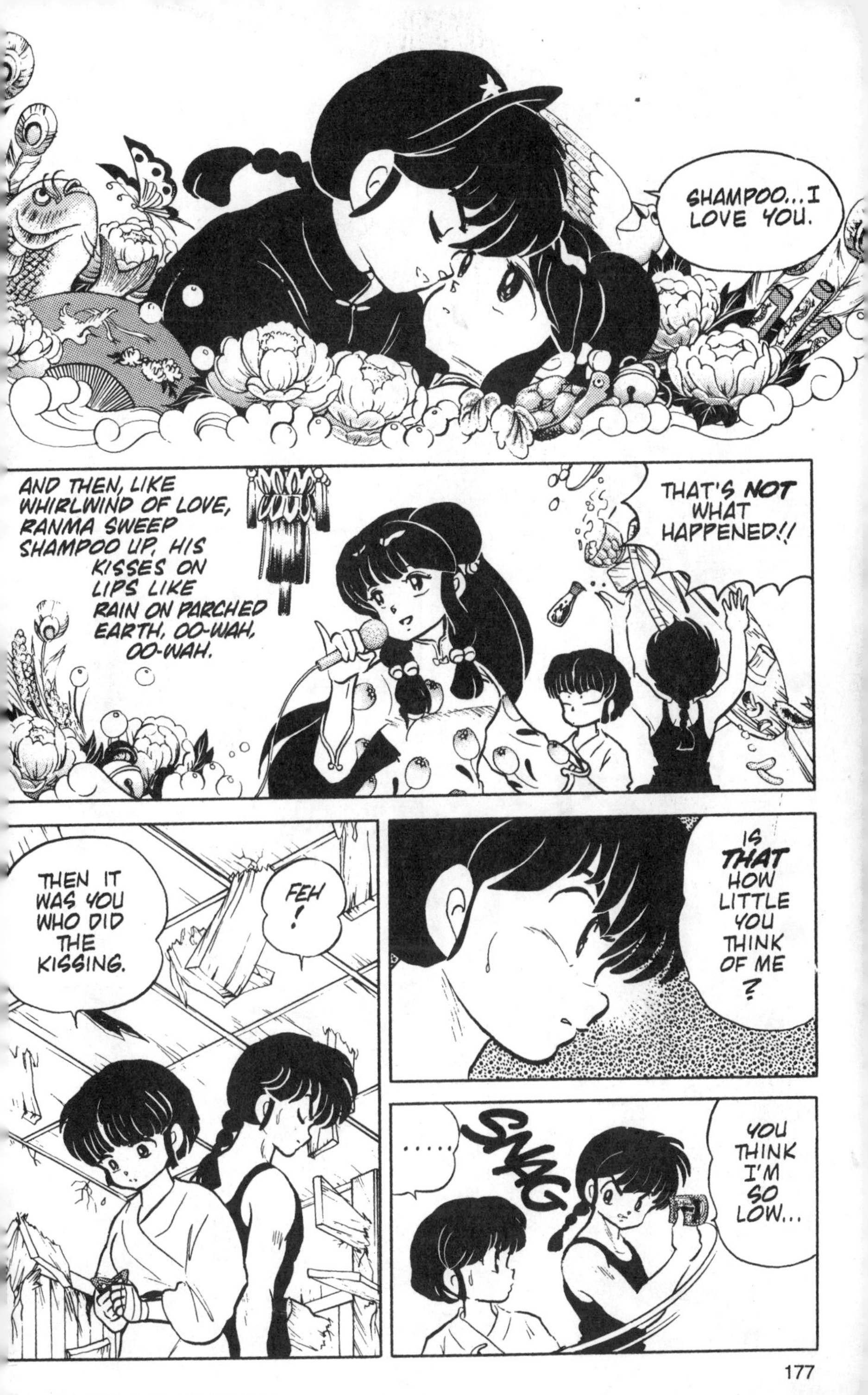
SHAMPOO...I LOVE YOU.
AND THEN, LIKE WHIRLWIND OF LOVE, RANMA SWEEP SHAMPOO UP, HIS KISSES ON LIPS LIKE RAIN ON PARCHED EARTH, OO-WAH, OO-WAH.
THAT'S NOT WHAT HAPPENED!!
THEN IT WAS YOU WHO DID THE KISSING.
FEH!
IS THAT HOW LITTLE YOU THINK OF ME?
......
SNAG
YOU THINK I'M SO LOW...

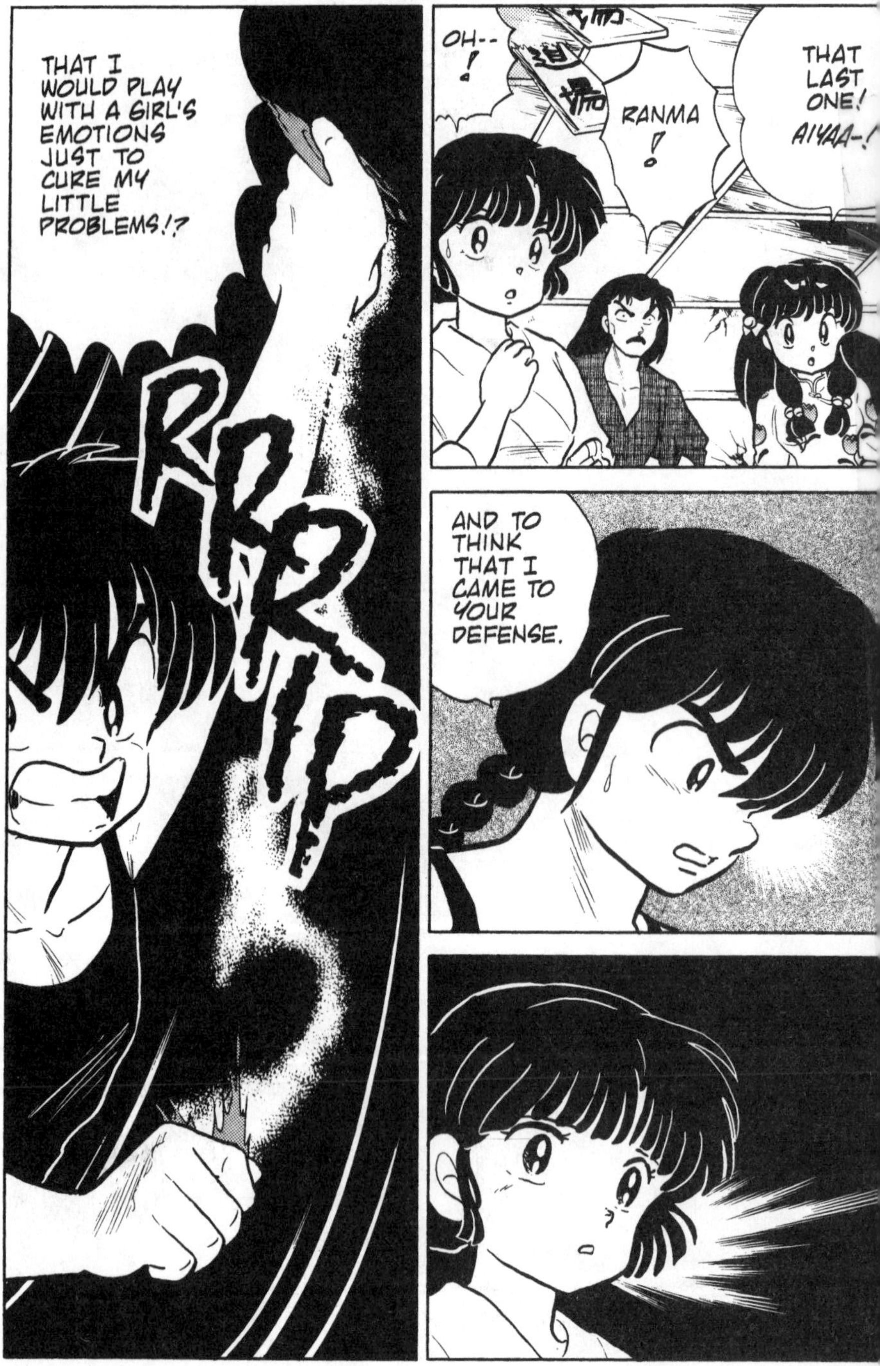
THAT I WOULD PLAY WITH A GIRL'S EMOTIONS JUST TO CURE MY LITTLE PROBLEMS!?
RRRIP
OH--!
RANMA!
THAT LAST ONE!
AIYAA-!
AND TO THINK THAT I CAME TO YOUR DEFENSE.

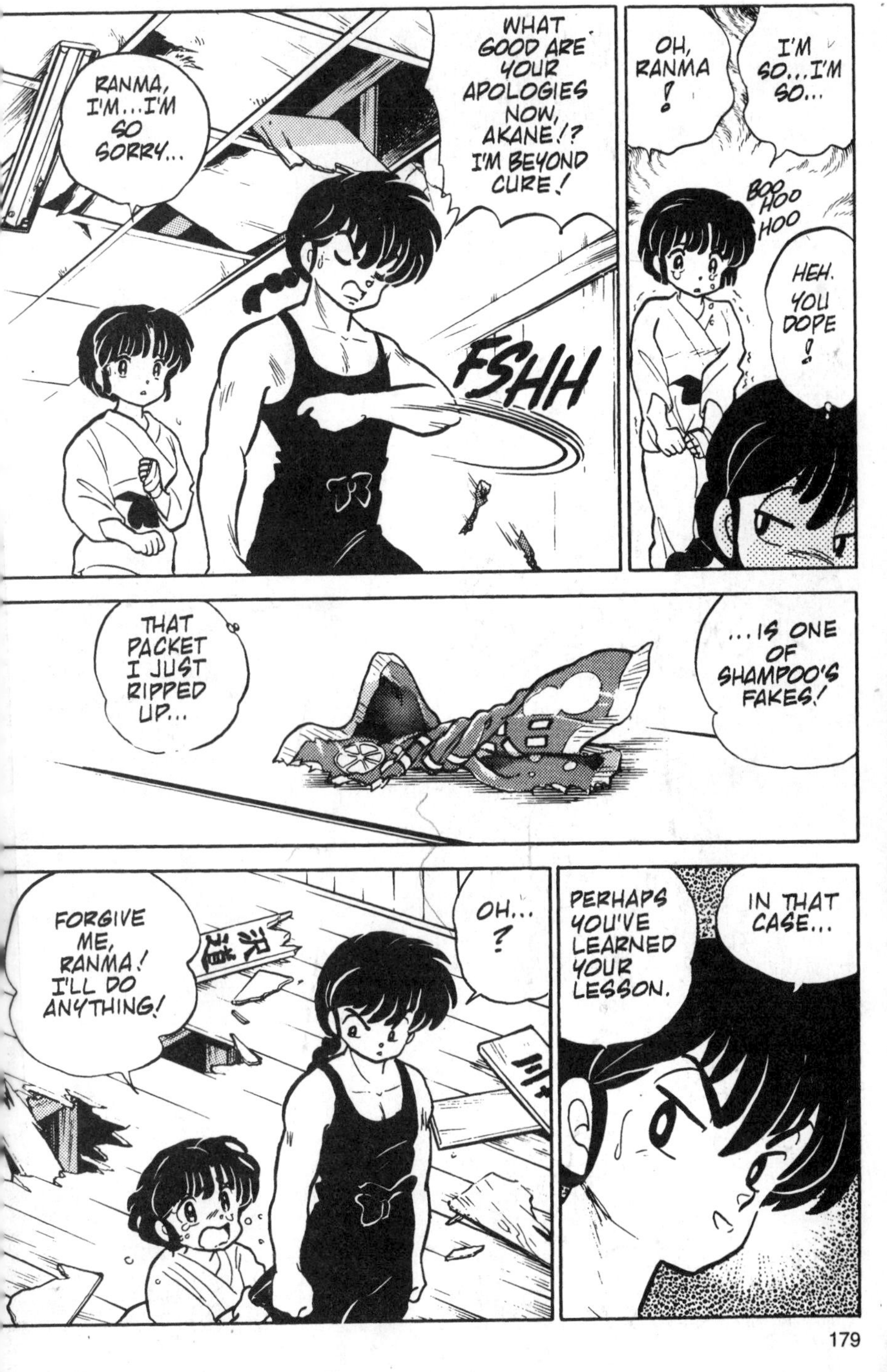
RANMA, I'M...I'M SO SORRY...
WHAT GOOD ARE YOUR APOLOGIES NOW, AKANE!? I'M BEYOND CURE!
FSHH
OH, RANMA!
I'M SO...I'M SO...
BOO HOO HOO
HEH. YOU DOPE!
THAT PACKET I JUST RIPPED UP...
...IS ONE OF SHAMPOO'S FAKES!
FORGIVE ME, RANMA! I'LL DO ANYTHING!
OH...?
PERHAPS YOU'VE LEARNED YOUR LESSON.
IN THAT CASE...

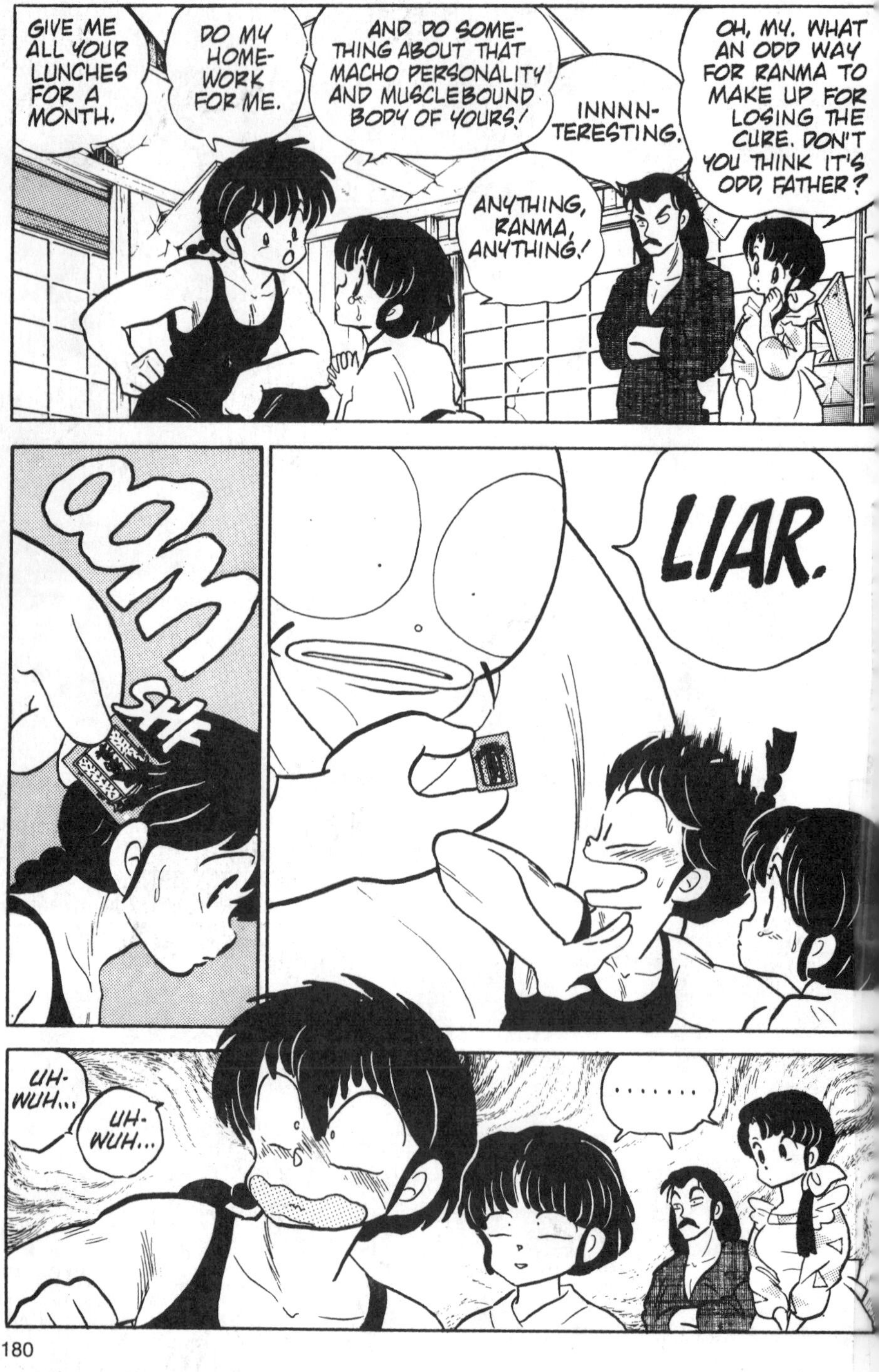
GIVE ME ALL YOUR LUNCHES FOR A MONTH.
DO MY HOMEWORK FOR ME.
AND DO SOMETHING ABOUT THAT MACHO PERSONALITY AND MUSCLEBOUND BODY OF YOURS!
ANYTHING, RANMA, ANYTHING!
INNNN-TERESTING.
OH, MY. WHAT AN ODD WAY FOR RANMA TO MAKE UP FOR LOSING THE CURE. DON'T YOU THINK IT'S ODD, FATHER?
OOM
SHF
LIAR.
UH-WUH...
UH-WUH...
....

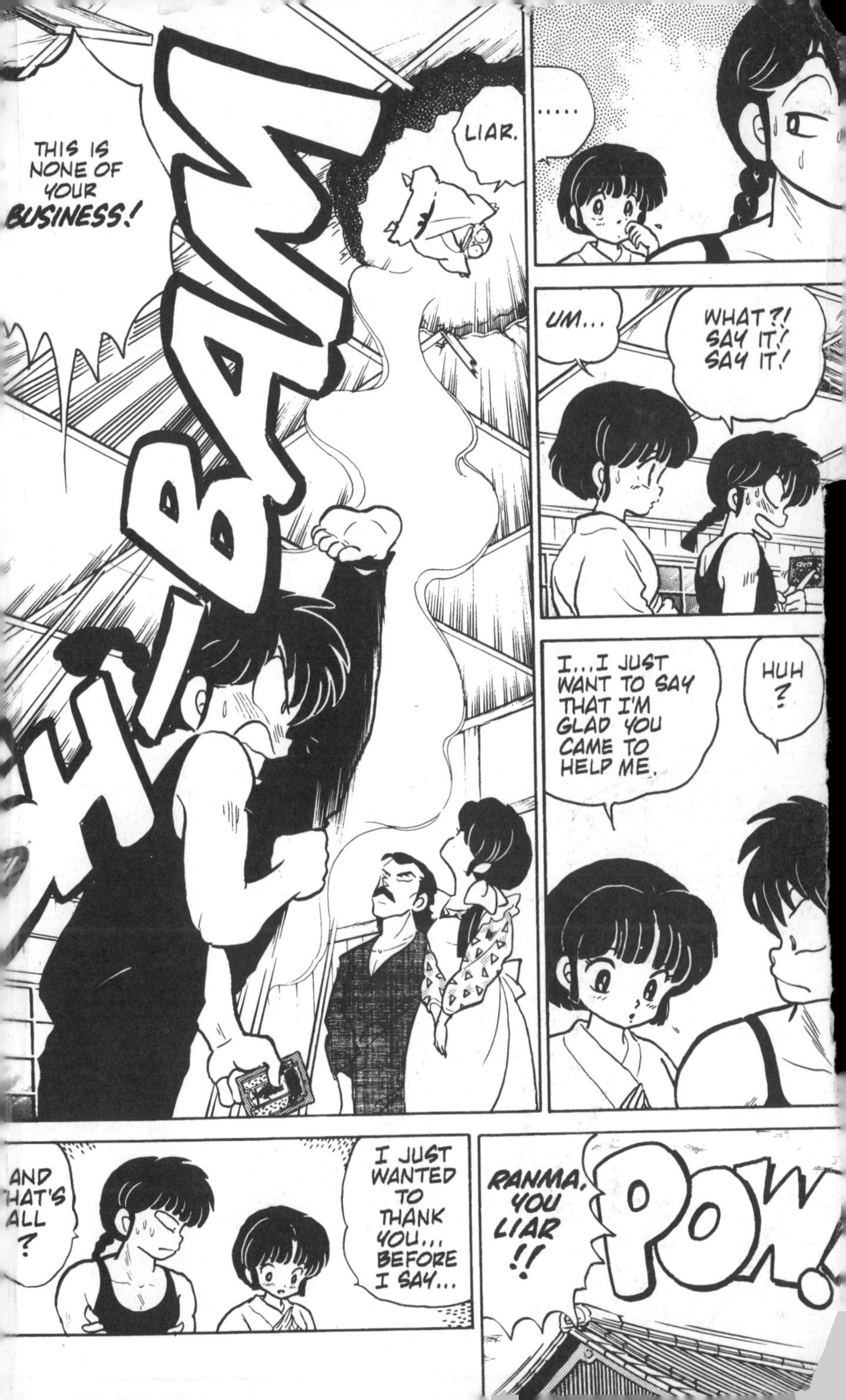
LIAR.
THIS IS NONE OF YOUR BUSINESS!
......
UM...
WHAT?! SAY IT! SAY IT!
I...I JUST WANT TO SAY THAT I'M GLAD YOU CAME TO HELP ME.
HUH?
AND HAT'S ALL ?
I JUST WANTED TO THANK YOU... BEFORE I SAY...
RANMA, YOU LIAR!!
POW!

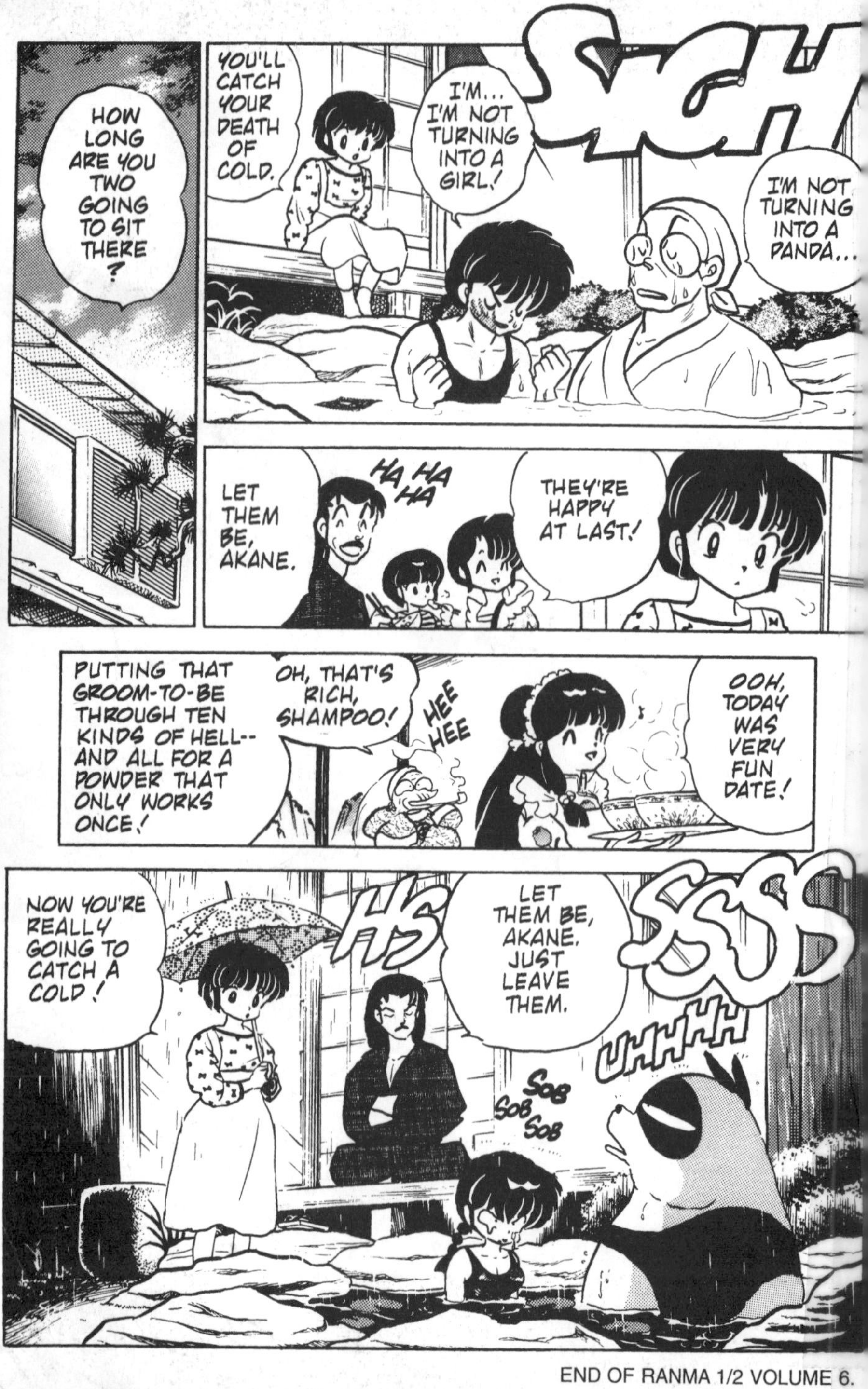
HOW LONG ARE YOU TWO GOING TO SIT THERE?
YOU'LL CATCH YOUR DEATH OF COLD.
I'M... I'M NOT TURNING INTO A GIRL!
I'M NOT TURNING INTO A PANDA...
LET THEM BE, AKANE.
HA HA HA
THEY'RE HAPPY AT LAST!
PUTTING THAT GROOM-TO-BE THROUGH TEN KINDS OF HELL-- AND ALL FOR A POWDER THAT ONLY WORKS ONCE!
OH, THAT'S RICH, SHAMPOO!
HEE HEE
OOH, TODAY WAS VERY FUN DATE!
NOW YOU'RE REALLY GOING TO CATCH A COLD!
HS
LET THEM BE, AKANE. JUST LEAVE THEM.
SSSS
UHHHH
SOB SOB SOB

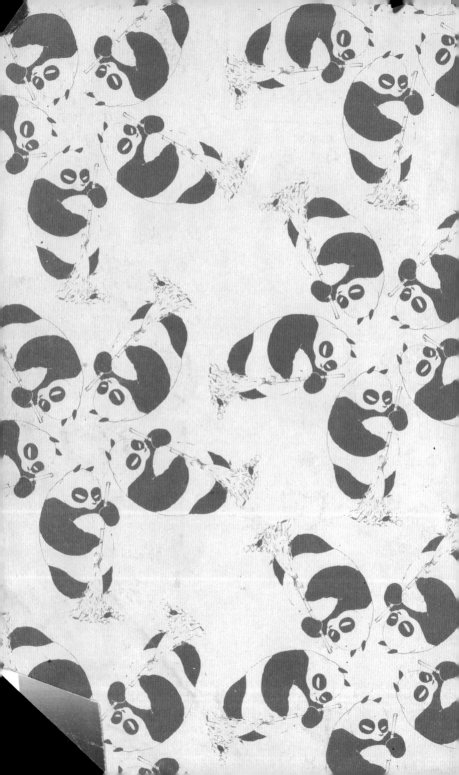